Baldur's Gate

BALDUR'S GATE

by

ELEANOR CLARK

PANTHEON BOOKS

A Division of Random House, New York

TO

Rosanna and Gabriel

. . . for the spirit of the living creature was in the wheels.

EZEKIEL 1:20

Part One

I

IT WAS SEEING JACK PRYDEN that afternoon, after so many years, that gave me the idea of going to see old Baldur Blake, the sculptor. I didn't know why. I hadn't even been curious about Baldur for a long time before, although I knew he was living in a boarding house only ten miles away, in Wellford, where I often went marketing. But then he hadn't shown any curiosity about us either. The story was that he was drinking himself to death, and when I thought about him I was only surprised that he wasn't dead already. I had wandered a few times around his house and studio, what was left of them, up over the hill back of our house, past the old cemetery. I would be up that way picking blackberries, or just for a walk, anything to get away from the house. It had been nine years before, a couple of years before I married Lucas, that he walked out in that strange way, after living there alone for about twenty-five years; but I hadn't seen him for quite a while before he left. If anybody in Jordan was going to inquire about him I suppose it should have been me, because he had been closer to my family than to anyone else and I had posed for him a lot when I was very young. It was my hands, my face and in a way my body, adolescent and always in the same filmy drapery he went in for, that you could see lying around scattered and broken in the mess on the studio floor. He had wrecked everything when he left. But how could I be curious, when my own life was just a bad sleep.

At least that was the way it looked to me that afternoon. Naturally I had heard that Jack Pryden was opening his aunt Adelphia's house, which had been closed ever since she died except for one year when it was rented, and that he was going to live in Jordan again, for the summer anyway. Old Beulah Wellman next door to us had helped clean the Pryden house ahead of time and she talked a lot about it. She had had a message too from "Doctor Pryden," as she called him now, asking her to hire somebody to fix up the grounds a little, so she got my husband Lucas to do it. It was funny hearing her call him that, but of course he'd been away too long for anybody there to feel familiar with him any more. For Lucas the work was just like the other odd jobs he did Sundays and late afternoons after his regular work, whatever that happened to be at the time; just then it was driving a tractor for Mr. Jarvis, a city man and new-comer in town, and at four o'clock he'd go and do gardening for Mrs. Hollister and some of the new people, dump their garbage and so on. Lucas had never laid eyes on Jack Pryden, and I had never told him that the plaster head I had rescued from Baldur's studio up the hill and kept in our parlor was of Jack when he was a little boy about twelve and still spending his vacations with Miss Pryden, his guardian. Not that he and I were particularly close then, al-though we saw each other all the time. He was small for his age, almost puny, and I was always proud because my brother Arthur was so much handsomer and better at everything, everything except books and horses. It wasn't till later, the summer I was eighteen and had a job in New York, that Jack and I were in love and going to get married.

Fourteen years before, and I had never seen him again until that afternoon, in the spring of 1952. I had seen his name in the paper, most recently in connection with his divorce but a few times before too, once with a picture. He had become famous, at least by Jordan standards and perhaps by any. At that time, I mean our summer, he'd been talking about psychoanalysis, but he went into research instead and was on some kind of medical research board during the war. And in all the years since that summer I had been inside the Pryden house just once, and then not by invitation. Around Christmas that year of our love, a little after I'd heard that Jack was married, I dressed up one day and went to call on Miss Pryden.

There had been no contact between her and my family for sev-eral years then. The scandal, or whatever they called it in town, that ended my mother's effort to run a boarding school in our house, had ended that friendship at the same time. Along with almost every other family friendship, and I have reason to believe that Miss Pryden at least had the loyalty to hold her tongue on the subject; as far as I know she never to the end of her life would join in the discussions about us, although some pretty strenuous efforts must have been made to draw her out. I am speaking mainly of my mother, but perhaps at the time of my visit to her they had already begun talking about me too as I know they did later. Not that there would have been any justification for it at that time, except as future mistakes live and grow in you beforehand like an unborn child and become plain to everyone. Miss Pryden, however, received me kindly.

Poor woman! It was lucky for her that my grandmother died when she did, a few weeks before that terrible evening at the school, instead of after it. Everything Miss Pryden had done for us had been done out of her devotion to my grandmother. They had traveled in Europe together when Miss Pryden was a young girl, and it was through her that my grandmother had met my grandfather while he was still in law school, and so eventually, with no preparation for New England life at all, had come to live in Jordan. There would have been a lot to undo, I used to realize, when I tried to remake the past with a view to preventing that particular marriage, and consequently my own existence; and of course before that I would have had to undo my parents' marriage, which was not as easy as it looked. Anyway, with my grandmother dead it was possible for Miss Pryden quietly to break off relations with us; and quietly, with no drama or explanations to my mother or to anyone, was the way she did it. As to withdrawing her financial support from the school there could not have been any words needed. I was only fourteen at the time and a good deal of what happened was cloudy to me, but I am sure there can have been no question in anyone's mind of the school's going on, after that evening.

I suppose my parents may have had some hope later that when she knew we were losing our house she would step in again, in spite of everything. How she had always admired our house! and she knew how desperately attached to it my mother was, as my grandparents had been. In fact that had seemed to be the only psychological difficulty in the way of setting up the school there. A boarding school was certainly a respectable enterprise, and this one was to be much more than that: it was going to have social prestige, the highest academic standing, everything. Besides there was an absolute necessity by then of something being done for the family living, but my mother didn't come to the idea just because of that; to run a boarding school, "the best in the country," had been her dream from the beginning. So when things came to the point, with nobody realizing how much too late it was, the trouble seemed to be only a division of feeling between the dream and the house. Perhaps I, at the age of twelve, most acutely, but the rest of the family too, had to fight a feeling of degradation at the thought of strangers being at liberty in our home, even if it were for something that was supposed to ensure our position instead of lowering it. My grandfather had been dead several years then, and when I speak of a "desperate" attachment I should exempt him. He and his father too had been born in the house, and although he had risen through years of hardship, after his father's early death, to be a judge, "one of our most distinguished men" as Miss Pryden used to put it—not quite specifying the area in question but in a tone implying at least a national scale—he had always kept the farm running too. He was so native to the place, I think he never distinguished between the house and life in general, and died in a despair that was all of a piece. At any rate he would never join in his wife's complacency over Miss Pryden's generous praise —of our doorway, "the most beautiful in town," or our living-room mantel which was "a museum piece" and "far better than any in Litchfield"; the house altogether was favorably compared to the best in Litchfield, the highest compliment of the neighborhood for anything colonial, besides having a more beautiful location than any house there.

As to that, some people might prefer being out a little from the center of the village and having a view down over the hills. Our house is just off the main road, and low, only a minute's walk from the green; the beauty is in the spaciousness around it, the way the land slopes softly toward the brook in back, and its being set much farther back from the road than most houses of its time; and the trees. It was only when somebody's appreciation turned on the trees that my grandfather would soften, and the long-smothered illumination of his nature would spark up again, making everything that was formidable in his long features, usually so locked up and stern and mysteriously suffering, vanish for a moment in the flow of tenderness that was almost like gaiety. On Sunday mornings when Arthur and I were very little, if he could win the battle to keep us from being taken to church, being a principled atheist himself, he would take us "calling on the trees"—a little joke at my grandmother's expense, for her flutter of weekly visitings; and with a running social parody that we helped to invent, of bows and curtseys and how-do-you-do's, made us familiar with their leaves and bark and habits, how they ate the sun and water and what certain insects did for them, along with their human and family history. Three of the four great elms particularly admired by Miss Pryden, between the end of the lawn and the road, had been planted by his grandfather; some of the maples he had helped his father put in as seedlings when he was a small boy; the two beeches were older, but the oldest of all was the grandis fir at the east corner of the house, shading the living room. That one had been there when George Washington marched over the hill, past the cemetery that would have been quite an up-and-coming one then and right down the lane. He would have seen that fir with his own eyes, "Unless he was busy looking at something else," my grandfather said. "And did he sleep in our house, Grandpa?" "Well you know it may have been the middle of the morning, and he wouldn't be dawdling"—one of the dreadful sins, almost as bad as telling a lie. "He could take a nap!" Arthur and I both cried out, and then shrieked with laughter at having both hit on something so brilliant at the same time. We were pretty sure that if George Washington went right by our house he would want to take a nap in it, and then one thing would lead to another and he would spend the night, so he would have plenty of time to look at the fir tree with his own eyes.

Oddly enough, the only person I have known who has cared about the trees the way my grandfather did is Lucas. My grandmother's love was mainly for the house itself, and for the wistaria vine that she had brought as a cutting in her satchel all the way from California and that before she died had a trunk like a hickory tree's; and my mother's for the garden, especially the bottom, by the willow pool, that is when she was not too worn out from hoeing in the vegetable garden and canning and all the rest of it and finally doing most of my father's work too with the few chickens that were left.

But when everybody in town knew that we were losing our house there was no word from Miss Pryden. Nor from Baldur Blake but nobody expected that; he had drawn into himself more and more and finally was seeing nobody at all as far as we could tell. The house wasn't sold; there was no buyer. But a man from out of town came along who wanted to rent it on a three-year lease, furniture and all, and turn it into a tearoom, with a three-year option after that. My mother tried to hold out on just a few of the best pieces of my grandparents' furniture, the highboy that had so long a story for us and the mahogany drop-leaf table and the four-poster from her own family's home in Massachusetts, but the man wanted his tearoom to have "atmosphere," "real New England class," and it was everything or nothing. So we had moved into a couple of upstairs rooms in the Howlands' house at the end of the green. My mother had stopped trying to make any secret of being —well, the word was not so familiar then and what people said was that *she drank*; and what Arthur had become, at the age of twenty, was public knowledge too: it could hardly have been much of a mystery, when he was living only three miles down the road. How could I have dared to call on Miss Pryden, to go and knock at her front door as I used to with my grandmother, as if nothing had happened?

But I did it. At least I was fairly sure that she wouldn't know about Jack and me, as she had never seen us together at that time and it wasn't likely he would confide in her. I had told him a few bare facts but I couldn't stand for him really to see what was happening, or to see it myself when all my unbelievable happiness seemed to depend on my staying calm and sure of myself, in order to believe in it. So all through that hot, dirty, glorious summer in New York, when the image was with me always like another heaven of our little tumbling river at Jordan, the Rapahaug, where the falls crash down through the gorge to the deep pool under the iron bridge, our swimming place, or of our own willow pool at the end of the garden, I made one excuse after another every weekend for us never to go there, never to be in Jordan that summer at all, even when my father sent a telegram saying my mother needed me even if I could only come for a few hours. My last evening with Jack, although there was nothing at the time to make me know it was the last, was the ninth of September, and my summer job at the department store was over a couple of days later. It was early in December when I learned by accident that Jack had been married nearly two months.

Miss Pryden herself opened the door for me, her secretary being off somewhere at that hour and the maid busy out in back. "Why

Eva, my dear, how nice of you to come," she said without the least look of discomposure. "Do come in," and holding the long gold chain around her neck that held her reading glasses, to keep it from swaying as she walked, a gesture I had always associated with her, she led me with no hesitation or questions into the living room, which was also her library. A pleasant fire was burning, in a fireplace and beneath a mantel almost exactly like our own but which she herself had always deprecated as "just a copy"; but nobody in our house had ever read as tranquilly by the fire as she had apparently been doing before I came. There had been something ferocious in my grandfather's insatiable reading, and it was usually in the midst of some kind of family eruption.

"Yes, that new life of Shelley," seeing my glance at the open book. "Preposterous man! I suppose I'd have been obliged to forgive Virgil if he had been a cad, but this creature—and his vulgar overdone Prometheus. But perhaps you admire it?" giving me one of her old sanguine brilliant looks that so graciously assumed the other person's involvement in the private flashings of her mind. "I remember I did extravagantly at your age. This is by a professor—well, no matter. I dare say I shan't finish it. No, do sit here in the wing-chair, Eva, you'll be more comfortable and not so far away. How well you look! College seems to agree with you. You *are* in college, aren't you? Good girl. And what a pretty frock. Did you make it yourself? You were always quite a little wonder with a needle, I remember; such pretty doll clothes you used to make, really quite extraordinary."

There was no nervousness nor any air of condescension in all this, nothing but the natural authority she had always had in all her relations, and seemed entitled to on the basis of charm alone if it had been by nothing else; and how much else there was to justify it, in more directions than the ones suggested by the enormous library around her and the somewhat sloppy stacks of papers on her desk, overpowered me as much on this visit as it ever had in my childhood. She had been too thorough in her accomplishments to need to parade them. Everybody knew, or if they didn't they weren't worth telling, that she had a Ph.D. in Latin, had published essays in learned journals on questions of French literature, and others on local history—a field a good deal less central to her than her affection for her French poodles but in which she could stand her ground with any scholar and could afford to laugh gently at the ladies of the

Litchfield Historical Society; that she had been a power in state
politics for some thirty years, and that her house, remote as Jordan
seemed from the center of anything, had been in my grandparents'
time and probably still was a meeting place for distinguished people
of all kinds. It seemed that senators, scholars, famous novelists,
would drive any distance for the privilege of lunching with her, and
I had never understood it as well as that afternoon, when instead of
any indication of her age, what struck me, and for the first time, was
something like a definition of her extraordinary magnetism. I suppose it was because I had just been in love myself for the first time
that the thought came to me. Not that I hadn't been just as dazzled
and drawn in when I was younger, and at times nearly paralyzed by
the sapphire beauty of her eyes, which neither age nor bookishness
had watered even at the time of this last visit. Once when I was
seven or eight I had been standing on the staircase when she arrived
in evening dress for dinner at our house, and after relinquishing
her cloak to my father, whom she undoubtedly thought good for
not much else, although she showed the same easy charm in the
gesture that she would have had for my grandfather whom she did
admire, she had glanced up with a still more scintillating grace to
meet my gawking eyes. The sensation of my jaw hanging down, of
not being able to close it or utter a sound, stayed with me horribly
for days. Her perfect posture which made her seem much taller than
she was, her creamy shoulders, the shapeless aureole of her dust-
blond hair, a little untidy as from a dispensation to angels, the
diamonds at her throat and the more thrilling thrust of light from
her blue, wonderful eyes, everything about her, since I had never
remarked that her clothes were designed to hide a rather dumpy
figure which was what I expected in older people anyhow, everything made her an apparition to stun me; and then most beautiful
of all came her instant acknowledgment of that fact. Almost as soon
as our eyes met she was saying "Thank you" with one of her loveliest smiles and a ripple of laughter, as if I had been not an overgrown
child on the way to bed but somebody old and exciting, one of the
celestial company whose praise was valuable, and she ran up the
couple of steps to where I stood and kissed me.

The flattery of that moment had bewitched me forever; and now
in the misery of that later December afternoon the words came to
me for what was behind it, what the subtle ingredient was that
could so entrance. It was the air of having been loved by many men,

and not having needed any; or if she had, and I remembered a strange whisper about her that I was not supposed to have heard and had myself witnessed a strange event in her house that might have borne it out, her powers, the mastery of her life and feelings, had only been heightened by it. What a marvelous headmistress she would have been herself—and in fact it was because she had long ago considered just that, founding her own boarding school in Jordan, that she had so generously, and as it turned out unwisely, supported my mother's project. She was born to power. But she had had money enough to pick a wider sphere; and perhaps after all, I thought, it was only that, only money and not any victory over turbid romance that made the difference between her and everybody in my family: made her so sure in everything while every one of them, of *us*, seemed to be always pushing in wrong directions and succeeding in nothing but suffering.

"How nice the garden looks in the snow," I said in a voice that sounded to me more like my grandmother's than my own, while Miss Pryden rang for tea. "Suzanne, le thé, s'il vous plaît. Eva, you remember Suzanne of course. Et les petits gâteaux, pour mademoiselle." Suzanne and I greeted each other without warmth, she with a hint in her eyes of what I took to be disapprobation of me and even of a dour pleasure in the cause of my long absence from the house. I had never liked her, but it had never occurred to me before what an anomaly it was for a French maid to be in Jordan at all, and one with an Italian gardener husband besides. They had just been among the appurtenances of the household, no more to be questioned than the French poodles, of which the one then reigning came bounding in, to be admired by his mistress and exhibited to me. Anything that Miss Pryden chose to do, even to her painting her barns pink in imitation of Italian villas, seemed by the mere fact of her doing it to be proper to Jordan, as much as George Washington's having ridden down our lane. Or the talk of crops, weather, new kinds of fertilizer and farm implements that she used to engage in with my grandfather, when they were not discussing points of law or exchanging Latin epigrams—a favorite game between them and much enjoyed by my grandmother, who would sit beaming with pride and understanding not a word. "Yes," reverting to the garden, of which I could see only a few fat burlap mummies where the roses were and down between the imported cypresses the fountain piece done for her years ago by Baldur Blake, "I've always loved it at this season. The renovating force of winter, as Thomson has it. 'Then would we try to scan the moral world.' Still, I do long for spring. Ah, here we are. Eva, do be a dear and pour for us, will you?"

I thought it might have entered her mind, as it had mine when she cut the subject short, how little my mother would be longing for spring that year, with her dear flowers inaccessible, and half of them in any case plowed under to make room for outdoor tables. For weeks she had not even been out for a walk, since to do so she would have to appear on the green and her main desire now was not to be seen.

But I chased the thought away, fearful that it would show in my face and confirm Miss Pryden in what must be her guess: that I had come to her for help, for my family, or even just for myself. I was determined not to tell her that I was going to have to leave college at the end of that semester. But I couldn't be the first to broach my real purpose either, although the framed photograph of Jack on the piano might have given me an easy opening. She would have to say the name first, and then that would be all, that was all I had come for. "Eva Buckingham came to see me," she would tell him, "and was very sweet." God keep her from telling him that I had been *very clever* instead. Not that there seemed much danger of that, when every subject I could think of mentioning bore on some other that must not be touched, so that mostly I was busy composing my feet and hands and handling my teacup in a way that would do credit to the remarks she had used to permit herself on my deportment. "Little Eva," I could hear her say, not so many years earlier, "your mother is a lady. Your grandmother is a lady. And yet methinks"—the smile and archaism were to sweeten the sting of the lesson—"methinks I have seen thee talk with thy mouth full." No: I had come for a little something more. I accused myself of meanness in the wish, but among so many self-accusations another could hardly matter, and I did wish to hear something derogatory to that marriage: that she was stupid for instance, or in the synonym I had acquired in recent weeks, "bourgeoise." I was only yearning for that small comfort to hang on my despair, as in a pause in Miss Pryden's comments about Hitler's marching into Czechoslovakia, and under the influence of her friendliness, I risked a remark at last on the statue in the snow: that I had forgotten how graceful it was.

This was true, although partaking of hypocrisy, and I could almost have taken her answer as aimed at my thoughts and all the summer's experience that was responsible for them, rather than at what I had said.

"I'm glad you can still think so," she said gaily. "Sensible girl. If my charming nephew were here he would be giving you a dozen reasons for its removal, and for putting a pair of marble toothpicks or something of the sort in its place. But evidently college hasn't yet made a barbarian of you. Unfortunately, most of the young people here in Jordan have so few opportunities to appreciate works of art at all, one would almost prefer to have them agree with my dear Jack, absurd as he is with his Picassos and goodness knows who else. I do believe before long we shan't be permitted to think anything beautiful unless it is done by children or the insane. Rubbish! But even so, there's nothing so dreadful as indifference, is there? I dare say a mistaken notion of beauty, even to the point of dismissing *that*"—glancing again toward the boy with dolphin that seemed to have been pounced on by winter in mid-spout, and perhaps meaning to indicate all the long Italian arrangement before it as well—"is better than none. I'm afraid I must admit that that is the authentic spirit of barbarism, and quite likely we shall go down before it again. It won't be Hitler, I'm quite convinced of that in spite of today's reports, but plain indifference. Ignorance of form. I do believe nothing is so despicable as a life lived without form, which is only a version of gallantry, isn't it? Well," laughing pleasantly as if I had really been the collaborator in her thoughts that the form of her sentence implied, "I hope we shall all go down gallantly at any rate. I can't bear a whine."

"Vous aurez ma tête, mais vous n'aurez jamais mes pensées," I murmured, quoting from an anecdote of her own.

"Precisely. What a good memory you have, my dear," and then she spoke once more of the statue, the clarity of her diction allowing her to speak so fast that all her other remarks had scarcely amounted to a deviation. "Yes, he had a lovely talent. I used to think it might even be a great one, and I believe it might if he hadn't had too good an income. And then that wretched love affair! Of course it was a pity she died, but he had no business cutting himself off from the world and letting it ruin his art."

"Was he really so much in love?" It was a question we had never been allowed to pursue in my family, although my grandparents, like Miss Pryden, had never joined with the majority of the village in ostracizing him because of the lady's long visits up on the hill. I only knew that there had been some reason for their not being able to marry.

"Oh, frightfully. And she was quite worth it, though it would have been rather more discreet of them both, if he must have her nude on his stone wall, the statue of course, to have put it in *back* of the house. Personally, I'd have preferred it not to be weeping too. Poor dear Baldur," with the only touch of the far-away in her reflections that I had seen that day, "I wonder what on earth will come of him; or is becoming of him now."

I had been afraid of this, as coming by analogy too close to home. But Miss Pryden was not given to gossip or to the kind of personal speculation that might verge on it, and was already dropping the subject when she was called to the phone, or rather was nudged to it by the dog who was sitting on his hindquarters beside her on the sofa with his elegant ruff showing to best advantage and his fine profile raised. "All right, Monty, and you entertain Eva a moment. Eva, do give Monty one of those little cakes like a dear, will you? I'm afraid he's too well-mannered to take one himself, though I've told him he may."

It seemed to me I could hear the photograph on the piano speak when she had left the room. Out the window beyond it Suzanne's husband was dragging a large Christmas tree up on to the porch; it would be brought in and trimmed the next day for Miss Pryden's annual Christmas Eve party, to which "the whole town" would be invited as always. "The holly and the ivy now both are full well grown," we children used to sing around her wassail bowl; and another line sang itself in my head as I watched the first flakes of a new snow lighting on the statue in the garden. "Love and joy come to you, and to you your wassail too . . ." Arthur and Jack and I and the Hollister children would be coached as the main performers, because Miss Pryden could not have borne to hear only "Silent Night" and the rest of the common repertoire, and loathed the sentimentality of adult carol-singing, although she would have to put up with a little of it before the end of the party. The rest of the decorations were already in place—the crèche from Naples in the window-seat, holly and mistletoe in the dining room, and at the front windows the wreaths of creeping Jennie like the ones we used to make for her house and our own, after gathering the vine in the woods all morning. How strangely tasteless her house was, really, inside and out, except for the garden; and some of the upholstered furniture was quite worn; most people who could afford to would have had it done over long ago, and would have ripped the side porch off too if they had known and cared as much as she did about "the best colonial." But that, as I took it in then, was just the point. The air of a power over life that one felt in the house, the same that had arisen from a treatment as different as possible in Jack's little apartment in New York, which was done in pale leather and bleached wood, with a de Chirico on the wall and not an ash-tray or any other furnishing that was not of the best modern design, seemed here in his aunt's house to come precisely from the flaws both of style, any style, and upkeep. The visible fact, carrying as it did the sense of the authority of money, was of her not having to bother unless she chose, since it was equally clear in what respects she did choose. Her table, for one thing, was famous; the teacakes had been marvelous.

I did as she had asked and offered one to the poodle, with a few words and the kind of smile that seemed in order. Not that I didn't feel friendly toward him; I had been very fond of him as a puppy and was anxious for him to like me again, now that we were alone in the room together. But he didn't want the cake. He turned away from it with a slow gesture of dignity and boredom, without looking at me, and the tears came spurting to my eyes. That nobody in my family would be invited to the Christmas party flashed forth as one with all the awfulness of the world, not exempting the talk of approaching war, which as I couldn't help overhearing was the burden of Miss Pryden's long and vigorous phone conversation out in the hall. The call was long distance and evidently from somebody important, who was trying to get her to use her influence with a certain congressman in some question of foreign policy.

I walked over to the window to hide my tears from the dog, and looking into the blur of salt water and falling snow, I was taken with a wild desire, to be loved and comforted by Miss Pryden. When she came back into the room I would tell her everything: how I had never loved my mother, and about last summer, and how horrible it was to look at the statue and think of Baldur Blake's life now, and that I had not found a way to make my life any good but I had never meant to be bad or do any wrong; and then more than anything I thought I wanted to talk about my grandmother, because surely there was no other bond so true between Miss Pryden and me as the love of her, and with every barrier broken down in the flood of my unhappiness I felt all the outrage of our having talked for an hour without once mentioning her.

The door-knocker sounded as she was finishing her call, and she stood conversing in the hall with Mrs. Hollister, who couldn't stay. She had only dropped by because she had been to Hartford to do her Christmas shopping and had happened to see "the most exquisite angel" and she couldn't resist bringing it to Miss Pryden for the top of her tree. "I hear the bridal couple may be able to come for Christmas with you after all. I should *so* love to see them. I hear she's perfectly charming. You know, of course, her mother is a niece of Admiral Thornton, who was one of Sam's cousin William's closest friends. How happy you must be!"

Miss Pryden said they would not be coming. But she had just received a picture of them taken a few weeks ago on their honeymoon; it was right there in the library. She turned the lights on.

"And here is Eva Buckingham who's been having tea with me. Why Eva my dear, how rude of me, I left you quite in the dark here. And Monty. Monty, say how-do-you-do to Mrs. Hollister. What? He wouldn't have a cake? Spoiled creature, I suppose you wanted me to give it to you myself." She did, and he snapped it up.

"Eva! Why how nice to see you, and looking so pretty . . . And how is . . . Well!" Mrs. Hollister lacked Miss Pryden's gift for hiding her thoughts, or having others instead if they were awkward; and she had been an intimate of my mother's for some twenty years. "Well now let's just take a glance at the picture so I can tell Sam about it, he'll be so interested because of the family connection, and then I really must go . . . Has Eva seen it? You two were always such playmates . . . Oh, that *is* a nice picture, Adelphia. How sweet she looks! perfectly charming! But you don't mean to tell me he's still riding? Wasn't it just a few weeks ago you told me he'd broken his collarbone *again*?"

"Foolish boy. But he will do it," Miss Pryden said with obvious pleasure. She was an admirer of recklessness. "And now he tells me he's buying a little two-seater plane, some sort of cub he calls it. However, it doesn't seem to be interfering with his work. Yes, she's very pretty and well-mannered. I shouldn't have picked her out for him myself, but then one never does hit the nail on the head in these matters. Actually I'd rather thought he wouldn't marry for some years. He's not easy to please, dear boy, and his life seemed quite full and interesting enough without. He's ferociously attached to his work, you know. But as you see," with a little laugh, "it's all irreproachable."

"They had a church wedding, of course?"

She nodded, "Even that," with a fond amusement in which I thought there might be a shade of something else, I couldn't tell what. "I should only be really vexed with him if he'd married a girl without spirit. But I gather she's quite independent in her charming little way. She's a pilot herself."

The picture had been taken just before or after a steeplechase. I knew the place, in Maryland; we had gone down to spend a week-end with friends of his there late in the summer. No, it must have been after the race; he was too self-conscious about his ugly teeth to be smiling so unless he had just won something. She was standing with his arm around her shoulders and was smiling too, or rather it looked as if they had both just been laughing very loud in the excitement of the victory when jokes would come easy. She was wearing a beautifully cut autumn suit that brought out a peculiar sameness of physique between them, as if they were brother and sister and both jockeys. I had sometimes minded our being the same height and my having a fuller build; it made me as nervous sometimes as if I had been fat, which I never was, and during our last weeks it had seemed that whenever we were together there would be something wrong with my clothes: a shoulder-strap or a zipper would break, or the jacket I had spent my last dime on would turn out to be just the wrong shade.

Miss Pryden remained magnificent, making her goodbyes so cordial and easy-sounding that for the moment I wasn't even conscious of the omissions: of her having still made no mention of my grandmother, or sent any word to my mother. It seemed to me that I wanted her good opinion more than anything, and I thanked my stars that I had been saved from showing her my tears and embarrassing her with my confession. She would never have forgiven that.

Mrs. Hollister was something else. I couldn't avoid letting her give me a lift home, that is to the house on the green, and she was sighing and pitying me and patting my hand all the way. It was only in Miss Pryden's presence that she hadn't felt she could express her feelings, which of course had nothing to do with the main point: she couldn't know about that. All her family were home for the holidays but she was going to come and see my mother as soon as she possibly could; and she did, a few days after Christmas.

"Betsy, Betsy, I implore you, *pull* yourself together," she went on, while my mother stared at her with the wobbly smile that had become the only variant to her chronic expression in those days, of sodden, vacant defeat. "I've got a brilliant idea, Betsy," jumping up, "I'm going to take you to the hairdresser. Right now! There's a little woman in Wellford that I've discovered who's been doing my hair, and it's going to be my treat. Now come along . . ." So for a couple of days my mother's gaunt, dismal face, which had never had any beauty except what was given by strength of character and a companionable warmth of humor, was topped by an incongruous mousy frizz that was a most hateful reminder to me. She had worn her hair that way during the few awful weeks when the worst of the trouble started—if you can ever speak of a start in such things: anyway, during the second and last year of the school. How could anybody who had known her and all her principles, who had seen her hoeing the vegetables and longing for the school all those years, have imagined *that*? Anybody who had ever seen the tenderness she always had, no matter what, for my father? I can't imagine it even now although I saw it: the girlish blouses she was suddenly wearing, the silly smiles, the excuses to be away all afternoon for her secret rendezvous—with Mr. F.! A fool, fat, half bald, the father of one of the girls besides. I suppose the novelty amused him, its being so clear she had never been treated like that before because there was nothing about her to attract a man that way; and he didn't have to live in Jordan afterwards. He was even boasting about it. She was the only one who thought it was a secret even when she would come back to the school prayers and dinner smelling of whiskey and making the girls giggle and look at me, she who hadn't had a drink in her life before those clandestine dates except Miss Pryden's table wine and the sherry my grandfather used to bring out before dinner on holidays. But it wasn't too bad until his visit in the neighborhood was over and he had walked out on the whole business, which she must have known was all he ever meant to do, although the way she took it she might have been imagining—but what on earth was there to imagine, even if he had not been what he was. She would never have left my father, who there later in the rooms in the Howland house, whenever he was not down with one of his head-aches, would make her cup after cup of coffee on the electric burner on the floor, the only stove, and bring covers and shawls to tuck around her while she passed out, and then would sit for hours waiting for any sound she might make, in case she should want something, or for any twitch of her face, any change of expression at all.

But she did have one other expression at that time, one directed only at me, and to me it was the worst. I would have given anything for her to go on being hard and unjust to me as she had been most of my life, when it was always Arthur alone who would be forgiven and could make her laugh no matter what he had done wrong; there was almost always an excuse for him, and never any for me unless my grandmother provided it. If I left a little bit of dust under the bed I was sent back to sweep the whole upstairs over again while he went ice skating even if he had done just as bad a job shoveling snow. I was "lazy" and "shiftless" and "a sneak" and eventually "boy-crazy" which was as bad as the rest; and some of it was true. She drove me into lying to her about almost everything even when there was no sense in it. But at that later time, the year of my visit to Miss Pryden, I was longing for her to scold me and accuse me of something however unreasonable, just to have a moment's illusion that her old personality and strength and moral certainties, as strict as my grandfather's and of the same stamp, were still intact. I would have loved, that late afternoon when I came in with the photograph of the honeymoon couple blazed on my brain, to be told I was a liar and sent to bed without my supper. But she looked up at me instead, as she did most often at that time when she was not too stupefied to look at all, with a twisted, humble smile in which she seemed to be asking my forgiveness for any hurt she had ever caused me in my life, and begging me not to hurt her too much in return. They didn't ask where I had been. They heard about it later from Mrs. Hollister who must have been dying of curiosity, but they didn't dare ask me about any of my doings in those days for fear I would get into a mood or say something cruel, so the visit was never discussed.

From that day, or perhaps it was from the minute when I saw the photograph, I lived in my dream, I don't mean a dream of hope but just a place of unrealities, until that afternoon when Jack

Pryden drove into our lane. Of course that is not quite true; nobody could live fourteen years, not at that age anyway, without some reality sifting through on to them, but it was the way it most often seemed. I had another life in my head all the time that was the important one, like the world of the set of paper dolls I had had as a child and would go off into when things were bad outside. The tearoom had failed and we sold some land and were back in our own house but without any way of undoing the damage that had been done to it. It was Daddy and I alone first, unless I should count the first week, the last of my mother's life; then Lucas after we got married; then Dickie who had just had his fifth birthday when the thing happened and the dream came pouring through.

It was because of Dickie that I happened to see. He was playing outside where the beginning of the lane makes the driveway to our gate, and when the car turned in he came calling to me at the kitchen window, naturally thinking it was somebody for us since no car had been up the lane in years. It was a little red foreign-looking car and I recognized him right away, I hardly know how when he didn't stop or even slow up much although the ruts were deep and still soft. I thought he must have arrived in town just that day and probably wouldn't know I was still living there; with so many city people moving in, a lot of houses had changed hands since he was in Jordan.

He went on up, and I began seeing it all with his eyes. Our house first, with the white paint peeling and the green shutters weathered nearly to black, and one shutter hanging crooked where a hinge was broken but that was nearly hidden by the forsythia. The lawn had gone to seed so it was all one big messy field all the way to the road, but the trees were the same, nearly; we had only lost one elm that was struck by lightning; and Lucas had recently patched up the little well house where we used to hide playing hide-and-seek, and had even painted it, I hadn't understood why when so much else needed doing. He would have to leave the car at a certain bend in the lane and would go farther on foot, between the old apple trees that were in the first days of blossom, or rather under them because they made an arch over the lane just the way he would remember them, unless he remembered more the way we used to go up there at night to see how frightened we would be by the black tunnel they made, and by the old cemetery at the top. He would be seeing all the center of the village from there, and it wouldn't look changed to him at all; it would be as small and green and pretty as ever, and it struck me then for the first time that that was true only of Jordan, of all the towns I knew. Everywhere else there were motels right at the edge of town or a drive-in or a housing development or something. The one gas station in Jordan you couldn't see from up there by the cemetery; the one store had been expanded and moved down on to the main road past our house, but it was still plain white and not much of a store; the only other new building near the center was the little fieldstone Pryden Memorial Library, Miss Pryden's bequest, which is rather an eyesore but not conspicuous enough to spoil the green. How peaceful it would look to him! and the hills spotted with orchards and cows, with the little May clouds skipping over, would be rolling away and away, blue but not like his eyes, as far as he could see. Then he would go a hundred yards over the side of the hill, I was sure he would, probably not knowing yet that Baldur Blake had been gone nine years or was gone at all, and would probably think he was dead, seeing the roof half fallen in and everything soaked and splintered and tattered all over the place; and even if he thought he was dead he would have to do some more wondering about it when he made his way on through the brambles in back to the barn that used to be the studio. He would be picking up plaster bits of me, my face and hands, "those beautiful hands, Eva, show them to me," around the floor.

I ran upstairs and changed to the only decent blouse I had, a pink nylon one I had made the summer before and never worn, and put on lipstick. I told Dickie I'd be back in a few minutes and to stay where he was and not go near the well house; he wanted to come with me and I had to leave in a hurry not to hear him crying. But when I got up to where I could see the bend in the lane where I knew the car would have to be I was taken by surprise. He had run the back wheels into the ditch trying to turn around, and Lucas of all people, my husband, was helping him out with the tractor; the field there was the one we had sold not long before to Mr. Jarvis and Lucas must have been manuring at that end of it when the trouble occurred. It made me almost laugh to imagine the two of them in conversation: Lucas bringing his words out so slow as he always did with strangers, as if he were hunting for the next idea at the bottom of a haystack, and probably with the twitch that was apt to come on in unexpected situations going about once a minute on the left side of his face; and Jack so fast in his speech and in everything else, making himself more agreeable than he felt, to hide his impatience. His hair, in the same old crew-cut so short it was almost a shave, was grey now, with a spot nearly bald in back. Lucas very tall up on the tractor seat in his dungarees and T-shirt, blond and strong and sunburned, looked from that distance a lot handsomer and a lot more than two years younger. But just for a minute. Something Lucas said, I couldn't imagine what, made Jack turn away from their parley with a big laugh, and then it seemed to me that his face was not old at all, I even had an impression of something in it more boyish than fourteen years before, and his step was still that of a person who has never been tired in his life. He looked as fastidious in dress as ever too, even in the old country clothes he had on then; I had remembered particular suits and ties that he wore, more than the innate elegance I was seeing now.

I went back to the house, wondering if he would be finding out that Lucas was married to me, and busied myself around the gate instead of going inside. Dickie had begun to be frightened and perhaps it was because of that, although he had seemed all right as soon as I was there again, that he didn't get out of the way of the car when it came down a few minutes later. He was playing with his pail and shovel in the driveway, the bottom of the lane, and it was coming fast but I saw him look at it when there was still plenty of time and even start for the grass. But then he turned and was running right back in front of it, perhaps just because he wasn't used to cars coming from that direction. There was a scream of brakes and I think I screamed too, as the car missed him. It lurched up out of the ruts and over the grass and then as if it hadn't slowed up at all was whirring on down the drive and into the main road. I was staring after it in a crazy way so I saw him glance back once to where I was sitting in the dirt with Dickie howling in my arms, and lift his hand I suppose in a kind of apology, before speeding on in the direction of the center and the Pryden house.

II

WHEN LUCAS CAME HOME I was playing the piano with Dickie in
the living room, both of us laughing at the clatter we'd been making,
and he fell in love with me all over again. I still had my pink blouse on,
and had taken some trouble with my hair. He was surprised to see us
in there; we lived mostly in the kitchen and the old pantry next to it
where we'd put the TV, and except when I had a fit of house-clean-
ing, had scarcely set foot in the living room or dining room in ages;
in fact Daddy and I had stopped using them before Lucas came.
The funny thing is that seeing his surprise and happiness as he
stood in the door, discovering in the deepening of his eyes what
laughter was in my own, I think I was in love with him too, and if
he had taken me in his arms quickly it would have been like long
ago between us, when often for a night, sometimes for days I used
to empty myself of any wanting beyond his arms and his goodness
to me. "Oh Lucas, you're so good," I had said out in the field our
first night together, "you'll never do anything bad, will you? will
you, Lucas?" He had just laughed, not noticing anything wrong in
the question or thinking of answering it. His face was promise
enough on that score; and now suddenly for a moment when I
least expected to I was seeing it that way again, not only as handsome, which it so movingly was, but with the something else that
used to bring such words as "noble" and "princely" to my mind. He
went on staring at me in the strange excitement of the moment
while I thought again, what familiarity had both confirmed and
obscured, how incapable he was of any meanness or deceit or
doubleness of any kind, so that whatever he chose to do could seem

a good and enviable thing just because he was doing it. There was nothing but candor and love in his face as he looked at me, and I had an impulse to run and smother myself against it.

But perhaps he distrusted my mood, not having seen me like that in so long. Or perhaps it was because he was dirty and sweaty, having gone on to another two hours of digging somewhere after his job, that he held back and didn't touch me yet. He seemed to be trying to figure out something about the room first, or about himself, and doing it in that slow way of his, although in some situations I had seen him act quickly enough. "Hey! All dressed up!" he said smiling as Dickie ran to be taken up on his shoulder. "Where's the party?" Then he was wishing he hadn't said that. We never talked about all the parties we weren't invited to, more every year with all the new people moving in. When I was little there had hardly been any parties in Jordan except Miss Pryden's or our own or the dances for everybody who wanted to go at the Town Hall, but things had begun changing around the time my mother opened the school. Sometimes I would hardly know I was feeling anything about it until I saw it in Lucas's face, saw him knowing I had somehow heard about a certain party and knowing what I was thinking, and he would be puzzling, just wanting me to be happy, because it wouldn't have occurred to him to want to be asked himself. "So *we're* having a party," he went on quickly, "aren't we, Dickie-boy? Music and all. The three bears are having a dance. Da-de-da-da . . ." He went dancing around with Dickie hanging on to his hair. One of the hundred jobs he'd had was playing the clarinet in a jazz-band back before the war and he could give a good imitation of a band all by himself. But then his eyes happened to rest on the plaster head of a boy that I'd kept in the living room all those years and I saw that he was getting ready to say something.

I told them it was time for them both to wash up, and began chattering as we moved to the kitchen, saying that Dickie had been playing next door at the end of the afternoon so I'd gone for a walk up the hill: as I had, for the second time that afternoon, to try to clear my head.

"I wasn't playing," Dickie said. "There wasn't anybody to play with. I was just sitting. The man almost hitted me too."

"What? What man?"

"He means a car," I said. "Some man going by in a car."

"You shouldn't play out by the big road," Lucas said gently, sloshing his face at the kitchen sink. It was the same old iron sink that had been there when my grandfather was young; a new one had been put in for the tearoom but they ripped it out when they left, and we had brought the old one back in from the barn. "You mustn't ever go out there by yourself. Whizz. Bang. Boom. Ouch!" He made his hands go like cars and brought them into a punch in Dickie's stomach, then grabbed him and threw him in the air and they were both laughing so that Dickie stopped trying to explain about the car, and that it hadn't been out on the big road but right in our lane.

"Do it again, Daddy, do it again!"

"Wash-time. Ting-a-ling."

"Why can't we have a puppy, Daddy? Tell me why!"

I didn't know why either. He was the kind of man who would naturally want a dog; it was just one of those things he refused and that we didn't talk about.

I helped them fill the tub on the floor and started cooking while he bathed Dickie as he always had done from the beginning, and always there in the kitchen because it was cold upstairs in the bathroom in winter; besides, Lucas wanted me near him when he came home. They had a game of washing each other and looked so alike playing it, I used to feel sometimes that I was no relation to either of them, only that Dickie's eyes were nearly black and wide apart like mine and like my grandmother Buckingham's. His tough blond hair was Lucas's, and the two strong squares of the chin and forehead and the upper lip much fuller than any of ours, and he was growing to have a lot of Lucas's expressions, even his trick of looking into distances the way farsighted people look at birds far away only there would be no bird. I didn't mind. I had hated every day I was pregnant, and out in the driveway that afternoon I had had almost an hallucination, that I was only pretending to be his mother, and I was looking around almost really wondering why his real mother didn't come.

Lucas was still happy. He looked up at me across the tub, his eyes, grey and very clear, telling me that I was beautiful and he loved me, and his hands wanting to reach for my shoulders. I had never known a man's hands as strong as Lucas's, so that I would be afraid of his playing with the cat and used to be astonished at their delicacy in love: as if he were "educated" I had found myself thinking—not very aptly considering some of the college graduates' and even professors' hands I had experienced. Actually Lucas remembered what he had learned better than I did, and had read a lot more too at some time or other, I never could figure out just when. It was certainly not since I had known him.

"So I walked all the way up to Baldur Blake's place, just for the exercise. I hadn't been up there in ages."

"It's a mess all right, I went by a couple of times last winter. I suppose Jarvis'll be getting his hands on it one of these days. Okay Dickiebird, all clean."

"It's awful seeing it like that, as if he were dead. He was always such an old maid about the place. My grandmother used to say he cut his lawn with nail scissors. And when he was making that rail fence in front you'd have thought every piece was a statue he was so particular. I went out to the studio too. There isn't even a lock on the door."

"You'd think he'd come back for some of that stuff, it must be worth something. Unless . . ."

"Unless what?"

"Unless he's too drunk." But that wasn't what he had started to say. "People get to hate themselves," he said speaking fast. "Have to kill somebody, or something."

"Yes. Anyway he wouldn't need the money; he wouldn't care about that."

"Say," Lucas said when he came back from putting Dickie to bed, "you know that head he did that you've got in the parlor . . ."

"Yes, I told you. I'd give it back to him if he ever wanted it."

"No, I mean there was a fellow with a car, kind of old-looking I thought he was at first, got stuck up the hill this afternoon. I was thinking I'd seen him somewhere, and it just came to me tonight when we were in there . . ."

It was strange the things I had told Lucas about myself; bad things. Before we were married I couldn't stand the way he would speak of my small wrists and ankles and my smile as if I were a princess and had never touched anything dirty in my life. I told him I was lazy, and a liar sometimes, and about the men I had slept with; and once I did happen to say that I had been in love one summer when I was very young. But after all I had never slept with Jack Pryden. I don't know if I would have if he'd tried but he never did, not from inexperience in himself but in respect for mine, which he seemed to feel as one with the other "purity" he claimed to love in me. I suppose really I was sexually backward then, or at least not up with my generation, having had so little life with people my own age. We would just lie on the couch together talking about how it would be when we were married and then he would put his tie on again and take me back to my room, only it was so hard to separate we would have to talk and kiss in the car a long time before I went in. We were half sick all summer from going to bed so late.

Perhaps if Lucas had been inquisitive I might have told him more, but he didn't seem to care what had happened to me before; it was as if both our lives were all contained in what we were seeing in each other right then and nothing else was interesting. I discovered one day that he had known for at least a year how my mother had died, and what she had been before, and hadn't thought to mention it. But I was just as indifferent and knew just as little or less about him. If he said anything about his childhood or running away to sea or the army later, I would half way listen and not press him for anything more; and he never did say much. It would be a passing mention and he would be embarrassed and go on to something else, as if to speak of the past at all were a form of weakness or ex-hibitionism. And perhaps it was because I felt that in him that I liked him right away the first time, just after the war, when he came around selling Happy Bread and expecting, as he told me within a few minutes, to find some crazy old maid living in a house like that, not a beautiful girl like me.

I let him joke along about my husband wanting some bread even if I didn't, and didn't tell him till the next time when I bought the bread and a cake too, although we both knew it wasn't fit to eat, that there wasn't any husband, just my father and me. He had a car lined up to borrow the next week but something happened so we went out on our first date in the bread truck. Then before long the company folded and Lucas began picking up odd jobs around Jordan and spending most of the time there, because of me. He couldn't un-derstand what a girl like me was doing buried away in a town like that without even a movie house; not that he wasn't glad or ever wanted to see a city again himself, but he couldn't understand it in me, he seemed to think it was too good to be true that I shouldn't be want-ing a job in the city and more of a life. I just told him I'd tried it; that was all; I'd tried it, twice, not counting the summer in New York way back, the last time in a war plant in Bridgeport until I got sick. That was true, and perhaps the rest of the truth I didn't know

well enough myself to tell: not that the boss was a filthy old man
but that I was lost in the city in a worse way; something was going
to come for me in Jordan, in that house that was as much a part of
me as my own blood, and I had to be there where it would find me.
Lucas didn't ask any more; and didn't tell why he'd had a medical
discharge before the end of the war when there was nothing wrong
with him. I think he didn't know or care, or cared too much to
stand knowing, the way it was about other things, because he was
afraid of his own temper. The fight he had at the gas stand in Jordan
because of me, when he was hanging around there on the lookout for
jobs before we were married, I heard about from somebody else,
never from him at all. I could imagine the kind of things they would
be saying, knowing Lucas was dating me; and so he had knocked
one of the boys clean out, without any warning, and was so sick and
strange afterwards we had to put him to bed in our house for two
days. The twitch was going all the time on the left side of his face.
But I know he was sick from his rage, not from whatever he'd heard;
there wasn't anything that I or anybody else could tell him that
would make a dent in his feeling about me. It was a long time after
we were married that something came out about his father running a
country carnival and making him do stunts until he nearly killed
himself and ran away. That was when he was fourteen and it
sounded as if he had never seen any of his family again.

My father went on living with us after we were married, looking
more and more like a moth, although he wasn't so old really, only
in his sixties, but he had begun looking like a moth, or a dead
dandelion, long before. He still kept a few chickens and would sit
in the kitchen after dinner very slowly sorting and wiping the eggs,
telling little jokes from the radio or the Wellford paper; he washed
the dishes as he used to for my mother, when he wasn't down with
migraine, and would think of other little things to be helpful, like
taking the spots out of Lucas's clothes with cleaning fluid. Lucas
would listen to his jokes and tell him some of his own, and I would
try to be like that too, because my father had never been unkind to
anyone in his life and I truly loved him, but sometimes the mystery
would hit me and I would scarcely know what I was saying or doing.
I would be feeling all my grandfather's perplexity and despair over

him, his only child: whose resemblance in features and courtesy of manner was all to my grandmother's side, only the power had gone astray, from either side. The money had gone astray too, most of it, even without his help; the tales and habits of grandeur, or what came in the echo to seem that, were from way back in my grandmother's young days in California. Still there had been no strain or struggle to send my father through Yale, majoring in chemistry, and set him up in a drug business in New York, where he employed another chemistry major, also from New England but a great deal more penniless and more determined, more like his father than himself— my mother, unbeautiful and without any of his social grace, who was working nights for an M.A. in education, having even then the dream of a boarding school. They went to the opera together, she for the first time. My grandmother, who had been to the best opera houses in Europe and could play and sing all the famous arias, must have smiled later at her enthusiasm and musical ignorance. But she had the gift of not expecting everybody to be like herself and was prepared to value her son's choice, whoever she might be, just so the heart was pure.

By the time I was four years old we were all back living with my grandparents in Jordan, with my father in the new role of gentleman farmer, or so my grandmother fondly put it, not in the least distrustful or disappointed by the change. It seemed he had been ruinously cheated by a partner, and there had been a slump in the stock market, also an unfortunate accident of some kind in the manufacture of a certain drug; and so on; besides he had an allergy to drugs, or possibly just to something in the city air, that was giving him headaches. "*Gentleman* farmer?" said my grandfather, who however was getting too old to go on running the farm by himself along with being a judge, and wanted time to finish his book on the legal history of New England. His other book, a thin little volume of verse in old-fashioned print, I never heard of until he was dead. "This farm needs more than a gentleman to run it. But I dare say, Edward"—looking at him with a bitter skepticism, in which there must still have been affection and some relic of hope— "you have better sense than to fall in with your dear mother's regard for Marie Antoinette." "Why, Thomas, how can you say . . ." "I am speaking of her only in her capacity as a farmer, my dear. The rest of her history can wait till we've mended the henhouse." My father was delighted, as he always was when his father made a joke, and said respectfully that he would do his best. He'd been thinking about the henhouse all morning and wondered what his father would think of buying new tar-paper for it; on the other hand, if they were going to invest in a milking-machine perhaps they'd better cut down the small expenses and concentrate on that; unless it should seem wiser to get rid of the cows altogether and build up the place as a chicken farm as Dan Pickett had done and made a very good thing of it. "Chickens get such diseases," my grandmother said, "and I do think, Thomas, that Edward needs his sleep; he's still not strong, you know, after that terrible siege last winter. Of course there's always Frank"—the hired man, who was gone by the next year, followed shortly by Bridget in the kitchen. "But whatever we do," looking around at everybody with brilliant and loving enthusiasm, "now that Edward's going to manage everything, we *must* have horses again. It's so important for the children."

She was clearly referring to a different order of animal from the one that my grandfather, at that time, would still hitch up to the sleigh when the snow was too deep for the car, to drive in a jangle of bells the ten miles to the courthouse; Arthur and I would rush out all joy and importance to help with the harnessing and wouldn't let him leave till he had flicked our initials in the snow with his whip. I believe he felt a great love for us on those mornings, and in spite of his disappointment in his son, who might have been supposed to make up to him for some of his own frustrations, something like happiness. Yet I think of him turning out on to the main road, in the crackling air and tinkle of bells, with his long face set as though in the welcome certainty of an accident to the sleigh that would make that his last sight of home. He had left us, as he still thought then, "security," no matter what should happen to the farm; his duty was done. As it was he lived to know that he would never finish his book, to see most of his investments turned sour and my father crumpled under worse headaches than ever, and perhaps even to have a suspicion of Arthur's character; in which he would have been alone in the family and particularly at odds with my mother's happy partiality. In almost everything else he had such a depth of silent accord with his daughter-in-law, it was a wonder that neither his wife nor his son should have felt their exclusion from it; but it was not in their natures; they knew nothing of self-scrutiny or resentment. It was enough for my grandmother that she loved and admired us all; and when the possibility of my mother's school began to be discussed, before my grandfather died, my father showed no pride but his pride in her. It was not necessary for anybody to try to make him feel that the plan and the need of it were no reflection on his own failures; it never occurred to him that they were, and he entered into the scheme, for which no backing was then in sight, with his usual tender and whimsical willingness to help. He had watched the cows and the hired help depart, and the chickens diminish, with the same look of innocent dignity, as uncrushed as a wraith would be by a falling rock.

It was the same later, with Lucas in the house; he was only smaller and greyer and slower. He hadn't thought to question our marriage, and when I searched his patient and always intelligent face for the scars that should have been there, some mark at least of my mother's suicide, it would seem to me that there was nothing. He still grieved for her, and missed her continually, but more as if she had been removed by some sleight-of-hand, which not being in the business he could naturally not be expected to figure out.

A strangeness would come over me, and for days I would know that Lucas was knowing I was somewhere else, listening for something else: because Lucas's kindness and love for me would become part of the one trouble. I would say cruel things to my father, or do strange cruel things, like not setting a place for him at dinner so he would come in in his quiet moth way and have to go to the cupboard for his own plate and fork and knife, while I went on eating or talking to Lucas or just thinking, as if there were nobody else there.

My father didn't say anything about it usually; but sometimes he did: "Well, girlie, I guess the old man's kind of in the way, eh?" or more jokingly, with his little faded smile, "Three's a crowd, eh? eh, girlie?"—pushing at me for an answer until I would feel my eyes going hard and think if he said "eh? eh?" once more I would have to break something. "Nonsense, Pop," Lucas would break in, hurrying to help him and clap him on the back, "Eva's just so tired tonight she can't count, she's been ironing curtains all day. Why, we couldn't get on without you, there'd be nobody to tell us what was in the paper. You don't mean that's *dinner* you've got on your plate? I thought it was a speck of dust. Here . . ." and he would heap my father's plate with more than he'd eat in a week, shrunken as he was, with the old businessman's suit he wore hanging from him so he wouldn't have scared a crow. "Well, I know how it is," my father would go on. "When you get old you're not much company for anybody. Just a

fifth wheel on the buggy"—smiling as if that were a pretty good
little joke that he'd made up himself. "But it won't be for very long.
That's one consolation, eh?" with a wink in my direction. "Eh,
girlie? That's one comfort, anyway."

"Oh for Christ's sake shut up!" I yelled once. Another time I
began to cry quietly and just sat pushing my fork around while my
tears splashed down into the plate. Then suddenly I was smiling
at him with all my love and running around to take his head in
my arm and rough it up against my side. "Oh Popsy, you old wretch,
as if you didn't know we love you and need you and want you . . .
Hey, Pops, remember when you got us the pony? remember? and
kept it hidden three whole days before Christmas? I was thinking
about it today out in the barn and started laughing; remember how
you made us all laugh about it on Christmas?" So then he and I
together were telling Lucas for the dozenth time all about the pony.

That had been in one of the periods when some mysterious
little recuperation, from a change in the stock market or rise in the
price of eggs, would bring us a short whirl of luxury that was always
assumed to be natural and permanent. There had been a fine new
victrola and a new coal range for the kitchen that same Christmas,
and once for a few weeks there was a French governess; because as
my grandmother mildly said, a fact so incontrovertible needing no
stress, "It will be such an advantage to the children all their lives to
have learned French when they were young." She herself had learned
too late ever to have a good accent and had always regretted it.
Arthur and I, accustomed to running barefoot around the farm as
we chose and who fought for the privilege of feeding the pigs,
dumped a pail of water over the governess's head as she sat brooding
under an apple tree, and so spared everybody the pain of admitting
that she could no longer be paid.

It was two years after the end of the war, and a year and a half
after Lucas and I were married, that my father was taken with his
fit, or whatever it was that gave him the fancy of having to visit
Arthur's grave. It was on an island in the Pacific that we had never
heard of till the notice came, after a Marine landing in '43. "My
God!" I said. My father had been very proud of the Silver Star that
eventually arrived and would recite over and over the few details of
the place and the battle that we had managed to pick up, much
as he spoke of the camping trip in Canada that he had gone on as
a young man. Since the camping trip he had never been farther than

New York. He had no urge to travel himself, and my grandmother's cultural impetuosity, which later just when the wherewithal seemed all gone sent me huddling off to Europe tourist class under her wing, had come to grief in his case, against my grandfather's rock-ribbed view that a man should stick to his profession: very narrow, to my grandmother's chivalric mind, but she was too wifely to say so and might even have half way agreed that a knowledge of cathedrals was mainly important for girls. My father in any case had been content to get his, such as it was, from the stereopticon. And how, Lucas and I wanted to know, was he going to pay for such a trip? So that was when it came out that he still had a little stock that we had never heard about, even when we were having the worst time over the mortgage; not much, just enough probably if he went very cheap all the way. "Arthur never wrote home at all, never once, after that night down there," I said nodding in the direction of the green because I never could stand to mention the Howland house. But my father didn't seem to hear me, and perhaps really I was only talking to myself.

Arthur had only come, that night, to say that he and his friend were leaving for Mexico. The friend had had a different young man with him when he first came to town and bought a little house on a back road outside the village; he was fat, mincing and old, at least in his forties, and he was said to be a decorator although I never heard of his decorating anything but himself and his own house. His name was Mr. Delacey, and he was called Spank. When Arthur began going around with him it was supposed to be a job; he had recently flunked out of college after a series of scrapes with girls, and now he was going to earn money to finish and go to engineering school as he had always meant to. He was "working for Mr. Delacey," landscaping, even building a new kitchen wing for him— there wasn't much Arthur couldn't get the knack of if he set his mind to it; and pretty soon he was playing the penny whistle and the guitar for Mr. Delacey's weekend parties and having to spend the night there more and more often. In the beginning he would bring money home, that is to my parents upstairs in the Howland house, or sometimes big bags of fancy groceries and other presents, and would be very cheerful, vaguely intimating that they wouldn't have to worry about the house very long; he was sure he was going to earn a lot of money on the side, drafting or something, as soon as he started engineering school. "I've been talking to a friend of Spank's who knows a lot of people in the army . . ." "Yes," my mother would say, "yes . . . yes . . ." and seeing how much he wanted her to be pleased with the rum cake or the green silk scarf he had brought she would rouse herself to smile and say it was nice, while her head and eyelids drooped like a sick animal's. He never brought Mr. Delacey there to see them but I was sure Mr. Delacey wanted him to, I don't know why; or why I was invited to one of the parties. I was the only female. Mr. Delacey, when he was not doing dances by himself in a Spanish shawl, hung around me all the time as if we were the tenderest friends, although I had scarcely ever spoken to him before, all velvety with attentions and compliments that had some bright little insult quick as a snake's tongue in them every time. Arthur began to pout about it across the room, an expression I had never seen on his face before; but finally he became angry more in his old way and took me home with such a look, I was sure he meant not to go back. I am sure even now that when he left us that night he was only going to return the car and get what clothes he had left there and walk home.

Mr. Delacey was evidently afraid of something of the sort the last time, and hadn't trusted Arthur to come and see us by himself. I went to the window to hide my feelings when I understood what Arthur was saying, and in the light from the porch saw him waiting beside his car, too nervous to stand still. "Stop this," I wanted to shout to my father. "He's your son. Stop him!" It had been a long time since Arthur had brought any money or presents home; I suppose it was too embarrassing for him, and perhaps Mr. Delacey, from not being invited into the family circle, had become less generous. But that time when I turned back into the room I saw two ten-dollar bills on the table. Arthur was explaining that he wouldn't be able to start college again until the fall anyway, and he had a friend—he didn't say "a friend of Spank's" any more—who had promised to introduce him to some mining engineers in Mexico, so he thought he would take advantage of that to get some "practical experience" for a few months. It was the first time I had heard him speak without seeming to believe what he was saying, and he looked hectic and half sick; his big outdoor face had become dragged and pouchy like an insomniac's, so that I almost felt, from the voice too, that some wretched double was there impersonating my brother, and was startled to hear my mother, who had been snoring a moment before, say quite distinctly, "Where's Arthur? I thought Arthur had come." Then I watched her get to her feet, wildly recollecting a scene years before, when discovering Arthur in a car at night with one of the "bad" girls of the village, she had gone out like a scourging angel and driven him into the house: the first time her wrath, which I knew so well, had been visited on her darling boy.

I thought it was about to happen again, and looked triumphantly at my father, ashamed for him of his role, but he was seeing better than I. Her hand was reaching for the money on the table and she was asking Arthur, whom she had apparently recognized, to go and get her a bottle of whiskey for a stomach-ache, although there wasn't a liquor store nearer than ten miles. "Yes, Betsy," my father said, "tomorrow . . . the first thing tomorrow. Come and sit down now. You want to talk to Arthur, don't you? He's going on a trip tomorrow, he's going to start being an engineer in Mexico. And he's going to spend the night with us now, so he'll get it for you in the morning. Aren't you, son? You'll stay tonight, won't you? Eva will make up the couch there . . ." I didn't say anything. We heard the front door slam and then Mr. Delacey arguing hysterically with Mrs. Howland on the stairs, she saying she wouldn't have him in the house and calling to her husband to throw him out, which in a minute was happening, accompanied by more indignant squeals and shrieks for Arthur. Arthur started for the door twice, looking sicker than ever, without the strength either to go through it or to stay. The commotion stirred my mother to a moment's consciousness, in which she looked at Arthur and said in a voice of agony, "If your grandfather had known . . ." "My grandfather! He was a stiff-necked old fool. He and his stupid poems! What did he ever know about me or my life or anything in the modern world? and what if he had known about *you* . . ." But he broke down right away. "Mother! Mother!" he began calling, bending over her. "Listen to me. I'm staying, I'm not going away tomorrow. He can go to hell, I loathe him, I loathe all his friends. I'm going to stay here, Mother, and we're going to go back to our house . . ." My mother didn't seem to hear anything, even the car horn that had been going in one steady blast for several minutes in the quiet night and must have woken everybody on the green. "My little baby," she was mumbling, "my little boy, my sweet baby boy . . ."

"I'll be back in a second," Arthur said to my father, and without looking at me ran out and down the stairs, and we heard the car drive away. My father made up the couch, and for a couple of hours went on waiting for his steps to be coming back up.

"My God!" I said to Lucas, watching my father in the other

room carefully turning the pages of the family atlas for the map of
the Pacific. But later I said, "We'll have to let him go. It's as good
as anything else, I suppose."

So we put my father on a bus for New York, all of us acting as
if that were as far as he was going, and never saw him again. There
wasn't even a postcard later than Ohio, although it was aboard a
freighter half way to Hawaii that he died. But it was before we knew
about that that I had woken in the middle of the night and heard
myself saying, childishly, "As if he had ever cared about Arthur . . ."
and then in a stranger voice, ". . . or anybody else." Lucas pulled me
closer to him and held my head gently against his naked shoulder,
and we went back to sleep.

"That's who it was," he was saying now about the head of Jack
Pryden in the living room. It was a curious work in one way, with
a child's features but as if Baldur in doing it had been seeing way
ahead into the life of the man too, or as if the child model himself
had been doing that; and perhaps it was true that Jack had never
been much of a child. It took only a little trick of vision to turn the
white face, thin, taut, intelligent, with something about the eyes
more than the nostrils that suggested a keen sense of smell, into the
face of the medical student some ten years later, or the one that
had broken into my life that afternoon. "I had to help him out with
the tractor. Turned out it was that Dr. Pryden you used to know, the
one I was fixing the drive for last Saturday." He pointed toward the
living room. "That's who it was."

"Oh. Well yes, I suppose it must be. He did pose for Baldur
once or twice when he was here staying with his aunt. I can't imagine
why he's come back."

"Not to be the town doctor anyway; I asked him. He said something about a new laboratory down near Danville. But he was in an
awful hurry. He tried to give me a dollar." Lucas laughed over that
in his pleasant, easy way, helped me dish out the dinner and pitched
into it as gladly as usual. "Baby, I'm sure glad you can cook. And
don't look at me like that when I'm busy. You'll be giving me
ideas."

I gave him back a smile like his own and pushed my hand over
where he could touch it and for a minute, chewing more slowly, we

stared at each other in a joke of love. I had a clear feeling of happiness in being with him, and wasn't thinking yet of the night. Nor of how he on his side might, before the real night came, be talking about Alaska and snow. There was something for him in the idea of the deepest possible snow that I hadn't tried to understand, but I had learned to recognize certain warnings of the thought coming on and making him like a stranger in the house: a stranger, I used to feel, in life, because I didn't think he really meant to go to Alaska. It frightened me; it was too much like a privilege that should be only mine. He was never so happy as in winter when he could be off tramping in the snow for hours looking after his traps, and I would go into a panic sometimes on those days when the light began to fail, as if I were engaged in a dim battle to bring him home, against the power of the snow.

But there were no warnings just then. He was very solid and hearty and at home across the kitchen table, and ready to listen to my inventory of Baldur Blake's house, as of that afternoon, or any afternoon in the last nine years, subject only to weather and animals.

Split-rail fence still perfect; lawn and path vanished; little front porch sagging but pump beside it probably still usable (he had never had running water); front door held to with a twist of wire. Living room, tiny like all the rooms, scene of great anger, but the leaks not too bad. Two downstairs bedrooms left more hastily; sheets and blankets only slightly rotted on a good four-poster, other covers and work-clothes mildewed on floor; kerosene lamp overturned, with broken porcelain shade; bureau drawers open containing a few ties, one pair gold cuff-links, laundry left soiled; in closet, officer's hat and pair of puttees, World War I. In kitchen, some cheap crockery left dirty in iron sink; a few chunks of wood beside stove that was for heating too (no furnace in that house which was perhaps as old as ours but was just a poor little lonesome farmhouse never meant to be beautiful); hanging, one frying-pan, two pots, a bachelor's kitchenware, who for twenty years never had a guest; broken panes on floor, from back window blown in. Little shed used for wood storage and chemical toilet, now encumbered with fallen roof and porcupine nest. Painted door giving on narrow stairs, to one room above, but it was scary there and I hadn't gone up. Back through the living room quickly, before the scare moves there, through the hour of the owner's final unbearable rage, whatever was left over after he had finished with the studio, and further scatterings from nine years' rain and wind, but he would have had to do the tearing and throwing down first: of letters but not many; cancelled checks the latest dated September 1943, so he had left in October not able to face another coming on of winter, of dark at five o'clock, in the company of an eighteenth-century cemetery and a pet duck; newspapers but none for his last two years there, the war in Europe was passing him by that time and maybe he was still being proud of his khaki hat and puttees in the closet and not thinking any other war worth reading about since he was not in it; annual volumes from the Century Club in New York, to which all those years it must have pleased him to pay dues so he could have the vanity of never going near it; a form letter addressing him as "Dear Member" from an artists' association, that being presumably the beginning and end of his relation to it; a volume of Nietzsche; a few volumes of the *Encyclopaedia Britannica*, which even before I was in college he had gone crazy enough to be reading straight through at the rate of about one letter of the alphabet a year; and in and around the old granite fireplace, ashes of other books; at the windows, still not all broken, shreds of curtains badly sewn by himself, although my grandmother had offered to do it for him.

No pictures; there never had been any; nor any trace whatever of the convivial except a couple of ancient ping-pong balls, recalling a championship that had once sat as high in his pride as his three years with the Prix de Rome. For all the later years there was nothing to see but the grim closing in of the one idea, which on that October afternoon he would discover at last was no idea at all: was just nothing. The pictures were in the old barn, the studio, and were merely photographs, a dozen or so, brought back all those years ago from Rome and now still tacked to the beams or curled among the rubbish on the floor—Michelangelo's Moses and some figures from the Sistine Chapel, and a relief of Venus rising from the sea, of which my grandmother had brought back the same photograph around the same time, to frame and hang back of the sofa in the living room where it still was. The photos nearest to contemporary were of some works by Saint-Gaudens, whom Baldur had known in his youth and gone on revering out loud ever after.

"Poor fellow," said Lucas, and I thought he was going to get up and turn on the TV as we did most evenings although he usually went to sleep in the chair in front of it. But he was happy for me to be talking, and still holding the moment of his coming home, when he had found us at the piano.

The studio—

"Yes, I know. The statue in the corner . . ."

Lucas often surprised me that way. I hadn't known before that he had ever noticed that horrid mutilation, of the final statue, and the only one that was still upright and not otherwise broken; the others had just been pushed over and had broken as they fell. But nobody else could have made such a distinction. The work of the last six or eight years, the "perfect goddess" that was to have finally justified everything, was different only in sitting cross-legged on a double leaf instead of standing. They were all the same prenubile nymph, with the same lovely adolescent diaphragm under ripples of chiffon and hands that a passing breeze would break, smoothed over to such insipid grace, it seemed preposterous I should ever have posed for her, or should have imagined until that afternoon that there was anything of me to be recognized there. Or that the magical *preederome*, without which in my childhood there could scarcely be a mention of Baldur Blake, at least in my grandmother's vocabulary and almost as surely in Miss Pryden's too, should have kept the power to awe me long after I learned to connect it with the city of Rome, which after all my grandmother had also spent a whole winter in, and even after I knew, or thought I did, how little value there was in the statues in that case.

Perhaps even now some tatter of that *preederome* of my youth, mystical and grand, beyond decay or belittlement by any actual fact, was influencing me as I remarked that I thought I might go over and see Baldur Blake in Wellford some day: not that there was probably much point in it.

"It seems awful nobody ever bothering. And we did use to see him so much. He used to play bridge here with Mother and Daddy almost every night."

"Sure, why not? Go ahead."

"You know I even had a funny idea"—I was smiling very straight at Lucas, too straight, though I didn't know why I should be feeling disingenuous on this subject—"that he might like to come here and stay with us for a while, so he wouldn't be alone all the time, and he could go back up there and work again in the daytime. If he just fixed up the studio a little . . ." I went on rather breathlessly, amazed at my own proposal and my excitement in it, as Lucas stopped looking at me, "He could pay board, we could even make a little something. And I'm sure he'd still have his own car. He always got a new one every year."

"Have a lush in the house? Baby, you're nuts. I'm through with that. If it's just for the money you mean, somebody to pay board . . ."

He got up and stood with his back to me at the window, looking over the bottom of the lane; the dusk was just coming, and we hadn't yet turned on the lights. The little edge of strain in his voice was as far as he would go, I knew, toward telling me how hard it was to go on meeting the payments on that big house and now on the TV besides, which neither of us had ever exactly said we wanted, only there had to be something in the evening. But our keeping the house was only for me.

"Oh for God's sake . . . No, it was just thinking of all that work and his caring so much about it, seeing it all broken up like that, got me feeling . . . Well, never mind." But in a moment instead of starting to wash the dishes I was bursting out, "It's awful living like this just with ourselves, never doing anything for anybody, not doing anything *good* at all or even thinking anything. We don't even see anybody. We haven't even got any friends!" Lucas didn't turn around, or say anything. I went over and put an arm around him and rubbed my cheek against his shoulder. "Darling, don't look so sad, please smile at me, because I have another idea. We're going to fix the house up! We'll do it ourselves, it'll be fun, we always *used* to talk about it. We'll paint it and make a lawn again and everything. I'm going to start clearing the garden tomorrow. There isn't any reason why it has to look so terrible, why we have to live like this as if our lives were finished, is there? Is there, darling? Tell me. Speak to me."

He kissed me lightly, almost smiling but as though something had slipped, making a distance between us. I saw that he had come home dead tired from his thirteen hours' work and had been putting all his strength into not admitting it until now.

"Yes, honey. Sure. I guess you're right." He looked at the window again, at the glass more than through it. "Jarvis's man was at me about the house again today. Sounds as if the boss were getting pretty hot about it."

"No!" I said with violence, but less than I felt. The year before too I had had the same earthquake feeling, nausea and the walls slipping, when the Jarvises were newcomers in Jordan, or at least were spending a fortune on the old place around the hill from us which they hardly ever came to, and I first heard how much they were ready to pay for our house too, as if one weren't enough and when they already had the best piece of our land. "Especially not now!"

"Why especially?"

"Just when we're going to fix it up. But I mean not any time; never. You didn't tell him . . . ?"

"No. I just told him it was your family's place from way back and we weren't figuring on selling."

"What did he say?"

"Nothing, he just looked as if he didn't believe it. I guess Jarvis is used to having his own way." Lucas paused and I thought he was waiting for the twitch in his cheek although it rarely came when we were alone. "I expect I'll be moving along pretty soon, maybe next week."

My heart stopped, as if I hadn't known that he was only speaking of the job; I had never known him to stay on a job more than a few months. "Why? Did he want to give you a raise?"

"Yes," he smiled, "but not much, and anyway . . ."

It was always like that; he would leave as soon as there was a threat of promotion, of his being put in charge of something and making more money, instead of being the nameless man at the bottom of the pile. Some day I supposed people would catch on and there wouldn't be any more threat, more offers, but up to now there always had been, sometimes inside of a week; because there was something in Lucas's face, more than his being bright and more than the peculiar air of authority that was around him in any job or even in doing nothing, that made people love him and want to push him on to something better. It was almost sometimes as if they were afraid of his gentleness, afraid of being ashamed of themselves for being more successful than he, though it was not likely there should be anything like that in the Jarvis case.

"It doesn't mean we have to sell him the house, just because you let him give you a better job. He seems to run all sorts of businesses aside from the farm here. Isn't he the president of some big company?"

"Sand and gravel. Cement. Housing developments."

"Whatever it is he could do a lot for you, if you'd just stick around a while . . ."

"Maybe so," Lucas said gently. "But I expect I'll sign back on the road gang next week."

I turned on the light, and it was as if I had never seen his face in profile before, it was so beautiful. A saintly face, I was suddenly thinking, and a little shiver of horror seized my spine at the thought. It was certainly not emaciated; even tired as he was, the slight curve in below the big cheekbones was only enough to keep his firm, fresh-colored cheeks, with their tracery of tiny scars by the left temple, from looking juvenile and the sense of strong appetites from being gross. Nothing ascetic at all; and he might never have heard of the Ten Commandments, he might be a thief and murderer for all the sentiments I had ever heard him express; if he was displeased with anything he would just move away from it without ever telling why, if he knew. Only it seemed that evil would die like a poisoned insect in the vicinity of his face as I was seeing it then. I couldn't understand it, it made me giddy, it seemed to take away all the substance of the world. But then as I moved toward him, frightened and fascinated, another kind of consciousness began to spread slowly like a stain over his features, and when I came to the window I saw that the light was striking on the muddy tracks where the car that afternoon had plunged up on the grass. He looked down at me a second but even his eyes weren't asking me why I had lied, letting him think it was a strange car out on the big road that had nearly hit Dickie; and perhaps I was mistaken, and he was not connecting the two things at all.

There seemed to be only tiredness, not anything hostile or suspicious in the silence between us as he began helping me with the dishes, but even so there was no peace.

"You're never going to do anything," I said with a sudden loud bitter clarity. "You're so afraid of being dirty! You'll never be anything but a handyman all your life."

He was looking at me, but with his snow look, as if I were just a form seen far off through a driving snow.

III

It was a week before I thought again about going to see Baldur Blake, and when I did go I didn't get past the boarding-house porch. I didn't plan the visit, but just went on an impulse after I had finished marketing in Wellford; it was the only boarding house there, and not far from the parking space in the middle of the green. I saw him through the window. He was playing bridge with three old ladies, very intently, and wasn't facing in my direction, and after I had stared at him a few seconds I tiptoed away. He had lost the chronic sunburn he used to have from puttering around outdoors so many hours every day waiting for inspiration, but otherwise his appearance was remarkably unchanged, and if he was drunk the old ladies must have had an agreement among themselves to ignore it. In any case, with the constitution he had it was apparently going to take more than nine years of that life to lay him low; he was close to seventy and at least in that stealthy view looked fifteen years younger.

The days were full and bright. It rained most of the night, the night after Jack Pryden drove up the lane; when I woke up, Lucas had made up his own lunch-pail and was gone, and I lay in bed a few minutes and looked out at the shine of the young elm leaves that had just opened. In the freshness of the morning it seemed to me a curse had lifted; the birds could sing and the brook, where I used to watch the sunlight for hours, was running again for the first time in years. I have never known water anywhere as lovely as it is in Jordan, in our brook and the spring up the hill, and the other brooks and the river. Long ago, before any of the worst of my family's troubles began, it had come to have a great power over my imagination and I am not sure it was not that more than anything else that pulled me back to Jordan twice after I had tried to make another kind of life for myself in the city. At least it is true that I had never felt lonely as long as I was looking into the water there or hearing it; and in the office I would sit half mesmerized thinking of it wriggling over the stones, and remembering the smell of weeds and iron in the river, as if everything I was missing in life would be somehow in its image. A bullfrog holding his breath at the rim of the spring, until I outwaited him and he dove through a fan of sunbeams to his secret slime, could cancel out every human impediment in his neighborhood, as in the fairy tales. But for a long time I hadn't cared. I hadn't even thought of the water in ages until that morning, when with the sound of the brook out the south window, just gently audible at the end of the field toward the Episcopal rectory, the old brightness suddenly filled the room, along with a flood of flashing projects and a conviction of strength in myself to carry them out: to do, it really seemed to me, anything I might set my mind to. I would make money on my own hook, for one thing, if Lucas would not. Since I was fifteen I had made and designed most of my own clothes, and with Jordan becoming so social I had thought sometimes of making a business of it, only the will or the nerve had been lacking, until now. For that morning, however, no better beginning of life proposed itself than to clear brambles until Dickie and I were both worn out, he having caught the infection and started on schemes of his own: we would dam up a pond, have a family of ducks, and so on.

In the afternoon just for fun we drove down the river road, not to the swimming-hole below the falls but a few miles upstream where the river is shallow and deep in woods, with a wooded cliff up on one side and no houses along the valley bottom for miles. The family, with my grandparents, used to go there for picnics, and nearby was a ford we used to cross on horseback, before a long gallop curving up the mountain and ending at the top of the cliff where the trees parted and the river was suddenly there again way below. Looking at the ford I felt through my body again the thrill of the horses beginning to surge forward at the approach to the other bank, all gathered for the gallop ahead that was hard to check, the riverbank at that point being the signal for a furious license that would begin to spend itself half a mile above. The picnics were exciting too, in another mode: lyrical, long, murmurous, with a sense of hours consenting and the sun lazy, among little staccato flurries from the telling of a family joke or the discovery of a missing package of sandwiches, all winding along toward a gentle readiness at last to go home. I couldn't remember any serious quarrels, or anything desperate or bad at all, on those excursions. If they could be run off now for somebody to judge, with the full cast of characters and no cuts, I am sure the verdict would deny any possibility of all that happened later and to some extent was happening then.

My grandmother, with her indomitable taste for an occasion and flair for making one out of a sow's ear if necessary, sits on a log in her starched gingham, with a matching ribbon on her high straw hat and a parasol, on the lookout for mushrooms and ants, as pleased as a hen with her chicks. My grandfather, when it comes time to open the baskets and thermos bottles, addresses her as "Lady Buckingham" and with courtly affection suggests that if she will stop fussing everything will be much simpler; to which, very sure in her womanly prerogatives, she answers with a serene "Nonsense, Thomas," and the touch of coquetry due in recognition of his manner. Previously, after a brisk splash in the river, dressed from neck to knees in an ancient bathing suit, which owing to an ill-timed absence of my grandmother one spring has for some years been a network of patched moth-holes, he has been leading Arthur and me in a strenuous series of setting-up exercises by the riverbank, although he has already been through them as usual in his night-shirt after a cold bath that morning. My mother is also in a bathing suit, which in spite of its long skirt and heavy lining fills her with an awkward consciousness of her drooping breasts and somewhat mottled skin, so that she is forced into inactivity by the urge to hide as much of her bony length as possible. But after a while, rarest of spectacles, the sun and my father's boyish pleasure in puttering over the picnic fire charm her into indolence; she smiles tenderly even at me, when I bring a wild flower or some other exhibit for her praise, and when the refuse has been burned or packed away, in the mystic hour of digestion before adventure may be resumed, is to be seen sharing a tree-trunk for a back-rest with my father. Being shorter than she, he has to sit straighter so that her head may rest on his shoulder; his hand in transit from a lazy scratch on the leg happens to brush hers and in the harmony of their snooze comes to rest there; somebody makes the kind of remark that is made at that hour, for the sake of the after-ripples, and a little joint murmur of laughter comes from my parents' tree, before his head sinks down against hers, his mouth opens, and as though all our destinies were in the safe watch of the little couples of butterflies that flicker now and then across the scene, he sleeps.

The picture was so bright I could almost believe that spring afternoon, returning there thirty-two years old with my child, that the spell had really held, and nothing not previsioned on those long lovely days had happened to any of us. They had, anyway, their part in the truth, and seemed somehow to sanction the happiness I felt in playing there with Dickie and knowing again the play of light in the river, like the running of steel knitting needles in my grandmother's expert hands. April was past but still left its chill in the water, under a summer sun that was wrangling with every stone in the river-bed and shattering the greens in the woods so the dogwood blossoms were hidden among them like trout in the shallows. But we did see a trout, and stuck our toes in the water, and squealed over minnows.

"They like me," Dickie said. "The fishes like me."

I said I liked him too, and with a hurt of jealousy that astonished me, of the fishes and anything he might trust more than me, I pulled him tumbling into my lap. He put his arms around my neck and snuggled closer as I kissed him, as if nothing uncommon were happening. "Mommy loves you," I chanted, entranced by the fullness of my heart and by whatever genius it was in his, duplicate it seemed of his father's, that made him not question it nor oblige me to think of myself as forgiven. "Mommy loves your nose, and your eyes, and your funny big mouth just like your daddy's . . ."

"Will Daddy be home when we get there?"

"I hope so, my sweet." I had never felt so close to Lucas. But he had gone to see about a new job and came late.

I saw Jack Pryden's car go by at the end of the afternoon, and a few days later I ran into him at the store.

He was just leaving. I heard his laugh first, before I had reached the door, and wasn't sure I could go on; then I thought of waiting where I was so I would meet him there alone instead of in the mail-time crowd inside. If I had heard that laugh in a crowd on the other side of the world I would have known it. It was more like a big man's laugh, not what you would expect from his face or build: a genial, generous kind of laugh, with loud separate notes not snipped off

or reined in but wholeheartedly ringing, although not to the point
of his ever doubling up with laughter or lapsing into it uncon-
trollably for a second burst once the first had died down. But his
face was still all given over to the funniness as we met, which infected my face too so that it looked as if the joke were our having
nearly collided in the door. "Hello, Eva, how are you," he said in
the easy way of anybody greeting a neighbor in the store, and with
the usual pleasant nod of such situations, nothing further being in
order at the moment and no offense taken, he went on out. After the
screen door had swung to he did half turn, evidently with a thought
of apologizing for the incident in our driveway the week before;
unless it was the evening I waited for him fourteen years ago that
he meant to explain; there would have been some little misunder-
standing that had made him miserable too, nothing serious, nothing
that five minutes together wouldn't undo. But then somebody
leaving the store greeted him and we parted, he walking off thick
in that conversation and I to resume my other life.

That evening when Lucas was giving Dickie his bath, I said I
had to drive to the center a minute to see a certain woman about
making a dress; the days had become long and that one had been
unnaturally warm so that people would be sitting outside. I kissed
them both and ran out and drove past the Pryden house. There
were people having drinks on the porch as I expected. The yew
hedge along the road, which Miss Pryden had kept clipped and low,
had grown wild since her death and afforded only a flash glimpse
up the path of the figures on the porch, among them the host fresh
from his pre-dinner shower and change of clothes, passing a glass
and apparently in the midst of an anecdote that was holding the
other faces turned toward him in the last stage of suspended laughter. I imagined it just breaking out as I left the house and in
another moment the village too behind, the street turning there
suddenly after the last house into one of the lonesomest roads out
of Jordan. But in the sociable scene that went on developing for me
as I drove on a little farther without pleasure or purpose toward the
valley, his face stayed apart from the general cheer and took on
instead the look I thought I had seen in it after the screen door had
closed between us that morning. It was a look I had known well in
our days of happiness, of a deep and most delicate appeal, not for
love but for the chance to be exposed and vulnerable in his own
love, as though in this there would be a release from some doom

that no speech, only his eyes would ever confess. I hadn't seen until later that the doom was in me and had been from the beginning. I had brought it myself into our love, and so was riding all the time on fear and deceit, afraid of his knowing my fear or hearing the prayer that was in me all the time, for his love please God not to stop. So it was only later, when it had stopped, that I grew into guilt and shame, seeing how little by little my whole personality had begun to go wrong in his presence, just as my clothes did; feeling myself going to pieces, I had had to make up other personalities for myself to please him, and lived in a dread of not sounding like myself.

An exact date, four years before that summer, had come gradually to fix itself as the origin of that feeling of being condemned, so that any happiness I imagined would seem meant for everyone but me, no matter how I pretended to be eligible too. That was the hideous last evening of the school, when the scandal was exhibited before an audience of some two hundred people and Miss Pryden, hastily grabbing up her cloak without a word to anyone, swept from our house for the last time; or more exactly, from our barn, which served as the school auditorium. At any rate, I never saw the scene without my cheeks burning and a silent cry for rescue filling my head—the cry had discreetly changed from Jack's name to a "Darling! darling!"—and without its bringing into focus automatically the other picture: of myself as outside the pale, humbly watching the magic by which the most ordinary people, not necessarily even good-looking or goodhearted, were capable of falling in love in reciprocal pairs, both at the same time. For me it seemed foreordained that something should be rock-bottom wrong, and so it always had been, with the boys I had dates with before that summer and the men after. They had to be ugly, sick, crazy, something; twice my age and married, a lot younger and weak; T. turned out to be a homosexual, and L. a thief. I used to fall in love with the relief of knowing the wrongness ahead of time, instead of waiting for it to be sprung on me, as if that were an insurance against being hurt, and then in the end I would be hurt just as much as if I had been really in love and had lost something wonderful.

But now I thought I had suffered enough to have grown out of those fears, and the lies they bred.

The valley became spooky to me; I turned the car around at last and drove slowly back. The last house on that side of town, nearly across from the Pryden house, had been bought a few years back by a pair of middle-aged maiden ladies that I had a speaking acquaintance with from meetings in the store, and having stuffed some dress sketches in my pocket as I left home I had an impulse to take them in there and try my luck, if I was ever going to try. Under the anaesthetic of suddenness I thought I could carry it off, and did, beyond any expectations. Miss Bean and Miss Troy were delighted, flattered that I should have thought of them, urgent that I should join them in a martini; they certainly did want some summer dresses and never could find anything ready-made to fit, would look over the sketches and come to my house tomorrow to discuss materials, etc. It was a triumph.

Dusk was settling when I left, the people had gone in from the porch across the road: to dinner presumably, and a fine French wine, if the host was as choosey in that regard as he had been as a young man. I felt exhilarated and very full of my powers, just as my grandmother must have felt, only that she never had known a lapse from hers, in everything she did, all her life long. I saw her through all her years in Jordan tripping up to that door in the gay certainty of her welcome, the door springing open before she could reach it as doors seemed to do for her everywhere, as soon as she was seen approaching; and Miss Pryden, to whom interruptions in general were so galling, glad in this one connection to lay down whatever she was doing, and come forward to greet her. For all their long easy intimacy she never failed to rise at my grandmother's entrance, as a mark of respect due to their disparity in years if not to something in the quality of their friendship as well, which put their intellectual disparity in the light of a thing of no consequence. If there had been only that side of the picture, the one predominant in the public view of the "learned," "dashing," "influential" Miss Pryden, her respect should have been chiefly for my grandfather, and she might have felt a certain contempt for his wife's mind, as being in cultural and public matters both hazy and cavalier. But something else bound them; some other sphere of wisdom was recognized by Miss Pryden, in which with all her charms and accomplishments she seemed not quite to claim a footing of equality with my grandmother, and seemed even to be the subtle recipient in any element of favor that might be between them. As far as I had ever seen, it was a tone unique in Miss Pryden's human dealings, and it was only by the touch of deference on her side in that one relation that one recognized the touch of the imperious in all her others, with the further exception only of her poodles.

In the bright, busy days that I was launched on now this mystery of my grandmother's nature stayed with me constantly, as though all her love for me had raised only echoes while she lived, and I was only now coming into true communication with her. Circumstance had certainly done what it could to shadow her, and introduce her to the possibility of defeat in life, and had utterly failed; she knew of no such possibility; nor could physical decay, any more than poverty, make her image less victorious. She can creep down the hall to the bathroom in her cotton nightdress, her white hair in curlers beneath a nightcap, her teeth left behind in a glass of water beside her bed and her aged face otherwise distorted by a sudden gastric attack, hands gnarled, legs veined and spindly, her breasts long since shriveled and scarred from the removal of tumors and allowed to hang exposed now owing to her haste and discomfort, which have caused her to paddle forth without stopping for her bedroom slippers; she is nearing eighty; her bladder muscles especially have weakened so that every social occasion has to be thought of in terms of escape and life is webbed with little lies covering retreats to the toilet. But the enduring presence is that of "the magnificent old lady," and even, agelessly, the "beautiful woman"; who was never really beautiful, her features having no classic regularity and her large splayed nose being almost enough to mark her as ugly. What she has, along with a stunning sweep of hair, white since the age of thirty, is the indefinables of beauty: the carriage, flash and sense of dress more often associated with a certain hauteur and at least occasional malice of expression. Their total lack in her is the final chemistry, so that to us in the family nothing seemed more natural than that the Queen of Italy, all one winter, should have bowed to her every morning as she stood on her hotel balcony across the street from the palace.

It would have been the natural recognition of like for like, that particular queen, so we were told, having been noted for her goodness and simplicity of heart. In a photograph from that winter, a year before her marriage, my grandmother is seated on a fallen column in the Roman Forum, between two other ladies of her party. No candid camera there; no running out sight-seeing in a sloppy dress either. The pose is courtly, the dignity too delicate ever to be caught in a lapse, even aside from a certain sense of higher responsibility that seems to attach to the making of a picture; the ladies' ankle-length pinch-waisted attire, beneath hats like accommodations for three setting hens, hides such a machinery of snaps, buttons, hooks and eyes, linings, whalebones, it is hard to see how there is time left after dressing to do more than exclaim over the Forum. Actually they have walked miles, and studied a good deal; the guidebook my grandmother holds in the picture has been thumbed to pieces; and in the afternoon, fresh as robins, they will be off in a carriage to Tivoli or somewhere to study more miles of stones, before meeting friends for tea and a stroll in the public gardens, and eventually going on to somebody's very special box at the opera or an ambassador's reception. Her circle of friends and acquaintances at the time, like those of her glamorous girlhood in California, might have come years later under the heading of "connections" if she had been capable of thinking of them that way. She was not, worldly situation having no bearing in her mind on the realities of friendship. From all but Miss Pryden she was separated later by geography, but she wrote and received her innumerable Christmas letters every year, full of family chitchat on both sides as if there had never been any break, and was even able to accept a one-sided flow of favors provided only they were for one of us, the family, not for herself. We *were* herself; if I tried later to see even a moment's worth of her image, a single gesture, as outside her love for us it would vanish, veils, hats, amethysts, knitting needles, the Roman Forum and all, like music without an instrument.

Hence, via my grandmother's correspondence, most of the enrollment in my mother's school the first year; and my own series of vacation visits, from the time I was ten years old, to Bar Harbor, the Adirondacks and Nantucket. She seemed hardly aware of any limitations of Jordan for herself, but couldn't bear to think of my girlhood as less privileged than her own; there should be dances, tennis courts, above all "young people." The phrase should have implied that our schoolmates in Jordan were in some mysterious way not people, and I came to wonder later by what mystery of innocence and lack of snobbery in her it did not; because she, most of all in the family, to whose lips the word "background" came most naturally, would have extended her love to Lucas without any thought of his—my father's acceptance of him being too ghostly to count. But I never could tell her the misery of those visits in the homes of her old friends; on which I was always the outsider, the wallflower, the one imposed on the "young people" by their parents; who didn't come from their kind of life. They had the hostility of animals for a creature of another breed, more so because their mothers admired my manners and through practice on Miss Pryden's tennis court I could get to the semifinals in their tournaments. The boys who were made to dance with me were always stuck, unless they dared to walk off and leave me, and sometimes I knew they were holding out a dollar bill behind my back. The worst time was a picnic at Lake Placid, when the group of four or five faked a game of hide-and-seek to go off and leave me, and after waiting a couple of hours until nearly dusk, I had to find my way down the mountain by myself. Afterwards I got up at night to stare at myself in the mirror, trying to see what was different about me, unless it was just that my clothes were never quite right and I had to wear my old polo coat for an evening wrap. That was the year before my grandmother died, two years after our trip to France. I was thirteen, and I knew the grown-ups thought that I was pretty, even that I took after my grandmother, so in the mirror I imitated the hold of her head and her most irresistible smiles, seeing myself as the girl at the dance who was cut in on every minute, as she would have been in California if they hadn't had cards instead, but my face was hideous from crying and after every smile I was back playing hide-and-seek on the mountain, discovering all of a sudden that there hadn't been any game and nobody else was there. There was a porcelain cat in the room. I took it to bed with me and between sobs lay theatrically crooning to it in French, my one accomplishment aside from a slight edge at the piano.

The family were all turned out to meet me at the Wellford station a few days later as if I had just been crowned the queen of something. They couldn't wait to hear every little thing about the wonderful time I'd had and my mother and grandmother especially wanted to hear the nice remarks I must have heard about my clothes, because they had both saved up for them all spring and worked hard getting them ready. It hadn't occurred to them that any girl my age would have an evening wrap. Only to Arthur when we were alone I told a little of what it had really been like. "The dirty sons of bitches," he said, looking very manly. "But you *are* pretty, Evie, you're the prettiest girl in town. I hear a lot of the boys say so." "This isn't Lake Placid," I said. "They can stick Lake Placid up their acid." We roared over that, and then he took all the money he'd earned delivering milk that month and came back pretty soon with a bottle of bootleg wine and a lot of fancy things for a party, just for the two of us. We took it up to a cave in the woods and before long we were laughing at everything under the sun, especially the ridiculous Adirondacks, and I was sure I had never been so happy in my life. The rest of the family assumed I was being modest about my triumphs and probably had a special reason to be secretive too. "What's his name, kiddo?" my father would go on at every meal-time. "This Mr. Tall Dark Handsome . . ." My mother, who had never had any beaux or much fun when she was young, fell in with the joke, watching me intently through these interrogations with a grin compounded of pride and sarcasm and incredulity, this first identification with me in romance making her aware of me for once as her daughter. "Does he go to boarding school? Did he ask you to the prom?" "Nobody says boarding school," I said. "They call it prep school." "Oh, I beg your pardon. Well, did he?" "Leave the child alone, for pity's sake," my grandmother said. "A girl has a right to her own secrets. Now you're not to ask her any more about it. But tell us about the picnic, Eva. I'll never forget an ex-cursion at Lake Tahoe when I was your age. There were about twenty of us, boys and girls, with a chaperone of course, and we met two mountain lions and a grizzly bear and a rattlesnake all inside of an hour . . . But I suppose you young people now wouldn't think of having a chaperone. Was that nice grandson of Mrs. Seward's along? Such a sweet boy. I do hope you were nice to him, Eva. He seemed rather a quiet type, and you're such a rowdy; you know sometimes when a girl is having a good time she can hurt people's feelings without meaning to. Of course it's true he can't have been above five years old when I saw him last. I think she wrote me he goes to Exeter now . . . I do wish we could send Arthur to Exeter for at least one year, he needs to meet nice young people too, it would be so valuable for him all the rest of his life. I think I might just write her and ask about scholarships."

I never told Jack the truth about those visits either, that summer in New York. I suppose I was afraid of his thinking I was in love with him for the wrong reasons; because of the kind of car and apart-ment and clothes he had, and the kind of restaurants he could go to; because he could afford to be so lordly and easy about things that were either a pinch and a scramble or else unthinkable in my family. Not that he hadn't known perfectly well since we were children what kind of life I was used to. Perhaps I didn't exactly lie. I would just recognize somebody, or pretend to, in a theater lobby or a nightclub—he was a wonderful dancer and we used to drop into places sometimes just to dance for half an hour, not even bothering to stay for the floor-show—and say in an uninterested kind of way, "I think I met him sailing once in Newport"; something like that; and drop it, as if summer resorts were as natural to me as the swimming-hole under the iron bridge in Jordan. Or I would manage to mention casually, in some other connection, a dance or party during one of those visits, without saying that I hadn't had as good a time as anybody else. Later the original humiliations came to seem nothing, or even funny, compared to the discomfort I felt over those deceits; I used to flush with shame when I thought of them. It seemed to me that there was nothing in my life I wanted so much to undo, and when I ran into Jack Pryden that morning in the store it had been almost on the tip of my tongue to tell him right then, as if it had all happened only the week before, that I knew what he must have thought of me and I was really not like that. I was sure that if he saw me at home now he would see that I had grown capable of the "simplicity" that he admired.

He had thought he was finding it in me in the beginning; and in fact the lies were more toward the end, when little by little I had begun to feel him judging me and to feel myself shown up as lacking and guilty, without ever knowing when the fault had set in or what it was. In the beginning we were so happy, I don't think I even noticed especially what kind of places we went to and whether they were expensive or not; and perhaps at that time, in that happiness, it wasn't even a lie to sound as if I had always been popular and at ease in any social situation, anything to the contrary being as though wiped out by the present. Or if that is not quite true, at least about a good deal in my life I did talk at that time just as it came into my head, without considering what he would make of it. We used to weep with laughter when I told him about the trip to France, for instance, and the dreadful pension my grandmother and I were stuck in without any money to leave, until we were rescued, of all people, by Miss Pryden. "Oh Eva darling, you're wonderful," he said. I had been describing my grandmother's dinner conversations with the other characters in the place, exactly as if it had been the Hotel Regina of her youth, and Miss Pryden's appearance as the goddess out of the machine. "She never mentioned that part. Just that you'd all driven down to the Riviera together, with a chauffeur who was a Russian prince." "Well, she and Grandma decided he was, it made it so romantic. But no, of course she wouldn't mention where she found us, and how she got us out."

That particular certainty as to Miss Pryden's character, that that was the kind of thing she would never tell, no matter what the temptation for her own wit, would have been enough to make me tell the truth. But perhaps with my grandmother so vividly on the scene it wouldn't have been possible to pretend, even if I had wanted to.

"Come along, Eva," I hear her saying as the ship nibbles up to the pier, and France, after all the talk, is about to be walked on by us. "Oh, those beautiful cliffs! oh, look at the café! oh my, to be hearing French again! Did you hear that man? Monsieur, monsieur, ici, les bagages! I wonder how much we should tip him. Eva, where are your manners, there's that nice Mrs. Hodge trying to wave goodbye; poor thing, I wonder if we shouldn't help her, she looks so lost. Goodbye, goodbye. Yes, hasn't it been a lovely trip, I don't know when I've enjoyed an ocean voyage so much. Why bless my soul, I believe they're playing the 'Marseillaise.'" The tears come to her eyes. "Eva, don't you ever forget this moment. You're in France!" And a little later, "No, no, Mrs. Hodge, that's the First Class line, we're over here. There; now I suppose there'll be a little wait, but French officials are so kind, I'm sure they'll do their best. I'm so happy for my granddaughter, it would have been so terrible for her never to have seen the châteaux. Think of it! We'll be seeing Notre-Dame tonight! Oh thank you kindly, but no, I'll wait my turn. Goodness, am I such an old lady as all that?" She goes off in a peal of merriment, infecting everybody in the line near us, to my embarrassment. "He acted as if I could scarcely stand on my feet." The gentleman had really acted, as others frequently did, as if she were entitled to privilege, like a prime minister's wife, or a pretty child. Sometimes later I thought of her myself as a child; yet it had been through an accident and not any foolishness of hers that we were stranded in the pension. A recluse cousin in California, whom she hadn't seen in years, had offered out of the blue to pay for the trip, and then died in the middle of it. The fault was only in our being peculiarly subject to such happenings, as some families might have a tendency to be caught in landslides.

But she, at least, emerges every time groomed and glimmering, still wearing her amethyst choker and a fresh lavender ribbon in her high-perched hat, which can be old as the hills and still, because she is wearing it, look like the latest thing; and scans the ruined landscape, pension or hen-yard or whatever, looking for the point of resurrection, of glamor of life that is surely there for the asking; and so for her it always is. Perhaps the ruinous night at the school would at last have crumpled even her, but she was spared that; and as to merely traveling in less style than she had once been accustomed to, and coming to the end even of that rope so inconveniently, she is not aware of anything about it that ought to try her spirit. On this trip it is a crone on a street corner in Montparnasse who says good morning to her every day, although for some days we have been having to do without our mid-morning treat of brioche and have nothing to give, and she answers without any undue graciousness, just pleasantly, being really pleased, as with the other acquaintances she is continually making in busses and on benches in the Luxembourg gardens where we sit waiting for the check that might possibly come in the mail: she holding her head, both before and after the disappointment of the mail in the black hall of the pension, in a smell of urine and boiled cauliflower, exactly as in the photograph in the Roman Forum some fifty years before.

"The chauffeur's name was Félix," I heard myself telling Jack Pryden seven years later, having been eleven the year in France, and now after another lapse twice as long, not being able to relive the earlier events apart from that evening's telling of them. It is not an elegant restaurant that time but our favorite one, a little upstairs place with red-checked tablecloths, where we sit sipping wine and holding hands across the table for incredible numbers of hours; no doubt his work is suffering somewhat, at any rate I haven't yet become jealous of it or started wondering every day if he isn't using it as an excuse and really doing something else on our evenings apart. "I mostly rode up front with him, with a pane of glass shut in back of us to stop the draft inside, while Aunt Addie and Grandma rattled away at each other on the back seat, gay as larks. I used to wonder what on earth they could be having such a good time about, when they were so old. Or what kind of secrets people could possibly have at that age; it couldn't have been just the monks and kings they were always reading up on. They were always changing the subject when I came in on them and your aunt would start making me recite *The Song of Roland*."

"That must have been in the Pyrenees. Thirty lines a day." We laughed, remembering the summer she had had us both memorizing Milton, and then were silent a moment, plunged in common thought, as far as our common knowledge went, of what had come between our families. But he had developed a certain antagonism to his guardian and would not have sided with her in that peculiar story; besides the faults and failures of our elders were blissfully far from us just then. "But go on . . ."

"What *did* they have in common? Grandma had never memorized anything but 'This is the forest primeval' and 'Gallia est omnis divisa in partes tres'; and a lot of Mendelssohn on the piano. She could still play it then, and did one night on a broken-down piano in the back room of a little hotel in Aix, by candlelight, very fast and with a lot of mistakes but it was thrilling just the same. The servants had all crept around and gave her an ovation afterwards, and the proprietor brought out a bottle of champagne, and gave a toast to 'la beauté Américaine.' And she was seventy-five! She was really just going on her style that year, too; my grandfather had died the year before, and her heart was broken. I hadn't ever seen his poems then, the ones he wrote to her when they were young, and I used to think it was all just a grim patience between them, nothing like love at all. It always fretted her so that he never wanted to travel or change his routine in the least, and never would make any flaming gestures; and when she interrupted him at his reading to chatter about something, the way she did every few minutes every night all those years, he would just hang on to his book and wait for her to finish, as if it were nearly more than he could bear, and the next time he wouldn't bear it and would take his hat and go off and die in an inn or a ditch somewhere like Tolstoy. But now I know they were really living those poems all the time, and nothing else mattered. That night in Aix was all a flirtation with him. She was sparkling for *him*, when he was dead.

"One day in a tiny French town, sitting at a café, we watched a funeral go across the square to the church. A wedding procession had come out of the church and crossed the square in the other direction about twenty minutes before, and she'd looked like a bride herself watching it, but when the coffin went by something

else came over her, the happiest look I ever saw. As if the two proces-
sions were really one, and all her life with my grandfather had been
in those twenty minutes, and she didn't want anything more. She
couldn't have let herself believe in an afterlife, considering his
principles, but if he was just nothing, then it would be heaven to
her to be nothing too. That was the way she looked at the funeral,
the way people coming back on a ship look at the Statue of Liberty,
when they've been away from the person they love."

The restaurant was ready to close, the proprietor was sitting in
shirt-sleeves at the corner table reading the paper; but he got up
cheerfully enough to bring the final glass of wine. He liked us
because we were young and in love and because we liked his place
best. Our fingers were still peacefully entwined and we were both
staring at them, scared for the moment of each other's eyes.

"Aunt Addie can't have taken it like that," Jack said with a
sudden little one-note laugh, breaking the mood off before it should
go murky.

"Oh no, she was busy reading about a twelfth-century abbey we'd
been seeing. She made a remark about 'the brute *trudge* of peasant
ritual' and the horrible dullness of those lives. It was a trudge all
right, there wasn't even a cart for the corpse or the bride and groom,
and they all had big clumsy shoes. So Grandma said, 'But you know,
Addie, if we had to use our feet more it might be better for our
heads,' and then looked terribly wise and pleased with herself, because she wasn't given to philosophizing. But I was just looking
around all the time for Félix and wishing he would sit with us. I
didn't care if he was a Russian prince or not. He was my first love
and I thought I'd die every time he was made to stop the car
because one of us had to go to the bathroom, especially if it was me.
I used to wait till I nearly burst rather than have him know.

"We crossed a mountain late one afternoon when I was riding
beside him. It was wild, with snow at the top; it began to get dark
as we went up and there were some red berries along the road that
were very exciting against the snow, under the headlights. It grew
on me that I had to tell him how much I loved him, I was going to
have to make myself say it, and it would have to be up there, before
we came down to some ordinary place, or it would all be lost. It
didn't strike me there was anything funny about my being eleven
years old, wearing socks and a middy blouse, when he must have
been thirty-five. I had the words all ready but I couldn't say them,

and he was thinking his own thoughts, so we drove about an hour without speaking. Now and then I'd sneak a look at his profile, so noble and handsome, and I'd get my mouth open but nothing would come out. It was awful, like when you used to dare me to walk across that high beam in the barn and I'd think 'If I don't do it I'll go shoot myself.' Finally we were beginning to come down, and I knew that pretty soon there wouldn't be any more snow or red berries and it would be all over. So I said it, looking straight ahead grim as death, with my heart pounding so it made my voice all weak and shaky. I said, 'Félix, je vous aime beaucoup.' He just smiled a little bit, not enough to be rude, and said, 'Vous êtes très gentille, mademoiselle.' That was all. We went on down the mountain, without saying anything more that day."

I left Dickie out in the car when I started to go into the boarding house where Baldur Blake was living. It wasn't clear what I was going for. Now that I was so busy with other things my earlier impulse to rescue him looked foolish from every point of view, so perhaps I was only thinking of it as a little sentimental or charity visit, because of old times. I kept remembering Jack Pryden's scorn for his kind of sculpture. But that wasn't what stopped me on the porch. It was an afternoon of brilliant sun; the Wellford green with its stores, bank, drugstore, bandstand, seemed suddenly paralyzed in ugliness, as though everybody there had gone into a horrid trance as of that moment and would never move again. The only motion was at the bridge table beyond the lace curtains, and as I stood watching it, seeing Baldur Blake's massive face intent on the slow laying down of a card from one of the old women's hands, it seemed to me that I had gone looking for somebody in hell. I wasn't thinking of him then as an "academician," a "failure." For me he couldn't be that; even if the statues were no good, I understood at that moment that he had always been with me as an image of a purity beyond anything possible in ordinary lives, and it was out of a yearning for some such purity in myself that I had come looking for him, and had thought to bring him back. But there is no way back from hell. He might go between the bridge table and the bottle hidden upstairs not for nine but nine hundred years and there would still be the same old women waiting to cut the cards and the same saxophone screech coming from the TV in the restaurant down the street, and I felt that in another minute I would never find my way back to Dickie in the car and would turn into an old woman there myself.

But sometimes it seems that once you have made certain gestures, or even just had certain thoughts, they go off on their own and you can't take them back or change their course. It was as if Baldur Blake had known I was there on the porch, and that a few nights later Lucas and I would have some time to kill before the feature started at the movie and would stroll past the bar opposite the station, where he would be standing with his fourth or fifth or fiftieth glass of whiskey of the evening, waiting for us, although in so many years of going to the movies we had never once happened to run into him before. He beckoned us in, and Lucas with all his hatred of bars, having been through his own hell some time before I knew him, for some reason pushed the door open for me with no hesitation and had us going right in, somehow knowing it was Baldur and getting into an easy kind of talk with him, about his place, right away, although he had never laid eyes on him before. I wouldn't have dared myself to mention the house and even less the studio, having imagined so often the way it must have been the day he left and went mad with destruction there all by himself, but he didn't seem to mind it from Lucas; who standing at the bar with a coke even spoke of the last goddess, the last seven or eight years' work, and how she alone was still upright and unbroken except for her genitals being bashed in.

"With your fist? Or a rock? A chisel would take too long." It was the first time I had seen Lucas in an unusual situation without the twitch coming to his face and his speech getting slow. It might have been he, of the two of us, who had known Baldur all his life.

Baldur laughed. He was weaving a little, and now close to under the neon bar-lights I could see the purple alcoholic webbing over his cheekbones, but he still had his old military carriage and his eyes were so glimmering sharp, he seemed not so much a drunken old man as a detective disguised as one. It wasn't a glance I remembered from the old days. There had used to be a continual stop and start in his eyes, and in his sequence of thoughts, which only a suavity of voice and in his choice of words kept from being too noticeable. Now his voice was harsh and jerky, not only from drinking, although he was already calling for another whiskey, and not an old man's jerkiness, but as if what mattered were only some far scheme and knowledge that I couldn't see into and that seemed to have brought us there that night.

It wouldn't be, anyway, that he was asking us to rescue him. When his eyes came up straight to mine I thought he was laughing at me for that, although not only for that.

"Or it might have been a croquet mallet, mightn't it?" he said with a gleeful croak. "Look at yourself, Eva," waving toward the long mirror back of the bottles across the bar. "Trying to be kind. You *could* just say 'I've always admired your sculpture so much,' that sort of thing, but you do better. See? You've made your chin small and your mouth sweet like a little virgin's and you've been thinking of your breasts as two little flowers. Trying to be the goddess I made of you, to give me back my self-respect as you imagine. Well, it's a sweet lie; thanks just the same. We can both do better now."

"How?" said Lucas looking rather cross. "How can anybody do better?"

"Mostly we spend our time drawing water in fish-nets and catching fish in hoops, assuming we care about anything, and it's something after all, it's better than nothing. It teaches us good habits, of patience and industry. But have you ever dreamed you were Nero? I have. It's refreshing, going the whole hog in adolescence, or call it self-congratulation, the same thing. The typical teen-age murder: kill mother, kill Peter Pan, but you're really proving to yourself that you made the world, if you can destroy it. I haunted the neighborhood of my grave for a thousand years, calling myself an artist all the time; I was the evil eye. Boring, you'll say; Lord yes, I died of boredom. It all comes down to sex. Deny it, indulge it, violate it, elevate it, pervert it, call it God Almighty so you'll get more of a squeal putting your boot through it. Poor us; when we try to break the connections, burn the bridges, it's always that, the rejected lover playing God. I kicked the poor little thing. She wasn't worth it of course, no more than a baby doll—excuse me, Eva, I see I've hurt your feelings again, but it wasn't you, you know. But when you've made the world and it's all lies and you're a lie you don't make much distinction.

"The dream, though, I see you've had it too"—this like most of his speech to Lucas alone—"so you know. It's refreshing, as far as it goes. To see ourselves as foul, petty, and sentimental for a thousand years. It helps, a little."

"And then what? You were talking about hoops, I think it was, and fish-nets." Lucas was smiling a little, as any kindly sober man might have been, but with something else too in his expression that was altogether new to me, and that seemed to exclude me altogether. Not the way Alaska did; the opposite; it was not distance in his face now but a smoldering, with occasional bright flashes, of disturbed presentness, a coming into play of some part of his being that never entered into that other presentness that I did know, of his love for me.

"Oh, then . . ." Baldur's head began to sag and his eyes had gone suddenly vague, yet even so as they turned on me for a second they gave me again a feeling that the drunkenness was only to cover some fiercely sober purpose beyond our guessing at. He roused himself to one more small effort. "But this man you were speaking of, Ja-Ja, Jo-Jo, you say he's after my place? Come to think of it I must have had some letters from him, or his lawyer, something. I don't read letters any more. What does he want with it?"

"Just to piss in the spring, I guess," Lucas said. "You know, a big shot. Wants what he sees."

"Oh, is that all." He tried to get off the stool and Lucas caught him and helped him over to a booth, where he called loudly for another drink and immediately fell asleep. They were used to him there and apparently had some arrangement about getting him back to the boarding house. I was nearly at the door but heard Lucas saying casually, as if he were talking to a fellow workman at the end of the day, "If you ever get homesick you could put up at our house." I was sure Baldur hadn't heard him and it wouldn't have made any difference if he had.

But I was wrong. A week later Baldur drove in and left his car by our woodshed where he always had, and started up the hill with a bag of groceries the way he always used to, as if there hadn't been any interruption in his life and work at all. He seemed to have forgotten or perhaps hadn't ever taken in that his house was a wreck.

I didn't call or run after him, I don't know whether more out of triumph or dread. Jack had never telephoned or come near our house, although I would see his car everywhere else, outside all the parties; perhaps I had only imagined the look in his eyes after we had run into each other at the store. But I knew that his opinion of Baldur's work in the past was not as strong as something else, and now he would have to come even if the first time it were only out of curiosity, and then he would know that no matter how guilty or lacking I had been in my life, the best of myself, which he alone had ever recognized or shared enough to love in me, I had never betrayed. Yet I was trembling more from another certainty, that whatever I had gone searching for at the boarding house, what had turned up was going to fool us all, even Jack Pryden, but me worst of all.

Part Two

I

BY THE TIME I saw Jack a few weeks later so many things had changed, it didn't matter if he was at the party or not, not really, not the way I had imagined all those years. It was pleasant and I was glad, but life had been all gladness to me since Baldur came back. I had never admitted before into what miserable laziness I had sunk all through the years of my dream, and now this other brightness had blown the dream away and I was working hard every day and really doing something in the work, not just pushing things around in dead circles and fooling myself. You could hardly have recognized our house, inside or out, from a month ago. But that was only part of it.

It was at Cluny Grey's housewarming party and I was standing in the garden with Cluny and Mrs. Hollister at the time. They were both wearing dresses I had made for them and were gaily boasting about them over the cocktails, and admiring mine too, when the car drove up, not Jack's little foreign one but a yellow convertible too big to turn up into Cluny's steep little driveway.

"Why there's the famous Dr. Pryden!" Mrs. Hollister burst out. "Hi, Jack, hi!" waving, with the rather incongruous youthfulness she sometimes fell into nowadays. "But what on earth is he doing with . . . Isn't that that vulgar Mrs. Jarvis and her husband who's trying to buy up the town?"

"Oh, but he financed the laboratory, you know," put in a Swedish countess, turning to join us. She and her husband had recently bought a house on the green.

"Of course it's a tax dodge," said the Count, who had shipping interests, "but still it's a fine thing for this section. Dignity. Something idealistic. And with the whole countryside going so commercial . . . Have you seen it?"

Mrs. Hollister said she had driven by. I had too one day, not in the spirit that had taken me past the Pryden house that evening earlier in the spring, but just because I happened to be over in Danville looking for dress materials and the laboratory was almost on my way. It certainly was an elegant place and a beautiful piece of modern architecture, at least it looked so to me.

"I don't think I should care to call on them just the same," said Mrs. Hollister loftily, assuming for a moment the mantle of Miss Pryden. It was one she dearly loved to wear although it didn't fit her very well, any more than her own clothes seemed to when she was adopting it.

The new arrivals walked up slowly, chatting and laughing, toward the garden; if you could call it a garden. Cluny had only recently bought the place and for flowers there were still only the same towering lilacs, past their bloom now, and the same wilderness of red ramblers I had known years ago, when my grandmother used to take me there on charity visits to crazy old Dill Polk and her seventeen cats. I don't know why the cats had always been spoken of as seventeen; anyhow quite a few had been found dead in bed with her a few years back and Cluny, who looked much too ethereal and ladylike to stand such a thought, made a big joke of the skeletons she was still finding all over the house. Half way up Jack saw us and lifted his head, smiling, in a most natural way, as I did too. Actually I was more struck by the quite different greeting, a mere flicker but bold and flattering, that I detected at the same moment in the eyes of Mr. Jarvis, with whom I had exchanged only three or four words in my life, and whom I had good reason to fear besides.

Mrs. Hollister, having to curb her impatience to be more intimately noticed, came back to congratulating Cluny on all she had done with the place. She was right, the transformation was wonderful, without your quite being able to see that there had been any. She hadn't gone in at all for the painted wagon wheels, wooden buckets and such, or what they were calling "early American pine," that some of the new people had around, but had just somehow brushed away the gloom. It had been a lot of hard work, mostly done by herself, "when I should have been painting," she had said with the playful desperation that she often fell into; she did like to think of herself as an artist.

"And you've painted your house too!" Mrs. Hollister went on, to me. "How lovely it does look, just like the old days. I noticed it right away from the road. The old Buckingham house, you know," she added for the benefit of the Countess, who murmured that of course she did know. "We always say in Jordan that it's the most beautiful house in town, at least as fine as any in Litchfield."

She tucked her hand under my arm and drew me to her as she spoke, being again for a moment altogether Miss Pryden, even to the slightly English intonation and the slump of weight to the hips. At the same time she made sure that I should see the pain in her eyes, a reference to my mother and the other sorrows of our house, or rather to her own sympathy in that connection; an embarrassment I didn't need to expect from anybody else at the party. Mrs. Hollister's dear husband had died within the same year as her dear, her dearest friend Miss Pryden, and she had emerged from the double loss with quite a new flair of style and spirit, very unlike her old noisy efforts at self-deprecation. It was true the style was marred now and then by certain incongruities, but still it was lively enough to have made her, almost alone among the old-timers of her generation, a fixture in the changing social life of Jordan.

The rest of Cluny's guests, except Jack of course and the old Dan Picketts who didn't stay long, were all newcomers in the neighborhood, most of them more nearly of my age, like Cluny herself, and all of them only recent acquaintances to each other although they didn't talk like it. Between Cluny and me there had sprung up a whirlwind friendship of the kind I had never had before, or at least not since I was about eight. She claimed to envy me, I couldn't imagine why, but I had to believe her, because she was as candid as a puppy, with all her Victorian airs and graces, and couldn't lie about anything. There was nothing artificial in her manner either. She was really made to move her legs as from within a rustle of long silk and her wrists as if she might die of a sudden noise or unrequited love, and since she apparently was welcome anywhere she cared to be, she could afford a great worldly unconcern. I didn't tell her how I envied that, or the almost outrageous toughness and daring that didn't seem to go with her appearance but were just as real in her. She had no particular beauty and didn't need it, she was so delicate and nurtured-looking instead, and yet she would use words I had never let myself say aloud even to Lucas; and if she was somehow lost, as she seemed to me at times, she wasn't worrying about it. It was what she wanted to be.

Perhaps I didn't entirely trust her then, but then I wasn't in the habit of trusting women in general, and I certainly enjoyed her company. I hadn't had anybody to talk to in those ways, perhaps I should say those reckless ways, for years, not since I lost Jack and my brother, and it was wonderful to me, as much so as anything else in that lovely month. And I had Mrs. Hollister, of all people, to thank for it! Cluny and I had met once as children at Miss Pryden's, where her father, a well-known historian, had been one of the visiting eminences, but it was Mrs. Hollister who reintroduced us—Mrs. Hollister, who had cut me so mercilessly ever since the night of my mother's death, and had been largely responsible, as I knew, for the town's version of that event. But it appeared there had been some reversals of feeling in Jordan that I hadn't known about before, cut off with Lucas as I had been.

In the beginning, however, it was nothing but Baldur's return that drew Mrs. Hollister to us, inducing her first to speak to me in the store and later to drop by with a little neighborly gift of cake: as though Baldur, a drunken old wreck as she still persisted in thinking him, had in some mysterious way wiped the stain from our house and even the awful guilt I know she used to attribute to me. I suppose really it was curiosity; she couldn't stand not to know what was going on. Or perhaps she had been waiting for some such excuse to be nice to me, because of something else, something that at first was a dreadful shock to me, harder to bear than her former opprobrium.

I discovered through her, as I would have long before if I had been seeing anybody, that Miss Pryden in memory was no longer the town goddess she had been in her lifetime. Mrs. Hollister didn't come right out with anything very precise, after all she had to guard against a charge of treason to that lifelong friendship and she was also the President of the Pryden Memorial Library on the green; but still in various hints and half-sentences she made plain enough what had come about in local public opinion on the subject, not excluding her own. After all she couldn't help knowing that she had never really been in the top swim of Miss Pryden's acquaintances, but only the sort of dear friend good for an occasional supper and for Christmas Eve. It must have rankled, making her all the more pleased to be playing first fiddle herself for a change, as the present "grand old lady" of Jordan. For the village in general the first horror at Miss Pryden's death and the manner of it—in a plane crash, when everybody beginning with herself had expected her to live to a hundred—seemed to have been followed very soon by a subtle feeling of liberation, as if they were ashamed to discover how they had let themselves be lorded over by a woman. As I began to see, nearly everything about Miss Pryden that either had been admired while she lived or else tolerated with a certain cranky community pride, was in for censure now: her pink barns and poodles and French maid, even her wit and her Latin, her culture in general, from which everything that was bountiful and public-spirited had apparently dropped from view, leaving only a picture of scorn for the intellectual level of her neighbors.

I shouldn't, of course, have been surprised. I, of all people, ought to have known what any reputation was finally worth in Jordan, even the one that had shone as the final standard, justifying the ruin of ours. Nevertheless I was stunned by this talk, and quite unhappy about it too at first. I had never stopped looking up to Miss Pryden, never, no matter what other bitterness I felt, and now it seemed to me that even my grandmother's character and memory must crumble if hers did. How well I knew too that my mother, right down to her last agony, would have been the last to blame Miss Pryden for anything that had happened to her; she had never suggested by so much as a sigh that Miss Pryden had not been right to withdraw her support from the school. And now to be re-habilitated myself at Miss Pryden's expense!

Mrs. Hollister's feeling and intention came exactly to that, and made me think of a quotation of Miss Pryden's about the fallen great and of how merrily, with that golden charm of hers, she would laugh as she said it. Among all the reprehensible items that were being turned up in her own case nothing was more so, at least in this version, than her treatment of my mother. She, with her newly discovered feet of clay, however undefined the nature of the flaw, had wronged my family, had been as responsible as anyone could be even for faults of my own: what could a young girl do, where could she turn, in such a fix? And Mrs. Hollister, evidently feeling a slight guilt herself in that part of the matter, was determined to make it up to me, even to the point of inviting Lucas, her part-time handy-man, to dinner. Jordan, I could hear her saying, was "a little New England village"; we didn't have social distinctions there and were proud of it. More peculiarly, at one of her dress fittings, catching sight of the sculpture in our parlor, she said sadly and quite out of the blue, there having been no previous mention of the Prydens that day, "Poor boy . . ." She didn't document her pity, which might or might not have entailed some further revelation, except to remark that it was wonderful what he had made of himself. She made it sound as if he had been literally the poorest of poor boys, instead of one who had inherited a double fortune, from his aunt and some years before that from her brother, his father, who had lived and died somewhat mysteriously in France. I say mysteriously because that was Jordan's view of Europe in general, but I must say that my grandmother had always been rather reticent about Forrest Pryden, although she did take me to tea once at his house in Paris.

However it was the "wonderfulness" if not the fortune, rather than the pity, that was uppermost in Mrs. Hollister's feeling as "the famous Dr. Pryden" finally made his way over to us. She was all aglow and very proprietary about him, even betraying the same touch of the obsequious, veiled in jollity, that there used to be in her relation to his aunt, and I was startled to discover, as I watched this exhibition, how much her gossip, or whatever it was, had worked on me. I had let myself get used to it and no longer felt any anger in thinking of it, nor even saw it as particularly ironic.

"And you remember Eva, of course . . ."

"Hello, Eva, how nice to see you." His hand, so small even for a man of his slight build, closed on mine in the grip I remembered, long and strong and authoritative, leaving you with a sense of strength in the bones and mind more than a casual contact of flesh, while his blue eyes, with nothing of sky or water in them but like valuable stones, held mine in perfect directness. It was only in the crinkles of sunburned skin at the corners of his eyes as he smiled that there was a hint of a more inward, private intelligence due to the occasion, but that was of amusement and had reference, not too unkindly, to Mrs. Hollister's behavior. "Is your husband here? I heard you were married."

"Oh, that heavenly husband of hers," Cluny put in. "The mystery man! Have you heard him play the clarinet? If I weren't in love with David I'd fall for him myself. But I'm furious with him for not coming to my party."

I explained that Lucas was working late. "He was terribly sorry. But you've met him," I said to Jack. "He pulled your car out of a ditch one day, up the lane."

He answered politely, "Oh, yes," not making it clear if he

remembered or not; and when Dickie, who had come along to play with Cluny's two children, ran up to me just then, Jack didn't show any sign of remembering him either, and that he had nearly killed him.

Later, some months later, that moment at the party stood out more sharply in my memory even than the scene in the lane, but at the time I just went on with my Scotch and soda and pleasure in everything around me. I kissed Dickie, and as he ran back to his playmates felt a little loving pride in having all those people notice his sturdy beauty and the sweetness of his face.

"We're all in love with Lucas," exclaimed Mrs. Hollister, once more drawing me to her, protectively. "I don't know what any of us old ladies would do without him. And he's so handsome! My son Richard was here last weekend—you remember Richard," this to Jack, "you know he's at Hartford Life, I'm so proud of him, and he was crazy to see *you* again— and *he* was saying that Lucas ought to be in the movies."

Jack hadn't been at the other parties I had gone to in the last month. Not that he hadn't been asked. He and his laboratory were one of the big subjects of talk around Jordan and everybody was after him, but he had always been working or away at conferences in Washington and other places, so they said. Perhaps that was why he had never phoned or come to our house either; the question, however, just flitted across my mind, without disturbing it.

"I couldn't get her to bring Baldur Blake either, stingy girl, I think she keeps him in hiding. I haven't even laid eyes on him. And I did so want a lion for my party, I mean another besides you, darling," to Jack. "But you must have gotten at him. Why he practically brought you up, didn't he?"

"Hardly. No, I haven't seen him lately. Isn't there some story about his having disappeared for years, something of the sort?"

"Why Jack Pryden, you young hypocrite," Mrs. Hollister coyly scolded, "as if you didn't know all about Baldur. Why he's the talk of the town. And they say he's actually trying to work again. Is that true, Eva? It was all Eva's doing," she explained, "I mean her rescuing him and simply saving his life. Oh yes it was, my dear, don't protest. I know all about it, how you went and found him in some terrible *dive* in Wellford and made him come home. I don't know how you did it, but you've been a lesson in charity to all of us." Her eyes were suddenly brimming. "If the rest of us had been half as charitable long ago I suppose it never would have happened. But we don't *think*. We just go along in our little selfish concerns . . ."

But before I could disclaim this credit, which I felt this time a great need to do although on several occasions I had let it pass, Cluny was dragging Jack away to serve as bartender. "Something awful must have happened to David. He was supposed to be here at three and he was going to do everything for me, you know he's such an angel about running parties. But he still has such trouble with his back, poor darling; if he's had an accident I'll just die." Cluny was divorced and talked a lot about David, her "fiancé" as she called him, but something awful seemed to prevent his turning up most of the time. At least something had every time I had been supposed to meet him. She and Jack went off and we were joined by a young navy officer and his wife, whom I didn't know.

"Was that the famous scientist we've been hearing about, the one who has the laboratory in Danville?"

"Dr. Pryden; yes," Mrs. Hollister said, "but he's from Jordan you know, why I've known him since he was just a tot. He more or less grew up with my two boys. And with Eva Buckingham here too," she thought to add, "I mean Mrs. Hines. Excuse me, Eva, I never can remember anybody's married name. We were talking," she rattled along, having begun to be a little tipsy, "about our other famous Jordanite, Baldur Blake, the sculptor. I'm sure you've heard of him. He had the Prix de Rome . . ."

"The what?" said the navy man.

"It was the *bottle*," Mrs. Hollister proceeded in a sudden dramatic whisper, shaking her stylish grey head, and then I had to listen once more to her version of the story, leading up to what a sister of mercy I had been, "even if it doesn't stick. They say it never does when it's gone so far, there's bound to be a relapse . . ."

This praise of myself, which heaven knows I had fought off as well as I could in the beginning, had like the slanderous talk about Miss Pryden gradually come to seem natural to me, or at any rate not worth denying. I don't mean that I had really come to believe that version of what had happened and of my own merit in it, but it was pleasant to be given some credit and consideration in general, after spending all my grown-up years under a cloud, and I had stopped feeling I must sort out the true from the false at every little point in the process. In those few short weeks, after years of not hearing anything nice about myself except from Lucas, I had become used to getting compliments of all kinds and from all sides, on my child and my own looks and my dressmaking talents, in one instance even on my "soul," so that this other tribute didn't seem as wrong as it would have all by itself.

Or perhaps that was even the one that I most wanted, wrong as it was. I have sometimes wondered if along with my other reasons I hadn't been reckoning, that day when I went to the boarding house in Wellford, on some such publicity as Mrs. Hollister was now giving me, for my "goodness." It wouldn't have seemed so implausible then, when my image of Baldur was as grotesque, as horribly mistaken as hers was still. In any case now that I knew better, knew at least that the charity and goodness and rescue had been all the other way around, I couldn't have made them believe it. It would have seemed a worse lie, and a good deal more insulting to Baldur, to have mentioned all his practical gifts to us, all the electric appliances for the kitchen, and Lucas's electric drill and clarinet, and even his having the house painted, when his real gift to us was something else, for which I couldn't have found any words; or if I could, it would have been a betrayal of Baldur's silence, if not of my own feelings, to use them.

"But what's this I hear about his going to *Brazil?*" In Mrs. Hollister's mouth this sounded like the most dire revelation of all.

"We're crazy about Brazil, aren't we, honey?" said the navy man's wife. "We spent a year there; it's terrific. We had a cook in Rio who . . ."

"Oh, for you young people . . . But Baldur Blake! Why he never went ten miles from Jordan in twenty years. You don't suppose he was really . . ." She drew a swig from an imaginary bottle.

No, he really had flown to Brazil, for only a few days, to see some modern architecture he was interested in; and to France too for the same reason and the same length of time, and one night he came in very late and said he had just been to Chicago. Between trips he was working furiously, at least according to Lucas who had helped him patch up the studio. I hadn't been up there myself, knowing he didn't want anybody to see what he was doing just yet, and Lucas hadn't managed, or rather as it seemed hadn't wanted, to give me any clear idea of it. "No, it's not like the old stuff," was all he would say, "nothing like that, that I can see." But I didn't go into that part of it with Mrs. Hollister, who in any case was too distracted by martinis and the company to pursue the subject further.

"Oh, there are those nice young Stimsons who've just moved to . . . Hello! Isn't this a gay party! Well now you tell Baldur I'm going to get up a nice game of bridge for him next week, that'll give him something to think about . . ."

"Where did you ever get that divine dress?" the navy man's wife asked as the Jarvises began moving our way.

Cluny's house, which for half my mind could still not be wrested away from old Dill Polk, as indeed all of Jordan still seemed to withhold its significant reality from these new inhabitants however happy I might be in their society, was low in the valley, a couple of miles above the falls. In the field across the road I could see John Purser driving his rickety old tractor, probably with his long face set in its usual snarling bitterness or a little more than usual as he brooded on the kind of cars and people congregated up here and on his wife's having been asked to the party. Hester was cheerful and very popular, and had recently been making a big social success, along with a snitch of a living on her own, from running a vegetable stand out on the main road; but he was a rankling man, always had been. He had made a horrid proposal to me once, but that was long ago. It was the river I was thinking of now. There was just one flash of it visible, down beyond his field at a short gap in the line of trees, where it formed one of its deepest pools before bending away for its secretive, shallow run to the top of the falls, and as my mind followed it there I felt a thrill of exclusive possession, as if I were the only person present who knew what the river truly was in that long hidden passage, hidden at least from the road and well protected too by woods and brambles, or knew the wonderful secret of the falls.

Of course I wasn't the only one. Jack knew, unless he had forgotten. He and Arthur and I used to spend whole summer days exploring the river, wading and clambering and shouting after watersnakes, and sometimes when we hadn't noticed how low the sun was getting we did go as far as the falls, although from there we would have to walk six miles home and would be in for a scolding, or worse: we might be forbidden each other's company or to go near the river for a whole week. I suppose just the risk of punishment was exciting to us, but there was a more majestic sense of risk, and of the forbidden, that surrounded the falls themselves, so that although we never spoke of it or of being frightened, we would look at each other with a certain wild and guilty triumph as we came down over the cliff's last barrier, of boulders and exposed pine-roots, into the full view of that water. The roar of it too, because by some acoustical peculiarity the sound breaks on you no sooner than the sight. A stranger would have to be right on top of it even to know it was there, but a stranger would have to be a fool to risk his neck as we did to climb down into the gorge, and we never did meet one, or anybody there at all; the trout fishermen would be out of sight around the bends, above and below.

The sides of the gorge were granite, so my grandfather had told us, going on to speak of its age and how long it had taken the water to wear down such a groove. "You mean it was there before the Indians, Grandpa?" I couldn't imagine anything before that in the world. He smiled one of his rare tender smiles and reaching down from his old armchair to where I was sitting on the floor beside it, rested his hand a second on my hair. "Well, we don't know just when the Indians came, but yes, little girl, probably before that. Long before." I used to say the word *granite* over to myself, much as I did *preederome*, to fill myself with the awe of it, and I got into a row with Jack and Arthur once, speaking of the hollows in the rock, like great lacquered bowls, that except in the spring floods showed alongside the twisted course of the falls, by saying that it must have taken "centuries" for the water to carve out even those, "considering that it's granite." "You don't even know what a century is," Jack said, "or granite either," and then they picked on me, both of them showing off by standing nearer the edge than I cared to, until I practically wanted to push them in. That would have been sure death. Nobody would have believed, knowing the rest of the Rapahaug, that such a peaceful little river could contain year in year out that horrible scene of power and violence, because the water didn't fall straight but tore gnashing down over the rocks like a crazy white segmented dragon, each part waiting to kill you, and really the boys were just as awed by it as I was, and just as much in love with its being somehow our secret experience, even though the fact of the falls was public enough; that whole area, which was almost unpopulated, was called Jordan Falls, and locally just The Falls. Only the boys preferred to express their feelings by guessing at the height of the uprooted tree-trunks that would sometimes get stuck in mid-drop and teeter there till the next spring, or

by telling each other for the tenth time about the cow that was
supposed to have fallen in and gotten killed "instantly."

It may have been partly that story, or my saying I was sick of
hearing about it, that worked Arthur up one day to jumping over
the falls. It was right at the top. The ledge on the other side was a
little lower than where we were but it had a steep slant and was in
the spray and the jump was longer than he had ever made even on
to dry ground. Naturally we didn't believe him or that he was
climbing up the bank behind us, as he said, to get a running start.
"I bet you a nickel you can't hit it from there," Jack shouted over
the bellowing of the water, referring to a pissing contest they had
had, and then there was a scrambled feeling and I was standing there
screaming, in a way I never had screamed before and have only once
since, as if I could scream it into not being true. Arthur had sneakers
on and for two or three seconds on the other side he was slipping fast,
not making it, and I was trying to scream to him then where a
handhold was. I never told him afterwards how beautiful that jump
had been. We were going to be the latest ever getting home and
none of us mentioned what he had done. Jack was cross and
sarcastic, and they had a long quarrel about different bores of rifles,
which neither of them knew much about.

That was one of the worst of our homecomings. It was long after
dark when we reached the Pryden house, and we were so dead beat
then, Arthur and I gave up and went in instead of going on home. For
the last mile or so we had all three been scared silly of the dark,
although normally we loved going out and trying to scare ourselves at night; we had become convinced that an evil dark-faced
man, with a knife and black whiskers and an old hat pulled low
over his brow, was keeping up with us on the other side of the
hedges and stone walls, and now and then looking out at us. But
if we expected comfort in that house we were wrong. Miss Pryden's
wrath was terrible; she scarcely deigned to address us at all, and as
we had been close to tears anyway, a tremendous love sprang up
among the three of us, and Arthur and I felt utterly exposed and
forlorn when she ordered Jack upstairs to his room. "Your supper
has been put away. I will hear your explanations, if you think them
worth my listening to, later." To us she only said, "I shall phone
your mother. Gelindo will drive you home at once," and when
Arthur who was braver than I, probably because he didn't worship
her as I did, tried to mutter something: "No blubbering, please,

you can answer for yourselves in your own home. I have quite
enough to try me with Jack's part in this." I am sure that my
mother, if left to herself, would have sounded much the same;
this was several years before her own condition had undermined
her notions of discipline, if anything rather more unyielding than
Miss Pryden's, and brought her first to the stage of pleading with us
and then to the more pitiable point beyond even that. But she was
not often left to herself in such matters, unless she saw fit to com-
pound the crisis, as sometimes happened. My grandmother, without
seeming actually to interfere, would manage to be passing through
the room on some pretext or other, and out of her deep diplomacy
would hit on something to deflect the course of retribution. "Why
they're white as sheets, both of them, and their clothes are sopping
wet! Oh, the poor children, what on earth . . . But we'll hear about
it later. I'll just go get some blankets, Betsy, while you bring the
soup, I put it back on the stove a few minutes ago, I just knew in
my bones that something terrible must have happened to them."
"All that's happened is that they've been disobedient and ought to
be punished," my mother grumbled, but she was overworked and
too tired to fight it out.

Another homecoming was more closely associated with the scene
of the party, that one in my grandmother's company and from this
very house. That was the only time I saw Dill Polk smile. We had
come down as usual in the buggy, because my grandmother never
learned to drive a car and anyway the ruts in that road were usually
too deep for one, and she was wearing her high straw hat and a
starched linen dress, just as she would have to call on Mrs. Dan
Pickett whose husband was President of the Wellford Bank or any
other lady of her acquaintance. Dill came to the door with her
pickle face, which must have been where she got the name, and
her hair matted with dirt and briars, anyway it looked like briars,
and said, "What you want?" "Good afternoon, Miss Polk," my
grandmother said with a charming smile, knowing better than to put
out her hand although she always made me curtsey to the old witch.
"We were just driving by," that being five miles from anywhere,
"and thought we'd stop in with this currant jelly." "Don't like it,"
Dill said. "Gives me the pip. Maybe *they*'ll eat it, save you the
trouble of taking it home." *They*, all seventeen or more, were all
over the furniture, including some rather valuable heirlooms that
you couldn't tell from anything else in the state they were in, so we

had to stand up, and it was pitch dark inside as always, the windows were so dirty.

My grandmother chatted along about this and that, and pretended she didn't hear when Dill said we'd better get along. She was used to Dill's making out that we were wasting her time. But that day a terrible thunderstorm was coming up that we hadn't noticed, and it was when the first crack came, as we were unhitching the horse, that Dill got off that one, unique smile. "Better take your currant jelly," she said, "you might need it," and she looked around, evidently to see if the cats were laughing too. It was a dreadful drive. My grandmother wanted me to huddle down under the horse blanket, but the horse was getting wild with fear and I knew she needed me on the seat beside her, since my grandfather was not there to protect her; and in fact I ended up taking the reins myself. My mother, who couldn't bring herself to make calls except among a few close friends, would have taken a fierce satisfaction and even joy in that drive, but my grandmother's mettle was of a different order. How I hated Dill Polk! She gave me nightmares. Nevertheless, after every visit I would start thinking how she wouldn't see anybody, probably not a single soul to speak to again for months, and I would get a crazy impulse to go back again the next day; I even set out once alone, on my pony, but I turned back half way. The last time I ever saw her was at my grandmother's funeral. Perhaps one of the Pursers had happened to drive by and tell her about it, anyway it was the first time she had been to the village in years; she washed her hair and walked six miles to the cemetery, and I imagine that from that day her spirit must have been broken. Or perhaps not; there were still the cats.

"And you," a man was saying to me. "What about that?"

It was the man who had once remarked on my "soul," a middle-aged Russian-born painter named Boris, rather worn in appearance and attractive in his sympathies. I was on the verge of telling him what I had been thinking about. But it turned out he was speaking of Baldur. He too; the publicity was going too far, and made me feel suddenly that I had been guilty of betrayal, of Baldur, and of some intimate vision of my own as well.

Out of the corner of my eye I saw Jack, very much the well-dressed man at a party, in his white linen coat and discreetly speckled tie, approaching with a tray of drinks.

"I didn't go after him," I said with what must have sounded

like irritation. "I started to once, but I didn't. He came back by him-self. He'd had a heart attack recently, though we didn't know that till a few days ago, and I suppose it had made him feel, well, you can imagine . . ."

"Yes."

"And perhaps even, I don't know how to say it, that there was some need of him now, except that he's not conceited. I think he used to be, but now he doesn't set himself up as anything at all. He's almost like a baby that way; you can hardly be sure if he even re-members any of his old life. But it's nothing like senility; he never seemed so bright before. Only sometimes, it's as if he'd been *made* to come back, by something . . ."

"He could be a saint," Boris said, with what degree of whimsy I couldn't tell.

"Who's this you're calling a saint?" Jack asked, coming up with the tray. His little grimace, not a disagreeable one, of mockery, was the same he had had most of the time at the party; he was still ashamed of his ugly teeth. At one moment that afternoon when I had caught sight of him not smiling he had looked as pure and dedicated as he used to sometimes as a boy when his intellect was aroused.

Boris shooed him away. "You wouldn't understand. It's not in your line."

"Baldur Blake," I said, looking straight into the valuable blueness of his eyes, and for a moment I felt that the great rock of the dead years between us had split right apart. But it was not so, and I was glad.

He let out a big hearty laugh. "Very likely. It's a pity saints are so unemployed nowadays. The gurus have driven them out."

Mr. Jarvis was turning just then to take a highball from the tray, before Jack proceeded on his rounds. David still hadn't come but Cluny wasn't as put out about it as she had been earlier; she had stopped talking about possible accidents, and even seemed to admire him for being so undependable. "Isn't he wonderful? He's probably fallen in with some fascinating characters and he'll bring them along to spend the night. That's one thing I adore about David, you never know what he'll turn up with next." One time when she had been wild with anxiety over him it turned out that he had come on a wounded pigeon by the roadside, and had been so sick with compassion he had had to turn back to New York.

"Haven't we met before?" Mr. Jarvis said to me. He stared at me with the same blunt, almost driving admiration I had noticed earlier, which somehow missed being coarse, it was hard to tell how, considering the indelicacy of his face.

His wife was trying to place me too, and as her sunglasses veered my way turned on me a glittering but uncertain smile. She had come to our house about a month before, with what I had taken in the first moment to be an invitation but she was really asking if I would serve as waitress at the dinner in question. I overheard her complaining now in what she thought was a low voice about what a "dump" Jordan was. "I don't know what Chuck sees in it. Of course we're not here much, thank God. You can't even tell people from servants in this town." Her husband, Chuck as everyone was calling him there, heard too and was embarrassed. "Marilyn's so used to Long Island," he said more to Boris than to me, "she's bored to death here. You can't blame her. I like a little village like this myself; something different; peaceful"; and to me: "You're not a native, are you? You don't look it."

In a minute, I thought, he would remember our one previous meeting, on a warm sunny morning late the summer before, not long after he had bought his place. Dickie and I had gone up our hill to pick huckleberries, and it got so hot we went on up to the spring and took off our clothes and splashed each other from our empty bucket. All my life that had been what I loved best in the huckleberry season. Only now the land around the spring was more overgrown, so I had barely time to clasp my skirt against me when Mr. Jarvis appeared. He was taking a walk, a purposeful one by the look of it, and not for huckleberries. "This land is posted," I said angrily, which was only partly true, we hadn't bothered to put up any new signs since before my father died. He hastened to apologize and turn away, pulling a tuft of Dickie's hair with a little hurried, sympathetic grin as he left, but not without a moment's frank and appreciative gaze at my nakedness. I had imagined him much older; he could hardly have been forty and he was not at all bald.

I had already known then that he had designs on our land if not our house too, but I hadn't yet heard the general talk around town about what he was up to, most of it rumors and guesses. The one fact behind them was that he had recently built a huge housing development on Long Island, and speculation had it that he was aiming to do the same in Jordan, though why he should trouble to start a farm and furnish a house there in that case I couldn't see. Some people were even saying it was our hill he had in mind and that his plan was for a thousand houses, as if there were a living anywhere near Jordan for that many people, and so of course he would have to take over Baldur's place and Beulah Wellman's next door to us too.

It sounded absurd, and yet there was an air about him that did raise visions of whole countrysides changing overnight, so that you could almost believe he might try it. The rumor alone was enough to make me loathe him and I was mystified to be finding him at the same time so agreeable, even when the great sledge-hammer swung close, at something five miles from home and for my feeling just as sacred.

"The falls must be right down over there," he said as if he were in possession of a sheaf of documents concerning them. "I haven't had time to take a look at them yet. Do you know anything about them?"

"Oh, they're nothing special. Nothing in Jordan is big."

"It could be. Will be, one of these days." Boris turned away at this with a look of disgust he didn't try to hide from Mr. Jarvis, who however took it in good humor. "Reactionary bunch, these artists; can't stand progress; it upsets them. That one's got a lot of talent, though. I just bought a big painting of his. Do you like painting? But here"—he took my arm and with no more than a courteous degree of pressure, even with a suggestion of timidity, drew me toward an old garden bench dating from Dill Polk's childhood, which Cluny had found deep under the lilacs—"sit down and tell me about yourself. Oh, but now I remember!" He backed away from me a trifle, looking boyishly pleased and just a little embarrassed, whether from having seen me naked or because my husband had been his hired man I didn't get a chance to find out.

There was a commotion over toward the driveway just then, and amid delighted shrieks from Cluny and a general burst of exclamations, David alighted from a New York taxi. The rather elderly little hobo who got out after him seemed to come up more or less to her expectations. She sent one of the children inside for her purse, and by borrowing from both Jack and Mr. Jarvis, still looking the delicate highborn young hostess, one would have said a widow, of another era, made up the taxi fare. It would just about have paid for the paint for our house. David apparently thought nothing of it. He was strong, blond, and as handsome as she had said, only his lips were a little too full to suit my idea of a "Greek god," and his limp handshake along with a droopiness of the eyelids, as he and the hobo did their round of introductions, would have struck me more unfavorably if it hadn't been so important to me to think well of him, for Cluny's sake. The touch of that handshake, like raw scallops, stayed with me a while as being somehow familiar, but the recollection if there was one was crowded out for the time being.

The shift of the company had brought Jack and me together near the garden bench, and looking suddenly drained of all general sociability, and even as though contemptuous of himself for having been so good at it up to then, he proposed with a weary sigh, "Oh, brother!" that we get another drink and sit down. A certain meaninglessness, not as unpleasant as his tone implied, seemed to have come over the whole scene including ourselves, giving our conversation and my thoughts the same commonplace character, or lack of weight, as anything else that might be going on in the garden. I asked him how it felt to be living in Jordan again and he said it was at least very pleasant to see *me*. Speaking seriously, he hadn't of course come back out of sentimentality about the place even if he'd had any; Danville had been a good location for the lab, near enough to the university that was partly sponsoring it, and far enough to avoid nuisances from that quarter, and so on, and since he happened to own a house only fourteen miles away it seemed sensible to use it. "Not that I ever liked it particularly. But it's all right." Apparently he had outgrown the fierce exigency of taste that had shown itself in his little New York apartment long ago. I thought of Mrs. Hollister's innuendoes, and wondered a little about his divorce and his having no children, without their mattering much, and in the same vein made some answer to his question, formal although friendly enough, about the deaths of my father and mother.

I suppose it was his failure to mention Arthur's death, which he must have known about too, that after riding along on the circuit of irrelevancies, suddenly rose up from them, with disconcerting effect. I recognized Cluny's fiancé, and in that instant the old chain of shames and horrors, and its concomitant, the yearning to prove and justify myself, seemed about to overwhelm me again. I felt for the moment the need to tell every truth no matter what it might cost, and an equal desire to keep Jack from ever knowing this particular one, of where I had met David and about my brother's life in that Delacey house. But that was nonsense. He must have known it all long ago just as everybody else in Jordan did, and if there were any embarrassment coming it must be only to Cluny now. So when I spoke again it was about something else and without any change from the weightless ease, the sense of things without contour, that had been established before.

"Baldur told me you'd gone to see him in Wellford, a couple of months ago."

"Yes."

"But then why . . ." I meant why hadn't he ever tried to see him here, but it didn't seem worth going into.

"I'm afraid of him. Oh, he was boiled as an owl that day, of course, but still . . ."

"You mean he's too good?"

He smiled, without any self-consciousness that time. "Perhaps, something like that. I mean he respects life too much. I'm not up to it. I don't go in for emotions, you know."

"Why did you go to see him at all?"

"Oh . . ." He seemed to consider it, then with a little humorous gesture, turning up his empty hands, said, "Why not?" and we looked at each other and laughed. A moment later he remarked, "I see you haven't changed, except that you're better-looking, as I suppose you know. You were always so complicated."

Even that didn't stir up the mystery of what he had done fourteen years ago. I was wondering more whether Lucas had come home and was glad that the party was almost over. Mrs. Hollister had already left, and Mrs. Jarvis, fretfully pulling at a lock of her shoulder-length peroxide-yellow hair and with her smile flashing less regularly, like a lighthouse in need of repair, was trying to nudge her husband out to the drive.

II

BUT OUT OF THE EMBERS of the party a proposal flared up and caught on like brushfire among the remaining guests, and so before long I was walking into the Pryden house. It was the first time since that sad December afternoon when I drank tea with Miss Pryden and saw the photographs, one on the piano, the other of Jack and his bride on their honeymoon. This time it was only an incidental stop to pick up a bottle of whiskey, as Cluny's had run out. The idea, which had been taken up with various degrees of hilarity, as if we had been drinking a lot more than we had and were setting out for the zoo, was for us all to go and burst in on Baldur in his studio. He usually came down to our house to sleep and sometimes for dinner, but he would be up there as long as there was daylight and often much later now that he had floodlights. I, of course, was the one who ought to have stopped it, but after a frown or two I was caught up like everybody else and at one point when the plan might have died down even fanned it up myself, though I was dreading Lucas's distaste when he should hear of it as much as Baldur's. It was as if the very unsavoriness of the expedition, once I was committed to it, had become an excitement I couldn't give up.

I had been feeling guilty toward Lucas anyway, I suppose just because I had been having such a good time, and for the last hour had been wishing he were there. Baldur's coming had brought us very close in one way, closer than we had ever been before. There had been a physical need and passion between us lately that I had never known with him or with anyone before. The little pretense of modesty in our undressing that we had never cast off till then, and

the real one that had kept us from ever speaking words to one another during our love-making or even most often from crying out,
were all gone. We came to each other at night as if nothing but
that single craving had been real to us all day, and were loud and
violent in our abandon; afterwards we drifted into sleep with our
legs and arms tangled close and shifting to the last to be closer,
while we went on drowsily murmuring our love and trying to stay
awake to murmur something more, as though to deny what we would
be to one another by morning. But I don't believe that Lucas was
really thinking of that at those times any more than I was, any more
than we did all day. In every way but that one we were so far apart,
it didn't bear thinking of.

Once in a while I did wonder for a minute what he was making
of my new life, if anything. Sometimes as he watched me do some
ordinary thing, like running to answer the telephone or putting pins
in my mouth as I worked on a dress, he would look suddenly intent,
as a person might who has just had a first suspicion of cancer, and I
would feel annoyed, as if I were being accused of something. But I
may have imagined the look, or there would be some other explanation. Once it was when he had just come home, and still grimy and
smelly from work was only waiting to step up behind me and pull my
body against his, with one hand up under my skirt while the other,
after pulling the shears from my fingers, plunged down under my
blouse. I laughed, embarrassed. Normally he was almost too fastidious about being clean. In all those years he had never before let
himself touch me, beyond a light homecoming kiss, until he had
washed up after work, but it wasn't his being dirty that I minded,
minded a lot more than I had my earlier misinterpretation of his
look. I was angry at my helplessness under such a power of attraction,
heightened as it was by the novelty of that sweat against my flesh,
not like the simple sweat from sexual exertion but strong with the
accumulated odors of the day, of hay and manure and grease. I
was lost in my own desire from the instant his hands were on me and
as we rocked on the floor, in a tangle of clothes only half ripped off,
was distracted only by the sight of my work-scissors across the rug
where he had thrown them.

I burst out as we got up, "You're killing me. I have to call you
my husband but I don't call you that to myself. I can't breathe.
I've got to have my life."

He stepped toward me, I thought to comfort me as he had so

many times though never for quite such a reason, and then I saw in amazement that he had been about to strike me. "As you like," he said wrenching his arm back, and left the room, and the house.

But that night we made love again and in the loving stillness of the long embrace afterwards, not even needing to ask forgiveness, listened happily to the bullfrogs down by the brook pool, and the million other little noisy businesses of the night. Lucas loved those sounds and could distinguish among them as perhaps Indians used to but not anybody I had ever known; he would name them, as he did the stars, and by patience and contagion would make me hear a dozen more, of wingbeat or insect percussion or even a field-mouse running, accompanying the owl or the wind.

"Oh darling, I'm so crazy about you," I murmured, and he answered, holding me tenderly, "You're my life." We were telling the truth, I mean a part of it but that was the only part there was at that hour of the night.

We had only one other quarrel at that time.

"I thought I might take Dickie to work with me today," he said one morning, and when I said what on earth for, what a perfectly crazy idea, he was silent and strange for a minute. Then he said rather sharply, "You're too busy. It's not safe for him here. As a matter of fact I was thinking of taking him fishing, not going to work."

I said that would certainly be fine for Dickie, to know that his father couldn't even be bothered to make a living. This was just a day or two after Boris's reference to my soul, and I wondered rather grimly what he would say of it now if he could see me in this ugly rage, but I didn't care. I felt ugly all through. "Besides I've arranged for Cluny to bring Paul here to play with him."

"That's what I mean. That and other things." Like his nearly getting run over, I was thinking. It seemed unfair that Lucas's anger shouldn't have any air of ugliness, but only made him more impressive and untouchable, like an avenging angel, though his right-eousness was only directed in this case against a six-year-old boy. But I knew better than to press him on his objections to Paul; he wouldn't have told, and anyway in the next instant he had come off his high horse and was grinning like a little boy himself, charming, affectionate and victorious. "Anyhow," and he paused to kiss the back of my neck, "I haven't got anything lined up till five. I quit Saturday. So now I'll go rig up my old fishing-rod for Dickie."

No, I don't think he was puzzling much over my new occupations and the change in me. I imagine he just closed his mind to it most of the time, as I did to whatever it was, unhappy and unfamiliar to me, that was going on in him. There was something between him and Baldur that excluded me, as there had been at their first meeting, and I didn't care to know what it was, but I couldn't help seeing some of the results. In all the time we had been together Lucas had always slept through the night like a baby. Now a little while after we had fallen so peacefully to sleep in each other's arms he would turn from me and begin to toss and wrestle, until sometimes I would wake him, crossly, thinking of my own need of sleep if I were going to accomplish all I meant to in the morning, but the incubus would only wait to catch him napping again. Or some time before dawn I would start up as if he had called me, and find him staring rigid and wide-eyed at the black ceiling, just as I used to picture my grandfather, alone however, having exiled himself to the back bedroom because of his notorious although unmentionable insomnia, silently battling through his interminable white nights, in a company that my grandmother was surely dealing with in her extravagant insistence that the room, that room more than any other, should be *thoroughly aired* every morning; if the mattress had not remained up-ended before the open window for a full hour before the bed was made she would unmake it herself and start over, knowing perfectly well that the spooks she shook out in the sunshine would be back in force at the stroke of nine P.M., when my grandfather would close his book and alone and proud in his sentence walk slowly up the stairs, to close the door once more on his horrible rendezvous. But Lucas had not come to any such terms with his bugbear. He was fighting and denying it, and falling into its snares. One night he sprang up wide awake and ran into Dickie's room in a panic; he was sure he had heard something.

Was it some such beast of his own that Jack was thinking of when he said that he too was afraid of Baldur? Only Lucas would not admit even the fact of his struggle, still less that the new presence in our house was anything more than good company. He had been unsettled, however, the very first night of Baldur's return, when after we had waited a good hour for him to come back down the hill, as we were sure he must when he had taken in the ruin of his place unless he had had a stroke instead, Lucas finally agreed to go up after him. He went reluctantly, as if he were seeing farther and more clearly than I, who was only thinking just then of the immediate scene and its pathos if not something worse. It was a long time before they came down, and then it looked as if Lucas were the one being helped, he was so uneasy, while Baldur, going on seventy and with every reason to be stricken by what he had just seen, was perfectly in command of himself and as cheerful as he had been ever since, only a little diffident, in a manner in part courtly but more that of a well-bred child, about taking up the offer of hospitality. His veins had gone back to a more normal color; he must have been sober the whole week since we had been with him at the bar, and for a moment, looking at the familiar features, the wavy nose somewhat bulbous at the nostrils, the long but sloping forehead with its big hillocks of bone above the shaggy eyebrows and two bays of baldness above, scarcely longer than years before however and the remaining hair seemed to have been arrested in its greying too, I had an illusion of being back in that other time: he had finished his afternoon stint splitting rails for his new fence, fed himself and his pet duck, and was arriving to play bridge with my parents. And with what fervor! They had to give it up in the last years, he had become so irritable over the game. Besides, that was when he had begun reading the *Encyclopaedia Britannica* straight through and he drove them crazy with his monologues on nothing but B or C subjects for months on end. He never did get beyond F.

But he used to be quite particular, old-maidish as my grand-mother said, about dressing for the evening; he would never have played bridge in the dirty poplin jacket and old dungarees he had on now. Not that they changed him much. He stood as tall as Lucas and from his stride and posture you might have thought he was still as obsessed as ever with having been a lieutenant in the First World War, and still just as scornful of potbellies and flabby muscles. I suppose it was that combination of scorn and physique, along with a mere weightiness of face, that had made him pass for handsome, when really if you stopped to consider it there was an almost gnomish distortion in everything from the neck up. I mean there had been, because the whole difference was in the new pair of eyes I was seeing, but perhaps it was rather that that was where the gnome had been lacking before. I kissed him, anyhow, as if he had come to the tree-trunk where he belonged and nothing could be more natural, which was evidently the way he looked at it himself; his politeness had been in the nature of a joke.

He must have taken some kerosene up the hill with him, enough to light the old lantern that had been lying around for years in the studio, and Lucas had found him there, among his broken statues and curled-up Greek and Roman photographs, singing: not loud, just absentmindely humming snatches of opera as he went about the job that would have made Hercules think twice, of straightening the place up. He got Lucas to help him dig a pit out among the bushes in back and they had quite a gay funeral there by lantern light, of all the dismembered statues, the pieces of my body, my hands and face as he had seen them long ago, including the more ghastly goddess that was all in one piece. But there was nothing mocking or ribald about it, I gathered from the little Lucas would say. Baldur just hadn't known what else to do with the things to get them out of the way, and of course the burial had its funny side, but he laid them in the ground rather tenderly. Somebody, after all, had spent a lot of time on them.

And that was that. At any rate, that was all I got out of Lucas.

Baldur still wasn't drinking at all, but the first time he disappeared on one of his trips that was naturally what we were thinking of, and I could have cried with disappointment, and at Lucas's relief. "You were the one who asked him to stay here," I said. "Not me. You know you love him as much as I do," and added without thinking what I meant, "Perhaps more." With Baldur gone, Lucas had reverted to his own true gentle nature, at least the one I had always known, and his clear grey eyes met mine with their old fondness, from which our present passion and alienation together were blanked out. "Forget it, baby. It's a damn shame, I hate to see a guy in that trap, but you did your best . . ." "I!" "Well, *we* if you like. Anyway there's nothing more to do, I've seen a hundred like that who tried and it's no use. So now we're back where we were, honey, and I'm going to start cleaning up the garden for you tomorrow . . ."—as if you could reduce Baldur to that skid-row image even if he did happen to be back in the Wellford bar or some other like it; as if Lucas didn't know as well as I did it was too late even if he were gone for good. We would never again be what we had been, because Lucas himself didn't want this reprieve, this resumption of comfort, no matter how often he wished that that strange disturbance had never come into our lives.

The presents were part of it, even the little ones he brought us that time from his three days in France, and all the others. I am sure that by nature I was just as averse as Lucas to receiving favors. For my grandfather, as for my mother until she lost her hold on life itself, that was a principle as dear as granite and more unalterable; my grandmother, whose principles lay with her heart, outside such strict accounting, had to more or less hoodwink them both, mainly by a series of non sequiturs and changes of subject too fast for their superior minds, to bring about the summer invitations for me that could clearly not be repaid in kind. But it was only that she knew her own riches; she had her granite too, in the matter of sponging. I suppose in the spot we were in after her death, if Baldur or anyone had offered help, meaning money and it would have had to be a lot, my parents would have taken it, sunk as they were then beyond the luxuries of principle and pride. But luckily those last luxuries were spared, for them and for me too; Baldur was as sunk as they were in his fashion and had been on the stingy side to begin with, and there was nobody else. Arthur, becoming more and more irritable at that time, called them damn fools for not trying to touch Baldur before the house was lost: he himself would be able to pay everything back pretty soon, and what was the crazy old bastard doing with all that dough anyhow, and so on; but I was sure that even for him it was the single remaining point of pride that they never did ask.

It was different now. I didn't feel needy in the least and I certainly wasn't being lazy. Besides, leaving out the small amount Baldur paid us for his board there was no money in question. Except for the paint, the presents were all things that he looked on himself as toys, ingenious and delightful ones that he seemed to have bought more for his own childish pleasure in their workings, in which he had a perfect rapport with Dickie, to such a point that no machine was safe from their worshipful examinations. It was Dickie's kind of pleasure that he took in the giving too, and if it involved a blessing of liberation, after all his years of never doing anything much for anybody, he never showed it. Nor was it possible to read into his gifts the slightest accusation of Lucas, any more than there was in Dickie's presenting his father with a piece of carpentry, and so again and again, most bitterly over the laundry machines which after all were for my relief and not his own, Lucas had to swallow his resistance and accept.

It was cruel, and made me suspect Baldur's innocence at times. I was perhaps more ready to because the sight of Lucas being goaded that way was both joyous and strangely unwelcome to me. But I could have looked much longer than I did into those gay lights gleaming beneath the thickets of Baldur's eyebrows without finding any recognition of what he was up to, and I am sure that none ever figured in the endless conversations between them, about everything under the sun. "Now Spengler says . . ." There had been at least some reading-matter to his nine drunken years. There had been women too now and then, not like the ones I had seen at the bridge table in the boarding house.

That was not such a surprise, though. The surprise was that Lucas was doing his share of the talking, and not in little hesitant bursts and questions as I would have expected. I took no part in their talk but I would hear his voice going on as long and energetically as Baldur's, and could tell that he was not feeling prodded or lectured, however much he was the one being led. Once in a gay mood he came out with a passage from the Bible, from Ezekiel he said it was, and Baldur got quite excited about it and urged him to keep on and to my astonishment he recited the whole chapter, all about wheels and wings and eyes, to "This was the appearance of the likeness of the glory of the Lord." It came back to me a little as I heard it, being one of the parts of the Old Testament that my grandfather used to consider particularly crazy; he said nowhere outside religion could you get away with a prose style based on genitives and refute science with the appearance of a likeness, whatever that might be. In answer to Baldur's question Lucas allowed to having known quite a lot of both the Old and New Testaments by heart at one period; he wasn't sure how much he would remember now. Other times the two of them would be roaring with laughter over some pun or fantasy, about rural development or something, and I would vaguely record as odd that with that much enjoyment of conversation and company, Lucas should have gone so long without seeking any.

Prodded or not, it must have been from that influence that he had finally agreed to work for Will Beardsley and his son Clifford, who had the only prosperous fruit orchards in Jordan and had been after Lucas for a couple of years. I was pretty sure that it was because he loved trees too much that he hadn't been willing before. He was afraid of getting to care about the work, getting too good at it, and he looked baleful and ashamed now when he told me about taking the job, as if he had been drawn into a crooked deal.

It was only two days later that he would admit the worst, that he wasn't to be just a hired hand. Will Beardsley, who had been a great friend of my grandfather's although younger by some years, was handing over all the management of the orchards to Cliff, with Lucas as assistant.

"Oh darling . . ." I was about to give him a kiss of congratulation and tell him how happy I was, and it wasn't his feeling about the job that stopped me. It was my own. The enthusiasm I had put into my eyes would have come there naturally a few weeks ago, and I couldn't have said what the reservation was that made it not quite honest now. "But don't worry, you won't keep it long," I said with a flippant smile, as though it were out of a deeper understanding and sympathy that I had changed my tack.

"No. Probably not." He sounded lonely and miserable, and that night while I sewed in the next room, told Baldur that when he was little he had gone by the name of Tod.

This was not like all the other moves, at night usually with the creaking of the trucks and carnival baggage for lullaby. How they ever did it with only two trucks he couldn't imagine; everything got capsuled somehow, beginning with the big tub and stands for the motorcycle act. Anyhow this time it was only the three of them, the mother and two children, Tod about three and a half, Rachel six, tearing along a craggy seashore, with no baggage at all and not a building or road or path of any sort to be seen the whole time.

No baggage, no jokes; it was a flight, the children knew that much. Later he always remembered the sun beginning to slip behind the shoulder of dunes above them, and the waves, which had been fun earlier, crashing with a new gnash and anger as though the beast in them woke with the approach of dark. He got it mixed up with what they were running from. By then they must have been at it, running wherever they could, for hours; the candy bars were all gone; for a long time the mother, who had eaten nothing herself, had not had to slap the children to stop their playing with shells and the other beach wonders they had never seen before. They had never seen the ocean before. They had never seen their mother like that before either. They were not to stop for anything; even *he*, when they were not learning their new stunts fast enough to suit him, never drove them more savagely than she that day.

Where did she think she was taking them? There had perhaps been some real refuge possible along that coast, which she seemed to have a groping memory of: a cave, a house, possibly a fairy-tale society that would appear around the next headland, with gentle voices and fireplaces. All she mentioned, however, in broken mumbles to herself as her dark eyes darted over the shifting shore, was an empty rowboat they were supposed to find, and a railroad track they could follow if the boat failed. But after a while even those images ceased and the hope was only of another stretch of sand beyond the point, one point after another telescoping on and on, each a jumble of huge rocks hopelessly set off by sheer sand-cliffs from the whistling dunes. The little boy had taken it as a lark in the beginning, in spite of the way she was. He ran every which way to tease her and laughed at everything. Now he kept climbing and stumbling, shivering under the spray, while the wee-wee ran down his legs and the tears down his face.

More likely some association stirred up by the sea, this being the first time in the children's lives that they had played a coast town, had caused her mind to crack temporarily, and they were not where she thought at all. It was from a coast town, a place of gloomy mansions and hateful aunts was all they knew of it, that she had been somehow hypnotized into running away with the great B. J. Hines and his company seven years before, when she was sixteen. But it wasn't probable that he would take her back to that exact location, and if he had risked it there would scarcely have been a welcome for her after what she had done, not from the aunts anyway; they had stricken her from their lives, merely sending the gardener after the troupe the next day with a pair of huge silver candlesticks that had belonged to her mother. Still, it might have been his idea of a joke, B. J.'s that is, their father's, to play her old home town or one near it after seven years just to see what it would do to her. But Tod couldn't know any of that. His sister was enough older to remember, in later years, some fierce quarrels around that time, because of their mother's singing with them and her expression during the knife-throwing act. That was all she was good for in the company except box-office work, standing in spangled bra and G-string against a board while their father outlined her with knives, and it seemed the act didn't go over unless they *both* looked happy, like lovers in fact. She was so bad in that period he was in danger of knifing her every night, and there was a lot of yelling, Rachel said, about her trying to make him do it on purpose so he would get in trouble with the police, worse than he was in half the time already.

They did come to a stretch of beach but the waves were terrible. The moon came up and he thought it was on a string that would break it was flying so crazily, and he was right, everything went black and they were out there with the hissing and crashing and the whistling through the grasses above, not seeing anything. His mother looked very queer afterwards, almost as if she could laugh about it, when she discovered that had been the night of the big eclipse of the moon. But no one had happened to mention it beforehand so the children thought it must always be like that at night by the sea. Dragons thrown up out of the ocean whizzed past their faces; little crabs plotted around their toes.

His mother had stopped nagging. For a while she tried to carry him and he fell asleep in her arms, huddled under the cliff, and she tried to shield them both from the spray, murmuring all sorts of love and comfort to them and telling them everything would be all right. "We'll never go back," she kept saying. "Never. Never. He'll never lay hands on you again." Suddenly Rachel howled into the black wind, "It's cold, I want to go home!" and so then Tod began remembering too how nice and warm it was at night in the truck and about the pretty curtains their mother whisked out at each new stop to hang around their mattress in the corner, and the laughing and loud-speaker music every night, and his nice special friends in the company who let him go to sleep on piles of rubbish in their booths or show-tents if he felt like it and carried him home to the truck when things closed down. But he knew it would be disloyal to say anything. His mother put her hand over Rachel's mouth, gently, and said, "Hush, baby, no. We're going to a lovely place and you'll have a pretty dress and go to a real school in a schoolhouse . . ." It felt more as if they were going to be snatched up by the dragons and hurled to the bottomest bottom of the black hungry ocean and never be heard of again.

How beautiful she was! Pressed to her in the blackness he knew it and wanted to save her; the hurt-child look never did leave her face as long as she lived; her hair was wavy auburn and she liked to wash it with eggs. God had not been fair with her. He fell asleep.

She never tried to escape from B. J. again, although he grew steadily crueler and more violent after that night. It was as though she had some terrible disease so that her spirit was kept alive only by transfusions of light, and the eclipse of the moon, the last thing she could have figured on, coinciding with her one superhuman effort, had finished her.

The next thing Tod remembered it was afternoon, probably the day after, and in a frenzy of treachery to his mother he was running to be swung up on his father's shoulder, at the entrance to the fairgrounds. B. J. stood huge and handsome, his black moustache curling around the same confident, majestic smile he turned on his public every night, as if nothing special had happened. Tod remembered it all clearly, because that was the only moment in his life when he had loved his father. There were many times later when against his will he admired him and was ready to risk anything in the effort to be like him, but that went together with the desire to kill him and was probably triggered by it, since B. J. was the winner in everything and you had to become just like him before you would have a chance of killing him. But that one time B. J. had looked like a real father, grand and calm and protective against all harm, and he had flung his arms around him in a passion of gratitude and relief.

It lasted a few seconds. B. J. pushed the children aside and began walking slowly toward their mother, his smile changing only around the eyes; on his mouth it was still easy and public. Disheveled and beaten, she had been standing with no expression at all, even of fear, but as he moved toward her his eyes were sending life racing back through every sad battered bit of her, just as they must have done the first time after she had climbed down the rose trellis outside the bedroom she hated in the house where she was not loved, and sneaked away to the fair. She took a step toward him, and another, and the children saw the little smile spreading on her numbed face, by which she would be alienated from them as by death. Then B. J. had her hand and was leading her up the back steps of the truck which was their home except that just then it was only for those two, and he was getting ready to close the door as if nobody were staring after them but a couple of the vagrant kids who always hung around the fairgrounds in every town.

Tod began yelling and fighting and biting for dear life. B. J. sent him flying with a kick in the ribs and his mother just turned away into the truck, with that smile.

She died in childbirth a few years later, one night on the road. The truck didn't stop for it. B. J. threw the dead baby into a field and woke up somebody in the next town who would bury his wife cheap while the company went on to where they were booked for.

For a long time then he had been bringing other women into the truck, but Tod could recall later only one act of rebellion on her part after the night of the eclipse of the moon. That was one night when he was five or six, and she sent him after a young redneck and his girl to give them their right change from the ticket booth.

By the time he was eleven he was not just riding with his father in the motorcycle act but standing behind him on the back saddle so at the top rim he was straight out sideways going seventy and over, thinking "Kill him! Kill him tonight!" You had to admit there was something grand about B. J. in that depression period, when carnival money was what more and more people didn't have and hardly anybody was too proud to count their change. He just wouldn't believe there was anything wrong with the country and it wouldn't be better in the next town, he was being handyman and everything else and still kept driving himself and what was left of the company to be faster, funnier, dirtier; afterwards there was always something to blame, even himself, because by God under the capitalist system a man got his chances and if he couldn't make good it was his own fucking fault. Tod believed in that power. His hands were on his father's strong leather-jacketed shoulders, in the tub which grew more and more dilapidated and dangerous; it was his father's thoughts that pounded in his head as the few faces up under the tent roof slid into a blur. "Success! Success! Success! That's the ticket, never mind the price. But you've got to be the strongest, you've got to be the best . . ." He'd show them who was the best. He had practiced the motion in his mind so many times, he was sure he himself would be hanging on to the rim as the machine pitched over.

But the accident came one night when he wasn't riding. He couldn't when the cops were there, and somebody squealed in town, or maybe they were just there. One of the loose planks must have come too loose. He and Rachel looked at each other once, grabbed the cashbox such as it was and were two states away in a boxcar by morning.

Another offer, very different from the Beardsley job, had come to Lucas that month. A jovial, husky man of about his age drove up in a new Chrysler one day and asked if that was the Hines house;

which incidentally wasn't the first time I had nearly said no to that, because I never did think of it as anything but the Buckingham house. Lucas, who instead of finding another job that week had taken to napping at peculiar hours of the day, sprawled on the couch or anywhere, came out looking groggy, almost sullen, and became rather more so under the man's puzzled stare. It seemed there had been some mistake, but then Lucas was rubbing and half hiding his face, in the gesture and with the same little pensive scowl he often had when he had finished shaving. It became plain in a minute that they had been close friends at some time, even if the boisterous pummeling and expressions of pleasure in their meeting were all from one side. "Damn it, Luke, you're the hardest man to track down; I've driven over half the state and went for two or three bum steers before that. Are you in hiding or something? Didn't you get my letters, you old faker?" He went on like that as we moved around the house to the porch, to give Lucas time to pull himself together and introduce me. "Lucky Luke! So this is the hero's wife! No better than he deserves, though . . ." "Lay off, Corey," Lucas said, suddenly wide awake and giving his friend a sharp look, which however didn't affect its target at all. "Captain to you, my boy," the man said with the same affectionate good humor, and that was how I learned at least that much, that this Corey I had never heard of had been Lucas's captain in the army. I could tell that he was a good man too, as well as shrewd, with some delicacy of feeling bound up in the rowdiness, and I knew that Lucas knew it, so it couldn't have been from any general condemnation that he'd told me the letters addressed to D. L. Hines were meant for somebody else.

Afterwards I thought I should have asked that man, what happened? how was Lucas a hero? why didn't you recognize him? You hear of men so aged by fighting or enemy prisons that people don't know them later, but that certainly wasn't the case with Lucas, who was always being taken for younger than he was. I had my chance to ask. The captain, or just Mr. Corey something now, I didn't get the last name, became quite insistent after a while about wanting a drink, and as there was no liquor in the house and no place in Jordan to buy any, Lucas had to go borrow some down the road; which he did with fairly good grace, being by that time more or less disarmed and able to trust us both well enough in the matter of confidences. "Ah, he's a great guy," Corey did say, looking after him with a fondness mixed as it seemed to me with a certain

canny speculation. "And I mean great. But perhaps you'd allow me
to call you Eva, considering what Luke and I . . ." He broke off
with a laugh, showing for the first time a touch of constraint. "Well,
you know your husband as well as I do. He'd probably kill me if I
said anything, even if he did save my life once, as he's probably
told you. A beautiful place you've got here . . ." I couldn't say no,
I didn't know my husband that well, didn't know even that there
was anybody in the world who called him Luke, but just that he'd
been a noncom, some of the time in the paratroops, and I didn't
remember how he happened to have mentioned that. I told myself
that I wasn't asking the questions because Lucas wouldn't want me
to, which was true in one way but wasn't the reason. I didn't ask
because in some awful part of myself I didn't want to know my
husband as well as this stranger did; I never had wanted to. He
didn't ask me anything either, but seemed to be satisfying his purpose,
whatever it had been, in sending Lucas away, just by chatting along
with frequent jerks and switches of theme, partly about the great
scheme that had prompted his visit.

Or perhaps he had really felt that much need of a drink, with all
the voltage of energy that was spitfiring through his heavy frame,
making him as uncomfortable to be sitting long in an armchair
as he was in his well-tailored business suit and apparently in the
landscape. The lack of outlets had made him pudgy, with the kind
of fat that would turn to toughness after a few days' proper activity,
and even seemed to be hardening under my eyes just from his pacing
back and forth on the porch yanking off a leaf at a time from the
box hedge, when he was not fingering his bald spots instead or
his wide moustache. "You don't know how lucky you are. Just got
through my second divorce myself. Nevada—Christ what a hell-hole.
Have a couple of children too, that's the worst of it; both girls. I
don't see much of them." He lit a cigarette and snapped the match
in two before tossing it away. "If this were a hundred and fifty years
ago, maybe even a hundred, they'd be looking for a man like Luke
to be a senator or something. Then I suppose he'd have wandered
off and gotten melancholia the way so many of them did, Christ
knows why but they did; loneliness maybe—woods, mountains; I
guess the plains were the worst, got them thinking too much. Did
you ever think how big this country used to be? Luke, he'd have
been a top shot even for those days I expect. What an eye! And then
all the rest, the Bible . . . why, even the Greek! does he still remember

it?" He laughed and sat down briefly in the wicker armchair but without resting, more as if he had intended to tie a shoe-lace and had been distracted by something outside. Far outside, across the hills, and you'd have thought the whole vista was a closet. "A lot of those old boys used to read Greek to themselves, out in the wilds. Isn't that something? Me, I went through a good university, and of course then it was too late to start learning anything; I was ruined, hopeless. I still read a lot of history though . . ."

The big scheme was a mahogany development in South America. He'd been in other ventures around the world for some years, in Africa and for a while in China, which was why he hadn't routed Lucas out before. But this mahogany business was the real thing at last and he was determined that Lucas without a red cent of capital to put into it should be his partner; a full partner; it would be just the two of them. He had the capital himself and had brought evidence of it, along with a briefcase full of statistics and maps, showing the dot in a big square of jungle, and the details: the river stations, the fifty miles of private railroad they would build; and blueprints. Corey himself, it appeared, had a degree in civil engineering.

I didn't think much about it afterwards. I was used to Lucas turning things down. But a few nights later when I came home early from a party, I found him with the maps and documents spread out on the kitchen table, so intent over them he hadn't heard me come in. "No, honey; it's nothing. I was just glancing, out of curiosity . . ." He wasn't asking me if I wanted to leave Jordan for the rest of my life; if I thought a mahogany forest a hundred miles from a village and that full of savages would be a good place to bring up Dickie. It might have been Alaska, and it was just himself. He took the job with the Beardsleys the next day.

I went into Cluny's house to phone him, half way thinking that if he were home it might somehow serve me as an excuse to backtrack after all and stop the migration to Baldur's studio. But there was no answer and in a minute we were off in a procession of cars, Mr. Jarvis insisting on driving me in our old beat-up Chevvy, a kind of vehicle so novel to him he looked as excited as a boy driving for the first time, while his wife Marilyn paired herself off with Jack in the convertible. Cluny's fiancé and his pickup were tired from their long taxi ride and weren't coming, so Cluny had wanted to back out too but gave in after some urging from both me and David, who wanted the heavenly dinner he was going to cook for her to be a surprise. A barbecue, he whispered to me; he had brought shrimps and a bag of hickory chips from New York. She had a woman there looking after the children and Dickie was to stay for supper, which for a moment, when I saw how the company was dividing up, pleased me even less than the rest of the plan. But he and Paul were way up in a tree and sounded happy, so I went on. I thought then that we would only wait a minute outside the Pryden house while Jack went in for the bottle.

It came about otherwise because of another painting of Boris's that Jack had in his living room, and that everybody wanted to see, there having been some discussion of it at the party. I should say, in Miss Pryden's living room. It was the shock of her presence there that opened my eyes, and made me feel like such a fool not to have understood long ago.

Perhaps it was because Jack didn't care to feel permanent in that house that he hadn't bothered to replace the older image with one of his own. Or perhaps he didn't want to feel identified with any place that was merely to live in; as I thought of it now, his earlier reference to the house seemed to sound with a more general contempt, of what I had no idea, not of his work anyway. He had gone quite stony when one of the women at the party made a teasing remark about the laboratory. But he became frivolous and even mocking himself, in voice and manner, as soon as he stepped into his own house or at least what had been the only home of his childhood, as though determined that it should be taken as nothing more to him than a motel cabin. He had replaced the copies of Dutch and Pre-Raphaelite paintings that Miss Pryden had been so fond of, and most of her books as I saw from a glance at the bindings, but that was about all. The wing-chair in which I had sat drinking tea on that last visit was exactly where it had been by the fireplace and had the same old olive-drab upholstery, which like the chintz on the sofa that the poodle had honored with his backside was scarcely more frazzled than it had been then. The little Sheraton tea table, the slightly threadbare Persian carpet with its border of open squares made from one line that ended in itself like space, where I used to fall down sometimes in the effort to make my feet follow every single right angle of the road—leading through the deserts of Arabia at least and maybe even Oregon—were as they had been all my life. So was Miss Pryden's absurd collection of lamps, one cloisonné, one a miniature Roman column, one a brass vase beneath a huge red damask shade with a beaded fringe. That one had always been imperfectly polished as it was now and had had about the same number of beads missing; Jack and I counted them once on a rainy afternoon. Only now it was a different spirit that allowed the things to stay, and stay in that condition, and kept Baldur's boy and dolphin still presiding over what was left of the Italian garden, waiting, while the fascinating voice and eyes flashed forth appreciations beside the fire, to be comforted with disguise under a clown's cap made of snow.

Not longing for it any more than I, on whom the mercurial syllables and not any comfort were falling again, although this was only the beginning of summer and another picture was superimposed now on the one of the newlyweds at the steeplechase. I had it from Cluny, who had seen something of "the Prydens" in Washington just after the war, and heard nothing of horses or private planes or for that matter of their ever having had any interests in common at all. Whatever their rapport had been, the kind I had thought I was seeing in the sudden heartbreaking lamplight that had blocked out the Christmas tree on the porch and all the rest of the world outside, the picture I had gone on treasuring for my torment through all the years, had either never existed or had gone by the board very early. The physical sameness that had been the second sharpest point in my despair had apparently been a delusion. So had all that was represented by Miss Pryden's word "irreproachable," which however she meant it herself had had a clear and cruel enough meaning to me in my outcast state. That had been the worst. I could admit it finally now that the fraud was exposed, only whether Jack too had been taken in or I alone wasn't clear from Cluny's sketch, which was only a little digression from some other subject: on this one at least I had held my tongue. The only point of correspondence in the two pictures seemed the most ironic. The couple had been very popular, as I had supposed, and had been asked out a great deal in certain fancy circles of Washington, but in what sounded like a burlesque of the social verities of Prydens and Buckinghams that had ruled my imaginings.

"A crud," was Cluny's placid expression for the ex-Mrs. Pryden.

"But smart in that vile way." She just loved to analyze people, almost anybody; rather prided herself on her talent in that line. "He was drinking a lot and she seemed to encourage it, I suppose it gave her a better hold. You always felt she was waiting for him to be drunk so she could pick his pockets—just spiritually of course. She has plenty of money of her own." "Spiritual" and "spiritually" had a big place in Cluny's vocabulary, often leading as then to her most raucous guffaw. "God, what a nympho! the worst I've ever seen. I swear she'd ring for the elevator boy if there was nobody else. I don't think Jack minded especially. As a matter of fact, I don't think he even minded being bored to death with her; she was practically illiterate, you know"—another favorite word, Cluny being a tremendous reader herself, with a scorn of anything but the most ponderous books. "He seemed to like it, actually. It left him free for his work. It was a pretty neat setup. Everybody said that was one pair that would never be divorced."

The photograph is dropped lightly on the desk; the perusal of it has been light too. This is not a character to detain for long the attention of the rightful mistress of the room, who is probably wondering what to make of the new painting—a sad little landscape, with a recognizable barn and hayfield, not my idea of modern at all but somehow piercing, the grey light being by some trick of technique the opposite of misty. But no, the picture is not quite for her, it dispels her, it is both too sad and too—what? truthful? too inward anyhow. It is the other less familiar voices that are going on about it: "yes, the stillness, but so charged," "that divine stroke of red," while Jack insists on pouring a round of drinks "for the road," and she for a moment is entertaining a very different group of guests in the dining room, to my discomfort. "Eva, do be a dear and run fetch Montaigne for us, will you? We'll settle it right now. Where? Just where it always is, my little goose," and from her seat at the end of the table, where all of us and Baldur too and some people I didn't know had been having a wonderful dinner, she waved me into this room. That was the new puppy's name, Monty for Montaigne as the later Monty would be for Montesquieu, and because she didn't mean him but something so absolutely hopeless and awful I wanted to go find the puppy anyway and run away with him into the woods. There were two million books in this room and I was supposed to find just one particular one, and make it snappy, if I were slow she would laugh at me and make me ridiculous in front of all those people; even my own parents wouldn't dare stick up for me in her house. I rushed along one wall in panic looking for M's and hoping the tears of rage would stay back, and then all of a sudden my father's soft voice was saying, "Let's see, girlie, I think I remember where she keeps that. Yes, here it is." He put his arm around me and whispered as we started back, "Let's play a joke on her in our house next time."

How enormous she looks, with all her flash and backbone, against these people who are walking now on her rug, on her head; she could crush any one of them with a glance, including Mr. Jarvis. Yet the only sign that Jack was aware of it was perhaps the extra pitch of banter he had fallen into there. Even Cluny, although she had never known Miss Pryden very well and besides had been in the house recently so that it shouldn't have surprised her, remarked on the persisting spell. "I can just see her sitting right there," she said looking like somebody over a ouija-board, "reciting Virgil . . ." Cluny had been brought up in New Haven, which was a long way for lunch in those days, and so hadn't been in this house more than two or three times in her childhood. But Miss Pryden had been much talked about in her home, as in a great many others, and Cluny had an extraordinary reverence for anything that touched her father's circle.

"Who was that?" Boris asked.

"Jack's guardian. My father says she was one of the great women of her time, and it's true. She lived here all her life."

"Good God!" Mrs. Jarvis shrieked. "In Jordan? And without even a man?"

"If she'd had your figure, Marilyn," Jack said laughing, with a bawdy glint in his eye that was startling and oddly attractive, "she might have escaped. Well, here's the booze. Let's go, if we're going."

"Come on, come on," Mr. Jarvis began ordering everybody. He could enjoy himself at a party when he had to, but he clearly wasn't a man to tolerate delays or confusions of purpose.

But Cluny and Boris's wife, a large friendly woman with no make-up, were looking at another painting, a small abstraction I remembered from the summer in New York, and Mrs. Jarvis hadn't finished with Jack's aunt. It seemed incredible that knowing him as well as they seemed to they shouldn't have heard of her.

"Hell, darling, even if she was Mrs. Roosevelt you don't have to keep all the junk. It's too fantastic. Chuck, look!" She went into a whoop of laughter. "Did you ever see anything like that lamp?"

"Any day you want to come around with a truck and clear it out," Jack said, "go ahead. Just leave me something to sleep on."

"And that old woodshed—I guess I've never been here in daylight before. Why, it must have been pink!"

Then I remembered the man.

Out the window toward the garden, across from the woodshed, I saw the kitchen ell half a story lower than the rest of the house, with an old crab-apple tree in the angle and the same old syringa bushes in a high thicket around the kitchen stoop. It was night. Jack was away at school and I, about ten years old, was spending the night in his room overlooking the ell because somebody was sick in our house. In my pajamas I climbed on to the kitchen roof and down the crab-apple tree, not running away, just for the adventure and thrill of risking Miss Pryden's anger if she should find out; which wasn't much of a risk because some late caller had turned up. There were several halls and doors between, but I was sure I had heard a man's voice in the living room a little earlier. My feet hit the ground and that same minute I was not play-scared but scared blue. A stocky wild-looking man with everything dark about him had come crashing out the back door although the lights in the hall had been out for a long time, and into the bushes, too crazy to look where he was going. He stared at me in the dim light coming from the living room, let out some kind of wild angry word that couldn't be English, with a fling of the arm that had to be foreign too, as though telling me I didn't exist, then strode away fast and I heard the steps on the gravel as far as the road but no noise of a car afterwards. He must have hidden it or else was going to walk ten miles to Wellford and stay wrought up all the way. Not from seeing me; for just a second he seemed about to grab me thinking I was some other child, maybe a boy because I had my hair shingled that year and wanted to look like a boy, but I wasn't and I didn't exist. I suppose he was about as old as my parents but he might have been handsome once before the devil got hold of his face; unless he was the devil, I joked to myself later. Anyway he hadn't been visiting the servants even if they were foreigners too, nothing about him was like that. That was one thing I knew for sure, that there was some terrible secret between him and Miss Pryden, and it was because of something she had said or done that he was probably going to shoot himself, or perhaps had already left her a strangled corpse on the living-room floor.

Now the syringa was again in bloom as it had been that night, and the sick-sweet whiff coming through the open window and the other opening of my mind had grown so strong, it seemed that even the Jarvises should have sunk down overpowered by imbecile delight. For me, however, the smell had a visual accompaniment that was anything but languorous. It was of two blades of light sharp as knives, one struck off from the coating on the man's few remaining locks of black hair, which until the furore must have been greased stiff across his bald top, and the other, in the same moment of his furious gesture in my direction, from an enormous jewel in his ring. I had never before seen a man wearing anything but the plainest kind of gold ring, or with such stuff on his hair either, hence no doubt their power so many years later to slit the covers of memory.

A hundred other scraps of recollection, conversations, atmospheres, changes of tone or face, references to Argentina and Biarritz, a certain look of Baldur's once when he was working on Jack's head, flew into place around those two knives of light under the syringa, and told me what Mrs. Hollister had been saying: what the whole town must have known even long before Miss Pryden was dead, only she had been powerful enough to hold them at bay until her grave was closed and make them accept or pretend to accept her whopping great lie. Even so she couldn't have done it if she hadn't been shielded in her hoax for twenty-odd years by my grandmother, the one person in Jordan who wouldn't just have guessed or known by hearsay but had actually helped to arrange the lie, having as I had heard many times met Miss Pryden in France that summer and shared a cabin on the boat coming home with her and the baby. It is true there had also been a helpful coincidence. Forrest Pryden had really been married although apparently he had kept it rather dark for some reason even in France, and his wife, a Russian or Polish woman, something like that, had really happened to die around that time and perhaps even really in childbirth as the story had gone, but if so her baby must have died too.

As to Miss Pryden's other lover, at the moment I only knew there had to have been one. Of this, under the two-pronged stab of the recollection, I was positive: that the man who had given me such a scare had had some nefarious reason that night to try to claim a son who was not his.

Boris noticed me smiling just then, and if he thought I was drunk he was perhaps half right; it had been a good many years since I had drunk as much as that afternoon. Or perhaps the blossoms outside were as strong as I had imagined and he was looking to see if anybody else were under the influence. But I had never felt less hazy. It was only that some tremendous weight seemed to have been lifted from me, from my body and my soul, something I had carried for years without even knowing it, and I felt if I opened my mouth I would break into a concert of beautiful laughter like a xylophone. I had felt such relief only once before in my life, the night Lucas said he wanted to marry me and afterwards alone in my bedroom I walked around to make sure I still could without my doom to hold me down, after I had been sure for so long that I would always be walked out on by anybody I could love and only the ones I couldn't stand to touch would want to marry me. But perhaps the weight that had fallen now was even greater. At least it went back farther, to the scene that had fixed itself for me long ago as the cause and root of that doom, that horrible night at the school when my mother for her ruin tottered to the platform at the end of the barn and Miss Pryden, snatching up a cloak that I remembered now as blue velvet, turned her back on us all forever. She with her sin, her tawdry romance, her shameless deceit! Well and was that so terrible, just to have had an illegitimate child? Some people might have called it courageous. But the thing was only to be felt in the terms set down by herself, in which she had reigned over Jordan and my imagination, ruining my whole family, my brother too whose shame had also been settled by that night, and my own chance of love. I had never been free of her, the threat of her judgment had been inseparable from Jack's, haunting me through him as I began to wallow in my small deceits, so trivial compared to hers.

We got back in the cars and as we turned in at the bottom of our lane, before walking up the hill to find Baldur, I was seeing our house in a brand new way. It looked as lovely, as much "the best colonial" as it had in my childhood, but brighter and younger suddenly, like a place to start a life in. "My mother," I said to Mr. Jarvis, "ran a boarding school in it for a couple of years," and that was the first time I had spoken of my mother with pride since I was fourteen. But when I laughed it was only at Mr. Jarvis's bewilderment and his features not knowing what to do with it, it was such a new expression for them. He evidently thought I was boasting about being poor.

III

"BUT DO YOU MEAN you really think there's a function for sculpture in the modern world, Mr. Blake?"

"Function?" Boris put in. It was the first time I had seen him annoyed. "What is that? Cluny, you have the disease of words."

"Nobody expects you to understand them, angel. I was asking Mr. Blake."

"Function. Hm." Baldur considered it amiably, leaning back in a contraption he had tacked together out of strips from an old leather coat, and looking very comfortable. He didn't seem to be minding the intrusion at all and wasn't letting me catch his eye to apologize for it. "Maybe not. But how are you going to stop it?"

"Oh of course it *was* a natural and necessary expression, for the Greeks, and dear old Chartres." Cluny giggled, but reverted at once to the nervous schoolgirl earnestness that had come over her at first sight of Baldur. I had never before seen her anxious to please, or caring a hoot what anybody thought of her conversation or of her life either, and I realized suddenly, seeing this new side of her, that I had made one mistake in her dress. It was an afternoon cotton with just the right note of the old-fashioned lady in its pastel stripes and in the design of little pleats I had worked out, a good job on the whole, but I should have covered her shoulder-bones more; they were too thin, and by calling attention to the element of bone, made her long nose overprominent too.

"Gargoyles!" intoned Mrs. Jarvis, striking a dreamy pose. She had once been an actress of sorts. "That's what America needs, more gargoyles. I can see them everywhere!"

"No Henry Adams now, Cluny, please," I said with a lame smile, hoping to change the subject. She was an Adams on her mother's side and tended to drag in Henry whenever possible.

Leaning forward from the edge of a crate, she was holding one hand up in the air and rapidly working the cuticles, the adjacent fingers taking turns on one another; such elongated fingers they might have belonged to one of those dear old saints. Baldur, with a sketch-pad on his knee, was observing them too. "Well, since you've mentioned him, it *is* interesting, after all that about the lost center and all, that he resorted to sculpture when his wife killed herself. I mean getting Saint-Gaudens to do the monument." That name made me nervous for Baldur, but he remained calm. "But still that's a kind of last gasp, isn't it? I mean of sculpture as personal expression. Wouldn't you say it was bound to die out now? I mean the way the novel, for instance, is obviously a dead form in literature. Now you be quiet, Boris, I know about Calder and Henry Moore as well as you do, and I can see Mr. Blake's work and how thrilling it is." Prim, bird-eyed, satisfied with her intellect and worried in her femininity, she glanced over the jungle of shapes around us, the products of Baldur's new life. "But who's going to want it? Where will it go? With the human scale lost to architecture . . ."

If Baldur found this either tactless or stupid he wasn't showing it. "On the contrary, I'd say we were on the verge of the greatest demand for it ever. The difficulty will be trying to keep the pea under the mattresses."

"The pee?" said Mr. Jarvis. "I don't get it."

Baldur had been more relaxed than I had ever seen him, both during the first noisy burst of reactions to his works, statues or what-ever they were, and later, lounging with a quart-size glass of iced tea on the floor beside him and a cigarette burning itself away be-tween his fingers as he doodled on the pad. Now he perked up and began to gesticulate, not with any impatience, just in interest and as though it were shared by everyone, even Jack, who alone had wanted another highball and was standing with it somewhat apart, back toward the shadows of the small low-raftered space where for so many years the last goddess had sat, mutilated, on her plaster lily-pad. Everybody else seemed to have lost the taste for whiskey, the whole mood of the expedition having turned abruptly as soon as we stepped into the studio. Mr. Jarvis had looked the most taken aback. "But this is great!" he said rather angrily. "Nobody told me . . ." and he looked around as if to find out who had been trying to make a fool of him. I don't know what I had been expecting myself, nothing probably until we were nearly there; I had been too taken up with Baldur's effect on me and my own life to wonder much about his work. Some kind of old-hat modern, I began imagining then as we made our way around the wreck of a house that he still hadn't bothered with except to board up the door, and in a spasm of disloyalty I half apologized in advance to Boris who was following me over the plank, across the swampy place. Baldur would have discovered abstract art of course, cubism, the "toothpick" school that Miss Pryden had deplored, and all the rest, along with everything else in the modern world that he was so crazy about, too late—oh yes, I was sure of that; it would be the kind of thing I used to see with Jack that summer in New York and that since then had made its way into all the ads and toyshops and even the one cheap furniture store in Wellford.

I was eating crow with the rest of them the next minute, standing in what was in fact something like a toyshop, enigmatic, funny, and all his own; and good—even I could see that. Baldur himself was most pleased by the notice taken of the electric refrigerator he had had lugged up there for his iced tea. He didn't care if somebody sat on an oak log he had begun to carve in, or when Mrs. Jarvis got the titters in front of one of the most haunting pieces, apparently unfinished too, a great leaflike shape on a long stem thin as a pencil. But then there were so many of the things, his imagination and his hands had been working at such speed, even without considering the time out for his whirlwind travels, he could afford to feel profligate about them.

"Of course it's no Renaissance we're heading for," he was going on. "Different time sense, different everything. And God knows we don't need to wake up in this country. We've been prodigiously awake, heroic really, and by God we've nearly reached the goal. Talk about austerity—no nation has ever voluntarily sacrificed itself the way America has. We've learned to do without taste in everything, even the most basic staple, *bread*. Pig stomach, pig heart, as the old saying goes. We've endured it all, but now we're nearly over the top. Right now—1952. It'll be one of the great dates, like 1066 and 1492. The year of the end of cost accounting." He made a quick grimace of mock sociology and the little laugh that went with it was catching, although the smiles around him hadn't been quite unanimous a moment before. "We've done what we had to do; had to be a clean sweep of course, we'd gone too far for patching up. Now at last, barring a few acres here and there, like these"—he gestured toward the open barn door—"and a few thousand in the West, we've achieved what no nation ever has before in the world. *Saturation ugliness!* and all that goes with it, in the way of mental crack-up. Now we can sleep a while, and dream our pastures new. The human brain . . ."

"Dr. Pryden over there," put in Mr. Jarvis, who had been solemnly following Baldur's every word, "can tell us about that. It's his specialty."

"Oh, is that so? Well, doctor, what about it?"

The last of the setting sun was striking through the woods and the newly screened barn door, on to his great gnomish head, lighting up each weathered fold of flesh around the jaw and the bumps and five deep furrows, three horizontal two vertical, of his forehead. But the light obscured his eyes. I was filling in the dark sockets for myself with their passion and knowingness, more unreadable to me after several weeks of familiarity than they had been the first evening when he was drunk, and never as much so as now among the works that might have explained him. They didn't. The purpose I had felt in him that night at the bar in Wellford, although it must have had to do with this weird burst of creativity, still didn't seem to stop there, whether or not he himself was conscious of having any particular aim, outside sculpture or even in it. You couldn't be sure, for all his insight in general. Or the whole business, statues and whatever else he was up to, might have been on the order of a huge practical joke. There was certainly something of that, so integral to all that was burning and to a rare glimpse even tragic in his new hold on life, that sometimes playing on his name I called him to myself Loki—the mischief-maker. But of course that wouldn't do. The amusement, which was always there and was still more unmistakable in the studio, wouldn't have been so disturbing if there had been any barb in it. As a younger man he had been scathing; I remembered it well, and how my parents had been often hurt and in the end bored by it; now that was all gone, together with the self-encirclement that bred it. His laughter had been the opposite of infectious in those days, and he used to look on all strangers, especially if they came to the studio, with a certain resentment. Not that I had been altogether pleased with his easy all-around welcome this afternoon.

Or perhaps the root of my jealousy, or pique, was something else; not his giving out as freely to these strangers as he did to Lucas and me, but thinking of all the times I used to ache all over posing for him, and that now his art seemed to have nothing to do with me. Egg-shapes, arches, hoops and bustles, kidneys, a fish, a flying saucer: there were approximations of them all in the toy world, leaping but strangely peaceful too, that he had been projecting out of himself up there in the woods, in metal, rock, wood. The ice-box was only one of the loads that had gone up the hill; he had been sending all over for materials requiring skills I never knew he had, and new tools, so that the barn had partly the aspect of a foundry. There were even a couple of constructions in papier-mâché, like sketches for some Martian carnival, but almost all the things had an air of sketches, intimations of forms caught on the wing and perhaps even human ones among them but they wouldn't be god-desses, they wouldn't be me, although here and there I saw a touch of the old virtuosity that had made him famous at one time for his draperies and human joints. But it wasn't just technique that had saved him from turning out a new kind of dead duck in place of the old one. He had caught up on modern art all right but there was no sign of its having dawned on him recently. Perhaps he had really been living it all of his working life, while he acted instead out of some crazy fake respectability, like Jack's in his marriage; or per-haps he toppled into it on the day of his madness when he tore the place up, and had been working through it every day in a drunken dream for nine years, in hell. However it had happened, he wasn't bumbling around in the tricks and dead-ends of an unaccustomed style. Everybody felt that; the imagination, whatever it might add up to, seemed to be working full scale without any awkwardness, saying just what it wanted to. It was "masterly," Boris murmured to me, and Jack, looking moved and at the same time peculiarly bitter, had nodded in agreement: "It certainly isn't banal." I wondered if he too was holding up his childhood days there against the baffling challenge and wit of these objects; more likely he was only miffed at Baldur's not having singled him out for any special greeting when we came in.

"The eye of God," I had once overheard Baldur saying to Lucas, I don't know in what connection, but here it was and it was the eye of a hardwood potato the size of a muskmelon. There was also a quite recognizable toad about twice that size in dark grey stone, the most naturalistic piece but with the same sly hint of the mystical about it: the "spiritual," as Cluny had promptly remarked. The first impression of all the things was of prodigious energy, coming partly from the treatment of the surfaces, which were not exactly rough but fibrous and muscular, so that the life process seemed immediate and taunting even in the most abstract shapes. But beyond that they all had too that same lucidity and quiet, snatched from the eye, if not of God at least of a bad storm, since the other general impression they gave was of speed, as if the work of the universe had been stopped for inventory and in a second would resume. Baldur's delight in his recent plane trips had evidently gone deep.

I never could stand being teased; it's a failing of mine. "I don't think that's funny, it's just mean!" I used to yell at Arthur when he played one of his dirty tricks on me, like getting me to look for something that wasn't there, and for a minute I felt that way about Baldur now. You couldn't stop looking at that big dark dented potato or the giant leaf either, they kept drawing you to the brink of something so grand and pure, just what the *preederome* was supposed to have been long ago, which had never existed in his work before and now that it did was only so the eye could wink at you, or wink at your expense. The little sense of loss and pique I had had spread out, until from the mere representation of my body or the idealization of my girlhood it had grown into a mourning for all the past, my own and everyone's, and all the simple beautifulness that was probably never in the world but anyway seemed to have gone out of it now. I missed it all terribly in that moment. It seemed all a happiness and I wished us back in it, myself back in my navy-blue bloomers not knowing yet that there was anything wrong with my mother and father or that they would ever die, and Baldur back in this same studio as he used to be, sarcastic, desperately serious, puttering away more slowly every year on another fingernail, another nymph. It was his old seriousness that I missed most. Pious and lonely, lonely for the understandable human shape, in my mind I was out among the bushes in back where the burial had taken place by lantern light, digging out the pieces of the old statues and trying to fit them together again. How graceful they were after all, and serene; not with this other, grander calm that acted on you like a trap; if only they had had a little more vitality, or something. But of course that was just it, they fell apart in my thoughts. Jack had been right long ago, though perhaps he needn't have been so cruel about it; there had been nothing there.

I wondered then, more precisely than I had sometimes before, thinking of that mock funeral, if he himself even remembered, more so as his behavior with his present guests gave me a faint suspicion that he might have moved in with any of them just as he had with us and showered them with presents in the same way. It was conceivable that some partial amnesia might have set in some time after our evening at the bar, perhaps the day or the moment when he stopped drinking; he never referred to his old life or work, and when he showed interest once in the head of Jack in our living room, saying it was rather good, it was without mentioning the identities of either the sculptor or the model. Of course I didn't quite believe it; he must be only choosing to put his past aside. Still, I thought it might be unbearable for him to have to face it. The whole structure of his new life struck me, this being the first time I had seen him in company outside our little family circle, as fragile and risky, open to all sorts of chance indiscretions that might bring it down in a heap, and I found myself monitoring the conversation as if I could have guarded him against any further reminder of what he used to be.

There was no occasion for it at the moment, however.

"I think what Mr. Blake means," Cluny was laboriously explaining for him, while he went on with what I took from the direction of his glances to be a sketch of her hand, "is basically what Heidegger says, that is if I understand Heidegger correctly. Please stop me, somebody, if I'm wrong. But I mean about the ultimate purpleless . . . purp"—she giggled again getting her tongue untwisted, and again plunged on still more earnestly—"purposelessness of creation, and human creations and activities having to take their purpose precisely from partaking in the universal lack of it. Only when you say cost accounting, Mr. Blake"—pigeon-toed under her intellectual effort, she threw him her best salon smile—"of course I know you're being funny, but I wonder if you aren't really getting a little too close to the pogical lo—I mean . . ."

"Hogical pogical," said Boris, and he got up to inspect one of Baldur's purposeless creations again. "Art is art."

"But then business would be business," Mr. Jarvis said stoutly. "And that sounds like an insult." Everybody laughed at him, but although he had been growing restless under these mystifications, he was too conscientious to let them fade out in a joke. He wanted the knot untied in plain view, right away. The determination, usual to him but being applied outside its usual beat, made his rather bulbous eyes stick out farther and brought a general bulldog look to his heavy head, on which ears, nose, chin, cheeks were all characterful but a little thick and amorphous—a good idea left unfinished, in a state of splash, so that in his sleep he must have looked altogether crude, whereas really the face was not undistinguished. It was saved by intelligence plus a quickness in all his responses, which although it seemed to entrain his will at every moment even among trifles, was accompanied by nothing sly or mean.

It had been growing on me as more and more likable, making it harder than before to connect him with the talk around town about what he was up to. Baldur, who knew the rumors too and ought to have felt just as threatened by them, had been showing a particular sympathy for him from the start.

"I agree, sir, names are not definitions. The fences don't hold. There's too much chemical interaction between our 'human creations and activities.' " The thrust at Cluny went with a smile so genial, it was more like a gallantry. She was enchanted. "In that sense, I take it we're in a constant state of transformation and danger, like the rest of the universe."

"Transformation and danger! You can say that again!" Mr. Jarvis slapped his knee and grinned with pleasure, as if he had just made a discovery of love.

"But you, sir, I understand you're in the building line. That's something I'd like to learn more about. For instance, sewage . . ."

Mr. Jarvis was too sensible to read any jibe into that, but his wife did and let out an unspousely hoot at his expense, suggesting a variety of secret disgusts. Cluny, in a different way, also misinterpreted Baldur's real, practical curiosity, of the kind that had made him send for electronics manuals to help him understand our new household machines. She smiled with subtle appreciation, as if he had made a metaphysical witticism. Meanwhile, with a hectic gesture and pretending to do it without thinking, she had rumpled up her neat little cap of short barley-colored hair, as though she were suddenly not sure that its flatness was becoming to her. She seemed to distrust everything about herself in Baldur's presence.

"But seriously, Mr. Blake, from the existentialist point of view, and I have to admit that I . . ."

"I thought you'd switched to Zen," interrupted Boris's wife with a bright but pleasant smile. She was not such a picture of wear and tear as she liked to make out.

Jack laughed, "That was last week."

"The trouble with you," she threw back at him, getting edgy, "is that you can't stand philosophy at all."

"Not in ladies, God no."

It was a few minutes later that the threat came again, just what I had been fearing, but with a very different effect. Baldur's memory was all there, and if there was any point in it that might be too sore, it wasn't the lost years of his work, but only Jack Pryden.

"By the way, Mr. Blake," Cluny said out of the blue, "speaking of Saint-Gaudens . . . didn't you once study with him?"

It was nearly dark. With a quick springy motion Baldur got up, and I thought he was heading for the bottle that Jack had kept on the floor near him and had just helped himself from again. It seemed the natural thing. He hadn't had to watch anybody drinking until now, and now the old failures had been let loose on him, through my fault. I had opened the way for it; I who had expurgated all my talk with him for weeks more carefully than I had realized until this gathering, and while I thought I was remembering everything had managed to forget, almost as if there had been some will in me to destroy him, that the mention of Henry Adams was bound to lead Cluny to this.

He stepped over the bottle. He had only gone to turn the lights on. They were very powerful lights rigged up at different levels, about a dozen of them with reflectors, and as they came on, shattering a second's fantasy on my part of Baldur and his present works having vanished under that question, as if he had died a few weeks ago in the boarding house and all this other were a minute's dream from which the name of Saint-Gaudens had wakened me, the new sculptures around him sprang into such life, they might have been taken all together for a modern and playful but not irreverent view of the Last Judgment. He himself, at ease and looking perfectly indestructible, was not without a magician's pleasure of an innocent sort in the working of his trick, which brought a "Well I'll be darned!" from Mr. Jarvis, and a general round of appreciative laughter and exclamations, over all that had been only half revealed in the pieces before. Perhaps he hadn't been above pulling that bit of showmanship just then on purpose, by way of demonstrating whatever he owed to the idol of his youth and how little he needed to worry about it now; anyway the question didn't trouble him. Still with his gleam of prankishness, he answered it in a few mild words, of which only the tolerance, his feeling no call to judge either the old master or his own errors, made him sound momentarily as old as he was. He had become benign. No, he said, he hadn't really studied with him but it was true he had visited him a few times as a boy, and Saint-Gaudens, then the "dean of American sculpture" and living in New Hampshire, had given him some encouragement. He added, "He was very generous in that way," and then turned to answer a different question from Boris, who was scrutinizing a column of red stone in which an upward spiral was just adumbrated. "Why, it's the baseball player," I said. A few evenings before he had been entranced by a super-speed camera shot of a man batting. "Or is it Lucas?" One effect of that strong light, coming evenly and without any glare from all sides, was that the most abstract pieces took on another dimension, something out the other side of pure form, which I supposed the critics would some day be calling either romantic or classical. "I call it Galahad," Baldur said.

"A moral vision," Jack had once said to me in a taxi, "has no place in art." The phrase, forgotten as soon as heard because being in love was more important, rang out now in my mind, and I felt like teasing him with it. Only that was from another past not to be revived.

"Yes," Baldur was saying, "it needs a little more off here. How about this?" He held his hand up to the still stone, making it whirl higher.

"You can call it Nearer My God to Thee," Jack said, and was evidently surprised by his own tension and the remark being such a flop. "And what's this going to be?" He fingered a flat openwork rectangle in wire, that was propped against a wall, discarded or just begun.

Baldur turned and they looked at each other straight for the first time that afternoon, probably the first time in many years, because whatever Jack had gone to see Baldur for in Wellford, whatever it was that I had known long ago was pending between them, I gathered Baldur hadn't been in condition to come to grips with it that time. Until a minute ago, I hadn't even been sure he had identified Jack, he had greeted him with so little interest. Now the line of the past had been laid open and in public, all the way to Saint-Gaudens, down through all the unfathomable joke that was in Baldur's eyes, and somewhere along it was some specific piece of unfinished business between them; something that for Jack, I was sure, partook of the nature of my own search for Baldur and of Lucas's relation to him, and yet at the moment had the startling effect of making Baldur seem the more vulnerable of the two, and the one who might flinch. But if it was true that his mischievousness had been pierced at the one possible point, and he had been on the verge as I thought of exposing a pain deeper than any in his old self-centered life, there was no trace of it a second later.

Oh that, he said, looking as wise and gay as ever and as lacking in afterthought: that was just for fun, maybe something would come of it. He had been fooling around with an idea for a gate.

"A gate? What kind of a gate?"

"Well, now that's the question—what kind of gate could make sense nowadays?—except for jails. It's a big problem when you come to think of it. The idea of gates goes pretty deep, way beyond any practical uses they ever had. It's an atavism on one level, but I'd say a necessary one; heaven and hell were based on it. It was a big psychological shock for cities when they discovered they didn't need their gates any more, and now look at the American countryside, if you can call it that any more, especially here in the East."

"We have a nice gate on Long Island," Mrs. Jarvis said, "but we can't keep a gatekeeper. They always marry somebody and turn up with a yacht."

"You should marry them yourself, dear," her husband said. "But go on, Mr. Blake, I'm with you."

"You snow me," Mrs. Jarvis said.

Baldur, enjoying himself and communicating his good humor so that even Jack for a while stopped looking so guarded, spun off into a discourse on all kinds of gates and their uses and meanings: cottage, garden, palace, cemetery, convent, factory, etcetera, and the sad little suburban gates you could see nowadays stuck at the end of the front walk with no fence for them to let you through, just a gate stuck up there with air around it. But after all those were not so pathetic, they were the symbol of the human necessity he was thinking of, a double symbol—of differentiation and welcome. It wasn't the lack of a fence but the TV aerial on the roof that made the gate look false; the air was swarming, the whole idea of identity and possibility of welcome was vitiated by that. "How can you push open a picket gate and get to your front door with any dignity when you're thinking about rockets—and bombs and bulldozers? Now what we need," Baldur went on, addressing himself mainly to Mr. Jarvis, who was taking it in as if he were paying for it, "is a gate that won't be a lie—that will take account of the idea we live with, and that, I think you'll agree, sir, is of solid structures vanishing. Nuclear physics and money pressure, in the form of the bulldozer . . ."

"Are taking over the function of religion!" shouted Cluny with more of her normal gaiety, but feeling she hadn't struck the right note she added defensively, "We certainly are as shallow and corrupt as the ancient Romans."

"And isn't it fun," Jack said.

Mrs. Jarvis, adjusting her bra, cast him a smile quite unlike her party one. "Oh no it's not," she crooned, "I'd much rather be deep and honest," while Boris with a wry grin at Mr. Jarvis sighed, "Progress!" Chuck, as he had insisted I call him, had relaxed under Baldur's sympathy into his natural and becoming role of the liberal young magnate, ready enough to go beyond his depth if there was anything to be caught there; a new kind of gate was something to consider in his business. In the matter of solidity, though, he hoped Baldur shared his view that there was a lot to be said in favor of the bulldozer. He himself had put up quite a number of low-income houses "of what we call the permanent type, that means a twenty-year expectancy," in fact, he didn't mind admitting he'd been a pioneer in new subdivision design, and people who called them the new slums were talking through their hats; before they got to be that the wrecking crews would come in. He'd been raised in the real old-time slums himself, so he knew what he was doing: "It's a crusade." As a matter of fact, though he wouldn't want to be quoted on this, he was looking forward to the day when people would think about houses the same way they did about paper cups. "Except they've got to express the individual. We're working on that. But now about this gate . . ."

Baldur resumed, as if he found it positively stimulating to think of all Jordan going under the bulldozer tomorrow. I knew this vein in him. I had heard him going on once or twice to Lucas, with what degree of naiveté you couldn't tell, about laying oneself open to one's own time, whenever it might be only we happened to be lucky in ours. What a time to be young! everything wide open, every human purpose and even the planet earth in question; why, the old days of the West were nothing to it. The trick was not to get alienated; that was a way of surviving once upon a time, now it was the surest way to be crushed. Another time when I mentioned having been to the supermarket in Danville he said, "Then you've been close to holiness."

It seemed that he had some holiness in mind for his gate and it wasn't only a comic conceit any more than his baseball player was, but he didn't exactly speak of it that way, holding the rack up at different levels to see where it looked most convincing; for design so far there were just some hasty curls in wire, like a notion of waves or birch shavings. "If it doesn't pretend to have any practical use you might begin to believe in it. And it mustn't be down on the ground. Most of the abuses of welcome, that make the real thing so hard, don't come up the front walk except now and then selling magazine subscriptions. They come over the air, telephone, TV, thoughts of astronomy, and the gate has to stand between you and all that. It says, 'I choose, or I don't choose, to be at home to this presence or proposition.' At most it might rest on a point, or a little stem, like this"—he twisted the wire into a fan shape. "It has to seem to be in flight, get rid of the lie of the fixed point that makes people so miserable. It's a waste of life, that 'uprooted feeling' when you or your neighbors get on the move again, or you wake up and find a motel in your back yard. You ought to be glad. If doubt, mobility, disintegration are the general condition, it makes a person sick to be pulling the covers over his head and thinking all the time, 'Not me! not my rock garden!' You have to dissolve the threat in yourself, be an Arab, make your gate collapsible like a tent and when the wrecking crew gets to it you wish them well. You have your car, and the symbol of your humanity; friends and flowers are everywhere.

"The paper cup! Fine! Of course twenty years is pretty long, but twenty years from now the reality will be far beyond anything we're saying . . . But now that's just the individual or family gate. What's harder to work out is an equivalent of the old city gates. You might say that with communities as dreamy as they are now, with all the changes of scene and turnover of characters, it wouldn't make sense. But that might make the community gate more valuable. Everybody coming through for a night or a year, or just stoping for gas or a forced landing, would feel the human bond, what they call togetherness. Maybe a gate lying in the air, way up . . . what do you think?"

Cluny was beginning to look depressed and I felt a little that way myself, even though I was used to Baldur's fancies and contradictions. He had given a lot of thought to rehabilitating our garden and bought some plants for it himself that would take five years to make any showing at all and ten for their full effect. He always spoke of it too in relation to the whole view up the hill, although the field we had already sold to Mr. Jarvis cut in there at the top. Now he sounded just as serious and was saying, "What do you think?" in the same tone of voice, holding his gate, twisted to a wobbly star or perhaps a sunflower, over an imaginary air-view of a countryside completely taken over by Jarvises. It was all going to be like the outskirts of some hideous industrial town like Hackasaug; the divisions would have to be arbitrary, but there was nothing wrong with that; anyhow the communal gates could be moved at will and would never be quite stationary. The important thing was for them to be "as beautiful as the towers of Chartres," and like them they must represent, he said coolly, memory.

"That's the hardest problem—human memory. Right now we're at the hit-or-miss stage, and that's the sickliest; it's not real memory, real history any more, just souvenirs, just enough to make people sad. As I see it there are only two ways to go about it. One is to perform some kind of lobotomy on every baby at birth so there won't be any question of it. The other is the communal air-gate, the symbol of continuity—because a big part of our austerity since the last war has been to turn ourselves into a people without a history. Oh well," he broke off, going back to his seat and his iced tea, "as you see, I'm just a sculptor in search of a function."

Mr. Jarvis grinned, looking boyishly pleased as he had getting into our old car. "It's not so dumb, just the same. You've got something there." He cast a piercing eye again over the other works in the studio, as though their commotion and mysterious stillness were also to be fitted into his scheme, and I was struck in spite of their great difference in age, by all that he and Baldur had in common, both physically and in their visionary grasp. "But just one thing. You spoke a while back of 'money pressure.' That's old-fashioned; sounds like commie stuff. What we're all up against is population pressure. Everybody knows the statistics . . ."

Jack, who ought to have been rather drunk by that time but wasn't showing it if he was, was sitting on the floor with his back against one of the hewn chestnut uprights of the barn. He had been following Baldur's proposals with a mild unflickering amusement, more at ease than he had been but very self-contained inside his still impeccable white coat, giving and taking nothing, and it wasn't any remark or look of Baldur's that brought him to his feet. There was some general talk about population and birth-rates and all society especially in America and Russia becoming "one big middle class of idiots." Then somebody raised the question of how much money was going into the effort to save human lives, and spoke of medical research and Jack in particular as "humanitarian." That got him. His emotions were still strong after all, for all his boast to the contrary, only he had kept the lid on them in response to the statues and even to the silly joke about his laboratory earlier, which had stirred him more. Now he dropped the sardonic cover together with his affability, and spoke with a hard conviction worthy of Baldur himself, only without Baldur's glee at the core.

It was wonderful how unmarked by life he was, as if the years of his marriage just hadn't registered, and nothing either good or bad had happened to him since the summer of our love. But then as with a quiet elation I took in the truth I had been half knowing for the past hour, it seemed that for me too the intervening years had blown away without a trace.

"Nonsense! Every ham and barker in the field will give you that humanitarian stuff . . ." He was pacing a line on the floor in short brusque steps, a couple of yards each way, his thin nostrils working and the blueness of his eyes stirred to a double depth and brilliancy; his mother's eyes, since I must use the unnatural word for her, but with a merciless singleness of drive that hers had never had. There was a prickling at the back of my scalp, a thrill of pure physical luxury such as I had always associated with a shampoo at an expensive hairdresser's. It didn't matter what he was saying. He would go to any length, I knew, to avoid being pompous and sloppy; he never could bear clichés, especially the "liberal" kind he used to accuse me of that summer after my one year of college. The point was his caring that much and knowing what he cared about. Baldur however wasn't taking it that way.

"Are you saying that any human being can afford to be outside humanity?" He still had his chronic glimmer, but the tone was one I had not heard from him before.

"In science, certainly; of course they can do what they like after working hours. Humanity in a laboratory is for publicity hunters. And the administrative boys who couldn't discover anything anyway, so they get the money and dole it out instead and have their pictures in *Time* and *Life*. Cancer, arthritis, schizophrenia, longevity, polio serum, tranquilizers. A miracle a week to keep the funds rolling and everybody happy, and there's always some so-called scientist who'll deliver . . ."

"Well now hold your horses, Doc," Mr. Jarvis broke in. Jack's indiscretion, considering who was paying for his own lab, rather awed me, not that he seemed to be risking much. Mr. Jarvis had indulgence to spare and anyway, as he had shown before then, wasn't a man for kid gloves. "All that may be true but you have to admit . . ."

"Oh leave him alone," Cluny said. "He's just playing monster."

". . . that this is the age of miracles, that's just a fact, and there have been plenty in medicine. Human suffering . . ."

"Is irrelevant to science, first, and secondly is a question mark."

"The alternatives," Baldur said, "are the exclamation point and the period." He was beginning to gather himself as for some imminent demand on his wits or even on his physical strength.

A moment before Jack had looked so exercised I had thought he was about to walk out, but perhaps he had reflected that a lay audience wasn't worth it. "Quibbles aside," he went on in a sudden reversion to good humor, "if it's results you want, of course there are bound to be some. Mongolians used to die at the age of two or three; now we can keep them alive into old age. Fine. We can control asthma and some other conditions enough to fill thousands of nursing homes with cases of geriatric idiocy. There's even some progress in medicine that isn't so ludicrous, but whether in the last analysis it lessens human suffering, as you call it, or adds to it is a moot point to say the least. If you're talking about real values in life any sensible man would prefer the eighteenth-century toothache, or a decent death from the plague, to present-day neurosis and senility. Anyhow it's not, thank God, for the scientist to decide, and if he claims to he's a fraud. Proteins and chromosomes—they're serious. The monsters in the field are the ones who play human, or humanitarian, as you put it. They're the ones who muddy the waters, confound the issues, take over the labs and fill them up with little technicians who are no more capable of a scientific idea than they are of flying to the moon on their own power. And I mean idea, not just the tricks of the trade, wrapped up in that bunk about the good of mankind."

He had stopped his pacing to pour himself another drink. The bottle was near the long up-ended box that was serving as pedestal for Baldur's melon-sized woodcarving, and as he set it down we both became aware at the same moment that the piece, which I had been calling a potato, was really an adumbration of a woman's head, round like an Eskimo's, not bowed but with its little wide eye turned up flat to the sky, and as I looked it seemed to have evolved just then, under my eyes, from a complicated and moving joke into the simple absolute of human grief. It reminded me strangely of the old nude Niobe, which had disappeared from the wall, I wondered how, a long time before Baldur's crack-up. Jack, passing his fingers in a quick sensitive motion over the head as though to take in its texture, let out a little laugh of surprise and pleasure. "Mater Dolorosa . . . It's a beauty." He smiled at Baldur in what seemed, for the first time, a perfect frankness of appreciation. "But there you are. What's good and beautiful in art can be fallacy and evil somewhere else. If we had the guts to think straight about the good of mankind, under present conditions, there'd be a lot to be said for genocide. I wouldn't want to organize it personally, it would be a bother and you'd probably get lynched. I don't care to be a hero. But it's rot to be squeamish about it, with miseducation and malnutrition and war doing a far nastier job now, and test-tube procreation coming soon anyway."

Except Baldur, who was slowly getting up from his chair, everybody began talking at once, saying, "Oh, shut up," "Even if there were too many people . . ." ". . . birth control . . ." "Who's going to decide . . ." and Boris's wife said with her incongruously pretty smile, "Too smart is dumb." I was holding my breath because that time Baldur was really heading for the bottle. The strength he had been gathering had left him, together with the last vestige of his humor, and he had become all of a sudden what I had never expected to see in him again, a confused unhappy old man groping for his one comfort, which this time I knew and he must have known too would be the end of him. But he didn't quite reach it. A little smile of contempt and almost of triumph appeared on Jack's face when he saw what was up, only for a second, but it brought Baldur's power flowing back through him as suddenly as it had gone.

"My boy," he said in a light staccato, staring full into those hard blue eyes, "there's one thing you might look into in your laboratory. That's under what conditions the human imagination dries up. I believe it's been known to occur also in rats." What was most peculiar, with their great difference of build and facial structure, was the physical likeness that emerged in the course of the long look that passed between them, which was not so much a communication as a trial of strength. It was only a subtle likeness. Only the mouth clearly marked the chip off the old block, and really it was more as if the old block had been facing down his own former self, the contempt that remained on Jack's lips was so like Baldur's in the old days, when he was the one despising the human obligation.

I understood then why he had let the plaster head stay in our living room instead of burying it with the rest, and it wasn't because it was the best. How well and even deeply the sculptor of twenty-five years ago had seen that boy!—with all the irony of his own refusal of the bond to give it a sharpness lacking in all his other work at the time and for years afterwards, until one horrible winter afternoon his fatherhood would come crashing down on his head, not through any love but probably by his not being able to bear the child's scorn for his works. All of them now buried in peace except that one, which he had come back to live with. A chilly pact it must have been, I was thinking, Miss Pryden being eight or ten years older and passionately and by her own standards squalidly involved, I was sure of that, with her Argentinian or whatever he was, a racetrack tout anyway by the look of him. But how like her, to have conceived a child not out of love or carelessness but in cool calculation, to mark her independence from that sordid enthrallment. And how like the Baldur of that time to have lent himself to the scheme, in the vanity of his aloofness and no doubt another vanity that Miss Pryden would have shared, of counting on the combination of themselves to produce a genius.

As apparently it had, and with a power of acid I had sometimes glimpsed when we were children but had never been afraid of until now. Nevertheless in the present tussle the victory went to Baldur, who was opposing to it nothing but an unashamed acknowledgment of suffering, on such a scale however that his huge erect form and ungainly features seemed to have grown in size, as though infused with majesty. Jack lowered his eyes, but not before his look had changed to one I knew much better, the one that above all I had kept knowing most vividly through all the years of his absence, in which he was himself asking for pardon and for the chance to love.

Baldur, his wits in full solemn force again before anyone else was conscious of his having lost them, launched on a charming improvisation on space and time, and how all we had to do in America was to invent a new kind of elbow room. "Here, these might amuse you," he said to Mr. Jarvis. He turned on another set of lights in the one section that had remained dark, a partitioned storage space still floored with sawdust from its days as an icehouse before his time. It was given over to a wholly different kind of disorder, of hasty drawings and cardboard models as for some labyrinthine children's game, for which an experiment in color seemed to have just begun. "What on earth . . . Why, they're houses, gate and all! And isn't that this hill we're on?" All focused now, he began firing questions, his eyes darting with predatory finesse over the jumble of notions scattered there. Baldur, rather apologetic, put the lights out shortly; it was just his way of resting, his bit of the hard-earned dream—of the pastures new, the imminent beauties of life; nothing serious. But it struck me that in that imaginary landscape with architecture he had been showing us the secret logic and motive of his new sculpture, which seemed no longer teasing as it had been an hour before.

"Oh it's great stuff," Mr. Jarvis said, and he kept going on about Baldur and his conversation in general as we made our way out by moonlight to the road and past the old cemetery. "He's my man. I'm going to make him great. I've got the dough and the know-how, he's got the rest . . ."

"For what?" I asked, letting him guide me by the elbow through the tunnel under the apple branches, although I knew every bump in the road by heart.

He swept his arm out. "A new kind of space."

I laughed, and called back to Baldur behind us, "Did you hear that, Baldur? Mr. Jarvis says he's going to make you great."

"Fine, fine," Baldur called back. "I'll be glad to hear your propositions, sir," and I didn't think that either of them was joking.

Part Three

I

"OH, THERE THEY GO AGAIN. The parachutes . . . six of them. Oh, how pretty they are!"

Jack came and stood beside me at the window, holding his dressing-gown around him. It was a Sunday afternoon in July and we were about to get dressed, after lying together for the first time on Miss Pryden's narrow bed. The other times had been more hasty, once up in the old cemetery that night after Cluny's party, then on the sofa downstairs or in the woods. "The poor suckers," he said. But he watched with a sudden bright edge of pleasure and a look of almost professional calculation, as the white blossoms struggled open and began the tug down. They fell nearly straight down, there was so little wind, and looked as if they had been meant to go straight up instead.

They were quite near, up on Fix Hill where a Mr. Larrick had bought an old farm a few years before and turned the top pasture into a little private airfield. It was being used that day for an inter-collegiate jumping contest, and practically everybody in Jordan was up there watching. But Jack had had to bail out of planes twice during the war and it hadn't been much fun either time. He didn't even care about flying any more, he said; it took too much time.

"It's a wonder Baldur isn't up there, though," he said laughing. "Parachutes would be his style these days."

"Yes, like the Jarvis business," I said. "I wonder if he's really going on with that, whatever it is. Did he tell you anything when he came back from Long Island?"

"No. But he can't go very far with it, even if he wanted to." I looked at him, questioning. He went on calmly, going back to his dressing, "He can't live long, at the pace he's going. A few months maybe. He knows it perfectly well."

"Oh you're horrible, to say it like that . . ." It hadn't been a very happy afternoon anyway and I didn't like being in that room.

He laughed again, not bitingly; it was just his nice big open laugh that I had always loved and had been listening for in crowded places so many years. "Darling, don't be ridiculous." However in a moment his tone changed. "Still, you're right . . ." He crushed his cigarette slowly in one of Miss Pryden's pin-trays. "You're right, the old man is rather grand. I just don't know if I'm up to it."

He took my hand and we drifted into one of our unpredictable spells of understanding, without talking for a minute. There was too much to catch up on, it was all too old and too new, for talking and telling to be much to the point, although we had done a lot of that too when we happened to feel like it, and it was wonderful how clear and easy it was, while it lasted. I hadn't half realized before what mystery I had been living in with Lucas, even around the littlest things not to mention the big ones. "It's lovely to be lazy with you. It's lovely to be with you, period. Shall we have a lazy drink and go for a lazy swim?" He was smiling at me, not even trying to hide his imperfect teeth. "It's a funny feeling, being happy like this. I'm not used to it."

What mystified me most in him, aside from his work but it was a pleasure to have that so far beyond my understanding, was the complete lack of tension or any complication of feeling that I could see in regard to his mother. He told me a little of the story in the most natural way in the world the second time we were alone together, and was only astonished that I hadn't known it long ago. It seemed everybody else had, and in fact as soon as the truth dawned on me I began hearing it from all sides. Cluny, for one, had known it so long and thought so little of it, she apparently just hadn't thought of mentioning it. But then Jack was one subject I had steered clear of with her, except the time she described his marriage.

"I just never saw anybody to talk to," I told him, to explain my innocence. "I hadn't been to a party in years till this spring."

"You do pretty well for a girl out of practice," he said smiling and kissed my fingers in a parody of his own party manner only with a different ending. "Your hair smells just the way it used to. But your family must have known. As I remember the story, your grandmother went to France with her that trip, to get me decently born."

"Yes. But you know how they were. They'd have had their tongues cut out, Mother and Daddy too, before they'd have gossiped about her." It was funny how those old shadows had lightened, even in the rooms and closets of our house, all in a few days. "I wonder if they knew about Baldur."

"Not from her, anyway. I'm sure she stuck to her bargain about that. I didn't know for sure myself until a couple of months ago." He made a wry little grimace, but that was only at having had to go through some bundles of letters that spring when he came back to live in the house; letters she presumably would have destroyed if she had had any idea of dying when she did, since she had a horror of any "splattering around" of people's private lives. It was a feeling he shared, but he had read through the packet concerning him, including one short letter from Baldur. It was a rather ill-tempered note, written when Jack was in his teens, reminding Miss Pryden of the conditions on which they had agreed to produce a child. "I can't imagine what she had done to make him write it, but it doesn't matter. He said he had all the paternal role he wanted with Carrie, his duck."

We couldn't help laughing. The duck had lived to a tremendous old age, and she and Baldur used to scold at each other year after year just like all the old maids living with a parent around Jordan. It was funny how many there used to be.

It was true that Jack's present feelings about Baldur were deep and ticklish enough, but then so were mine, and Lucas's, and for that matter so were the storekeeper's and the Episcopal minister's. His return had sent a shiver of something through the village, you couldn't tell if it was more of love or fear or shame or just novelty, which was beginning to show. Lately a group of high school children had been sneaking up the hill to see him. But Jack wouldn't admit to any particular shock or interest on more intimate grounds; human origins were always fortuitous, he said, and he didn't happen to be making a study of heredity. "He disturbs me as an artist though, very much, and I'm not sure I like it. I thought I was through with that years ago. But the other day, in the studio . . ." For a minute his face was as young as that other summer, and bared to its own peculiar beauty, an intensity of spirit without any strain, as it used to be during certain moments of music. It was a look of humility, I thought, which was not less so for being somewhat regal, like a very large butterfly deciding to alight. "Well, you were there. You saw it all."

Miss Pryden herself had told him only about her own relation to him, when he was fifteen and setting off for a visit with her brother in France. It had been a very happy day for him and he still remembered the scene in great detail, in spite of his casual poise in the matter.

"My dear boy," she had said when he was closing his suitcase and the chauffeur was already waiting downstairs, "just to avoid any embarrassment between you and poor Forrest, I think you ought to know that he's not your father." Jack told her he had never thought he was, and said grinning, "Goodbye, Mother dear," which was the first and last time he ever used the word to her. He had been hearing things from Suzanne and Gelindo all his life. Miss Pryden laughed, "Poor little kitchen souls, how they do love a tale. But I must put you on your guard against them," she continued, "in one particular. They very likely have it that your father was a Mr. de Lima, whom you may remember. He has rather lost his charm in recent years but he was a man of considerable quality before you were born. In any event, he has nothing whatever to do with you." Jack had suspected before then that it was Baldur, but he didn't say so. "Unfortunately I'm not at liberty to tell you anything more. That was the understanding and I shall have to honor it, even at your expense, my dear child. I shall have to expect you, I do expect you, to live through your life creditably without knowing who your father is." She sat herself on his refractory suitcase lid to help him close it, and in that absurd position added in her ingratiating way, as if they were intellectual equals and more or less the same age—oh, how I knew that magical gift of hers, and what it must have done to him then! —"I dare say it will seem hard now, but you may grow to think of it as your good fortune."

"And did you?" I asked him. I had been looking into the cold fireplace while he talked, but I turned to smile at him then, just comfortably. There wasn't any challenge or afterthought in the question, I wasn't trying to make him admit anything or thinking he had anything to admit, or thinking of whatever had gone wrong between us the other time and why it might have been, and he knew it and answered just as comfortably, getting up to fix us another drink.

"I don't know, I suppose it may have had some advantages. I've never thought about it very much one way or the other."

When the suitcase was closed she had kissed him goodbye, and I could imagine through his few words the dazzling clarity and self-confidence of her kiss. Then as an afterthought, at the top of the stairs, she had said, "I must leave it to your own judgment, Jack my dear, whether this fact should be made public, now or in later years. A certain deceit, as Catholic countries know so well and we old Yankees know quite as well, may be more than a convenience. Even the poorest life has treasures that are not for the marketplace. Your uncle Forrest, I know, would a great deal rather go on with this one than have a family scandal, and I must say that I prefer it myself. I believe it allows us all more freedom for our work, and for the wider decencies. But I'm quite aware that your world will not be what ours was. It may have greater honesty, or less, I can't judge of that. I do know beyond any question that general exposure brings a general cheapening of *all* experience, and I'm afraid, alas, that we are heading for that. I hope I shan't live to see it, but you doubtless will. And you may not be able to stand up to it. It might not even be wise that you should. For that matter," and here, as he reported it, she had taken one of her flashing turns to pure pleasure in her own play of mind, which were always so contagious, "there may be some gem of purest ray serene hidden away in cheapness and vulgarity, which my generation was too stupid to discover and yours will bring to light."

She was, and intended to remain, an "old fogey," she had concluded cheerily, and that was it: one of her masterly scenes. No pathos, no exhibition of conscience, not a trace of those regrets and confusions of meaning that she always called, along with other human wastes, the *mire*. As for her own reputation, it didn't occur to her to mention it. She only wanted him to consult his own feelings in the matter; which apparently hadn't been hard for him to do.

That was the first time he had felt really grown up, and he went off feeling so elated and somehow privileged, he could hardly distinguish between what she had told him and the fact that he was traveling on a ship by himself and handling his own passport and ticket for the first time. Only when he was getting engaged he thought he should tell the girl, and her parents had made quite a fuss and refused to have Miss Pryden at the wedding after they failed to prevent it. But as it turned out it was their conventional little daughter, Jack's wife, because for her it was all a big joke and nothing else and at the age of nineteen before knowing Jack she had already had two abortions, who eventually set the talk going around Baltimore and Washington, even before the famous plane crash that finished the worldly poses of Miss Pryden and forty-two other people and allowed even Jordan at last to say what it thought.

But they only knew half of it.

Mrs. Hollister, who by this time was talking openly instead of in sighs and hints and who was also very anxious to take on the role of motherly favorite with "the famous Dr. Pryden," had hit on the happy idea that his father was a Russian prince, which of course gave a different cast to sin even for New England. So she went on about the sufferings and courage of the Russian aristocracy, much as my grandmother and Miss Pryden herself used to talk about the Dauphin, who was supposed to have settled near Jordan at the time when our house was still fairly new, and of whom as the story went Dill Polk was the last direct descendant. At least until recently you never could get anybody in Jordan to say a good word for a going nobility but they certainly did love one that had had the stuffing knocked out of it, and the same with kings. Anyhow, although I don't know about Dill Polk and the Dauphin, Mrs. Hollister's idea came plainly enough from some garbled recollections of talk, around the Pryden house and ours, of the Russian driver we had that time in France—my "first love" as I used to call him to Jack.

Cluny's parents, so she told me, had run into Miss Pryden twice in Europe with her "South American lover," once in a general group in Biarritz and another time by coincidence in an isolated place in the Alps, and had always assumed the child was his. "My father thought it was magnificent of her. But you know, now that I've seen Mr. Blake, or rather heard him, they don't look much alike, but their voices . . . Jack's no spic if you ask me. But my God, she'd have been so old and Mr. Blake . . . What did he use for tail in those days anyway?"

Cluny had been at our house more than ever since the visit to the studio, in the transparent hope of meeting Baldur, which she did once or twice. She pumped me about him continually, and kept telling me about her disappointment at having had to leave us all that evening, instead of staying for the dance that had developed at our house. Everybody had told her what a wonderful time it had been and she wanted to know every last thing about it, what kind of sandwiches we scared up for all those people, what Lucas played on the clarinet and how Cliff Beardsley was at the piano and whether Marilyn Jarvis had gone on making a play for Jack, and especially everything Baldur said and did and what time he went to bed. "He danced too? with Beulah Wellman? Isn't he wonderful! Oh, I could vomit. David would have loved it so too, that's the kind of party that's just made for him, and there he was instead having such a time, poor angel. But you and Lucas have it so good, you can't understand. By the way, Jack's a superb dancer, isn't he? You'd never think it to look at him."

David had been having a time all right. When we got down to our house that night Lucas had just arrived, and to my astonishment, after all the years of his never bringing a soul home if he could help it, he had his old truck full of people, including Dickie and Cluny's two children, also the baby-sitter, sobbing and with a black eye. I had begged Lucas that morning to stop by at Cluny's party after work, so he had, just to please me, taking Cliff and Hester Purser whom they found closing up her vegetable stand out on the main road. They heard the shrieks from way down at the head of the road. David's pickup, the little hobo, was crazy drunk and chasing everybody with a carving-knife. They had left the two of them fighting it out. Of course we tried to keep the children but nothing would do for Cluny but Mr. Jarvis must drive her right home to help her fiancé, taking Paul and little wide-eyed Isabel too—Cluny murmured something about its being educational for them—and except for the loss of her car, retrieved a week later, it was all right. They found the house empty.

"It was so fine of David to clear out like that, to make things easier for me. I'm sure it was all that fool baby-sitter's fault anyway, she must have said something tactless." She looked suddenly intense and worried. "But *please* don't tell Mr. Blake about all that. You haven't, have you? Of course I know he must have heard something about it that night before he went off to pee, but still . . . It's just that he's of another generation even if he is so sort of ageless and outside of time—you know what I mean, really young, and I'm afraid he might get it wrong. And the friendship of a man like that would mean so much to David."

"Damn it, Cluny," I finally broke out, "why don't you stop kidding yourself. You've already had one husband like that."

"Eva darling," she smiled mildly, her poise all recaptured, "how you do generalize. Sometimes queens make the very best husbands, and anyhow what else are you going to find nowadays. That doesn't mean anything necessarily. Besides, he is *trying* . . ."

"Besides he's already run through half your capital."

"Did I say that? Well, it wasn't his fault he had a slipped disc, I could hardly refuse to pay for the operation, and of course he's going to pay everything back as soon as he finishes his novel. Why, he's got half a dozen lead reviews promised already. And then . . . Oh, by the way, it's a small world. He just told me the other day that he used to know your brother."

"Baldur Blake certainly has changed," old Beulah Wellman said one day when she was over cleaning house for me. "Can't hardly believe he's my age to look at him now but he is, pretty near to the day," and then in a voice no older than it had been when I was a child, it was always like cracking hickory nuts, she told me something that had happened nearly ten years ago, a little before Baldur disappeared into the boarding house.

Beulah herself, tall, gaunt and with only four or five teeth left, had changed since the night of the dance. She had come running right over when she heard the racket outside, because she loved Dickie in a pouncing, spinsterish way and was always on the alert for any threat to him, and then she stayed to help get him to bed and after Baldur had danced a waltz with her she became the belle of the ball. Not by way of the grotesque either, or not mainly, though she had on a dress of my mother's that had been already half a rag when my mother died and carpet-slippers older than that, bone hairpins slipped from her meager topknot as she danced and her steel-rimmed spectacles were askew. She looked like a piece of Queen Anne's lace in November, with her rattling old head as erect as that on the tall stick until the whole thing would topple together, but that was her night to be more white and green than ever in her real youth, which had been miserable. The Jarvises' house guest, a TV producer who hadn't gone to Cluny's party and started out being a sour apple at ours after they phoned him to come, couldn't get over it. Beulah was "terrific," the best dancer there, and she had him in stitches with her rather wicked mimicry and storytelling, about al-

most anybody and anything in Jordan. She knew it all, goodness
knows how when she had been ostracized so long, even more than
I and my family.

Now she was talking of having her hair dyed and even buying a
set of teeth if she could ever afford it, although in her twenty-odd
years of living with "my boarder, Mr. Brown" I had never seen her
look in a mirror. She must have loved Mr. Brown though, faithful
old dog that he was, to have faced down the town and her own
father for most of the twenty years, because of his already having
a wife in the insane asylum. He was getting ready to die before
people stopped seeing the scarlet letter every time she set foot in
the store: the change came in the backlash from Miss Pryden's
death, when that fresh scandal took the juice out of the old ones. But
Beulah had never showed that she had minded, there was nothing
vengeful in her gossip, and her one big hate was for the person
who had most defended her and tried to help her from the beginning.
That was Miss Pryden. Beulah had done her washing for years because she needed the money, but she did it in her own home and
one time when Miss Pryden took the laundry there herself instead
of sending the chauffeur, Beulah just refused to do it. Even now if
she had to say the name she looked as if she were biting off a thread.
With her sixth sense for a story, to feed her artistry in repeating it,
she had probably known a good deal about Miss Pryden's life long
ago, but in that one case hate was stronger than art. She preferred
to act as if there were no such person, and so kept mum, as for ten
years for some other reason she had about the episode with Baldur,
which came out now not at all in her usual comic style but almost
as a reverie, in the aftermath of the dance.

He had gone into the Wellman house late one winter night,
because he was out of gas and wanted to phone, and she had seen
right away that he was half dead, with pneumonia it turned out.
Her father Si Wellman, scion of the oldest family in Jordan and
himself the last of the mighty there, with his great beard and slow,
famous wit and hands that were said to have brought down full-
grown trees with three strokes of the axe, was dying upstairs, aged
ninety, while Mr. Brown shuffled around waiting for his meals, but
she took Baldur in anyhow and nursed him for a week. He was
delirious a lot of the time, she said, and kept raving about an
imaginary son. "Well, so finally I said I'd get hold of this son, he'd
been begging for him so, you know I thought maybe my boarder

Mr. Brown would do if I turned the lamp down, but then if he
didn't turn turtle and want to kill him. He was hollering to get at
him, just like that with his own hands, and I tell you he's powerful
even with a hundred and five. I don't know if we could have got
him tied down, anyhow he gave up first and just started to moan.
'He's dead,' he says, 'I can't ever tell him now,' and then he looks at
me and says, 'Are you his mother?' Yes, I says, and the boy was fine,
nothing wrong with him, so he sort of nodded and went to sleep."

"Did he say anything about his statues?"

"Ayuh. I was them too, some of the time. They were walking
around the room and this son he thought he had was laughing at
them. 'Make him stop that laughing,' he says, and then the statues all
come up close around his bed and they were kissing him and calling
him Daddy." Beulah's voice was as usual, crackety-crack lickety-split,
but she was dusting one chair over and over. "Another time it was
Germans. Seemed like they'd took Jordan and they were breaking
into his barn, going for the statues with bayonets, and what do you
know if his son didn't get into that one too. He was the German
captain. Oh well," she broke off, and I knew she was about to tell
a fib and probably had never told all she knew about that story
except to Mr. Brown, "a person's bound to get dotty being alone so
much, like he used to be. I get dreaming things myself since I buried
my boarder last year. It was company."

I didn't tell Jack about that, or Lucas either of course, although
I was going out of my way at that time to be conversational with
Lucas. But that was what I was thinking of when I said to Jack one
day, looking around his living room, "Oh, I hate her!"

"Who?"

"Aunt Addie . . . your mother."

"That seems a waste of time," and he tacked on in a way to make
me laugh but it sounded happy too, "darling."

One thing clear was that there had been no pretense of love
between those two, on either side. It had been a cold-blooded deal,
naturally with no money in question since they both had plenty of
that. It was a transaction in egotisms, with an extra purpose for her.
As I had guessed, she hadn't been so free of the mire after all. Her
relation to Mr. de Lima, I learned from Jack, had been thoroughly
degrading for years before she managed to get free of it. She had
lent him large sums of money which were never returned, chased
him to Europe and once to his own country, and had even given

social introductions to his other mistresses rather than lose him. She had "begged and wept like any housemaid"—the phrase was her own, in a letter returned from one of the wrong addresses he had sometimes given her; until at the age of forty she had decided that only having a baby by another man would release her, and had picked on Baldur, as being both handy and suitable.

Obviously, as Jack said, there was nothing he needed to honor in any of that.

"But now," I said, thinking of Beulah Wellman's story, "I mean when you went to see him in Wellford a couple of months ago, it must have been right after you read the letters . . ."

"I went to touch him for money for the lab, that's all."

I stared at him. "You mean you thought you could, because he was your father?"

He laughed. "What a little Portia you are! Well, yes, that's about the size of it. I'd heard he was drinking himself to death, the lab takes a lot, and I wasn't sure Chuck Jarvis was going to be too dependable."

"But that can't be why you've been seeing him lately, almost every day . . ."

"Well . . . no . . ." It was funny to hear him drawl, he was usually so rapid in his thought and speech. He looked and sounded for a moment exactly like a Yankee farmer of my grandfather's period considering the weather and with a lot at stake in it too. It made us both break into a grin. "Oh Eva, what are you doing?" he said holding out his hands, while as naturally as the two principals in a spiderweb we were drawn together. "I was so safe and empty until a little while ago, and now look. I'm almost in love with you."

"You're so lovely, Eva," he had suddenly been saying as we danced together that first evening, and I knew he had picked that time with all the people around because it would have been too hard for him to have to look into my eyes. "I should have married you when I had the chance . . . How can you stand me?"

I asked him where he'd learned to dance like that, at his age, and he said he'd known a prostitute in Manila after the war who had taught him. I said that was a funny way for a scientist to be spending his time.

I had been having such a good time dancing with Lucas and all the other men, I don't suppose I looked as if I had ever needed Jack or missed him. Hester Purser had said to me a little earlier, putting her arm around me, "It makes me feel good in my bones to see people dancing in this room again, and you looking so happy," and she really meant it. She was a lot older than I and used to come to my family's "village parties" years ago, when Arthur and I would hang over the banisters in our night-clothes listening to "Who" and "Avalon" and "Sam the Old Accordion Man" on the victrola and the people laughing and joking, and we would be dying to be big enough to be down there too, and instead when we were big enough there was no such world left for us and in our separate miseries we had lost even each other. But I knew that Hester was one who had never blamed me or Arthur either for what happened to my mother, whom she had loved, and I wanted to hug her for being what she was, only the TV man was asking her to dance. "John'll take a switch to me when he hears about this," she said, and stepped out as merry and highhearted as she used to be at those other parties, although what she had said was no lie. John Purser never could bear to see people enjoying themselves.

"Oh baby," Lucas said, getting his breath after a long number of his own, and he pulled my head against his shoulder a second, which was the first time he had ever done anything like that in front of other people. I gave him a little rub back with my cheek on his coat and we looked at each other and smiled.

I hadn't ever seen him as attractive as that night, or putting himself out that way for company, not from out of his distance, politely, but because for the first time in our life together he was really there and liking it. He had been practicing on the clarinet a good deal lately in the evenings while I worked at the sewing-machine and he was playing like an angel, with Cliff who used to play for the high school dances doing well enough at the piano, but it wasn't just that with Lucas. I knew as soon as I saw him that evening, in spite of the mess he had run into at Cluny's, that he had kicked over the traces in some way and had his heart in something besides me, and then I found out from Cliff what it was. It was a plum tree. They were going to try to get a new hybrid, and although it was already late for transplanting he had brought a couple of the trees home to set out at the end of our garden where there was something special about the soil. He had been doing some soil analysis recently but without taking much stock in it, it would be just another of those things he would fiddle with for a while and drop, when he had proved he could have done them if he'd cared enough, and then all of a sudden that day had been bowled over. As Cliff described it, very pleased in a paternal way although he wasn't much older but just solid and settled by character, it had been the old stroke of lightning. Lucas had fallen in love with the idea of that tree, "and when he gets his back into a thing nature better watch out."

It was all his doing that the party had come about in the first place, or rather his and Baldur's. After Cluny lit off with her children there was an awkwardness of fatigue and satiety and incipient goodbyes, with everybody standing in the dark and still unsettled, half of them by the mess at Cluny's house and the rest by the visit to the studio, so that they really wanted to stay together and not be tired yet and all jumped, as though being positively rescued, at the thought of food and music. Baldur and Lucas came out with it at the same instant and in so much the same tone and manner, of a natural, healthy hospitality, you'd have thought they were the ones who were father and son and that neither of them had ever behaved otherwise toward strangers at the gate.

Perhaps if Baldur had stayed to the end the evening would have turned out differently for me. I don't know; anyway he had suddenly had enough around ten-thirty and without a goodnight to anyone went upstairs to bed, and then it seemed all sorts of impulses, in almost everyone there, that had been kept in order as long as he was in the room, began to catch and go off. Not that things got rowdy at any stage; it was all just gay and obscure.

A sequence earlier that should have been peculiar, somehow wasn't because of his serenity in it. That was when we first went into the living room and everybody recognized the head of Jack as a little boy, and began asking questions and wondering about it. Even Lucas seemed to be taken for the first time by its quality, or perhaps by the fact that I had salvaged it. Of course there were questions then about Baldur's other works of that period: this one was so fine there must be others, in what collections, and so on. Lucas, no doubt thinking of the funny funeral when they buried all the broken pieces by lantern light, just smiled a little in an offhand familiar way at Baldur, and Baldur himself was as cool as ever, even when Boris's wife insisted on Jack's posing beside the statue. "No, no, don't *smirk*," she scolded him. "This is serious. Be as you were then, you were how old? ten? Ah, that's better . . . look!" He held the pose a few seconds, glancing at Baldur and then at me out of the child's fierce rectitude and fearless sweetness and even the ache to recapture those ways of being that Baldur had anticipated so long ago, out of an ache of his own that I had only that day had any reason to imagine, and all the events and meanings of our lives seemed in that moment sifted back through the long difficult mesh to that time, becoming clean and unconfused as a handful of water from the spring. It was only a minute later that I felt Jack guessing why the head, which he hadn't seen in many years and might even have forgotten about, should be in our house. But Baldur displayed the same spendthrift air he had had about the things in the studio that afternoon. No, he said, there weren't any more from that period, at least he didn't think so; he had gone astray in his middle years, but he didn't say anything about Nero and the years being a thousand. The music started, and he and Beulah opened the dance.

Boris, dancing with me, said with his gentle, joyless smile, "There will be a lot of sharks coming into these waters. The dealers . . . and others." He nodded, with a little look of distaste, over in the direction of Mr. Jarvis, whom I supposed he meant although his glance seemed to take in Jack and the TV man and a spread of dark pasture out the window too. "You will have to protect him. And maybe yourself," he added more whimsically.

"Oh, that's the last thing he'd want. It was being protected that killed him before. Now . . . No, he can't be hurt now by anything as simple as a shark."

"Sharks are not always so simple. There will be some who love him." A moment later he said, "You are thinking of something wonderful. What is it?"

"Only some words I just remembered . . ." I smiled. " 'And ride in triumph through Persepolis.' " It wasn't quite so that I had just remembered them. The phrase had rung often through the years of my dream and my defeats, like that other golden word *preederome*, only from what point of origin in my life I didn't know.

He laughed. "I had heard about your husband but I didn't connect him with you. It seems you are not often together."

"Well, we are at night, like most people I guess. What did you hear?"

"It was from that Mr. Farr, the minister, I think; yes. He said he had great powers and was wasted here, he should be in the church."

It was no funnier than some of the others, I thought. "They'll be wanting him for a royal consort next. But he likes it here."

It was true that the prince of the evening was Lucas, who until Baldur's advent had allowed only two forms of happiness, his own alone in the woods, preferably in the snow, and ours in an isolation from the world to be sealed a little more tightly every year. But that night there was something outside even the more recent extension of his nature with Baldur, and more than the subtle authority of glance and manner that always bothered people around him. He had come shining out with a whole other magnetism of high spirits, reserved before only for the most hermetic home scenes with Dickie and me, so that when he called for a square dance it became everybody's pleasure to fall in with it, although besides himself only Hester Purser and Beulah knew the figures. Later he really cut loose on a solo improvisation that brought the house down, and he hadn't drunk anything either, he never did. The end was terrific. He jumped an octave and a sixth, went on up in four long shrieks slower and slower, and then in a glorious burble just like the river at the rapids below the falls brought it all tumbling down home.

There were cheers; stamping; calls for more. Lucas quickly put a record on the new hi-fi set Baldur had installed and gave me a whirl around the room to cover his embarrassment, smiling into my eyes. We had only danced together a few times before, in a dreary little steak house with a jukebox outside Wellford. He wasn't much of a dancer, he kept good time but his step was too loping and he didn't like it especially, not the way I did, but it didn't matter that time. Everybody must have thought to see us we had been living a seven years' honeymoon. Dickie, who had been hanging over the banisters, came down in his pajamas at the end of the solo, yelling "Do it again! Daddy, do it again!" and began dancing in circles all by himself in a trance of joy. Mr. Jarvis couldn't hide his frustration at Lucas's having eluded him a couple of months before, and wanted me to tell him he was ready to talk turkey with him any time. I said oh, was he going to make him great too, wasn't Baldur enough, and hurt his feelings, not for long though, he was so elated over his discovery of us "natives." The TV man meanwhile was talking about putting Hester Purser and her vegetable stand on a Saturday afternoon show called "Our Daily Bread," she had just the kind of natural, homey personality he was looking for, and Mrs. Jarvis, who was something of an amateur blues-singer and had volunteered a number earlier, had switched her seductions to Lucas; she seemed to have forgotten that she had come to see me there once before. He, to my surprise, considering his usual shyness, was taking it with a calm air of experience. He hadn't been struggling for words all evening.

Jack, of course, wasn't missing a thing, although he couldn't know what a novelty it was for Lucas and me to be publicly admired and courted as the "handsome young couple," or for us to be having people in the house at all. I don't believe he really knew until almost the end, any more than I did, what triumph and treachery we were heading for. He kept cutting in on me and gave it quite an air of a contest, more under the influence of Lucas's playing and Mr. Jarvis's flirting with me than anything I said or did, but that was just lighthearted and a joke. There was no real contest, and no suggestion hanging between us, until the dance when Lucas confided into my eyes and Dickie, looking more than ever like his father but with his small hands lifted as though an invisible angel were leading him in his dance, and his handsome little face transfigured by a smile of mysterious delight, was weaving close to us, never looking up or appearing to see anything but his heavenly partner, yet he was clearly glad that Lucas and I were dancing together then and he managed to keep us near.

That was the signal Jack couldn't resist. I had seen his face once at the start of a steeplechase and I saw the look again then as he stood watching us, small, neat and smiling, against the white cut-tooth mantel that Miss Pryden used to admire and that Mrs. Jarvis, after being told by Jack that it was authentic, had been trying to buy from us all evening. She just loved those "genuine old things," she said, and would have liked to write a check and have the mantel hacked out of the wall then and there. That time when Jack cut in, dropping his conventional style that once and going all out, as graceful and fast and sure of himself as Lucas had been on his instrument, it was pure provocation, and so was his mentioning the prostitute in Manila, and I knew, oh yes I knew then that my dream had become real again and for fourteen years I had not lived in anything else and I was not going to lose it because of a plum tree no matter what, not even if Baldur should hate me for it, because if I did and let myself be trapped again I would never, never get out, and would go on being just the last of the Buckinghams and living with my dead the way I had gone on doing for seven years with Lucas. There has just got to be some point to life outside yourself and that's a fact, and not just children to go on being as meaningless as you are. Don't ask me why, I was sick and tired of all the wondering why, about that and a lot of other things such as that I really did love Lucas too. I wanted to *know* for a change, and I did know. I was as sick of wondering as I was of being poor, and I was so sick of that I used to think sometimes in those years "I would sleep with anybody for a fur coat," and would almost say it aloud to myself although it was a damn lie and I always did just the opposite, I mean I had a perfect genius for latching on to men I had to pay the carfare for. But it takes a lot of sides to make a dream. It takes a lot of waiting to make Persepolis.

So an hour later, when Lucas had gone to drive people home, without any words over it and scarcely a look, only with Jack's hand tight on mine and the knowing going through us in one current, we were on our way back up the lane to the old cemetery, where on the scrubby ground between the graves he spread his white coat for me. It seemed that was inevitable too, that it should be there, in that place, which had had the same hold on his feelings and mine most of our lives, and long ago, when we used to wisecrack with phrases like "the consummation of passion" but were really shivered in our timbers by them and moving in a golden haze, was where we once imagined the scene. I suppose it was because it was on the very crest of the hill, looking over maybe a hundred miles of ridges so wooded there were hardly any house lights to be seen, only a few far away and scattered like fishing-boats. Yet it wasn't too exposed. On the side toward the village the woods came right up against the tumbling stone wall to give protection, to us and the dead. The dead of so long ago, the last of them buried in the 1820's, they were way past being jangled by any living memory and at most might figure in a scrap of handwriting that could turn up some day in an attic somewhere in Jordan and inspire a moment's wonder at there having been such people, before it went on the fire. They were good clean bones and peaceful, not like the stamping newly-dead but altogether absorbed both flesh and spirit into the spaciousness of the hills, and so were fit to preside, along with the stars and the living brambles and the old plain uninscribed stones in the wall, over a journey of love.

"I used to try not to keep seeing your eyes, and your hands," he said after the first dry kiss that had all that waiting to dispel. "I thought I had managed. Perhaps I did, some of the time."

"But then why . . ." I was smiling a little, it had all turned so airy and easy and really I wasn't asking a question, any more than the leaves of the trees were. His short-cropped skull with its bald spot under my passionate fingers felt too small, and risky as a glass container, for all the brains he had. "Then why," I went on murmuring, "did you keep me waiting that time . . ."

"I suppose I had to prove something. I don't know. It doesn't matter any more, does it, Eva? Oh Eva, dearest, nothing matters. Not now . . ."

His body pressed down on mine and up above the Big Dipper, past his sweating head and my adoration, I was seeing Dickie's face turned up in its lovely happiness as he danced around and around.

The sexual act, on that occasion and later, was just so-so, but I knew myself too well to expect much else right away, and as a matter of fact I didn't too much care, with him, if it were always like that. That wasn't it. There was a little trouble of some other kind between us, now and then, during those first weeks.

Before I married Lucas I used to have a recurring dream, of which the scene was that same hill, a little below the graveyard. I would be going up the lane, under some necessity of reaching the top but getting more and more out of breath, when from the open field there, across the stone wall, I would see a great white bird rising, heavy as an airliner and beautiful, and I would cry out to it in ecstasy and try to run after it, but either I would fall among the stones and brambles or the bird would get up only a little way and crash in the next field, and I would wake up crying. I hadn't had the dream or thought of it in years, but now the image came back to me off and on in my waking hours. The beautiful soaring flight didn't come off. We were happy on the whole, and confident, and drifted often into good talk and good silences. But we kept being jarred by the need to snatch our meetings and sneak to them, and there was some trivial sparring between ourselves too, which began right away that first night coming down the hill. It only reached a momentary edginess of voice that time, but later it brought us to a couple of near-quarrels, one growing out of a mention of astronomy of all things and one over a kidnapping case that was in the papers that week. I told him he was trying to be "above life," and he accused me of wallowing in sentimental confusions; it sounded just like the quarrels we all used to have, he and Arthur especially, when we were children. I half guessed even then that it was Baldur we were arguing about, at least some of the time, and the argument was important, but it didn't sound that way and when we were actually speaking of Baldur the trouble rarely came into the open.

The worst hour or so was that Sunday afternoon in Miss Pryden's bedroom, where I had an impression that the most personal feminine belongings of a lifetime had been swept out pell-mell only that morning, and where I became dully, silently angry at Jack's waiting for me to take my own clothes off instead of caring enough to fumble with them himself as he had done in the cemetery. "I think I'd rather . . ." I started to say, but I didn't know what I would rather, except to be at the fair in Pittsfield with Lucas, who was overseeing the Beardsley exhibit of peaches. Dickie and Baldur had wanted to go too, in spite of the attraction of the parachutes that day, and as I stood taking in the unfamiliar hair and nail utensils lined up straight and sparse on the dresser top, formerly a clutter of jewels, creams, lotions, gadgetries of all sorts as well as fountain pens and unanswered mail on a lace runner, and through the dressing-room door the rack full of rather small-sized men's shoes stretched on shoe-trees and each beside its mate, I felt first annoyed, then sorry for myself, for being left to that methodical betrayal while the people I loved were off having fun without me. To the shoe-trees especially I took a real dislike. Lucas's shoes were always unpolished and strewn around any old way, or almost always; before taking his latest job he had passed through a fit of giving a lot of slow, exaggerated care even to his oldest work-boots, but he had forgotten about them again now.

Afterwards, lying with a cigarette on the newly crumpled sheet damp with perspiration, Jack was the one more detached. Not hostile or indifferent exactly. I had had one lover who was horrid that way after making love and he was the only one I came to loathe in the end. Jack just had a distaste for languor and was a little too prompt to talk brightly about important things that had nothing to do with us, which at first was more moving to me than any tenderness. That he should have come back to me out of the greatness of the world and his own achievements was still something I could hardly believe, but there it was and I fell into a bliss of humility before the fact, lying with my head on his shoulder and my arm across his body but lightly, avoiding any pressure that would seem a demand for intimacy. I would have liked to put flowers around the room and find one of his socks with a hole in it so I could darn it.

But after a while the impersonalness began to weary me, and I felt the beginnings of a fear peculiarly like the old one of so many years before. Somehow in that room, itself so impersonal now, my victory seemed to be slipping away, and my youth too, just when I had thought I was finding it. I had thought we had both suffered and learned and everything was going to be different, and instead the old thought was insinuating itself, that no matter what had happened or was happening, *they* were still the winners, and we the ones who would pay.

The bed was too narrow for our bodies not to be in contact, but I removed my head and arm to the edge and lay on my back, the sheet pulled up to hide my breasts, oppressed by the heat, the past and the neighbors. The man beside me was becoming more alien than when we came into the room and I couldn't keep my mind on what he was telling me, some story about the medical board he had had to do with in Washington. The mere mention of Manila, even aside from the prostitute, had thrilled me that first evening, but now the thought of far places was oppressive too, like the heat. I wanted to talk about ourselves and Jordan, and was thinking sex was probably a mistake in the afternoon, anyway in the summer.

"I wish we were riding," I said and turned back to him, in love again as soon as the thought hit me. "There's a nice little stable out on the Lincoln road . . ."

"You mean just get on a hack and jog around in the woods? Darling, you're so romantic." He went into the bathroom, wearing his nudity like a costume, a trim one but not quite his style. He must have taken to setting-up exercises, I thought, to keep so pared down and springy, with the life he led. Outside the lab he smoked all the time and by my standards drank a lot, but it told only in the dryness of his lips when we kissed.

Out the front window I saw the leaves of a big elm across the street dead still and glistening, and then out of the Sunday quiet, from down toward the grade school and the Town Hall, came a chicken's mournful squawk. Only two or three cars had gone by while we were there; Fix Hill had drawn all the traffic. I heard a dog barking way over by Mrs. Hollister's place a mile away, and from the big brown house next door, the only one along there uglier than the Pryden house, there was a faint jibber of TV, where old Jell Seeley the storekeeper, who used to be so fat he had to have a special steering-wheel on a hinge so he could get into his car, lay shrunken and addled after his stroke, dying. He had been a mean, selfish, grasping man and nobody ever said a kind word about him till his heart got broken, when Jell Jr. turned the family into managers for a chain-store with the new location down on the main road. Old Jell never knew his way around his own merchandise again, he couldn't get the idea of vegetables in cellophane or why the potbellied stove had to go, and looked as if he were crying all the time.

How queer to be naked on that side of Jordan, right over the village street, if you could call it that with no sidewalks and not more than thirty buildings the whole half-mile length of it not counting the barns in back. Still there are street lights, a dozen or so, and the Episcopal Church stands square at the end where the road makes its right-angle bend into the green, giving a certain formal weight and sense of community judgment that begin to let up out our side. When the store moved, taking the Post Office with it, and half the people you would see there were beginning to be city people anyway, it used to seem that "the center" didn't really exist any more. But it did. It was still a definite pressure area, say in a half-mile radius out from the Civil War monument, a place where you watched your step, and your step was watched, more closely than outside; which Miss Pryden must fully have reckoned with in all her doings in that house, and that bed. I hadn't felt the pressure myself in the same way since our two years upstairs in the Howland house, almost across from the Congregational Church; not to mention the little jerry-built Roman Catholic one just beyond, which in my childhood I used to pass with something of the feeling I had, and my pony had too, about the lonely barn where Mr. Berman the butcher did his slaughtering. Something sinister went on in those two buildings. Under the sunny surface of Jordan ghastly rites were being permitted, better not to think about. But in that period when our house was a tearoom I spent quite a lot of time with the O'Briens and the Wienowskis and the new Rossi family, all Catholics, whom I had never thought of being friendly with before. It was my own fault that I never saw much of them later, after we went back to our house.

My grandfather, to tease Miss Pryden, used to say there was some excuse for peasants like them to be benighted, coming from the countries they did, more than for her being a pillar of the Episcopal Church and always twenty minutes late to it besides: if she meant it why didn't she go on time? But on religious matters she preferred to draw, as she said, a veil, and she continued to stride down the street on Sunday mornings with her English walking-stick, always late but never missing; never remiss either in her donations, or in her regular dinner invitations to Archdeacon Collins, rector there for some forty years, too dreamy and erudite to want a bigger parish, who was no doubt enjoying her food and exchanging Latin verses with her when she was already letting out her dresses in her pregnancy.

The phone rang for the fourth time in an hour; twice it had been the young Italian, Dr. Sanseverino, who was Jack's assistant at the lab. He hurried out of the bathroom and I listened to him making a weekend date with some friends of his whose names weren't familiar to me. There was a certain pleasure and intimacy of fun with these people on the phone that struck me as more solid than anything in our relation, and he didn't say anything to me afterwards about the weekend I heard him arranging.

I had seen her in that bed only a few times, once on the morning after my escapade, when I had discovered her old lover storming out the kitchen door. I had been more or less right about that visit; he had intended to use her son as an instrument of blackmail and it may have been that very morning that she had decided to expose her whole intimate story to a lawyer, and so contribute to Mr. de Lima's ending in the penitentiary. But if so she hid it well. The other times too I had seen her a trifle harried on waking; everything was as usual; she didn't suffer from any such insomnia as my grandfather's, but her eyes would be somewhat drawn and her charms a little awry, like her hair, for the first hour. She almost always wore blue, and that morning like the others was in a blue silk bed-jacket, taking her café au lait and her daily spoonful of honey from the breakfast tray, and graciously receiving yesterday's *New York Times* from the poodle's mouth, since today's didn't arrive in Jordan till noon and she preferred in any case to read the news with a day's perspective. Of whatever furious occurrence there had been the night before there was no trace, and she burst into her merriest laughter at my being tongue-tied: had I seen a ghost? was there a fly on her nose? "What an odd little creature you are, Eva. You look positively homesick . . ." The room smelled of nothing now, but for half a minute, as Jack wound up his phone conversation, the old distinctive odor was there for me, very unlike my grandmother's lavender and linen freshly sunned and ironed. This was a more confused smell, of perfume, always the same and not much of it, old paper, a whiff of dog, and close to her person, in contradiction to the nearly chronic ink-stains on her writing fingers, her lifelong brand of French carnation soap.

But the image that was growing most urgent to me was not of her, and not of the famous night at the school either. It was of myself, exactly a week after we had gone back to our house, driving home alone in the family's old rattletrap Ford around three in the morning after the most loathsome few hours of my life, with X. in a roadhouse the other side of Danville, to find Mrs. Hollister and the rest of them there and my mother's body, her hair and clothes still dripping from the willow pool, laid out on the living-room floor. It was less than two years after the summer's affair with Jack and I had been calling his name aloud in my wretchedness all the way home, not thinking of my mother at all or if I did for a moment it was only to blame her and hate her for what was becoming of me; not thinking or able to bear the thought of anybody in the world but Jack, who was alive somewhere even if we were never to meet again. I must have been just about at the Housatonic bridge, crying out to Jack not to come back but only not to despise me, only to understand that it hadn't really been me in the roadhouse and the motel cabin behind it that night, because nothing had been real to me since that day I waited for him: at the bridge or not far from it, when my mother, already nearly unconscious probably, having crept downstairs barefoot so as not to wake my father, clumsily knotted the rope around the rock and her waist, got the last pills down on top of the quart of whiskey and managed somehow to fall in. My father never could tell what woke him and sent him out searching. Beulah Wellman said afterwards that she had heard a scream and thought it was a cat. Or perhaps very slowly, too slowly, up through the layers of his sleep, wayward as a feather, there had drifted the sensation of a last touch of her lips on his forehead. Even groggy as she was, she would not have left him without that much goodbye, of that I am sure. She would rather have risked waking him, and postponing once more her only possible relief, than not to tell him in one kiss, before she dragged herself away, that she knew herself forgiven for her only other betrayal of him. On her side, wonderfully enough, there was nothing to forgive. She never had blamed anyone but herself, had never thrown his weakness, his failures at him in so much as a look, and until that night, for twenty-seven years had never been able to sleep without his arm around her and their heads on one pillow. How could one drunken kiss sum up so many sweet goodnights?

For three years after that I couldn't stand for a man even to touch my hand. I would get an attack of nausea and my face would start bloating like a drowned person's. Then it was over and in my few months away from Jordan I had three men in succession, in love each time with the image I carried in me, which I would not tell myself was Jack although after each breaking off and for that matter after each time in bed, my head would be full of his name. So for another two years I wanted nobody and thought I never would want anybody again, till Lucas came by.

There had been a few people at the funeral, besides my father and me, but no word or flowers from Miss Pryden.

After that day we took to meeting most often by the river whenever he could leave his lab in the afternoon, and then he would go back to Danville and work again all evening. His devotion to his work was ferocious, as Miss Pryden had said long ago, and marvelous to me. It wasn't at all like Baldur's present joyous profligacy of output and effort. Jack reminded me more of my grandfather and the way he would be unstrung when some household matter delayed by half a minute his setting out for the courthouse or his leaving the dinner table when he had work to do at home. There would be such a charge of suffering impatience in him at those times, I used to think the telephone wires out over the road would snap if he looked at them, and it baffled me in later years to realize that in spite of all that passion, and the distinction of mind that everybody rightly attributed to him, he had after all ended his days as just a minor county judge. Jack had made more of a name for himself, and had his work written up in the learned journals, and the newspapers too, before he was thirty. He was trying to isolate some kind of substance in the brain, and naturally didn't attempt to tell me much about it, but he let me go to the lab once and it was exciting to me to see his face among all the tubes and bottles and pickled or pow-dered brains, and to think of some truth about us all hiding there in hints and atoms until his own brain should find the trick, to bring it together. The social whirl he went in for, or at least what passed for that in a place like Jordan, and the obligation he seemed to feel to be everybody's charming host and guest, was only in spurts. He hadn't been to a cocktail party now since Cluny's. I would see his little red sports model rushing by toward Danville sometimes at six in the morning, and quite often he slept on a cot at the lab. But he was always first at our meetings, and smiling when I came.

I was the one who was apt to be late; getting away from the house wasn't always easy. Once I had to take Dickie with me to the appointment and make up an explanation to Lucas afterwards. Jack took the intrusion in his stride, but although in our younger time together we used to talk about having children, he said now that he hadn't ever wanted any and it was clearly no pleasure to him to have one around. When Dickie brought him a handful of little stones for a present I had to make him hold out his hand, and then he hurt the child's feelings by asking, in the wrong kind of voice, if he was supposed to turn them into gold. No, said Dickie, they were supposed to be just stones, and he took them all back. Another time I was nearly an hour late and only managed to come then by leaving Dickie at Cluny's house, which I wasn't too happy about. I wasn't admitting it to Lucas, but he had been right, there was some-thing peculiar about little Paul; or perhaps it had begun only re-cently, since Cluny, saying it was so important for the boy to have "a man's company" and not be smothered by females, had let him go off on a week's camping trip with her "fiancé." It wasn't the switchblade knife that bothered me. It was Dickie's face when I happened to find it among his socks, after the two of them had been playing together. I couldn't make him tell me what he had traded for it, although he was utterly open by nature and his impulse until then had always been to tell and show and make presents of everything. He was sitting up in bed, in the summer twilight, holding the dirty old teddy bear he had slept with since he was a baby, but with a horrid little knowledgeable glitter and half-smile, in which along with the twisted darkness of his secret and his triumph in keeping it, there was a further calculation as to how far the teddy bear would be useful in disarming me. I had to remind myself that he was five years old. Otherwise I could have believed, under that tortuous look in his eyes, that he was even counting on my having some reason to dispose of the knife, as I did, without mentioning it to anyone, and so supporting him in the first deceit of his life toward his father. The next morning he was all loving candor and chattering as usual about his new family of ducks, and Lucas was only surprised later that he didn't want to sleep with the bear any more.

"Didn't your wife want children either?" I asked Jack one day. We were at our usual discreet place by the river, around the bend from the main swimming-hole, from where I could just see the strange up-ended boulder we called the Moses Rock, against the corner of cliff facing the little spillway at the top of the gorge. I had always loved that rock, which for some reason was never budged by the spring floods and which really did look like the one in the picture in our child's Bible, and it comforted me now in a contradictory sort of way to see it while having to work at not being seen. There was getting to be quite a crowd near the bridge on those hot afternoons, more of strangers though than Jordan people. There would be five or six cars nosed in among the pines at the top of the cliff, some on weekends from as far as New Haven and Bridgeport, with awnings stretched out from the side of the car and all kinds of paraphernalia that unfolded or got blown up. I suppose the process had been going on for several years, ever since the road was turned into a hard-top one connecting with the main highway, only my feelings about the place went so deep I hadn't been able to admit it. Now that I did, and could see that the scene of my childhood there was gone and short of national catastrophe would never come back, even without the schemes for a dam and a lot else that Mr. Jarvis was supposed to be cooking up with the power company, I didn't really mind, not the way I would have a few weeks earlier. In a way I almost welcomed all those city cars, and the tough voices and picnic litter around them. I felt somehow freed by them, I couldn't tell quite from what, but it was exciting, like Jack's laboratory. Some awful constriction of life had let up and new scenes were opening to me at last, not a bit like the dismal, haunted ones I had moved into when I was actually working in Bridgeport.

Jack had been half asleep in the sun. He took the towel off his head and rolled over, his body feeling out the rock for points of comfort, till we were both on our stomachs with our heads on our arms and our elbows touching. "Good God no, she was no fool. In fact she's a very sensible and honest girl. Not that I object to people procreating if it suits them." He smiled at me along the length of our two forearms, looking wise and bright and attractive as he used to after making a precocious crack when he was about fifteen. "I just heard she got divorced again. I suppose I should send her a telegram, of congratulation or something. But you're looking awfully deep, darling. If you want to get back to your handsome husband why run along, I can't stop you. I'm sure he would beat me in a duel. Or are you still worrying about Baldur and me? It's not that interesting."

He was lying, but I didn't feel like saying so. "No. I was just thinking about that English tutor you used to tell me about. You know . . . the moral scrap-basket."

"Oh yes; a splendid fellow. I've always been grateful to him. He froze to death on Mount Everest a few years ago."

Miss Pryden had picked out the tutor for him the summer he spent with his uncle in France, to drill him in classics, but he had learned something else from him, on the order of saying your prayers at night or figuring your bank balance. The idea was to make a quick note, before you went to bed, of everything you had done wrong during the day, from crimes to faux pas, add up the losses and gains and then wipe the slate clean.

"And are you still doing it?"

"Certainly. It saves me a lot of time." But in a minute he was back to Baldur; it seemed he was with us all the time, almost anything would lead around to him. "And it saves me looking for a parent to blame for whatever I may be. That's what most people use them for nowadays. The age of the alibi . . . I'd rather just blame myself."

"You'd rather not have to love him, or love anyone, I think you mean."

"Possibly. I love your figure in that bathing suit, anyway. Did you make it yourself?"

I had, as at certain other moments that July, a cool and rather delicious feeling that I was cured and about to call the affair off, on a nice friendly basis of course. My long dream had popped open as a little meaningless fling that I could stop any time, and sometimes I thought that was what I was happy about. I missed Lucas, who was too engrossed for a change to be paying much attention to me. Yet every time I was going to meet Jack I thought I must have stopped the clock by watching it and my heart would be pounding so I couldn't keep my voice right. Beulah Wellman, who was doing almost all my housework now, said to me on one of those afternoons, "You're killing yourself, taking so many orders at once. You could try and get Nanny Beardsley to help out, once they're basted. There ain't many left around town can even stitch a seam, but she might." Until I was seeing his face it would be a craziness, and it was for him too. He broke down and said so once, looking quite sheepish about it although you wouldn't have guessed it from his behavior with Lucas the time we were all together at one of Mrs. Hollister's more and more lavish dinner parties. It turned out the two of them had been in the same general area in the Pacific at some point during the war and they ended up exchanging funny stories about that with no strain at all, as if I didn't exist; which was the first time I had ever heard anything, except from Corey Leonard, about where or what Lucas had been in the war.

We had just climbed the cliff that day on the way back to my car, which I managed to hide on an old woodcutters' road above the falls, when we saw them starting across the bridge, walking. They had come in Mr. Jarvis's car and left it on the other side. Lucas was behind with Dickie and pointing out something to him in the water below, while Mr. Jarvis, with the same wide commanding gestures with which he had conjured up his visionary transformations on the way down from the studio, and holding Baldur firmly by the elbow with the other hand, explained his projects for the gorge. He really had been bitten by Jordan; apparently it charmed him so, he couldn't bear to leave an acre of it alone. I could see the water level rising as he told it to, right up to where Jack and I were crouching behind a clump of laurel, as fast as if it were all a bathtub, and little prefabricated cottages each with its own float and canoe and combination washer-dryer jumping into place along both banks. Baldur was taking it all in, his big gnomish face glimmering as usual with whatever thoughts of his own he wasn't expressing, but he was evidently asking some practical questions too, as if the astonishing rapport that had sprung up between the two had actually brought them to the verge of a deal. But just then I was only wondering, as they stood concluding their conference in the middle of the bridge, what on earth Lucas was doing with them. They kept turning to ask his opinion on this point or that, and although he didn't look particularly interested, and was mainly busy balancing Dickie on the bridge rail, he would follow the direction of their gestures each time with his far bird-watching gaze, that always seemed to pierce the skies and would surely penetrate a screen of laurel I was thinking, and would give an answer that they seemed to think worth considering.

The bridge was some thirty feet above the water, and I was so worried the talk might make him careless about holding Dickie, I didn't take in, until they had gone back to the yellow convertible and driven away, what had been happening to Jack. His eyes must have been on Baldur's face alone the whole time, with ravaging effect. He turned to me slowly, with no attempt to hide the sudden rupturing of all his hard-earned poses and presentabilities. "I wish he cared that much about *me.*" We walked single file across the pine-needles, without his saying anything more until we had almost reached the car, just within the sound of the falls, and paused to glance over the steep edge at the grinding water below. It was still scary, and wonderful, and almost secret; it was going to take a lot of dynamite to flatten out that bit of Jordan in the public interest, but it would be done and it looked as if Baldur might help do it. "Perhaps I've cared too much about work, in the wrong way; making a splash; being known. Do you know what he said to me in the lab the other day?" He was looking down across the falls, toward the rock that Arthur had jumped from that day so many years before, and it struck me that never in childhood had his face shown the fierce unhappiness that was in it now. "It sounds absurd, but I wanted him to be proud of me. I had no idea how much till he got there. I've done quite a lot; my name was up for a Nobel last year. I thought he would be, well, impressed." He glanced up at me a second, then made himself go on. "He said it was just like his old statues—the nymphs, whatever they were."

"Oh, no! Don't be ridiculous. How could you do anything like that? They were just what you used to say. Anyway how could he tell about your work?"

"He knows more about biology than you'd think. Not much of course. But the funny thing is"—he could hardly bring the words out—"he was partly right." In our silence the noise of a woodpecker working close by separated itself out from the bellowing of the falls and took on a silly importance to me, so that I was half sorry when Jack's voice made me lose it again. "I don't know what happened. About a year ago something went blank; I just didn't have the knack any more. I was riding on my reputation, and I guess fooling myself with it too. I thought getting this lab started would give me a lift again, but you might say I raised the money under false pretenses. God knows the work is important enough, but I didn't really have hold of anything. That kid Sanseverino has come up with more than I have, only he doesn't know it yet. He will, though, and so will the university. If something doesn't break for me soon . . . You can't imagine what it's like. I wake up in the night and see formulae, combinations, and I can't find my way into them." The woodpecker had stopped. I saw it fly away with food for the family, and then the roaring water, that had been as though muted by the little near strokes of the bird's beak on wood, seemed to grow louder every second as though we were slipping right down on top of it. Jack smiled a little. "Thanks for not saying it. Father-craving and all that. Maybe that comes into it. But when I was seeing him so much a while ago that wasn't the idea. We never mentioned it. I wished he would once or twice, but it was just a wrestling match. Your husband"—this with his only injection of bitterness—"is more his type. I suppose we both figured it was too late for babying, and there had to be a miracle or nothing. And I kept expecting it, almost . . . Something about his work, and the way he's in it; I guess I thought it would be catching . . ." He managed once more to look me full in the eyes. "Eva, are you disgusted with me? You're not going to give me up, are you? You're so clear and straight . . . When I look at that wonderful honesty in your face it makes me ashamed of everything I've been. But if you'll give me a chance I might learn, to be alive again, not to be empty. If you'll help me, you and . . ." He hesitated; *my father* I was sure he was going to say, at last. ". . . your paying guest," he said.

I giggled, it was so unexpected. "Oh, if you're going to think of him like that . . ."

"Well, don't push me too far; give me time. It's no joke to be born again, as he discovered. But at least I know how to think about *you.*"

"How?"

He pulled my head slowly against his, and the word was on the tip of his tongue, but it was too late. The great loud moment of certainty had just brushed us and flown on. "I think you're my dear sweet girl and I don't deserve to be so lucky. You do love me, don't you? a little?"

II

WHAT A SOUND OF BEES there was that summer! Nothing seems to take itself away as far and fast as that sound after the goldenrod blooms, unless it's the particular water that was traveling by at the same time in the brook, and that's the way the happenings of that season are to me now. But at the time the buzzing of the bees went with a delicious sense of postponement, as if there were no inevitable end or need for decision in anything.

I suppose there weren't really any more bees than usual around our house; I was just hearing them more. But at the Beardsley place there were hives and I was there quite a lot, because Nanny, Cliff's big bony handsome wife who had six children and energy to spare, was helping me with my dressmaking as Beulah had suggested. They had moved back there after Cliff's mother died, to keep the old man company. We would lay the stuff out on the screen porch and work there in a gabble of geese and children, theirs plus nieces and nephews and neighbor children, and a racket of farm machinery coming in and out, and the old man would be sitting in his shirt-sleeves in the shade of a big maple just outside reading *Les Misérables* or the latest tracts from the State Bureau of Agriculture, when he wasn't having political conferences or mending broken objects for his grandchildren. The house was only two down from the Pryden house, and as nobody ever used the front door and Nanny insisted on fencing her petunias against the sheep and the collies on that side, it managed to turn a fairly respectable face toward the street, even though it only dated from the 1850's. Everybody came in by the barnyard and the back stoop, including once long ago, toward the beginning of Will's tenure as First Selectman, the Governor.

There was a lot of important coming and going again now, because he was retiring next spring after forty years in office, and for the first time in my lifetime they were saying the Democrats had a chance to get in and Jordan was split wide open. But the old man, who had had the build and certain other characteristics of a scarecrow ever since I could remember, wasn't hustling for his visitors whoever they might be. He could have stepped lively if he'd wanted to, and his face, stuck on like a big walnut shell, had such a beaky brightness coming through the cracks, you always thought he was about to; he said it was all the injections of bee-sting he'd had in his early years that had kept his joints so spry, and he'd work a couple of them like hinges to show you there was no rheumatism or arthritis in the "contraption" as he called it. He just didn't feel called on to change his pace for the town people and the others that summer from Hartford and Litchfield, or for Mr. Jarvis who came around one day when I was there, any more than he would have thought of putting on a necktie. He had one, for funerals and once a week when he sang in the Congregational choir. At other times his shirts opened onto a chronic leathery V, above which the skin of his neck seemed poked out to bursting by his sharp little Adam's apple. He would give both the apple and the V a little absent-minded scratch when a car pulled up at the gate, as though putting something to rights about his person, and then eventually would get the parts of the contraption working together so that he'd be on his feet and shaking hands very pleasantly, even if it were a Democrat, but whoever it was always found himself in a position of having stopped in just because he happened to be passing by and had some time to kill.

Nanny said he was worried about what Mr. Jarvis was up to, but he didn't look it. He talked to him under the tree, as he did with anybody, about bees and peaches and where Jean Valjean had got to on the page where his marker was; he read the book over again every two or three years and there was nothing wrong with his memory but he always treated it like current events. None of this took many words; eight or ten in a row from Will and you thought the pipes had burst, except when he was singing, in a tenor voice that was still clear and beautiful. It gave you goose-pimples, issuing from such a face and frame, but he had used it rarely outside of church since his wife died. In business and politics he had it rigged so his captive audience did all the talking while he sized them up, unless it was another like him. Then they'd wander along inside through the mess in the dining room to the worse mess in the room beyond, in which for all those years the public affairs of Jordan had been run from a roll-top desk, in a jumble of antique firearms, arrowheads, timepieces, butter churns, etc., also batches of old papers concerning the Jordan history that he and my grandfather had worked on together for a time. Before the vacuum cleaner snorted across that sill there would have to be a rout, and the rest of the house while clean enough wasn't much tidier. Not that Nanny was a slattern by any means, and Cliff's mother could have been the old-fashioned model housewife if love hadn't hindered. It was a draw, inside and out. The spick-and-span, kept alive as an idea and continually imminent through the efforts of their wives, was continually disintegrating in the good-natured presence of Beardsley men, and nobody minded much in either camp. The men left the screen doors open in summer and tracked snow in in the winter, and the women closed the screen doors and mopped the puddles up, and that was that.

Mr. Jarvis, who was mostly leaving his wife on Long Island those days and flying back and forth by himself between there and Fix Hill, looked for the first few minutes of his visit like the man who fell in the swamp on the way to his wedding. He kept glancing at his wrist-watch, couldn't decide whether to turn back or bull it through, and ended up, in a resounding victory over his own nature, by just taking it easy, unlike the young lawyer he had brought with him from the Valley Light and Power Company. That one got sheep dung on his briefcase the first thing and talked as if Will were deaf. As they strolled inside, Mr. Jarvis, with the look of real boyish interest that made his somewhat shapeless and ruthless face so appealing at moments, was saying he certainly would like to see Will's collection and he wondered if he could tell him something about the monument on the green. Cliff and a couple of the other men had come in meanwhile with a load of something from the fields on the north edge of town, where most of the Beardsley land was, and were cooling off at the iron-handled pump that was about the last one still in use in Jordan, and Joey, aged fourteen, who was doing a summer's work with the men, took the interval to straighten out a sagging planet in the model of the solar system he was making on the porch. Then Mrs. Hollister, in a rush as usual, blew in with the notion of getting Will to declare an Anti-Nicotine Day in Jordan, but she couldn't wait. "Oh but my dear, isn't he a *Jew?*" she said when she heard who he was talking to. She was also wrought up about "those terrible Russians" and thought we should get up a town petition about them, to be sent to our congressman. However she left on a happier note. It struck her, "like an inspiration," as she observed what Nanny and I were doing, that we should put on a fashion show in connection with the fall exhibition of the Garden Club, and she proposed to start organizing it at once.

Next old Mr. Peck turned up as he did every week or so to report on flying saucers.

The humming of the bees swelled and receded, all the time, in little surges of busyness; finches fussed among the sunflowers down at the lower end of the patchy, overtrodden lawn, kicking up light like the children in the shallow brook beyond; everything was speckled, hot, and in the interstices between so many kinds of motion, still, as if our odds and ends of talk and occasional laughter on the porch, because we were doing a dress we thought was funny and it put us in a mood to remember other funny things, and all the little needs and crises that kept the screen door flapping almost without pause, were really part of a wonderful suspension of happenings. Nothing had changed much in Jordan or our lives; nothing was going to; or rather, yes, there was a waiting, but as delicate and illusionistic as the batting of hummingbirds' wings outside the screen while their long needle-beaks sucked at the hearts of the dahlias. That was before we knew how sick Alice was, Cliff and Nanny's second child. She was just a little languid and tired then; Nanny mentioned a tonic the doctor in Wellford had prescribed and wondered if they might ask Jack Pryden's advice since he lived right down the street but she didn't suppose they ought to bother him. The rope-swing broke with a niece, one of Angie's Catholic children, in it and we had to get a band-aid; one of the rabbits died; George chased Pugsy with a blacksnake; a pot of gooseberry jam burned out and nearly started a fire in the kitchen. When a breeze came up from that quarter you could just faintly hear the TV in the Seeley house, the same I had heard two or three times now from the bedroom on the other side, mingling with the sound of the bees.

It was like joy. It was so like it, the Beardsley family's own sorrows, and even the touch of a strange despair I thought I detected sometimes in Cliff's bluff, humorous grip on life, as strong as his father's but otherwise as different as the two men were to look at, seemed lightweight and short-lived, like the bees themselves, or children's prayers on their way to heaven. Of course they weren't like that, and even Will, who failed as a perfect Yankee type through having no inclination to bad temper, had been capable of a rumpus or two in his time. He had also been known to move in a hurry at least once. That was one winter day when Cliff and Angie were tiny and the team ran away with them from in front of the store; they were in the old farm sled, low on the runners and open at the back. Will raced the panicked horse all the way home over the snow and ice, and leaped in and pulled them up a second before the crack-up, at the turn into the barn. Nobody could see how he had done it. They said he wasn't even out of breath afterwards, and he wouldn't let the story be used in the next election either.

It nearly broke his and Mrs. Will's hearts when Angie turned Catholic to marry one of the Rossi boys. That was one rumpus, and he still looked as if he were seeing a rattlesnake when that set of grandchildren mentioned the Blessed Virgin. "They gut her mixed up with Tom Edison," he said. "Or mebbe the President." But Tony made his way up with no help to owning the town garage, and was a good husband; Angie was happy. So was Elizabeth, the quiet one, in spite of poverty. Her rumpus was over going to art school, after which she came home, slightly saddened, and married her high school sweetheart, Fred Nelson the carpenter, who mostly got shutters to paint so there was usually green paint under his fingernails, but he whistled beautifully and was a Congregationalist. Horace, the most home-loving of them all, made out the worst. He married a city girl, built a little house for them with his own hands on the prettiest part of the Beardsley land and nearly killed himself over it, because she wouldn't come to stay in Jordan with him at all until it was finished, and then she only stayed a few months—"in high heels," so the family said, and there wasn't much worse than that you could say of a woman. She hadn't even cared to take their child, so now Nanny was bringing up that one too along with her own six, and Horace was in the army in Korea.

Then there had been John, the oldest and the one who would have been the most like Cliff, if his years in a wheelchair hadn't scooped out his powerful face that had never had time to be young, the way the river ground out the big bowls in the granite below the falls. His eye-sockets always looked enormous, perhaps more than they really were; the great sweetness of expression that he had in common with his mother, and the loving, minute concern he had for any living thing that was brought near for him to handle, plants and tiny fish and small animals and wild birds his brothers caught for him to tame and which he never had to cage past the first day or two, seemed to belong with a milder bone structure, like his mother's: not those awful hollows and protuberances fit to house, when he was scarcely in his teens, the conception or overthrow of a republic. Instead he was often culling berries and shelling beans. It was just inevitable, with so much to be done all the time, that somebody should always be saying, "John'll do it," "Ask John," and he would lay down his toad or thrush or book, or the battered fiddle he was able to play till the last couple of years, and would take on the job and the indignity with his kindly smile, which he couldn't strip of its embarrassing perspicacity, but which at least was free of any trivial sensitivity. Angie especially made all sorts of coy, secret bargains with him that she didn't always keep her part of, getting him to do her homework or some sedentary chore, in exchange for four-leaf clovers or an ice cream cone from the store, and Elizabeth would get teary and overnoble in protecting him from such exploitation, so the sisters grew up quarreling over him. He would say, "Take it out to the henhouse, girls," and loved them both, Angie perhaps a trifle more. But he and Cliff were the closest.

He would be out there on the porch when the weather was good, and otherwise in the bay window where the plants were in the dining room, for sixteen years, having been stricken when he was three, except for the times when the pain was too bad and he stayed upstairs for a few days, and everybody missed him and got edgy and nothing seemed to go quite right in the house till he was down again. It was some kind of meningitis, they said; not polio anyway. He grew a little thinner every year, so that by the time Cliff was fourteen he didn't need his father's help to carry him up to bed although John would have stood taller than he, well over six feet, and Miss Pryden sent down oranges from Park and Tilford's and special eggnogs and every few months swooped in with a new proposal: a new doctor or discovery, something she begged them to try, at her expense. They were not hard up and preferred to pay— for the trips to New York and New Haven that she arranged, and everything else, until John couldn't stand any more, and Miss Pryden found herself beating like a giant moth outside Will's polite refusals, which as in other matters had the quality of a springlock, and the mother's luminous acceptance of death. "Impossible!" it seemed to their brilliant neighbor, who along with "Noblesse oblige" and "Altiora peto," cherished as a moral foundation-stone, "Never say die."

She professed, however, an enormous admiration of Mrs. Will as she was called in the village, and often spoke of her as the only "pure angel" in her acquaintance. It was not beyond her own notice that when driven to specify she would rest the case mainly on Mrs. Will's endurance of male slovenliness, and she would even add sometimes that angels were apt to be rather literal-minded. Still she had been known to sit in the Beardsley kitchen for an hour at a time watching that one at her endless baking, and had even turned her hand to peeling Beardsley potatoes—"like Henry at Canossa," as she once put it herself. But the most angelic thing I ever saw Mrs. Will do, when I was about six years old and could see only the cruelty in it, might have seemed more in character from Miss Pryden; it was only after my own mother's death that in a sudden recollection of it I grasped the absolute difference.

It was around the time they had given up hope of saving John, and he and everyone knew it. He was playing his usual repertoire of reels and chanteys on the fiddle when my mother took me in there on some errand, but it didn't sound like him at all. He played only by ear, with the same kind of sociable easy-going talent that Cliff had at the piano, and had never applied himself to serious music nor listened to much, except as Will's singing ran a gamut indifferently from certain Bach and Handel airs to "I Wandered Today to the Hill, Maggie." There was a lot of casual music-making in the house that John took part in, mostly of the "Sweet and Low" barbershop school with comical variants, all of it pretty good although only Will's voice was exceptional, and in the last year or so of John's life all but that was suspended; the heart had gone out of it. But that was the period when his father sang most often, for John's pleasure, and one of the last things John managed to ask for, when he was upstairs slowly taking his leave at last, all skull and drumsticks, was "My Heart Ever Faithful." Cliff had to play the accompaniment on the rackety old square Chickering in the parlor. His father stood at the bottom of the stairs by the parlor door, "looking like the goddam tin woodman" as I had lately heard Cliff tell it, in a spell of passionate confidence rare from him—"if he'd cried it would have been clinkers," and very high and softly sang the slow song through.

But that time I went in with my mother John was only fifteen, and had four years to go although the doctors were only giving him a few months. I never saw him before or after in such a mood. He was playing everything off key, with awful scrapings and scratchings, on purpose, to be obstreperous. Apparently he had been getting on everybody's nerves for some time before and he still refused to stop after we came in, as if he were much nearer my age and determined to try his mother to the limit. It really was queer, when already for years he had been the depository of everybody else's problems, more like the family counselor than either of his parents because he was more available; his father had been treating him like a man and discussing the town issues and points of history with him, which he never did with his wife, since John was eleven or twelve. He seemed to be trying that day in one bang-up fit to make up for all of it, and even to decompose his rocky, adult face back to childishness. I was of course delighted, and showed it, whereupon he winked at me and launched into a worse caterwaul on the E-string. There was so little flesh left on his fingers, his left hand looked to me like a huge crab burning its feet on the fiddle's neck, and I screeched with laughter, as if he were making his bones like that too for my amusement. "John Beardsley is dying," "John is going to die," all of us children had been announcing to each other that spring, always getting into squabbles over who had known it first. Then when the first flush wore off we began making up details, trying to pump up the feeling of importance again. That was why the sounds he was making were so especially funny.

There was a particular, quiet radiance around the relation between him and his mother, like a little extra and more shimmering sack, enclosing a further degree of intuition, within the family enclosure, itself somewhat special in town through the fact of John's existence, although in the way of common fun and common works they refused nothing. My own family had always been far more choosey in their doings. Mrs. Will had had the sense, or perhaps it was more like heroism on her part, not to spare or pamper him unduly, and a precocious gratitude in him for that seemed to figure among their subtle silences. But this time he was asking, outrageously, in the presence of witnesses, for more, and she gave it, at a cost to herself that I understood years later. She didn't mind what he was doing. There was very little irritability in her anyway, toward any of her children, and in his case I believe she would have given her ten fingers to buy him his allowance of childish tantrums. She would certainly have given a lot more than that to have him out wrecking cars and fooling with the town whore and in general worrying both his parents to death, as Cliff did two years later when he was fifteen. However, I didn't know it at the time, nor that if love were good enough it could make a liar of any woman, nor that when she rapped his skeletal knuckles with the yardstick, making him scrounge up his face with pain, it was only because there were so few possible gifts and comforts left to give him, and she would not let herself refuse him that one.

She put the violin away on a high shelf, brusquely, and I began to snivel.

"And now," she said, "before you go into the kitchen, you will apologize to Mrs. Buckingham."

He began maneuvering the wheels of the chair, not obeying the rest of it for a minute. Then when his back was to us he mumbled to my mother, "Excuse me," rather savagely, just the way either of his brothers would have said it.

"Can't get the straight of it," Will muttered to nobody in particular.

This was some time after Mr. Jarvis and his lawyer friend had left, both of them looking a bit disgruntled, and I thought the old man was still talking about the abandoned mines by Jordan Station. He had raised the subject right after they left, asking if there might be anything bearing on it among my grandfather's papers, as if that merely historical matter, the mines having been exhausted long ago, were all that the two men had come to see him about.

The area was still called The Station and the station building was still standing, although the last train had come through when I was quite small and gradually, a small stretch at a time, the over-grown tracks were being taken away from the woods and along the riverbank. It had been a branch line but a busy one, dating from the most recent of the two flourishing periods in Jordan's history, that is a time centering in the Civil War when the mines were being worked full tilt. It was manganese, with some iron, and not much of a vein, but enough to have given Jordan a sense of importance for some thirty years and to have started the Prydens' fortune, which they went on increasing by lucky speculation and by branching into paper mills in other parts of the state after the mines had given out. But it all began in Jordan, where they arrived in the late 1840's, upstarts and failures only one generation over from England and trailing a bad odor of some kind besides, I never knew from what. There were two brothers then, but they quarreled and the stronger, just as the mines were beginning to look good, drove the other, who was the thinker of the family, into the gold rush and an early death; he and his whole family were lost in a blizzard in the Rockies in '49. By the end of the Civil War, Joseph was rebuilding the present Pryden house and giving Jordan its equally ugly Episcopal Church out of his own pocket and on the choicest spot, on the rise overlooking the green, which the Congregationalists had somehow missed out on more than a hundred years earlier, putting their lovely building by the lowest road in the center where there could be no way around it and no good view even of its front. According to Will, one of his ancestors with a piece of bad land to unload had been responsible for this dreadful mistake, so out of keeping with Congregational practice elsewhere at the time. So between the two of them, a Beardsley and a Pryden, Jordan had forfeited its natural claim as one of the most beautiful villages in Connecticut. It was just in the "almost perfect" class.

But there was no great mystery, that I had ever heard of, about Joseph Pryden's activities and Jordan's decline afterwards; the mines just weren't paying off any more, and I wondered why the old man should suddenly be mulling over it. The point that he and my grandfather used to squint and scowl over together was what on earth had happened to the town's population, and all but a few of its buildings too, long before, after the Revolution.

It seemed the records were strangely lacking for that period. There had been a large contingent of Jordan men at the Battle of Saratoga, under the command of Silas Wellman, also from Jordan and our one still acknowledged hero. But several others had been killed with him that day, including Will's great-great-grandfather, perhaps the very one who sold his swamp to his church. He was buried in the cemetery up our hill, alongside the usual brood of dead infants and the smaller brood that had managed to grow up. Possibly their house then had been one of those you could still see the cellars of, or parts of cellar walls anyway, in our upper fields and the other field we had sold that year to Mr. Jarvis. A lot of the objects Will had from the end of that cèntury had been handed down in the family, but accompanied by no memory or written clue as to their exact point of origin. Not that he cared on sentimental grounds. "I like the things they used," was the principle of his fondness for antiquities, and the key word wasn't *they*, meaning anybody else as much as Beardsleys, but *used*; something about the way he said it made you glance down at his horny, scrawny hands, and the pestle or flintlock or whatever it was would seem a fine and necessary invention, brand new. All his cherished things were tools, not ornaments or furniture. But he did care in a general sense where the house had been, because of the mystery of all those other houses, from their traces apparently as big and well-built as ours, and the dearth of graves over a thirty-year period. The new cemetery down below didn't get going till well on in the nineteenth century, and was a slow starter at that.

There was a corresponding gap in both the Buckingham and the Beardsley Bibles, as if they had been thrown in the attic and forgotten for a long time. My grandfather had himself gone poking through walls of cobwebs and cat-stench in Dill Polk's attic to find hers; it was her mother's family's and did have a French name, no doubt the origin of the Dauphin story, cryptically entered in the 1790's and a bit of rotted French lace pinned to that page; the Frenchman had taken his wife's name soon after, there were children, and then again nothing until the middle of the century. Then the two of them, Will who was about forty then and my grandfather a little before he died, got on the track of a Jordan family that had moved in a wagon train to a little settlement in the Sioux country, called, rather pretentiously, Minneapolis. They wrote letters to descendants and found that the original pioneer, or exile, had sent all the way back to Jordan for elm trees to plant along what they were beginning to call "avenues" out there, in the hope of assuaging by that means his bouts of melancholia. His agent had reported that there were so many houses empty in Jordan then, he could have taken the trees "from the very green itself, close by the graveyard"—so the original green as they suspected had been way up there, by Baldur's house—but he had thought it better to move the younger elms from around the Post Road Tavern at the fork below, "much dipressed and dilapedated, sir, since your sad diparture."

Fire; epidemic; the West; too many deaths of young men for a single village to sustain, after they had marched up our lane which was the upper stretch of the Post Road with fifes and drums going while the girls and mothers with no flag yet to wave waved anyhow, from our gate at the bottom turn of the road and the gates of the other houses that nobody knew anything about any more. The British did no burning around Jordan, which seemed to have been unique only in its number of casualties. Then sickness and the rest of it, probably a little of everything once the manpower was diminished and the fields had to be made smaller and the fine houses couldn't be kept up to scratch, and most of all, so Will Beardsley finally concluded, a creeping discouragement—"dyspepsia." His own great-grandfather, the only one of the Revolutionary sergeant's sons who reached manhood, seemed to have been addicted to the Book of Job. At any rate it was in its margins that he scrawled his only two surviving sentiments, one written as a young boy, on the "Convention of Swine and Vultures in Philadelphia" with an exclamation mark, the other, years later, apparently referring to the taking of cordwood from the ruined green: "O Grand Old Friends, our Forefathers Shade and Pride, Adieu!" On a different date he had added below that, "Disastrous Drought. Carried ten barrels water in wagon to elm saplings on South Road." But he hadn't bothered to enter his young wife's death in childbirth or the births of his children who must have been of a late second marriage or anything else in the book.

However the farmland was eventually reclaimed and its netting of stone walls, "taking in the whole township, about the mileage of the transatlantic cable," my grandfather said, brought into the open again, as good as new, and after the mining and Civil War good times there was no such dramatic flop again, except in our family because my great-grandfather Buckingham lost a leg at Appomattox and it never healed right although he kept going eight more years.

The green stayed mowed through that period, there were no houses empty and no new ones built; things just got sleepy and cash was short.

I said to Will Beardsley, "The straight of what?"

"Mr. Charles Jarvis," he said.

Nobody said anything. He would explain if he had a mind to, otherwise not. Cliff was with him under the maple alongside the porch, having a beer while he waited for Lucas to come back with a shipment of new crates, so they could go to the orchard together. It was always a good feeling having Cliff around. He was getting a little paunchy, and his hair, straw-colored like Lucas's, was already thinner than his father's, but he spilled a nice kind of energy and careless good spirits and pleasure in his family; he enjoyed his father, let his children tumble all over him, and still kissed Nanny at least on the back of the neck every time he came in, as if they were newlyweds.

We spoke of a pair of hawks that were wheeling beyond the corn-patch and of finding a piano teacher for Alice who was eleven, and I pinned the unfinished dress on Nanny to give the two men a preview. "At the Chicago Exposition," Will said, "you could git a ride in a thing like that. For ten cents." Alice had had her heart set on cleaning her raspberries for the deep-freeze all by herself, but she gave up and came and lay on the swinging settee on the porch beside her mother, saying her wrists felt funny.

"I was saying to Eva," Nanny said, "maybe we should ask Jack Pryden, I mean just the name of another doctor or something. They say he knows all about those things . . ."

"We don't need him for that," Cliff said. It was the nearest to curtness I had ever heard from him, and I was sure he was thinking of his brother John and Miss Pryden's persistence in that regard. But he looked thoughtless enough as he came up on the porch a minute to stroke the child's face, wrinkling his big handsome nose at her to make her laugh, and examined her wrists, which were a little swollen.

"Tony came by this morning," Will said after a while, and Cliff, who after sowing his wild oats had gradually fallen into John's role as his father's sounding board, sat prepared to wait whatever time was necessary, staring into his beer glass. "They made a mis-take. Tried to buy him." Everybody knew that Angie's husband was working for a change in the zoning laws so he could put up two motel cabins back of his garage, and apparently Mr. Jarvis or the lawyer or somebody had thought that because he was a Catholic and a Democrat he would go behind his father-in-law's back. Will smoked a corncob pipe just like a caricature bumpkin's or a real scarecrow's, and was now slowly cleaning the bowl with a broken penknife he carried for that purpose. "Mistake number two. Sent one of the Leightons to make the offer."

"The Leightons!" we all said, although the old man's remarks hadn't been addressed to anybody but Cliff, and then all of a sudden he was laughing, a real belly-laugh, and it was such an astonishing sound and sight, after the little dry crackle of his speech, we all began to laugh as if we had never heard anything so funny in our lives, even Alice, because any child over five in Jordan knew all about the Leightons and always had, at least as long as anybody could remember. There had just always been Leightons, all of them, no matter how many there were at any given time, in one filthy wreck of a house four miles east of the center off the highway. There were always carcasses of cars, or in the old days wagons, around the yard, and usually a few of animals, and the number of broken windowpanes, like the number of convictions for theft and presumptions of incest, stayed about the same from one generation to the next. The only recorded murder in Jordan's history had occurred, in my childhood, in the woods a few hundred yards from there. A traveling salesman was shot and robbed, but the Leightons got off for lack of proof.

"And what did they want from you?" Cliff asked. There was a faction that wanted him to run to succeed his father, but he wasn't interested. He cared what happened to the town, though.

"Nothing that took much brains to think up. That lawyer boy ain't earned his pay yet."

"*Hasn't* earned," said Georgie, who had come over to show the family the blacksnake, hanging now with a broken back over a stick. "Dad, I've just got to have that taxidermist kit, I just can't wait to earn six more dollars, it's too long." He was on the verge of tears.

"It's too long because you don't finish the jobs," Cliff said, but affectionately. "You get that lawn-mower buzzing right now and you'll be a lot closer. Get along, your grandpa's talking."

"Same old horse-trade. We give 'em a free hand, they put our man in, whoever he is."

"*They* put a man in!" Nanny snorted. "In Jordan? Who do they think they are?"

"They're rich," Cliff said. "That's who they are, and you can't say Jordan can't be bought either. Things aren't what they used to be."

"Never were," Will said. He chewed on his pipe stem a minute, and scratched once at his Adam's apple although nobody had arrived. "There'll be a zoning change all right. Good thing too. It's the city folks paying taxes here now make the trouble; want to keep the town dead; pretty to look at; kind of sanitarium. Nothing for young folks to do." I had heard him in this vein before and guessed he was thinking of Horace. But then he was speaking to me, as if the breeze had jerked his head and his line of thought. "Baldur Blake still got that naked woman up on his wall?"

"No. I don't know what happened to it. It just fell in the bushes, I guess."

"A queer duck," Will ruminated. "In the old days anyways. I hear he gut a new lease on life. Happens once'n'a while." He scratched at his neck again and this time got his joints into motion too because John Purser, who was our tax collector, was at the gate. "You might tell him I gut a question I'd like to ask him. Any time that suits him." That meant urgent.

Quince-faced and rude-mannered as always, as though perpetually put upon, John Purser was nevertheless sufficiently of Will's breed to have to chew the rag a while, as a preface to other business, on the afflictions of bees, and then by a natural sequence on the elm-blight. The process in that case, there being no love lost between the two, consisted of a single, scarcely perceptible bite to a side before the rag was passed back, amid long scannings of sky, leaf and fingernails, and an occasional equivalent, by word or look, of a right hook to the jaw. It wound up with John saying, "Hear anything about chestnuts coming back?" and Will answering, rejecting the peace terms that the question implied, "Nope." In this way they had successfully collaborated for a number of years.

Lucas was down at the barn unloading the truck and I thought it would look better if I spoke to him before leaving. Dickie was there too, playing with Tommy Beardsley; they were going to take lunch-boxes to the orchard with the men.

"You look all beat up, honey. Something go wrong this morning? Prick your finger? Lose your thread?"

His smile was all right but there was something wrong in his voice. He might be thinking of what happened the last time he tried to make love to me, or just getting ready to move along, as he called it, from the job, as he had from all the others. It was about time; this was already as long as I had ever known him to stick to anything. But the day had begun turning into a weather-breeder in the last hour, and perhaps he was just feeling the weight of it or thinking a thunderstorm could spoil the peaches.

Past his head and the red Seeley barns the back ell of the Pryden house was partly visible, and no doubt he saw me glance in that direction. It was unpleasant to think how I had to hide my car way over in the woods by the old cider mill and walk a quarter of a mile through the back fields, alone unless Jack had gone over to wait for me. But I had been there only once since the afternoon of his strange confession, if that was what it was, and hadn't met him again by the river. Perhaps the novel experience of baring his soul, or at least airing his fears, had brought on the miracle he had been hoping for from Baldur; something, anyway, had opened up for him in his work, making the intensity of his drive earlier look rather sick, like a self-flagellation, compared to the new excitement that was suddenly carrying him along. Still we had been together a few times, avoiding any mention of that day or of Baldur, and once when he had had a few drinks he phoned in the middle of the night, at the risk of waking Lucas, to say that he intended to marry me: "Take your time. I can wait." It was true that he didn't seem to have any recollection of it the next day, and when I teased him about all the phone calls he was getting from Long Island said, "Why not? She's amusing. Anyway you know perfectly well you're not going to leave your husband, so why should you care?"

The telephone in general had begun to prey on my mind, he had so many friends in so many places, some scientists, some not, who were always "driving down from the Cape" or "stopping by on the way to Boston" and for whom he felt the need or desire to make himself available, no matter what was going on at the lab or what had to be postponed with me. He never told me anything about them, acting as if it could be of no interest to me or were even of none to him, yet with all of them he had the same tone I had heard that Sunday in the bedroom, of good-fellowship, of some generous, solid and comfortable rapport that was like a critique of sexual love and certainly suggested a relief from it. Alone with me he never laughed with the kind of wholehearted abandon and pleasure that I heard when I drove by another of his dinner parties, which I hated myself for doing but that time I was too stung to help it; in fact I set out with half a thought of barging in on the party, to see what would happen, and it was perhaps his laughter heard from the road that stopped me. There was a couple in Wellford that he hired as cook and bartender for these occasions and I used to imagine them taking over the kitchen and dining room that I knew so well.

I drove by the lab once or twice too, feeling equally at fault in some vague way. It was not exactly *his* lab, I had learned, though it had been his idea; he was aiming for bigger things but had wanted to set this up and head it for a year or two, as an experiment in interdisciplinary something or other; he had a young Dutch engineer and a couple of mathematicians and physicists working with him, as well as the other biochemist, Dr. Sanseverino, the genius of the lot Jack said and the youngest. I was puzzled by Baldur's remark there, as reported; he and I had never so much as referred to the lab, or to Jack in any way, and the treacherous thought crossed my mind, even though Jack himself had called the cruel comment justified, that he might have been paying him back for the contempt of earlier years. The building alone, small but beautifully set back from the road, elegant in glass and concrete, as Cluny said the only decent piece of modern architecture for fifty miles around, seemed enough to refute it; it filled me with pride to drive by and think of him in there. Not to mention the almost worshipful attitude toward him among the younger scientists. At least on my one brief tour inside, Dr. Sanseverino, tall, shy, with curly blond hair and an abrupt and oddly angelic smile, had called him with unmistakable candor and feeling "one of the best," and without being at all obsequious treated him accordingly, clearly feeling himself privileged to be in his company. He and his wife were sometimes at the dinner parties; so were the others, I gathered; but Jack rarely even identified his guests to me, though he did happen to mention once that his ex-wife had just been there for the weekend "with one of her boyfriends."

However, we spent a day in New York together, when he had to see about some supplies for the lab, and I started to tell him the truth, that I had never been there since that summer with him, but didn't; it would have made me sound somehow needy and dependent. I hardly recognized most of the city but we found our old restaurant with the red-checked tablecloths and the same old proprietor still there. We held hands across the table the way we used

to, and after a minute the old man remembered us and naturally
thought we were having a wedding anniversary, from our behavior.
So there were drinks on the house and of course he wanted to know
about our children. "Oh yes," Jack said, beaming, "we have five
strapping boys. I think it's five, isn't it, darling?" I didn't tell him
either, considering that he had been married to a pilot, that I had
never been in a plane, even a big commercial one, and made myself
trot along after him on Fix Hill one dark night as to the manner,
I mean the air, born, which was not easy knowing he was not exactly
sober; if he had been he wouldn't have acted on that wild impulse,
after I proposed it for a joke. He didn't even have a license to fly
any more, but had made friends with Mr. Larrick at some point and
somehow persuaded him it would be all right to borrow the Piper
Cub; as it was, but I wasn't sure then or later that Jack fully intended
it to be. Judging from his expression throughout, our coming down
alive was possibly in the nature of a slip. At any rate I got my first
look at Jordan from higher than any hill, and saw that it was very
small. "I adore you," he said thickly, seeing me off in my car back
of the cider mill. The next day I was violently sick. But to be honest,
my little joke, that got us into that situation, was really a taunt;
I had felt, all of a sudden, a need to hit out.

There was one other date, a week ago now, when he was particularly insistent on my sneaking off to go to an outdoor concert at
Briarwood, in Massachusetts. He was a fast, nervy driver and I loved
being beside him in the MG; people would look at us on the highway
the way I used to look at well-dressed couples going by like that,
when I was poking along in the old Chevvy or Lucas's truck. The
afternoon fell, to put it mildly, into two halves. The glory part
lasted to the intermission, past a Vivaldi choral work that nearly
undid Jack. Miss Pryden had had little taste for or knowledge of
music and the intensity of his appreciation for it, mainly via a huge
collection of classical records, had seemed to define his vague rift
with her in his New York period. He looked close to tears on this
occasion, as he had under the impact of Baldur's statues or after
seeing Baldur on the bridge that other afternoon, only this time
what flowed forth was such a tenderness of love for me, I thought
if my life should stop then and there it would have had joy enough.
A few minutes later, as still in thrall to that music we smoked in
silence out on the grass, he caught sight of a group of friends at the
edge of the crowd, and with a bland, "Oh, just a second," went over

to join them, turning on the instant into the outgoing, charming and sought-after character I knew from the telephone and glimpses of evenings on his porch. I supposed he would bring us together in a moment; there were still ten minutes of intermission; the minutes passed, and he came back as the bell rang to hand me the keys of his car. His friends didn't care to stay for the Beethoven and had invited him to go and spend the night with them. "I hope you don't mind, darling. There's plenty of gas in the car but here, just in case . . ." He fished from his wallet a ten-dollar bill, which fluttered to the ground as he turned to wave once, cheerfully, across the now empty lawn.

That night I yearned for Lucas's body as I used to often long ago but never with so little of myself withheld. It was his body I loved, then and perhaps all the time, nobody else's. Oh yes, I had craved sex with Jack and was wounded when he evaded it, I had wanted him to be mine and my body got its signals confused like a dog but a dog would not be the kind of receptacle he made of me, the rare times the stimulus got strong enough to bother. My breasts, tongue, stomach, all parts of me were sore with neglect and insult afterwards, while I smiled in my indubitable happiness; he never suggested there was anything more he might have done or I might have desired, and perhaps after all he was right and I had not wished for anything more. But with Lucas I did, I did, and knew what it could be. Two or three times earlier that summer I had pushed him gently away with a sweet kiss when he turned to me in bed, saying I was worn out from work, which was not altogether untrue; quite often I had had to set the alarm clock for five in the morning to finish a dress on time, after I had spent the afternoon by the river. He had been more tired than usual too, perhaps from the obscure, continuing challenge of Baldur so near, so we got in the habit of patting each other goodnight every night, as if it would be different another time.

That other time came then, for me, after the bitter drive back alone in Jack's car from Briarwood. Since the night of the dance Lucas had seemed to have leveled off from the earlier upheaval, had been looking cheerful and confident in the daytime and sleeping soundly through the night. But it was only some kind of worry that had subsided. Deeper than that, past the new cool style of affection that his grey eyes exposed to me that night, there had come to be a calm that was not trustworthy. I didn't want to inquire into it. I only wanted him to desire me totally as he used to and carry me with him into the whirlpool, over the falls, to where for a little while that would seem like forever no questions could be. I pressed myself to him, murmuring the old delicious incoherences, and after a while he was ready but not for long, not long enough, and he turned away from me without even a sigh. In the third year of our marriage it had been like that for several months; I never knew or knew if he knew why, as it wasn't among the kinds of things we talked about, only then he would groan and curse over it and sometimes beat his fists on the pillow. This time he said goodnight in the usual friendly fashion and went almost immediately to sleep. There had been no overtures since, from either side.

Now he was smiling at me beside the Beardsley truck, handsome and blonder than ever, hair bleached and skin deep brown from all the work in the sun, making his little joke about my needles and thread. The tiny scars by his left temple, which I used to caress with my finger but never ask about, made just the faintest white tracery as of a patch of lace through the sunburn, and perhaps because he saw me noticing them the slight twitch came to his lip and he raised a finger to it in the old way but still smiling. I realized that we weren't far from the beehives and the buzzing was loud and constant, not fitful as it had been from the porch only I hadn't been hearing it until then. It wasn't so comforting, close to. The pleasant picking and choosing and expertise of the bees in their travels, when each was on its own, gave way to what sounded like a frenzy of self-immolation around their doors, as though their wonderful commune were based on more than its share of anxiety and anger. Or perhaps they were all saying "After you, please." I looked up into Lucas's far-seeing, charitable eyes, right to the deep threshold beyond which his strength and his refusal to be strong were the same thing only the shutter was there and I couldn't see past it, and I thought, he knows, he has known all the time, maybe all the seven years, and why not come into the open right now, both of us, when there is no time or privacy and it would be easy. It would be only a quick flash, no more than a bit of broken mirror might make in the noon sun.

"Something happened," I said, and smiled too, "but not as bad as that. Chuck Jarvis came around just after you left, looking for you, and tried to kiss me."

"He's a good picker, then. I'm surprised. Well, solong." He didn't say tell him I'll take a poke at him if he tries it again.

"Solong. Are you sure you don't want me to take Dickie?"

The soulscape he revealed to me for a second then was brand new and black, like a black rock.

As I started toward my car I met Will coming down to collect honey, wearing, in spite of the benefits he ascribed to bee-sting, a tremendous square homemade mask that wobbled with weird dignity on his spindly shoulders. I stopped to tell him what he looked like, a voodoo dancer or maybe a walking squirrel-house, and he grinned at me through the wire netting and then suddenly, without opening its door, mentioned the mines again, as if we had been on that topic the whole time. "Your grampa ever tell you why his pa gut out? He'd 'a' been a rich man if he'd stayed partners with Joe Pryden. Might 'a' lived longer too."

I said no, I didn't know he'd had that much of an interest. The story in the family was just that he'd sold out early, at a loss, and they'd always been friends.

"After a fashion. Luther Buckingham had a big streak o' cussedness." He started to give his neck a think-scratch, which you couldn't tell from the company kind, and encountering in place of the usual objective the swathing of old strips of inner-tube and scraps of harness in which his head-box terminated, he decided to unlatch the door in front of his face instead. My great-grandfather had been dead several years when Will was born, but it was like his old muskets or the plot of *Les Misérables*; when he hooked on to a thing the moss had to drop off. "They were partners before Luther went to the war; he was a good bit younger. It was Joe Pryden's idea to buy up the mines and bring the new methods in; that's so; it was a hand-cart business before, just dozing along. But he wouldn't 'a' gut far without Luther Buckingham getting his father, the one was Congregational minister, to give him a name at the bank, and around the county." It was hot in his cage; the sweat was beginning to find channels across his face, every way but up, but he seemed to expect that in bee-work. "Luther came home with his leg shot off. Joe'd been busy; getting out cannon-ball material for the Union; did it his way—no worse than the rest of the country, generally speaking. Salted the mine, to finance the branch line over from Danville. Watered the railroad stock. Irregularities. Luther had to cover up for him; protect the stockholders, till they made good. Didn't do his health any good, I expect—the Buckinghams were always long on principle and short on the grab. It was a close shave. But they made it, by the barest. Luther unloaded quick then, at the worst time; gut out no worse off than he started I guess except mebbe in his mind." Will tried to wipe his face with his sleeve, forgetting the cage again, and then had trouble getting at his handkerchief in his spaceman's gloves. I fished it out for him. "Ned Purser was cashier," he said as though in conclusion.

I did know that Ned Purser had shot himself, a little before he was to have married my great-grandfather's sister, who consequently died, at the age of eighty-five, an old maid. "How could they stay friends, then?" I hadn't been paying much attention, but for a minute I had to try to imagine it, the two men sitting evenings in our living room as I'd heard they used to, and the spinster sister either sitting with them or closing herself in her room upstairs until Joe Pryden, who had murdered her lover or as good as that, went away.

"It was good riddance, far as Ned went." However, Mrs. Will had been a Purser too, so it wasn't that he had it in for the whole tribe. "What kept 'em friends?—just Luther's cantankerousness, I guess. Loyalty. He was the kind of man, if a mule kicked somebody down the street, he'd work till he gut it on his conscience. Must 'a' figured he'd had a hand in the business, and he'd stick by him. Mebbe even had some respect for him, spite of it all. But here's what I'd like to know. Who stopped Joe Pryden putting his paper mill down here at the falls?"

Then I saw where he was driving. "I didn't know he wanted to."

"Had the land. And the water rights. Cheapest water-power in the county; right at the door. And if I'm not mistaken, he'd 'a' given a mint o' money to have your great-grampa in on it, account o' Ned Purser and the talk. Instead o' that, next thing you know he gives the land to the town with a whole lot o' stipulations; tied it up for eighty years. Your grampa claimed he never heard about it. But wa'n't nobody but Luther Buckingham had the hold on him, to make him do it. Must 'a' been last thing before he died. 1872." Will began warming up an elbow, preparatory to closing his cage. "The way I see it, Luther was Joe Pryden's good and loyal friend, and he was damned if he was going to turn over in his grave watching him and his son Warren do business in Jordan. Warren, that's Addie's father, was coming along then. Chip o' the old block."

I helped him latch his front door, and for a moment, with his canny squint on me so close, I had a suspicion that what he was really talking about wasn't Mr. Jarvis and his schemes, and the eighty years being up now or perhaps just about to be. There was nothing womanish in the old man's snoopings, but still, the Pryden house was right over there; he could have seen things. But probably it was just that he'd done more talking than he usually did in a month of Sundays.

"Where was it they started the mills instead? Hackasaug, wasn't it?"

"Yep. Bloody Hackasaug, they called it in the eighties. Gut to be the richest small town in the state." In the same impulse we both glanced up across the sunny fields to the blue rim of the ones beyond, and I guessed he was thinking that Jordan, which had had only one murder that anybody knew of since it was taken from the Indians, had been about the poorest, except it wasn't even a town. "Had to stop spraying for beetles. Kills the bees. Trouble is, if the fellow down the road's using chemicals, throws the balance off."

For the first time I phoned Jack at the lab, although I hadn't heard from him since the Briarwood episode, and practically begged him to meet me by the river, but he wasn't free. On account of work, not friends that time, something was in process that he couldn't leave, and from the way he spoke I could believe it. Nevertheless, in dread of hanging up, I went on to talk somewhat hectically about Alice Beardsley.

"Christ, Eva, what's come over you? You sound like Mamie Hollister. I'm not the village doctor. Anyhow, if the Beardsleys wanted my opinion, they know where I am."

"Cliff won't ask you. You know why. Nanny's worried. If you could just help them find out who to see . . ." My voice was strained and weepy.

"If you expect me to stop my work for every case of measles, and meddle where I'm not wanted into the bargain . . ." Once before I had heard him that mad, when he was twelve and one of the Seeley boys accused him of cheating at croquet. Of course we all cheated once in a while, and I was never sure if he had in that game or not.

The click on the wire left me faint; the bowl of warmed-over stew I had put out for my lunch revolted me. My dream had only progressed to a new torment, I would never be out of it. Had I really thought I was caring about Alice Beardsley? Did everything I tried to do have to be a lie? I didn't even know if it was Jack's voice or Lucas's eyes that had put me in this state. It began to seem important for me to deliver Will's message to Baldur right away, instead of waiting for him to come down from the studio at the end of the afternoon.

III

HALF WAY UP THE LANE I struck off across the fields, to wash my tear-smudged face at the spring and delay the confrontation, as it had come to appear, with Baldur. There was no clear reason for anything of the sort. It would be the last thing he would ever propose, I was sure, with me or with any of us, and what on earth I was either wanting or fearing from him I had no idea. He certainly hadn't come back from his hell to arrange our lives for us; had never intimated by the slightest word or look that they were any of his business. True, in our better times together there had gone on hanging between Jack and me, like an unspoken pact, a sense of our relation being in some way a betrayal of Baldur, and sometimes when I was alone I would come out with it and tell myself that I didn't care what he thought of it. Until I realized what I was doing and stopped myself I would get quite angry with him in those silent monologues. He's not God, I would be thinking, he's not my guardian; ask anybody in town; they all know he's just an old family friend we rescued out of the gutter. But I wasn't thinking anything like that when I set out for the studio.

I hadn't been to the spring in over a year, and the sumach and brambles had grown so thick I had a little trouble finding the place. The timbers we had put there years before to roof the spring against falling leaves had rotted a lot over the past winter. I pulled the worst of them away, and cleared from the surface of the water the patches of brown powder they had dropped, before lying on my stomach across the stones and the grass that stayed emerald there the year round, the way Arthur and I always did together, one on each side of the little spillway. Then we used to count to three and slowly lower our faces up to the hairline in the shivery water and each count three again. That had to be done first, before we started splashing and being Indians, but it was a private rite and we never did it if anybody else, even Jack, were there. I didn't want to count or remember. I had been there often since he died and even in the worse period before he died without remembering too much, but this time his warbly thirteen-year-old voice, almost ready to change, was saying the numbers right by my ear in the excited way he had, as if we were about to do something thrilling instead of just getting our faces wet, and the silent count underwater came of itself, only on three I kept on pushing slowly down, not sticking to the rules, until my head was all under and the icy tickle was going up my backbone. I pulled out in a hurry then and lay still, while the nausea and the other memory came and passed, and pretty soon I was just looking at every bug-track on the surface and every bulge in the wall and pattern of leaf-mold at the bottom as I always had, except that I had never felt such distaste for my own face. I had never felt so lonely either, there or anywhere, but I would have been glad to be still lonelier if that were possible, if it could have brought me back my clarities. I thought I had had some once, looking over the record I couldn't have said just when, but some time, and surely not just as a child.

A deer, a big buck apparently, had been drinking there not long before; the grass still hadn't begun to straighten in the tracks. All kinds of birds big and little were calling and talking in their sporadic middle-of-the-day fashion, but one catbird on a branch nearby kept reiterating the same note, piercing all the rest. If I had been younger I would have thought he was like me. I pushed the dark wet strands of hair back from my forehead and tried to study my face in the water but it didn't tell me anything. It looked healthy enough, neither good nor bad. My "well-molded" chin and forehead and nose slightly crooked in front view didn't show any trouble, and the little creases by my eyes if I squinted were no more than normal for thirty-two; my eyes looked unusually large and black, rather tragic, but I had always been able to make them like that when I wanted. It looked like a regular person's face, not one like me that had stopped having any natural business in life, and I was glad when a frog, that had been holding itself paralyzed until then, finally jumped and broke it up, making me study him instead. It seemed that everything I had done in the name of clarity had been murky and a lie, and I thought that if I could hold still like the frog and try to see some object straight through that perfect water or just the refractions of light in it, perhaps I would get back to the starting point if there had ever been one, and see what to do.

But all I could see to do, or to talk to Baldur about either, was nothing.

Something else had been holding still—a partridge in a bramble-bush, right by the spring. It gave me a start when it went whirring up, reminding me of my first meeting with Chuck Jarvis, when he had come on me naked there with Dickie a year before. The scene came back to me with extraordinary vividness, his confusion and apology and instant of pleasure at the sight of my body, and the playful yank he gave Dickie's hair as he turned away, making my anger at the intrusion seem rather silly. He had had somewhat the same courtesy and even diffidence that morning when he tried to take me in his arms, along with a powerful sexual assurance that I hadn't been immune to that day by the spring either when it was only in his eyes, only now there was premeditation and will behind it, too much to be put off by a mere no. He flushed only a second and stepped back, saying good-humoredly, "That's all right. You'll come around."

"Oh no I won't," I said, not sounding quite as convinced of it as I meant to. He was wearing a rather ridiculous Hawaiian-type shirt and a pair of Italian sandals, exposing both a luxuriant black tuft of hair on his large chest and an expensive pedicure job on his toenails. It struck me that he had chosen his country garb with care that morning, to please me, and it made me sorry for him, when his face and bearing were so attractive.

"Yes, you will. Because you're married about the way I am and that's . . ." He flicked some imaginary little thing off his fingernail. "And you need me. Right in here."

Suddenly he was behind me with his two big positive hands shaped to take my breasts, but luckily he had the grace or blindness to move away at once, without touching me.

"So you're just trying to buy Lucas off, is that it?"

"Not *just*, dear. I don't play single stakes if I can help it. He can be very valuable to me if he chooses; if he doesn't that's his tough luck. I won't do him any harm."

That made me laugh. "As if you could. Why he's so good, he's
. . ."—"almost idiotic" was on the tip of my tongue but I said instead, "You couldn't touch him, he doesn't live in your world," while
Jarvis just looked at me with eyes flat and inscrutable like features in
a child's drawing, although I thought there had been another dimension to them a moment before. "What are you aiming to do
around Jordan, anyway?"

I didn't speak with any hostility. That was early in the morning,
before I had heard that he was getting the Leightons to do his dirty
work for him—that being the only kind they would know how to
do; and I was thinking how good he was, really. Ignorant perhaps and
liable to do some damage by mistake, but grand and somehow selfless
in his tremendous drive. The right woman might be enough to keep
it on the side of decency.

Apparently he had only been waiting for me to show some
sympathy for his projects, and burst out then with the most disarming enthusiasm, "Would you like to see the plans? Honestly,
there's nobody's opinion I'd rather have. I'll tell you the truth, I
wasn't aiming to do anything much here till I latched on to your
friend Blake. I had the farm, you know—a tax dodge and hideaway.
The Doc put me onto that a year and a half ago when the lab thing
was first up, but I only did it for Marilyn. She thought it would be
cute—different, something like that. She got some antiques and
Scotch tweeds to go with it and her picture in the society mags,
with the cows. But I wasn't thinking of *business*." He laughed
cheerily at the absurdity of it, looking out the window at the quiet
fields, and the brook and white steeple beyond. "I'd just wound up
a thirty-million-dollar deal in Boston, and had plenty of other real
estate boiling in New Haven and Chicago, and the hotel in Cuba.
I've got to run down and see about that tomorrow, by the way, so
if you'd . . ." But he bit that off, with a grin. "Excuse it. I'm not
used to . . . It was a slip."

It was that first meeting with Baldur that had changed everything. Marilyn was bored stiff with the place by then, and he'd
been about to get out. Of course he'd gone on buying up whatever
came to hand around his acreage, like that upper field of ours, and
had hung on a few months longer than he'd wanted, in the intention
of getting Baldur's place. It just wasn't in his nature to unload anything exactly as he'd found it, and that way the place would have
had some value as a development property.

"Not with the zoning laws in this town," I said, and again his eyes had that perfectly flat, paperlike quality.

Baldur had given him the vision, he said, his boyish eagerness flaring right up again. That was the only word you could use for it: a vision. "Between the two of you . . . Oh yes, you were in it too. You made me feel, it took me the longest time to dope it out, ten minutes maybe and that's more time than I've spent being puzzled in a good many years. I tried to imagine myself without any money and what you'd see in me . . ." And Baldur had given him the key. God, he interrupted himself, there wasn't anything he wouldn't do for that man; you could have your Gandhis and Schweitzers; the great man in *his* life was Baldur Blake. They would do something in Jordan that would be a model for the whole U.S.A.; he didn't even care if he lost his shirt for it. "This used to be a beautiful country, and I'll say frankly, I've done my two bits' worth to make it look the way it does now. It's hell and I know it. Out on Long Island we laid the stuff down like gridirons, miles of them, anything in the way had to go. If they wanted a tree they could buy one and water it, only the houses aren't built to last that long so they mostly haven't tried. I thought I was doing a pretty good thing too; didn't know any better; anyhow in wartime anything you did was public service.

"But now . . . Well, I'm not exactly Rockefeller yet, but I can afford to be altruistic." I could tell the word wasn't a new one in his vocabulary. He took my hand delightedly in both of his, with no sex about it that time. "I knew you'd be pleased. What was it he said that day? A new concept—of space . . ." He was really moved by the phrase, probably more than by anything since his boyhood, and for a long time by his standards, several seconds, went on holding my hand as he gazed dreamily out over the view that his glance had described as peanuts a little earlier. "We'll teach this country to be lovely again, so it'll be a pleasure to drive around in it. You know I'm on the President's Commission for Juvenile Delinquency, I mean against it, and Baldie connects there too. Boredom; ugliness; it all figures, just like he says. I guess I wasn't being quite straight with you when I said I got this place here just for Marilyn. I went to a head-shrinker for a while, I'd gotten so depressed it was making me impotent if you'll excuse a technical term. And you know what the trouble was? I'll give you three guesses. Mother, no; father, no; wife, no. Not even infantile sexuality. I just couldn't stand driving through my own developments on my way to work every day. Cost me eighteen grand to see that and here's old Blake giving away a lot more for nothing. Doesn't make sense, does it?"

Before he left he even told me some of the details, strictly in confidence he said, since the whole scheme, the "vision," would be wrecked if certain parties got wind of it ahead of time. They were going to start with three hundred houses; had a contract ready for signing with an aircraft company, for a plant to be erected on the site of the old mines; another contract for a lake below the falls. And oh yes: schools. He had thought of everything.

"We'll make ourselves felt all right," he concluded. "It won't take long. Even in the cities . . ."

"Each with its gate," I said.

He didn't smile. "Right. There'll be one here to start with, in Blake Acres. How do you like that?—ache, ache. But I guess it sounds like bursitis. We're having a trial one cast this week."

"A gate—of Baldur's?"

"Well . . ." He looked a trifle embarrassed, for the first time. "He slowed up a little; an artist's privilege, you can't push them too far, you know, so I had to get another fellow in on that. But it's all his idea, he won't mind, and if he doesn't like it we'll junk it. His word goes, he's the boss; I'm just the legman this time."

"Do you mean to say Baldur has agreed to all this? that he's actually helping you?"

He smiled with a certain effort of patience, as to a child. "It's the chance of his life, isn't it? What other sculptor in the world has had such an opportunity, since his friend Michelangelo and those boys? Statues everywhere; fountains; trees—that's where your husband comes in; I'll give him his start here and move him to one of the other projects later." He was so used to moving real mountains, he didn't bat an eye saying that; evidently he had never yet met anything that refused to get out of his way, or even showed any displeasure in doing it. "And Blake's the artistic director of the whole show. Why, he'll be one of the great names of the world before I'm through, like Le Corbusier only better. To see a man like that rotting in this obscurity—it's criminal!" With only the most delicate change of voice and expression he threw in a question: "Has he said anything about signing the contracts? Well, I'll see to it before I leave tonight."

From the doorway he reached again for my shoulders with that astonishing gentleness and equilibrium, that seemed to show him up as only a mock bully for all his horsepower, conceded to the shake of my head respectfully, and departed, like a good, reliable pirate. He would be back.

The personal part of the encounter scarcely rose to my mind a couple of hours later when he appeared on the Beardsleys' porch. It didn't matter. I had had a lot of come-ons of that kind from rich businessmen every time I was away from Jordan, beginning the summer way back in New York, and half the time I couldn't re-member their names afterwards. But now I looked deep into the spring and suddenly, exactly as if I had come through to the joyous purity I half remembered and was searching for there, the dawn of a smile was on my face and I was discovering the very opposite. I was seeing straight and whole for the first time, or so it seemed, the filthy meaning of the word *temptation*. It had never made much sense to me before, except in regard to trivial things, candy and croquet and such. Now I was seeing a possibility that filled the whole cylinder of the spring, miraculously driving out the hopeless vision of trouble and failure that had drawn me under, and the moss was just as green and the water as transparent as the minute before.

The catbird was still calling the same whiny note, although it had moved to a different tree a little farther away. But it was chang-ing. It became unlocalized, and then was replaced altogether by Arthur's young voice saying my name plaintively, "Eva, Eva . . ." It was awful having it come from so far away, when I knew how much he wanted to help me and was needing my help too, to undo his own years of mistakes and suffering. When we were young we were always able to help and comfort each other; even our grand-mother hadn't entered quite as fully into our troubles, whatever they might be, as we did for one another, being so close in age, even if we didn't look much alike except around the forehead and chin. He was lighter in coloring, with fuller lips and a bumpier, coarser nose, and in adolescence passed for good-looking much oftener than I, in spite of scabs and pimples one year, various scars from his more than normal share of daredeviltry, irregularity of features and a total lack of my "soulful" look. It used to annoy me no end. What he had instead for his handsomeness was a quickness of expressions, seldom disagreeable and even more rarely doleful, although of all of us he was the one most responsive to troubles outside the family, which in my grandmother's hierarchy of love had to take second place after her concern for us. But how little, it occurred to me, that rough and ready and always immature face ever advertised any sympathy; where others feared to tread in their pity he would go in with jokes, usually practical ones, like the most thick-skinned fool; you could catch his pale hazel eyes wheedling, lying, anything but pitying. Yet quite often when he was thought with good reason to be out raising hell, it would turn out he had bicycled all the way to the Station to take vegetables to the one-legged and half-starving old widow Mrs. Trowbridge, who scared me almost as much as Dill Polk, or had been playing chess for hours with John Beardsley.

I wished for his face to be beside mine in the spring, serious as his strange catbird voice was, as his face used to be for a little while sometimes over schoolbooks when the rare impulse to learn overcame his laziness. We would go back to that strange point where we started failing each other, and all would be different. We would walk together through the door that is always there at the bottom of the spring, down the long corridor to where the great dogs sit guarding their mystery chests, and this time we would have the wisdom to choose the right one, instead of the one full of shame and lies. "Eva," I was hearing again, but more faintly. A rumble of thunder in the east dispersed it altogether. The surface of the spring was becoming cryptic with clouds, and a hatred of my brother came to press on me, as if it belonged with the gathering storm in the air. Probably he had never forgiven me either. So we were quits and equally despicable, except that he had the luck to be dead.

I slapped some handfuls of water on my face and got up. No, whatever else I might do wrong it wouldn't be moving to Long Island; I wouldn't go that far, and in any case the errand I was on didn't even require that much clarity. It was simply to tell Baldur that Will Beardsley wanted to talk to him. Then I would go.

However, I had to wait a little. Gordon Farr, the minister, was just winding up a visit to the studio when I arrived, and as he turned away we saw some of the high school children, two who had sought out Baldur before and two new ones, approaching, as if they were afraid of being seen, around the back of the house. The sight of the house a minute before had already given me a queer feeling. It wasn't boarded up any more; he had been having work done on it. It had been tacitly understood right along that he wasn't going to park with us indefinitely and would move back up there as soon as he got the place habitable, but I hadn't faced the prospect, vaguely assuming he was too busy to be bothering with it and content with things as they were. It was something else to see material signs of an event more or less imminent, though just what was disconcerting about it I couldn't have said. I had perhaps been counting on a certain area of obliviousness in him, which the work on the house seemed to deny; some degree of personal judgment and calculation, beyond his not wanting to be a burden to anyone, must have entered into his calling a carpenter.

He stood in the open barn doorway watching the children, benign and interested, but with a little look of fatigue too that I hadn't noticed the night before. He was usually out of bed and on his way up the hill by six, so I hadn't seen him that morning.

"I don't know what they want of me," he said, mildly humorous about it, although the words seemed to have ridden on a sigh. "But don't go, Eva, they won't stay long. Have you time? I've been hoping you might come . . ."

One of them said right away what they wanted of him. "It's Values, Mr. Blake. We're just not getting enough . . ."

"Not *any*!" the girl interrupted with an angry shake of her ponytail. She was the oldest Wienowski child, the one who had caused such a fuss in town being born two months early, just after our house became a tearoom. Now she was in rolled-up jeans and maroon nailpolish and was rather flat-faced but pretty. She seemed to be paired off with Tom Seeley, Jell Jr.'s boy, the one who had been talking. It was a queer kind of talk to be hearing from a Seeley, but I was more surprised to see the older Rossi boy, named Will for his grandfather Beardsley but called Tiny. They were all about fifteen.

They had gone right along inside, but were too eager to tell Baldur their problem to look around much.

"We're supposed to have Values in school," Tom Seeley went on. "It's in the prospectus . . ."

"We don't get any from our families," Tiny said, but he crumpled fast under the look he got from the other three.

"What do you expect, Fluff-head? Be realistic. It's supposed to be in the second term in Improvement, I mean like real Philosophy, but they gave us Mulch instead." Tom had the hard-driving Seeley look and the hard family fat was incipient over his jowls and chest, making his sense of injury more impressive. "That's the human half of Human Relations, you know. Of course that's just what we call it; they call it Getting Along—like how to act at dances and all like that."

"Honestly, Mr. Blake, we're being shortchanged," the third boy said. He was a lanky kid named Bud Raymond, fairly new in town, whose father was in real estate. "All they talk about is life. We want something better."

"If we don't get it," the girl said darkly, "there'll be no way out but the Minks," and in one startling motion she plopped into a tragic pose on the barn floor, as though expecting Baldur to start sketching her at once.

"Myra's exaggerating," Bud put in, but he looked at her with longing. "We're not like that. They're just dumb delinquents . . ."

"Like the Leightons," said Tiny.

"See, if you don't want to string in with 'em, stealing and making bombs and all, you've got to be able to dot 'em in an argument, you know, make 'em feel . . ."

"*Inferior*," Myra said with a strong effort of accent.

"That's right, it's tough making guys like that drop dead when you're not laced for it. I mean with Values, like Tom said. See, we're not supposed to read sentences that have more than fourteen words in them. Of course that's all right for history and stuff but . . . Hey, that's sweet," Bud broke off, suddenly discovering a large statue under his right hand.

"He means it's cool," Tom explained. He was evidently the captain of the non-Minks. I asked him if they had a name too and he said "Naw . . . ," looking put out about it. "We thought of Woodchucks, or Pueblos; something to take the nose off the whole idea. But we're not really organized yet. So far we've just got these . . ." His jowls bunched, exactly like his father's at his age, as he glanced down at that section of his two-hundred-pound heft, and fingered his brand new satin jacket. The other two boys were wearing the same thing, windbreaker cut and striped in yellow and rose. "Myra's family won't give her the sauce to get one. They only cost twenty-eight fifty. You'd think they wanted to *drive* her to the Minks. So we're going to pile in and get her one."

The children, or whatever they were, all turned their attention for a minute to the things around them, saying "Whammo," and "That's streamy," and "How do you do it, Mr. Blake? I mean like where do you start getting an idea from?"

The place seemed less mischievous than it had two months earlier, I suppose because all the pieces had stayed so alive in my head and had come to feel only natural and right, and because the kids weren't having any trouble digging them. They liked some better than others, and aside from the girl's posing, just went on being themselves, as unperplexed as four ducks in a pond.

But then Baldur had slowed down some too, as Jarvis had remarked, or at least had moved into a new phase, more deliberate. He had also put a halt to his splurge of traveling; his last trip had been the one to Long Island, to look over the Jarvis developments. He seemed to have been working as hard as before but mostly on the pieces that had been unfinished or tossed out as mere sketches on my last visit; there were only two or three new ones, one a long horizontal bolster shape in plaster, in which some alarming yeast or smothered creature seemed to be at work, and one a little metal haystack he said was just an experiment he would probably melt down, over in his foundry corner. The earlier things, especially the baseball player that had such a feeling of Lucas about it, had been changed so delicately, I thought at first the difference was only in me. Some of the surface roughness was gone, not too much, and something else; a certain initial noisiness, a slight sense of impediment had been taken away, I couldn't quite see how, making them both faster and quieter than before.

They were like weapons, I was thinking, even if Cluny still persisted in speaking of Baldur and his works as "spiritual." Her engagement was broken, as she put it in her fin-de-siècle fashion, David having blown to Europe with some of her money, a boyfriend and no warning, so she had time on her hands and was proposing to work up a Baldur Blake show in New York. He had dismissed it in a brief gesture, in which for the first time I had seen a trace of the strain and weariness I thought he was showing today, or had been until his young visitors were at the door, and so far our friend Boris had managed, more or less by force, to keep her from bringing her dealer acqaintances around.

Tiny Rossi had picked up a handful of clay and was rapidly turning out a copy of Baldur's toad. The others had had all the art they could use for the time being. Bud, as though under the influence of cyanide, broke with a low moan into a ten-second spasm of rock-and-roll and stopped as abruptly, evidently unaware that it had happened. It left a desperate blankness in his pimply face and need for action in his limbs, and he looked for a moment as if he were about to throw himself upon Myra, who was on the floor again, apparently trying to enact the imprisoned spirit in the bolster.

Baldur was all absorbed in what Tiny was doing and looking neither critical nor approving, although the job was surprisingly skillful. "More thumb. There. Good," he muttered, and finally broke into a smile. The boy looked at him worshipfully for a second, looked another second at his toad as though just discovering what he had done, then noticing the ominous forces converging around him, squashed it into a cow-patty on the top of his own head and began leaping among the statues yelling, "Walla, walla, walla, walla, walla!"

The other boys groaned "Throttle it, Beanbag," and "Ma, the pacifier!" but Myra, in a unique show of protectiveness, told Baldur that Tiny wrote songs too, "like Bunny Sereno." She had her reason. His prize song, which Tom then rather grudgingly ordered him to perform, began "Let's go down to Myra's house and see what's cookin'." He got it off in a shy growl, with the clay still in his hair, accompanied by a lumbering beat of his spindly shoulders and certain compulsive bumbs and barks from the other three, who on the last note all turned to Baldur and under an identical bewitchment said solemnly, "What should we do?"

The coincidence scared them momentarily. They looked at each other and then at Baldur and at me, to see if it had really happened. Then we all laughed. A curious peacefulness came washing through the barn, from no source you could tell. Baldur, not tired at all any more, was looking just friendly and innocent. He had been listening to Bunny Sereno records lately, over protests from Lucas on musical grounds and on different ones from Cluny, who had become quite proprietary about how he spent his time.

It was as if the statues at a certain moment had begun letting loose their secret on the air, like green things in the evening.

"What do you want to do?" His visitors looked at each other again, encountered nothing but the same question mark all around, so looked down at their cigarettes, each scowling at his sudden separateness. Tom their captain was failing them. Myra, leaning back on her hands to give her pudgy body a maximum spread short of total collapse, her chin and bosom tilted, suddenly thought of being ingenuous. She looked up at Baldur with eyes like two daisies, and sighed.

"I know one answer," squealed Bud. "Solong pals." He jumped

up, deftly hanged himself in effigy and sat down again. "Mr. Bud Raymond, alias Wayworn, fell victim in the flower of his youth to the disintegrative forces of, oh bullshit . . . Seriously, Mr. Blake, what I'm sick of is the future. Pull it down and I'll piss on it. Has it got forty-eight stars or something? Kee-ryste! There must be some respectable way of getting around it, or . . ."

"Being," Baldur murmured.

"Like Tom here, all he hears about is taking over his old man's store when he's a hundred and eighty-five, and me, I'm supposed to trepan myself to get into college just for the fucking f-u-t-u-r-e that's supposed to be in it."

"I should think Tom would do very well in his father's business," Baldur said in a surprisingly schoolmasterish voice, "and you in college. You can't hang the wash without a line. But I'll tell you a story." He got up to get them some iced tea, and while pouring it began: "A long time ago, in an inaccessible part of China, there was a famous philosopher. Probably he lived in a cave, or it may have been a swineherd's hut; that sounds better. A young man came to see him one day and said he wanted to learn the meaning of life. The philosopher slapped him on both cheeks. That was the first lesson. The young man still said he wanted to learn—by that time he had learned better than to say what. The teacher gave him a letter to deliver to a friend of his. The friend lived about two thousand miles away, in another desert. The young man walked a year or so, dodging lions and bandits and floods and famine I presume, and presented the letter. It was only to tell the friend to send him back again."

"Dope," Tiny said, "he should have opened it on the way," but the others stamped him out once more. "I wish I hadn't flunked Thinking Readiness," Bud said. "I might get it." But Tom Seeley wasn't sure they were getting their money's worth. "Would you call that Values, Mr. Blake? I mean, I can see it's not Facts . . . But now this slapping. I don't think I like that."

Baldur nodded. "I agree. It's too forthright. We Occidentals have a congenital, it may even be a fatal, need for good manners, or you might say ceremony, in our approach to meaning, I suppose to make up for our crudeness in living. I dare say our pragmatism seems unbearably tortuous to the Chinese. Our taboos, in regard to the thought of death for instance, are too complex for them." His visitors looked at him with dawning pleasure. They didn't mind

being crude and complex; it was being called Occidentals that threw
them at first, but now the term was growing on them and Tom,
with a glance at the three identical satin jackets, was clearly considering it as an alternative to Woodchucks. "We Occidentals"
would be almost enough in itself to dot a mere Mink. "Now in
ancient Greece . . ."

I still marveled at the tone, remembering his old condescensions
and impatience, and his deep stinginess. This easy air of mutual
inquiry and pleasure in it was the same he had with Lucas, with
everyone, not excluding Mrs. Pickett and Mrs. Hollister and the
other ladies about town who would think of any excuse to pester
him with invitations; he always managed to decline them, yet in
such a way that the ladies would go off looking as if they had just
laid a fine glossy egg. Toward Jack alone, in their few meetings I
had witnessed, was there a suggestion about him of anything labored
or withheld. For the rest, he had done with scorn; he had let the
eagles peck it speck by speck from his entrails, and now in his humility was taking on all of the great world. It was too much, I thought,
watching the teen-agers hungrily gobbling at his words and his
soul, like so many sparrows. I didn't see how he could work at his
sculpture at all any more with so many demands coming in on
him, though he had asked for it; it was his own doing that Jarvis
wouldn't leave him alone and even the Episcopal minister, whose
predecessor wouldn't have dared set foot on the place even if Baldur
had been on his deathbed, felt free to barge in on him in the studio.
But it was enough to kill him. I thought of Jack's remark a while
back about his health and felt a twinge of something like panic,
although I couldn't have sworn the feeling was that simple.

The work he had been doing tended toward the same intimation,
as though at some point recently he had measured his time, and
decided to bring the statues that were there to a finished state, so
that they might live after him. Or perhaps Cluny had persuaded him
to let the dealers come around, after all, and what he had reached
was only a resting point.

At the moment, the sight of him was reassuring enough. The
somewhat drawn look that had worried me earlier had fallen away.
He was going on about the Greeks and the Romans, apparently as
indestructible and pleased with everything as on the night of his
return, with one difference. Probably because of the nature of his
audience, his discourse had taken on a touch of the old pedantry, of

the days when he was laboring through the Encyclopaedia and doling it out in yard-lengths to anybody who would listen. He seemed to catch it himself in a minute, and veered off into another fable— "a fish story" he called it. Vibrant, mobile, weathered, the deep folds of his face and his wild whiskery eyebrows in continual motion up, down and sideways as he talked, he looked as perennial as Santa Claus, just as he did every night making up stories for Dickie, when they had finished putting his patched khaki pants and smeared shirts through the washer and dryer that still fascinated them both.

In those stories there was an ogre named Grou, a princess who couldn't sleep and three other characters including a bear. The last few evenings Baldur had made puppets of them, which Dickie had spent hours painting and stringing up. The show, I was reminded, was to be that night.

"There's just one thing, Mr. Blake," Tom Seeley said when they were at the door. "All this about China and Greece and everything . . . I mean you don't seem to care much about America."

Baldur laughed. "Well, I think I can still recite the Declaration of Independence."

"Oh, I know about that," Myra said. "That's who our school's named for. Abraham Lincoln."

"Goda'mighty!" It floored him, for a second. "We'll have to give them something, Eva. What can it be? Can't let them go off like that. Haven't got any books up here . . ."

He glanced all around, eagerly, looking for something to give, and seemed on the point of handing them each a statue, if there had been four that they could carry. But then his eye lit on a rubbish-heap off in the dark stall where the last goddess used to be, and he pounced on it and brought out four dusty curled-up photographs. They were his old reproductions of Michelangelo. "Here. You can flatten them with a damp cloth, but not too quickly; be careful. Then look at them. Or you can throw them away."

"Do you like it? I'm not quite sure, but it might be a garden bench." He had picked up a tool and was rounding off one of the humps in his bolster thing.

"For Blake Acres. Oh, haven't you heard? That's what Chuck Jarvis is calling it anyway." I caught another flash of the *preederome* era, of annoyance this time, but he mastered it quickly. "By the way, Will Beardsley would like to talk to you, as soon as possible. Jarvis was there this morning, with a lawyer. I guess Will's heard you might be working with him." I didn't care just then what would ever happen to Jordan, but I asked nevertheless, "Are you?"

He laid down his tool and then stood in his soldierly way lighting his pipe, glancing past the flame at an aluminum construction like a large fan, which I saw now was a development of his gate. "I don't know." He spoke with a simplicity more startling than if he had sounded tired and sick, which he didn't at all, although this had evidently been worrying him. Something about it had assailed him in that new region of his being, the source of the gleeful reserve I hadn't dared look into and was missing for the first time. "But I'll go to see Will before dinner. Be glad to."

The last blue patch of sky was being covered over, and it looked as if the rain would break any minute. We needed it; the brook was as low as I had ever seen it and the garden was suffering. Lucas had been out at all hours nursing his plum trees. Baldur was waiting; I turned in from the barn door at last.

"Why are you so cruel to Jack?" I asked, and before I knew it I was crying in his arms. It was as if both our ties to Jack, his and mine, had been a well-worn topic between us. "Baldur, please help me, please. He's your son, you made him, now make him human, for me. You can; you started to. Why have you given up?"

He went on holding me lightly, his arms giving what patient comfort they might and it was so like the comfort my grandmother had given, the person in the world most contrary to him, it made me cry out inconsequently as though it were all one grief, "They're all dead! It's too much, being the only one left. I can't straighten out all their lives for them."

"Poor Eva," he said with a little friendly smile, and offered me a handkerchief. "It's not very clean, I'm afraid."

I smiled too after a little, took some of his eternal tea and sat down on what was not certain to be a garden bench. His eyes, set wide and shallow under their curling thickets of eyebrows, were strangely without color. I had a hazy recollection of them as somewhere in the greenish-brown class in the old days, but if they had paled with age they had also undergone a more striking change from what he had made of his age, so that it seemed not physical frailty but the brilliance of candor alone that had taken the color out. I had been right; something today had driven through the gnomish element.

"Jack went to see you months ago, in Wellford. You remember that, don't you?" He nodded, and I rushed on, "There seems to be nothing you won't do for us and everybody else, even those kids who have nothing to do with you. He needs you more than any of us, and he went to see you first. But you wouldn't make the effort then, for him, for your own son . . ."

He didn't flinch, but just said, "My son, yes," so placidly I had almost an impression it wasn't he who had spoken. It was again for a moment as if the statues had taken over, and that transcendental voice were theirs.

"You had never laid eyes on Lucas in your life, and you did it for him. You went through that awful struggle—at least it can't have been easy, I've never heard of anybody giving up drinking overnight like that—and came back. For him. Didn't you?"

"Well, and why not for you while you're at it? You were always a favorite of mine. But no, no, Eva, it's nothing like that, and it's not worth the bitterness I hear in your voice. It's hardly worth speaking of, you know . . ." He really seemed to believe that, lounged as he was in his homemade chaiselongue with his feet up, his eyes following the vagaries of his pipe smoke. If it was distasteful to him to be forced over this ground he was not showing it, but he was taking no relish in it either. It was only for my sake. For him the past in all its failure and agony was resolved. He was better than free of it, he was free *in* it, or so his stance and voice implied. Yet I didn't see how that could be, when Jack was the crux, as he had shown so plainly that other time in the studio, and he was failing as badly on that score as in the old days when he washed his hands of it. He went on, "We don't do things, even easy ones, for the needs of others. We do them out of our own needs or for our own fun and when God gives us the strength. I claim no more than the sparrow's share. Still He may have had in mind, in sending Lucas at the right moment, to mitigate a more shameful interview."

"Shameful!" I burst out. "Because he wanted money for the lab? You could hardly expect him to love you, at that point. You might at least respect his work, his caring enough about something . . ."

"I do indeed, it's very commendable, as far as it goes; I wasn't speaking of that." He paused, as though to ruminate but it was perhaps more to let me steady up for his next blow, and I thought the little far glimmer, as of some huge mischief whereby everything was going to work out all right, was in his eyes again for a moment, but I couldn't be sure. "Or I could say just as truthfully," he continued, "that in the end, after everything else, it was Arthur who gave me the strength."

"Arthur!" It was uncanny his touching on that fresh longing and hurt, not even an hour old. "He was nothing to you. You never even wanted him to sit for you . . ."

"I wasn't up to it in those days. Dear foolish inarticulate Arthur, in all his scrapes and messes, with that grin and his animal pride and the fine unthinking heart. If I could have done him fishing . . ." He shot a glance out across the studio, as though asking himself if that were part of what he had captured at last, so late, then swerved to the point. "I mean that the news of his death, in the spring of forty-three, put an end to a world for me, privately speaking. It was a shock. I'd been waiting, you see, to hear that Jack had been killed. I might say I'd been hoping for it. It would have been a great relief to me. But they got the wrong boy."

I had to get up to walk off my impatience. "I guess you never heard," and that time I could hear my own bitterness, although I was still aware that this was nothing better than a chore to Baldur, he was doing it for me, "what kind of scrapes and messes they were, the last few years."

"Yes, I did. He told me quite a lot himself. I'd seen him not so long before, must have been just a week or so before your mother died."

"Where? We never heard from him. He never came home then."

"Not to your house. But he came to Jordan. Sneaked up the back way here to see me. He wanted to borrow a rather large sum of money."

"Oh, it's horrible! He couldn't!" All our time in the Howland house was before me, with the full blast of that misery and my parents' last trickle of pride.

"Look here, Eva, you little prig." He got to his feet then too and was suddenly both direct and cross. "Do you think he was so unlike you that he couldn't feel shame? Not enough perhaps, never mind. He told me he'd gone over to the spring on the way here; had a hard time saying it, he was never much with words. Something about the two of you washing off your sins there together, and how he'd felt so rotten and dirty when he got there he couldn't stand to take a drink. He was looking seedy enough, that's true. Very likely had a friend waiting for him in a car over the hill, getting ready to laugh about how they'd rolled the old man. His resolution might or mightn't have lasted out the evening. What of it? It was real then. He was sick with self-disgust and longing for all of you; begged me to help you and your parents, whether I'd help him or not. Poor fool, what a time he picked. I didn't just refuse him, of course, wasn't in condition for that. When one drowning man grabs at another . . ." He had become quite exercised for a minute, for my benefit, his own feelings about this episode too having no further power to gall, and was back now to his own grave and special order of jollity. Massive, erect, the bumpy antedeluvian landscape of his face solid as through the work of centuries, he seemed scarcely to be associated with any such personal recollection; anyone might grab at him now; everyone did.

"It was quite a scene," he went on, and I saw that for him this was not a digression. It would take him back to the real subject presently, and also to whatever else he had wanted to talk about. "I literally threw him out, pretty near bashed his face in too; had what you might call a tantrum. He howled out there like a stuck pig for a few minutes, called me every name you could think of. Our Lady of Redemption, what faces she can wear! He'd offered me the chance, you see, and we both knew it in a way, but he had to die to make the point stick. To have lent a hand to anybody's erring son—would it have mattered whose?—the shoddier the better, just so the heart wasn't altogether fouled, so it could be done with no thought of the returns; to give as a parent does, unhopefully, against reason . . . But there was one thing he probably didn't know, so he couldn't understand my anger. Here, I'll show you something."

His voice had changed so abruptly, I thought the whole business of human relations past and present had become too tiresome for him to go on with and he was about to show me a new piece of sculpture. He led me instead to the oldest one of all. There was a trap door in a corner of the barn floor, in the old icehouse section given over to his landscape sketches, with an iron ring that had been covered with rubbish in recent years so that I had forgotten about it, although we had loved playing in the black pit underneath when we were children.

He shone a flashlight down into it.

"Niobe! What on earth is she doing down there?"

"Weeping, I expect," he said, with a note of mild and half-humorous affection for the old thing. She might well weep, corrugated as she was by her years out on the stone wall, yet still beautiful, and without a trace of the anemia of his later time. "For all our children." He added, "I overlooked her that day"— I didn't need to ask what day he meant—"and now, she does no harm."

He let the heavy door fall with a clank and a thud, as though on some old oubliette being shown to a tourist, and now he did seem in a hurry to get on.

"I misused her terribly. Oh, not the lady herself perhaps, but her memory. Addie Pryden was right about that—a brilliant and fascinating woman, as you know, but somewhat strenuous in her cures, for herself and others. In this case the patient was willing, for his own good and private reasons. Yes, I'm coming to your question. What a joke, what a triumph! what an offering to her"—he gestured toward the trap door, obviously referring not to the once living model, whatever she had been, but to the poor weathered stone that seemed to have shed tears from every inch of its surface until it was half worn away by them. "What a splendid way to prove one's devotion; not just to stay outside the human rigmarole, it doesn't take an artist to do that. But to create flesh of your flesh and be indifferent to it, every day, every hour." We had both sat down again. In his brief silence, in discomfort at what was coming, I looked down at my hands and for a second was taken by the conceit that they were turning boneless and white under my eyes; they were turning into the hands he had modeled from them and a fit of anger would be enough to knock them off. "I hadn't yet learned, Eva," he said quite cheerily, slipping over his nine years' absence, "that we have to accept the curse of our humanity. If we deny it, the best we can do is fail. The worst is to create a monster, for our own and the world's devouring."

There was a little wind but no rain yet. He got up to adjust a couple of awnings that were flapping and pull some pieces of sculpture back from the two big doors.

"You're being rather dramatic." It was right there where I was sitting that somebody had said monster, for a joke, after Jack had broken into the conversation that day. I thought, he would never talk to me about Arthur the way Baldur has, I tried and it just irked him, "It's too bad," was all he would say.

There was another chore that Baldur had performed for me recently; I hadn't realized at the time that he knew what he was doing. He had cleared a path to the willow pool, merely saying he'd like to be able to cool off there once in a while if we didn't mind and looking so innocent about it, I'd assumed that nobody had ever told him; I hadn't myself ever told Lucas where she did it. I had one of the old fits of vomiting, watching him out there with the scythe, from an upstairs window. But after he got it cleaned up so nicely Lucas and Dickie and Cluny and everybody began using it, it was five feet deep in the middle even with the drought, and pretty soon I was going too. Those had been the gayest times all summer, like long ago when my grandparents were alive.

I said harshly, "It sounds to me as if you'd come back just to disown Jack all over again. Not to help him but to fight him."

He had carried a stepladder over to fix one of the awnings and was busily up on it, with his back to me, looking so toned-up and agile, a healthy fifty at most, I could understand Cluny's delight on her first sight of him in bathing trunks. I knew she had visited him a few times in the studio too, but still I wasn't prepared for the sight of her jeweled lipstick, a present from David, which my eye fell on just then, on the floor by the couch.

"To counteract a little, if possible, the evil he might do? Is that what you're saying?" He looked down at me with a rapid twist of the head, half way grinning I thought but inscrutable as a monkey; and he did have some resemblance to one, with that nose and forehead. It suddenly struck me as funny that he should have been getting off all that lofty talk. "Perhaps, if it came to that . . ."

"I could kill you," I said, and wasn't far from meaning it. "So it was true, all you care about is Lucas. And what is he going to do for the world?"

Baldur finished the job, hopped down and was beside me, definitely grinning. I seemed to have given him back his mysterious relish momentarily, which as usual was free of either charity or spite. "You wanted help, you said." The word tickled him so, I thought he might double up like a real comedian and I could at least lose my respect for him. It would really be funny if it were just that military carriage that gave him such a hold on all of us. What kind of game was this, after all, when he had just spoken so earnestly of Arthur's giving him the chance to help? "I'm not a nurse's aid, or a stargazer either; you're in the wrong pew. And no, I haven't got a secret bottle hidden up here, as you've begun to suspect. I can tell you just this, for what it's worth. If it were Jack who wanted to kill me—if he could hate me so it was ripping the guts out of him the way your brother hated me after I'd bloodied his nose for him and flung him out there on his knees, if he just once had it in him to call me the names I heard from Arthur . . ." He turned away, merely smiling; the glimmer had died out. "So far, the best he can do is to admire me." With scarcely a pause he went on as if it were all one subject, as perhaps for him it was, "There's one other thing it might help you to know about Arthur. He first learned about sexual aberration"—he was looking at me very straight—"from me."

"Oh stop. Don't."

"One rainy day here when he was ten or eleven. I've been less drawn than most men, probably, that way. I seem to have naturally gravitated to the opposite sex." He saw me glance at the lipstick on the floor, and smiled, possibly also from reading my thought of the other ladies who had been figuring in our conversation. "But that day I found myself caressing his legs, and perhaps would have done it all if he'd been willing. Of course he wasn't. He ran like a rabbit and never came here alone again until the day I've told you about. As a matter of fact"—I felt he was wanting me to meet his eyes squarely again—"I offered him a dollar that rainy day. So he had some reason all those years later to think he might collect."

I felt my lips tightening, and after a horrid silence heard him answering that grimace: "But why the surprise, Eva? Did you think we could get into hell through the actions of others?"

It was a few minutes later that Dickie arrived, white and frightened in the rain, and out of breath from running up the hill.

Baldur was saying, meanwhile, that he didn't think Lucas would kill himself. "There's something he owes you though, before he leaves." There was no hint of apology in this remark. I myself, after all, had been begging him to interfere, before he dealt me that worst blow of all; compared to which I thought no further revelation could have much power to hurt. So his Niobe must feel in her black pit.

"Leaves?"

"Oh, it's not easy for him. He's the kind of father—well, no matter. But how he does love that child; like two pins, aren't they?

It's hard to imagine them apart." He shook his head, sighing a little. It gave me a suspicion, as clear as the one he had put his finger on earlier about the bottle, that he was lying. Any suspicion could seem in order now, in the train of the large one he had so carelessly—or was it with calculation?—put before me, as to what had drawn him to Lucas in the first place, and kept him in our house, and why he had kicked his last goddess in that particular fashion. "But you know better than I, it's been touch and go since that last letter from South America. That Lucas! It didn't tempt him much when it looked like clear sailing and an easy haul. Now that he's heard about the fever and cannibals and his friend Corey whatever his name is being done out of all the machinery . . ."

I hadn't heard of the letter; it too might be Baldur's invention. I looked hard one after the other at the stone toad and the long cedar leaf and the other wooden thing that was like a potato or the eye of God—"Mater Dolorosa" Jack had said—thinking that even now by some miracle they might cast forth their deep serenity again, but they refused me; as the spring had; as Baldur himself had. I remembered the sensation of sweetness in my face when I used to pose for him long ago, and how easy it had been to come by. "We don't owe each other anything."

"Only for him to tell you who he is."

"Well, he doesn't know who I am either. I know enough—all that about his father and the carnival . . ." It all flashed before me, lurid and precise for the first time.

"And his Eskimo wife and baby," Baldur said, "dying in his arms in the blizzard . . ." I hadn't heard that one.

I looked around at him sharply then. "You mean it's not true?"

I had hardly noticed the thunder and lightning and wild sudden downpour until Dickie came in.

"Let him go!" I shouted to Baldur, but he was off and I had to follow as best I could with Dickie in my arms, he was so shaken. It was the knife, he managed to say, and at last permitted a few tears to squeeze out, not because he had been ordered to go all that way alone in that awful storm but because his father had found the switchblade knife I had hidden in a bureau drawer and wasn't going to be there for the puppet show. Behind us I heard the studio doors crashing in the wind and then a sharper crash of some big metal thing, the gate perhaps, blown over inside. Almost in the same instant came the deafening crack and geyser of flame; an elm by the graveyard was struck. I was dressed like Dickie, in shirt and shorts, and I implored the water lashing our huddled flesh to wake me and make me whole again, but although I was nearly blinded by the rain my skin felt dry as a bone.

"The truth?" Lucas said. "What truth?" He hadn't figured on Baldur's being able to make it down the hill so fast. The truck was by the gate, with his gun and fishing tackle and a packed duffel-bag on the seat, and he had become a stranger in the house. It was like the day he first came by, handsome and glib, with the twitch at his mouth and the same deep reticence in his eyes, selling Happy Bread. Only now he wasn't noticing me. "It's not what you live through, it's what you live *with* that makes the truth of a life. But I don't have to tell you that." He looked at his watch, with a lot more impatience than he had ever shown about getting to a job on time.

"Mr. Farr, as you've probably suspected, has been getting letters from someone about you."

"The snooping son of a bitch." He was smiling, however; it didn't seem to concern him. "You mean he's been writing letters. There couldn't have been anything if he hadn't started it, not with this face." He rubbed his cheek, where the tiny scars were. "He's welcome to them"—because he was on his way, he meant, and it wasn't a jungle but the snow I was seeing around him. He had freed himself at last and was striding out into the white swirl as somehow I had always known he would, transfigured, glorious, loosed into his own unfathomable goodness and carried along by it as on wings of snow, to where no evil might ever reach. We were in the entranceway; the rain was still beating down outside. Baldur too was aware of the spirit that had claimed Lucas and seemed loath to make any further move to stop him. He stepped away from the door sorrowfully, his head bowed, looking the antithesis of the gleeful character who had been living with us. "From someone who knew me," Lucas added as he reached for the door-latch, "in the pen, I suppose. Which one? Atlanta? or just that little time in Danbury?"

But he didn't leave just then after all. By the time I was through fainting he had missed his inner cue and the spirit had been debased.

In my faint-dream a mob was doing something terrible to Dickie, and Lucas was trying to rescue him but kept being tripped up by a network of wires along the ground. Then in the other disorientation of coming to, on the living-room sofa, I thought I was in a house and among people I had never seen before, and cried out, "Where is Lucas?"

He sat on the edge of the sofa beside me and took me in his arms in the strong familiar way, in the embrace that had undone a thousand little wars and disturbances, saying in the old deep loving voice, "I'm here, honey, I'm right here." I clung to him hard, while the room shivered toward recognition. Then suddenly he was on his feet and I heard a hard, sardonic laugh, like the laughter of the mob in my dream. "That was a neat trick," he said in the fury I had glimpsed once before. "You never told me you could do that."

Baldur pulled him gently back. I drank the brandy they had put there and sat up. I had fainted half a dozen times in my life, from tension and lack of food, but hadn't happened to have done it in his presence before. "Go on," I said.

He did; he knew he had let his moment pass. "Pure little Eva— you really had me fooled. Look at her. The poor thing faints dead away, because she thinks she's been married to a common criminal, maybe a murderer, and as it happens she's right. That's what she's been married to. The truth, you want! You can have it; name any variety you think you could understand and I'll oblige. A knife wrapped in underpanties in a bureau drawer—that's your level. You found the right school for your son, to train him to be yours, only yours; taught him to like the taste of filth, a little more every day, and under such nice appearances. A playmate his own age for a change, cocktail parties for the grown-ups. A working mother, so successful too, has to leave her child somewhere, doesn't she? especially with a husband who can't even afford a dishwasher or a coat of paint for the house. He'll be the one to blame if she makes a mistake . . . No, Baldur, it's all right about the stuff, and thanks; it doesn't matter who paid for them, she needed them; you can see how happy she's been since she got respectable again. A mistake, like a child of five getting little doses of poison dropped into his soul. You don't think so? You should have seen his face up there; he never looked like her before that I could see but he did this time, a perfect picture of his mother coming home from one of those excursions lately, sweet as honey, as sweet as he really was up to a while ago. Oh no, he never saw a knife like that before, how did it work, maybe it was an old one of his grandpa's. Then quick as a lizard, to get back in with me, he said, 'Let's throw it in the garbage and not tell her.' Perhaps you never thought what your son traded for that knife. Did you? Would some more brandy help?" He looked at me, cold as a judge now, waiting. "She can't imagine, she's never been out in this dirty world. Well, I have, I've seen plenty of switch-blades change hands, for value received. Your son isn't missing any valuable toys, is he? A dump-truck or anything like that?

"But I'm off the track. It's my lies and crimes we were getting at." Baldur, standing by the fireplace with his hands in his pockets, was listening with monumental gravity, piercing and patient, as though the revelations of an hour before were from somebody else's life. Dickie had been upstairs getting off his wet clothes, and now that the rain had lightened, appeared in the living-room door in his yellow mackintosh, the clasps mismated and rubber boots on the wrong foot, carrying a paper bag. Nobody said anything to him and after a moment's scrutiny he trudged on out, to feed his ducks perhaps. Lucas's face contracted. But he got a grip on himself and said lightly enough to Baldur, "By the way, old man, the boys stole ten dollars from your wallet the other day—Dickie and his friend. I replaced it," and to me, "I'm afraid the Doc's going to let you down if I size him up right. None of my business of course . . ." He went over to one of the front windows, at which that morning when Chuck Jarvis appeared I had been hanging the freshly starched white organdy curtains, and stood there with his back to us, looking out across the long lawn that he had reclaimed from hay that spring, to please me. "Looks pretty now, doesn't it? Like everybody else's; like one of those magazines. You don't have to be ashamed any more." His big sunburned fists came down with no passion, only a dullness of misery now on the window-frame.

"Lies, my lies . . . Pretty good, weren't they? They ought to be, I've seen plenty. I liked that part about the sea myself. The carnival stuff was too easy; I've worked in quite a few, been practically every-thing but a geek. It's easy anyway. I was brought up with lies, lived with them a long time before I even knew it, like an eel under the lily-pads. Took me about twenty years to hit open water and I scuttled back a few times even after that. Every damn thing was a lie; big ones, little ones; about love, about money, didn't matter what, there wasn't anything else." Dickie's voice reached us, call-ing to the ducks; Lucas turned back into the room, in a new access of pain and anger. "But there was never a howler like this one. Oh, there's no blame, only it's funny. I thought . . . Well, it doesn't matter . . ."

"That we loved each other so much," I said, "it would be like the beginning of the world and we would do without the rest of the world, forever and ever."

He seemed surprised, as I was, at my speaking at all. "That's pretty fancy. I thought we could be honest, if that's what you mean. That we'd live in the truth, yes, and nothing but the truth. Thanks for the illusion; I hadn't ever had it before. It took us both seven years farther along anyway and that's something." He started toward the door, not as he had earlier but sadly dragging, with something in him broken by his own talk. "Oh, speaking of honesty, I suppose you're wondering, and about this face I've got . . . Sure, I had to tell a few stories to make it all possible; in the interest of higher truth, as Jesus Christ might say. As I said before, if a man could be allowed to judge his own truth, then that's what I told you." For a minute the sadness lifted from him, while his eyes followed something far away, off through a speck in the wall over our heads; it was the look that he and Dickie used to share, and that Dickie had lost now, at the bird that wasn't there. "I once spent a night like that by the sea, running away from something and the moon going black. I was fifteen, I guess . . .

"Well, cheer up, I'm not a bigamist anyway. Got a perfectly good divorce. She wasn't an Eskimo either; just a girl from down the street. And if you must know, I haven't done time—not more than a night or two now and then; a little vagrancy, disorderly conduct, a couple of strikes I got messed up in. Had a habit of losing my temper. But I never made the grade, the way you were thinking; had the impulse plenty of times and I wish I had; it was just some weakness —of character." He shrugged, looking more drained even than a moment earlier. "I'm no better than Charlie. We both waited for the war, to work out our criminal tendencies; at least I heard he got some medals too. But you haven't heard about Charlie, have you? I was forgetting. He's my brother—the fellow I turned off the TV the other night, and you remarked on the name. Some merger, or something . . ." He glanced around briefly as though to see if there were any little thing he had laid down and should be taking, and all at once was the smiling ideal jack-of-all-trades again, whom everybody would always be trying to push into a better job. "Solong," he said to nobody in particular.

Baldur hadn't moved in all this time, and didn't move now to intercept him but only to walk out with him to the gate. I stood on the stoop watching silently, as I had when my mother's coffin was being carried out, and never did know if Baldur had had some last word up his sleeve to keep him or delay him or if he just thought by then, no matter what hurt or failure it might represent to him and on no matter what grounds, that Lucas was doing what he had to do. The motor was going when one of them noticed the hump under the tarpaulin in the back and they found Dickie with his paper bag, chained and padlocked to the truck. He had only been calling the ducks to say goodbye. It was an old padlock he had found open, with no key, and he fought them both tooth and nail while they hacksawed it off. He was sobbing terribly then, so in the end Lucas carried him back into the house and on upstairs, with Baldur following.

I don't know what went on up there. They came down after a while, all three looking rather wrung out, and Dickie stayed tight beside his father. Lucas still acted as if the house and I were completely unfamiliar to him, except that when I touched his bare arm by mistake putting down a cup of tea he drew back in a spasm of revulsion, then quickly said, "Excuse me." It was only to Baldur that he said after a while, glumly, "Seems so long ago, that night when I agreed to it. I must have been soft in the head—you know, the shoveling, and all those arms and legs we were throwing in . . ." His hand went up, not to where the twitch might come but to cover the whole left half of his face. "And I didn't foresee its being so pointless."

IV

THEN CHARLEMAGNE GOT DOWN from his horse, and on his knees prayed to God to make the sun stand still so that he might have time to overtake the retreating Saracen horde, and God granted his prayer. The sun stayed still in the sky, and only when the last of the heathens lay dead on the field, or in their panic had rushed on top of one another into the river to drown, did darkness fall. It was one of Miss Pryden's favorite points in the story, and she told it with even more emotion than usual as we approached the Pyrenees that time with my grandmother. The proximity of Roncevaux touched some strange chord of tragic elation in her, as the scene of a single great love might in a more ordinary woman, but whether her attachment was more to Roland or Oliver I was never sure, in spite of all the talk that used to go on about their differences of character. Or Charlemagne himself. It would all have been twaddle, she once said, without that mighty figure for scale, and the way she said it, with an inconsistent little pout of contempt for youth no matter how heroic, you felt sure the only type of man she would ever go to bed with would be one who could make the sun stand still. Actually the scene of Roland's death affected her just as much, and it was thrilling to hear her tell of the sound of the horn across the mountains and Charlemagne's great line—*Ce cor a longue haleine*. Against such sounds and powers we were to measure the ignobility of our behavior.

I don't believe any of us was praying that evening, but it seems as if the sun, which burst through quickly after the storm, must have stayed for hours just over the brow of the hill while Lucas told

his story, and after. Neither of us interrupted him; I was sewing all
the time except when I went for a tray of cold supper. It seemed
he must have talked through half a night by ordinary time, and perhaps it is a blur of memory that makes me see dusk and no lights on
yet when he stopped. But no: because Dickie had gone upstairs after
a while to do some last work on the puppets and he and Baldur
put on the show after all with Lucas and me for audience, laughing
and providing the applause just the way we were supposed to, and
even after that there was still time for Baldur to keep his appointment with Will Beardsley although Will was always in bed by nine.
I still didn't quite need a flashlight when I went back up to the
studio then, while he was gone, because of our having left everything open there in the storm. I don't know what I expected, perhaps something awful like years ago when it hadn't been a storm
doing it, but all that was broken was a windowpane and a couple
of glasses; the one statue that had blown over wasn't damaged. I
suppose really I was giving Lucas that chance to go ahead now and
leave and take Dickie too if he felt like it. It wouldn't have surprised
me, and it didn't surprise me to find him still in the parlor, only with
all haggardness gone and a peaceful freshness as of morning about
his face. It became him so, I thought serenity must be his native
stance and I had never seen it before.

There was not to be much further occasion for it that evening,
through no fault of his. What happened took us all without warning, since the news Baldur brought back from the Beardsley house
struck me as interesting, considering Jack's tone to me at lunchtime,
but nothing more. There was nothing to make it alarming, except
in regard to Alice. He must have left the lab almost at once after
hanging up the phone, to go and do what I had asked, what he had
said he would never do, as if Pryden interference in Beardsley troubles had never occurred before. Then after looking at the child he
had made some phone calls to New Haven and had driven her
himself to the hospital, with Cliff and Nanny along in the car too.
Whatever symptoms he saw were enough for that, although nobody
would have said so or given a name to the suspicion, if that was all
it was; there would be tests and nothing more Jack could do after
getting the case into the right hands, except to drive Cliff home.
Nanny was going to spend the night in a chair in Alice's room at the
hospital. So according to his own long-established and cherished
regulations, Jack should have wiped the matter out of mind and
gone calmly home to bed or else back to the lab to resume what-

ever he had walked out on in such a hurry. But after all there was a crack in that elegant moral system of his, which hadn't been much in evidence for me lately, and without trying or wanting or even knowing about it, by nothing but the spectacle of his own suffering as the two of them drove home in silence in the dark, Cliff Beardsley drove through it.

It was, at last, quite dark. The sun at some point had slipped on down and we had a few lights on in the house, although we had nothing more to say to each other just then and were only waiting for Chuck Jarvis to come in with his ultimatum or whatever he would call it, so we could go to bed. Baldur had evidently talked a few minutes with old Will about that business, in spite of everything, but he didn't tell us what his answer was going to be and we didn't ask. I sewed a little more, yawning, while Baldur thumbed through a magazine that happened to be by his chair and Lucas in the other room tried a couple of TV channels and then turned it off, perhaps yawning too. In the quiet I heard the whippoorwill very loud and distinct across the brook, and it made me think as always for a minute, until my ears rejected it, of the night of my mother's death.

I screamed as I did nearly everything at that time, for the wrong reason. I had to pretend it was at the violence to Baldur I was on the verge of witnessing, while I stood not even raising my hand, but really I think I screamed a second or two later, over something else. As a matter of fact the something else may have been all Jack had in mind when he came in and it was only when his weapon, the brass and marble lampstand, was already raised that he had the impulse to swerve and bring it down on the living head at the back of the armchair instead, because Baldur either hadn't chosen or hadn't had time to collect himself to get to his feet, and his skull was there at striking level, eggishly inviting. Somehow Lucas made it in time, with the poker from the fireplace too, but it wasn't by an accident of the struggle that the sculpture was broken. It didn't just topple. This I saw clearly, that as soon as Jack had to let go the lampstand, he turned his anger on the white plaster head I had been taking care of so long, grabbed it in both hands and hurled it across the room. So I screamed, as if that would keep it in mid-air, intact; I just couldn't believe it could happen to me, that that particular object should be getting ready to crash into so many pieces it was practically powder, on the hearthstone.

It wasn't the action of a drunk but he was looking like one and a bum besides, tie yanked down crooked and his fingernails packed black as if he had been on some mad spree of gardening out in the night. "Let go of me," he snapped, and Lucas did, since the contortion of Jack's face, while if anything more furious than in the first minute, had passed beyond the physically random or primitive. He even laughed, for once as though taking pleasure in showing his ugly teeth.

"Jack, for heaven's sake . . ." I started to lay a beseeching hand on his arm. Baldur, from his look the whole time, might have considered being nearly brained no more than a fitting filial tribute and sign of precocity.

"You stay out of this. You're no better. As if you gave a damn for that brat of yours." I thought he was looking for something else to throw across the room, but the dementia, which must have driven him to some unaccustomed exertion before he reached the house, seemed to have played itself out. He slumped to the footstool, seething merely with acid, more like himself. He was even able to look Baldur in the eye. "Don't worry, I wouldn't have given you the satisfaction of having me up for homicide. That old ego-stuffed skull of yours didn't really tempt me that much."

"You weren't about to miss it just the same," Baldur remarked amiably, putting a hand over the part in question, as though still not quite sure it was intact.

"Then we can both thank Mr. Hines. You're not worth any such inconvenience."

A giggle burst from me, and another and another. It was almost like the girlish giggling fits I had had once or twice, to my mortification, at Miss Pryden's table. "Look at us, will you? All because of that nineteenth-century thunderstorm. Both of you, on the same day! Oh, my God . . ." I bent over shaking with laughter.

It was true that in this second, rather weary stage, Jack's explosion had an absurd resemblance to Lucas's of a little while before, reminding me of the kind of superstition my grandfather used to scoff at, about the influence of weather. But Jack wasn't rising to any comic relief. "That Cliff. A grown man like that. Crying; because his child is going to die."

"Die?" Lucas asked, and I realized it was the first word he had spoken since finishing his monologue.

Jack shrugged. "Nobody told them but he knows, he understood."

In a few bitter words he gave an account of his afternoon, beginning with Cliff holding Alice in his arms on the way to the hospital and telling her stories about all sorts of funny animals they had had at one time and another on the farm. I knew the stories. There was a little pig that fell in love with a goose and tried to learn to swim; and a puppy they'd sent for all the way from Tennessee to be a hunting-dog, who used to bring fawns and baby skunks and once even a young fox home as playmates; and the pair of mink that came back every evening after the Beardsleys gave up their try at mink-farming and had set them free. It was on the drive home when they weren't talking that Jack had known Cliff was crying. "But you wouldn't understand that," he wound up in a new thrust of animosity, at Baldur. *"That"*—indicating the broken sculpture—"was all your sacred responsibilities ever called for. And you were rather evil-tempered, as I remember it, about that. And after Midway when you heard I wasn't missing after all you went crazy with disappointment. It had been such a relief, the other way, hadn't it?" His voice had gone still quieter as the dangerous wildness worked up in him once more. "God damn your soul, answer me! Hadn't it?"

I was hearing the answer from that afternoon, and waiting now for Baldur to lie. He was rising, rising: how when he was moving steadily could it take him so long to get out of an armchair? and Jack's face with that horrible look on it seemed to be getting pushed back and back out of his way by some invisible power about us in the room, and the bass voice strong but soft seemed to be issuing from all about us too, from the whole house about us and above us, saying, "Yes, my son, my son, yes! It's true!"—he smiled, but without irony, at the novel words—"I hoped you would be killed." He was growing taller than any man could be, and under the radiance of his joy, all of us who had been in fragments were becoming whole for the first time, because the word had opened the way for all of us and we were all three without distinction truly his children, and would be redeemed. So it seemed. In the dazzle of that welcome, that calling forth of our truest selves, surely there could be no failure, even though watching the hard puzzled beginning of an acceptance of the gift in the two faces, Jack's and Lucas's, I knew there had to be failure somewhere among us. So I bowed my head, thinking not yet, not yet, and opened my heart as never to anything in my life before, to the blessed light that was going to burn away all my lies, as it had consumed the last hateful residue of my afternoon tête-à-tête. He had come back from the dead for us; all debts had been paid.

"Let us pray!" It was a raucous shout, followed by a violent smash of men's laughter, like the sculpture being thrown all over again; because Jarvis hadn't come alone. There were two of them laughing. "Are you all in a trance or something? So this is how you spend your evenings—calling up spirits, huh? I wouldn't have thought it of *you*, Doc. Well, well." Another round of laughter, every piece of it hard and fast and aimed at something. The other man was Fred Leighton, smile and hair done up fit to kill, dressed in a brand new bright-striped sportsman's garb that would have cost a year's living by any Leighton's previous standards.

There was some fast talk. "I've got Chuck's plane warmed up for him on the hill," boomed Fred in his new pride of henchmanship. "I guaranteed I'd have him off the ground twenty minutes from now." But Chuck Jarvis's voice was as charming and reassuring as ever, and after some scanty preliminary it was saying, "So this is it, Baldie. It's now or never. What about it, old boy?" He grabbed him by both arms in a flush of enthusiasm as fresh and innocent-looking as on the first evening of their acquaintance, when the whole grand scheme had struck him. "You and me together; it'll be a new day in rural development, a model for the whole country. And you'll have the veto on the art side, the architects understand that . . ." It was the speech I had heard that morning, the same boyish conviction, the same clear other message conveyed by the voice, of an *or else*. That was the aspect that Fred Leighton was counting on, very obviously; whatever fool caprice in his new boss had led him to approach such a character as Baldur wasn't worrying him, now that they stood face to face. After all Fred was no newcomer to Jordan, he knew the Blake story as well as anyone and probably had seen Baldur plenty of times at the station bar during the Wellford years; if ever there was a sitting duck . . . But Fred wasn't figuring on needing any ammunition of that kind; Baldur's age alone, he was plainly thinking, would keep him out of anything so ambitious, and the triumphant look he didn't bother to keep off his face was really just a generic Leighton sneer, with something to justify it for once. A Leighton was hitting the big time at last, and wasn't aiming to go to jail for it either. He was beyond that; he was a Jarvis man.

There was still no way of telling what answer Baldur was about to give. He was looking quite untroubled, however, as if nothing at all were pending, and his trace of a smile seemed only at the way the deal was being presented, with that bundle of human smut tied to it; such a blatant paste of evil held Fred's sleazy good looks together, it really was funny, unless you had to be afraid of it. But I was agreeing with the thoughts I read in those little pig-eyes. Baldur was too old, he needed to be left alone now, and what good could he do anyway, it would only kill him. So they would go their own way, nobody could stop such a machine as Jarvis when it got moving and it certainly was moving, and what we were about to hear was the announcement of the end of Jordan. A year, two at the most: nothing would be left there that we had loved, or that anybody could ever love.

"I'll go in with you, Chuck, if Baldur will."

There were two of us there who didn't show any astonishment— Jack, who was brooding in a corner, in disgust at the intrusion, and Baldur. No wonder he had been so calm. This was exactly what he had foreseen and must have gambled on in talking to Will Beardsley; of course—if there were a Lucas in the picture they wouldn't have to try to block Jarvis, and wouldn't have a right to; he was offering progress and prosperity, after all. But both of them were too old, nobody but Lucas had what it would take to keep a Jarvis in line, and why, Will must have speculated, should they think he would want to take on such responsibility all of a sudden: the drifter, the handyman—had he ever wanted to be anything else? And Baldur, I was sure, had as good as answered for him: I think it will be his own idea and he will do it, now.

The four right hands were coming out for a round of shakes, over the new fellowship of the enterprise. Fred Leighton couldn't avoid that but he looked as if he had been struck on the mouth. That tone of equality from Lucas, that easy use of the nickname that had drawn such a queer glance from *Mister* Jarvis when Fred tried it a few minutes ago, and worse, Jarvis's response to the strange turn of events: he was more than pleased, he looked positively exhilarated . . . Still I couldn't believe until I was seeing it that Lucas's hand would actually clasp Fred's. He could still pull out; I knew the long breath like a groan of nausea that would come and the shutter dropping over his wide grey eyes in the split second of his removal a thousand miles away, while the hand would fall back limp at his side. But the gesture he made became, in the instant of happening, far more familiar, as though I had dreamed it over and over. A sudden animal secretion had brought an oozy glisten to Fred's palm and features, and whether from dope or merely the new stress of his situation, his dark, rather puffy hand was trembling slightly, as was his lower lip in its crooked one-sided smile that left the upper lip in a cataleptic snarl of its own. However, he was able to muster up a little glitter as of a snake's tongue, under the cool blast of confidence and good spirits with which Lucas sealed their partnership.

It was done, the improbable handclasp had occurred, and I had seen Lucas look full into the eyes of an old antagonist, one who had appeared under several names in the story he had told that afternoon. As a matter of fact, it wasn't their first encounter in Jordan. It was Fred Leighton that Lucas had nearly killed in the fracas at the gas stand seven years earlier, for his innuendoes or whatever it was about me.

As the two left, Jarvis threw a calculating glance at the seedy figure in the corner. Distaste seemed to have overcome all Jack's native diplomacy, he didn't bother even to look up, either when they left or when Jarvis indulged in a bit of youthful exuberance by buzzing the house shortly after. "I'm afraid," Baldur said, looking at him with an affectionate concern I had never seen between them before, "our friend won't be keeping much interest in your setup, with this 'new day' going through. Financially, you know . . . You may have to start looking around."

"No, I won't." He explained, smiling again now as the hush of happiness that had been disrupted began to sift back about us, "Except for a job eventually. I won't starve."

"But the lab, it was your baby, and this breakthrough you were just on the verge of . . . or weren't you?"

"And suppose I didn't have a job . . ." Atlas must have risen to his feet with just that look when Hercules took the load from his shoulders, and I knew that the weight he had dropped for his salvation was the one Lucas had taken up for his. It was the dirt of the world's ambition. "By the way, I'm afraid I've wrecked your garden piece too, with a sledge-hammer. Sorry about that." They had ended up speaking so softly I could hear a mouse nibbling in the attic, but only for a second because the silence broke over the other way, on the side away from any noises we could make or recognize, into the weird vibrations of joy like an annunciation, that we had nearly captured and nearly lost earlier, and as though that music were hands working in clay, I watched Jack's face, which for a second I had seen as exactly that of a mouse, turn into a living replica, with all its youth and purity and gaze beyond any mere worldly appetite, of the one that was in smithereens around the fireplace.

Baldur was changing too. He had grown very tall again but now had a cloak and long white beard and his hand rested on the hilt of a tremendous jeweled sword. As Charlemagne, however, he receded shortly into a great ball of heavenly light, reappearing after another interval as an equally majestic lion. Jack had meanwhile turned into a seal and was having trouble balancing a ball on his nose, while beside me the white horse that was clearly Lucas stood pawing and fretting, evidently irked by the tawdry plumage and spangles he had been got up in. The music as it grew louder had turned to brass, playing "Yessir That's My Baby" and then some clumsy rock-and-roll for the dance of the elephants wherever they were, or perhaps they weren't, anyway our director Miss Pryden, in high patent-leather boots and rhinestone bodice, seemed very angry with all of us. The light flew in daggers from the tiara in her unruly blond hair as she stamped and cracked her long whip at us one after the other. The others obeyed as best they could—the lion squashed his hindquarters into the armchair and pretended to snarl as she approached, the seal tried desperately to keep the ball rolling, but when she turned to me, whip raised and blue eyes ablaze, I couldn't remember what I was. I heard that high bright merry laugh, laugh, laugh over the clash of the band and felt the celestial stilettos in my skull, and would so willingly have done my act, to avoid the whip, but what, oh what was I supposed to do?

In my fear I tried everything, jumped, danced, begged, rolled over, even squawked like a chicken because I remembered a trained chicken that had amused her once at a country fair, but nothing was right and I couldn't even be sure that the others were pitying me. At last, beyond hope of pleasing her and acting only on the dictates of my misery, I threw myself to the floor and began trying to reassemble the hundreds of chips and pieces of the plaster head. Then the telephone rang.

Lucas answered and came back with the message, for Jack. Something had happened at the lab; he was needed, at once.

"Sanseverino?" He had gone grey.

"Yes." Lucas was keeping his face averted from him. "They say he must have taken something this afternoon. They've been looking all over for you."

Part Four

UNTIL DECEMBER 1929, when Tod was eleven, it was a fairly ordinary God-fearing, golf-playing prosperous family, only a little less scrupulous and more principled than most. They lacked nothing in the way of comfort and appearances; when they moved it was always upwards. Both parents were outstanding in their good looks, force of character and lack of love, and used the first two traits to conceal the third. Aside from this, and the monstrous ambition that had drawn them together in the first place, they had little in common. The mother was frigid, the father ruthless; they thought divorce would hurt them in their chosen and to themselves not nebulous calling, which was to be on the top, and gradually the bitter quarrels the children used to overhear at night subsided. The mother's club work became more prominent, the father's mistresses less. Rachel, Charlie and Tod, whose real name was David Lucius Hines, were sent to good schools, exhibited for company, and learned slowly that although unwanted they were necessary and therefore prized, like the peacock wallpaper in the guest bathroom. They were dimly aware of the grueling work and vigilance by both parents that kept the show going and the phone ringing, and were proud of it.

They also knew that their strict attendance at church had nothing to do with the basic ethic of the household, which was a simple and absolute intolerance of failure. A tramp at the door, a soprano beginning to lose her voice, the rumor of a businessman refused credit or a species of bird about to become extinct, anything on the skids would set the lights flashing; moral repugnance would abound, of different origin in the two parents. The father had never known failure; he had been well enough off to start with and had ruined several other men beginning with his own uncle before he was five years out of college, always by methods that left him blameless and only the victim contemptible. Society and luck had always been with him; the poor and powerless were his prey or they were nothing, and he would sometimes remind his beautiful wife that he had rescued her from that category. She knew it only too well but didn't need to be nervous; outside of business it was her tone that had made him. She visited her own parents and spoke of them as little as possible. Her father was a dreamer and cracker-barrel philosopher; everything he touched including the family hayfields turned to straw; the nearest to success he ever came was being defeated for the New Hampshire state legislature and he had managed to run even a little country store into bankruptcy. She grew up loathing the smell of chicken dung and dishwater and the sound of her mother giving piano lessons, knowing her beauty and determined to prosper at any cost. As it turned out the cost was not much. She violated nothing but her breeding, very briefly, and broke only her parents' hearts, by secretly entering a bathing-beauty contest in Miami, where she captivated the uncouth young industrialist D. C. Hines by her innate scorn, her love of money and her distaste for necking. They were married within a week and installed in a new house outside Chicago in another.

Of her family background in that time she merely told him that her parents would never consent to the marriage, allowing him dimly to imagine an elm-shaded street reeking with just the proprieties he craved. She saw no need to mention her brother, who nearly upset the applecart by blowing in a few times in later years, obviously hoping to borrow some money and enthralling the children with his tales of Alaska and the Wild West.

Her father was just weak and incompetent; Uncle Dan was a real bum. He had been a logger, a trapper, a rancher, had panned for gold, went around with a guitar and a copy of Homer in Greek, would tell bawdy stories in front of the wrong ladies and give up steady employment any day for the pleasure of hunting and fishing and living in some Godforsaken cabin by a mountain stream. He was as tall and handsome as his brother-in-law and a lot more charming, so the few brief visits he made were agony all around, except to Rachel and Tod—Charlie was born knowing which side his bread was buttered on and aped the family opprobrium. Engagements were broken, Mr. Hines being damned if he would bring his business friends around with that rotter in the house; the loan was refused even before he asked for it, that is his sister, whose poise nothing else could mar, would bark at some point, "I warn you, if you try to get a single dollar out of David for one of your crazy schemes . . ." and there were some ghastly incidents. Finally, arriving without notice in the middle of the night, unshaven and dirty from a fishing trip and accompanied by somebody who could not have been his wife since he had none, he was refused admittance for good. The children, in their night-clothes at the window above the porte-cochère, heard their father threatening to call out the dogs, and had one glimpse of Uncle Dan's hurt, incredulous face as he turned back to his waiting lady-friend in the beat-up car. He looked thin and worried, really on his uppers that time. "That'll teach him," said Charlie. "Hee hee."

Tod's big scene with his father was a little after that. That he was happy only when visiting his maternal grandparents had been plain for a long time, and also that of the three children he was the most suspect to both parents, but his hatred of his father was not yet explicit and he tried hard to please him: ridiculed the poorer boys at school, memorized stock-market quotations, called Jews kikes, was rude to the maids and bright for the guests, became a sub-junior or "pixie" star at tennis and baseball which he disliked. These efforts made the father's anger worse when the occasions for it arose, because the anger was chronic, always waiting to break out; the boy was not of his breed, he knew it and felt cheated and humiliated by it all the time. The worst of it was that Tod was popular, without even trying, as he himself had never been. The leather belt came out, over some minor incident, but this time Tod whirled on the word "liar" and not only gave his father a size-able shiner but spilled all the beans too, thereby convicting himself as an eavesdropper, which he naturally was; it was quite a dossier of frauds he managed to hurl out, with reference to sex, business, God and social life, before he was quelled and on his way to military school. After the hiding he crawled to his mother for comfort, for the last time, being then nine years old. She was dressing for a dinner of some importance to both herself and her husband, and although not altogether inhuman and for a moment tempted, she knew the stakes too well; in that one second, with her husband's dinner jacket in her mirror, she could have lost everything but alimony, so she made the sensible move, on the side of her interest and of peace. Such were the deep sacrifices she felt she was making for her children.

The house had a long paved terrace and a couple of acres of lakefront landscaping. That was where the auction was held. Nobody had much thought for the children that day so they hung around the edges and saw some of it in grim fascination, which hardly grew when their own toys and better clothes came up for bidding. Tod had been pulled out of military school only the week before; they hadn't been told where they would sleep that night, everything had happened so fast. Their father was ruined, whatever that meant, and the man he played golf with most often had shot himself, so had some other people they knew, but it was not nice of Rachel to say that they were all going to jail. They went to a couple of rooms with rats and no furniture and a toilet three stories down, and gradually furnished it with boxes and old broken things, and for a long time it seemed that nobody was allowed to talk at all any more, but except for being hungry and Charlie crying so much, Tod liked it. He liked public school and began getting good marks for the first time and he could play in the street and make friends as he liked just so he didn't bring them home, and he even brought in more groceries than his father did, by going over to the quarters where they used to live and doing chores for the people who still lived that way, or by playing the banjo in the shopping district. Only Rachel knew where he got the money. His parents didn't ask, and the mother didn't ask the father what all the hurry was to get out exactly on time every morning by the insurance-building clock they went by after he pawned his watch. Not pity, certainly not any belated inkling of love, but a furious rigidity kept her with him, in that nightmare version of what she had fled from in marrying him. Not a word of accusation or complaint fell from her; if they borrowed from former acquaintances it was only in the beginning; they knew the rules of the game they had played and abided by them now, like two angry ghosts, sharing their mattress and their torment, who had had separate bedrooms for years.

Irritability reigned, made sinister by hope; there was always a prospect, a contact in the offing, but family conversation for the most part consisted of "Don'ts" and "Stop its," "Can't you see," "Did you hear me," "How many times do I have to tell you . . ." or talk of diarrhea and scabs. The mother became obsessed with the children's diction, her correction of it carrying her only note of near-hysteria, and with ironing her husband's threadbare shirts, as if it had been done out of love, yet they were never unwrinkled enough to suit him. Somewhere he got money for stamps and in great secrecy mailed out two hundred copies of a job-hunting letter that Tod contrived to read, listing his university degree, corporation directorships, etc. Then in two or three weeks when the daily disaster of an empty mailbox had passed, but not the haste to get somewhere on time in the morning, Tod discovered how his father was spending those mornings. He found him on a park bench, with the stance and visage of an equestrian statue and a robin pecking for yarn through the hole in his shoe. He was around forty then, but his hair had gone suddenly white at the sides and to the boy he looked ancient and somewhat insane. When another of the unemployed joined him on the bench and tried to start a conversation he came to and rose at last, with the same disdain he had always shown in such company and had now for the hollow-faced men selling apples on street corners, and then Tod saw an extraordinary thing.

In the square at the edge of the park a tremendous soup line was forming, already of several hundred people and growing fast although the booth had not yet opened. He saw his father approach it like a sleepwalker, hesitate, go on again and at the last minute, on being hailed with a jeering "Hi, Mac," by one of his former office boys, wheel back to the park, emptied now in favor of the soup line. On the path in front of him a squirrel was squatted, cracking open a peanut. An expression of animal cunning came on Tod's father's face; he went slyly forward holding out his hand to the squirrel, in one lunge seized it by the tail and the next moment had swallowed the peanut and crushed the squirrel's skull against a tree. He wrapped the little corpse in some paper from a trash-can and with Tod racing behind him to keep him in sight, headed off to a dump under the elevated highway, where a colony of tin-can and packing-case shacks had grown up and there were always a few bonfires going. He was evidently known there. He pushed in around one of them, borrowed a knife and within twenty minutes had skinned, cooked and devoured the squirrel, with the loss of one piece handed over in silence to the owner of the knife.

Tod lay awake a long time that night, trying to think of some way to cheer his father up. The next morning he collected half a dozen of his new friends and led them to the park. They sneaked up around his father, then all at once leaped out and began dancing in a wild circle around the bench, yelling, "For he's a jolly good fellow." His memory of the big thrashing a few years earlier was mild compared to this. His father on this occasion was like a falling oak tree, a dam breaking in a flood, a mechanical monster turning on the humans who had created it. He picked up the trash-can by the bench and hurled it in the midst of the boys, and would have thrown the bench if it hadn't been chained; he picked up the nearest boy and tossed him in the brush; he sent them scuttling up into the trees and out over the fleet of peeling rowboats beside the dying casino, and locked the door against his son that night.

After that Tod stayed away many nights, often with a Negro orphan his age named Carl who played drums on old pots and kettles and slept in doorways, his aunt and uncle having gone off with a lot of other people to look for farm work in the west. The boys were both crazy about making things grow and had a secret vegetable garden in an abandoned lot, until the owner ran them out, and they formed a club with some other boys called the MHS for Mutual Help Society, to share whatever they had and fight together when necessary, but one of the boys died under a bridge one night and two others were jailed for stealing. Tod and Carl talked a lot about the pros and cons of stealing and on the whole were against it, which lost them the rest of their club members, but sometimes it was the only sensible thing and it was after they had taken some seeds from a grain store at dawn one day that Tod messed up his face, which hadn't been symmetrically handsome like his brother's to begin with. An alarm went off, a watchman with a gun appeared from nowhere and Tod slipped getting over the high fence topped with broken glass. They got away, and he didn't quite lose his left eye, but it left a bad twist over his cheekbone and into the hairline on that side. His father meanwhile was doing occasional errands, some involving women, for his former bootlegger, who had used to come to the back door and now made a point of keeping Mr. Hines waiting at his. Rachel was turning fourteen and told her brother about propositions she was getting from men in the street after school. She wasn't taking them yet but she knew plenty of girls who were and so were dressing and eating better, and she cried talking about it.

Heaven opened then. Uncle Dan, who had been making out just about as he always did, tracked them down somehow and with scarcely a word about it whisked the children off to their grandparents, who at least had a cow and a few pigs and chickens and their own house. For three years there they had the strange experience of being sung to and tucked into bed at night and funny stories at mealtime and people liking one another and haying and canning and a grandfather making paper boats, and a lot of the time Tod was off in the wilds, in Idaho and Oregon and even Alaska, with Uncle Dan, who figured he could teach him as much as the schools did and that the authorities were too harried just then to interfere. He taught him Greek and the Bible, not that he was religious but he had a trick memory and happened to know a lot of it by heart, and about animals, trees, rocks, stars and how to live off the woods which they did, selling a pelt now and then for cash. Charlie, who didn't go on those trips, never quite stopped boasting about the kind of house they would live in again when the depression was over, and it turned out that he was right. All of a sudden their father was running a string of companies again and it was as if nothing had ever changed, except that they were in Pittsburgh instead of Chicago and Tod was not made to go to military school any more.

Probably only D. C. Hines knew by what wild stroke of genius and daring it had been done. Whatever it was, even a series of crusading reporters in the New Deal years never quite managed to pin anything on him to the point of prosecution. It could only have been the tiniest steppingstone in the process that his wife, on her only visit to her home town in the three years the children were there, had persuaded her parents to mortgage their small house, to raise cash for a certain deal that was going to start him on the way up again; and perhaps by some mystery of finance, appearances to the contrary by then notwithstanding, he was really not able to prevent the foreclosure. Uncle Dan who was ignorant in such matters didn't think so and made a terrible scene about it, not knowing that his mother and father were performing a little miracle of their own and it was too late. They died only twenty-four hours apart, one of kidney trouble and one of heart failure, the week before their eviction.

Tod, or David Jr. as he was called then, ran away when the telegram came, in the first of many disappearances. He hitchhiked to somewhere on the Atlantic coast and then started walking but there was an eclipse of the moon. He was first in his class that year and captain of a baseball team.

It was as if nothing had changed because the changes were too deep; nobody had really forgotten. The queerest thing was that the mother had another baby, and while her feelings toward the older children had if anything shifted a little from indifference to hostility, with Judith the baby she was a caricature of her own mother, unquiet and voracious, cuddling and gooing all the time and leaping up at the slightest squawk. If in this bewitchment she bore witness to the murder of her parents, the fact was betrayed in no other department; she was a ranking beauty, hostess and member of committees as before. The father was away on business trips a great deal of the time, and beyond some novel and weird efforts at jollity when he was home and a certain fussy anxiety to be sure that everything there was of the best, especially the illumination in the house for which he called in a series of lighting engineers, he entered very little into the family life. For the older children, even Charlie, the secret strands of authority had snapped for good in the unmentionable period; to keep up appearances was all that could be expected. Nothing was said about David's absences or Rachel's affair with a middle-aged and married longshoreman. They came back to a hot bath, a good dinner, talk of sports, school, the club dance. In this darkness guilt grew like a huge poisonous mushroom and the boy could not stamp it out nor do anything without tasting it, if he had fled from pole to pole it would have spread before him. Most often he felt guilty toward his father, blaming himself for the terrible lack of communication between them, haunted by the image of that desperate courage and solitude in the time of ruin and his own joy in being taken away, yearning for the reprimand that would no longer come.

He went off and spent another summer with Uncle Dan and the taste of the mushroom was there too, as though the boy had connived in the death of his grandparents. Not that either of them believed this, but an area of silence lay between them that made their duets sound false so that they gave up playing after the first night. Also there was a note of bitterness, something almost crochety in Uncle Dan's speech now that embarrassed David. "I guess I'm not much good to anybody when you come right down to it," he would say; or, "Don't listen to me, I'm just an old daredevil that never made the grade"; and finally he said, "What you want to be skinning coons up in this nowhere for, boy? Better get yourself a respectable education while you can, it won't keep." Still worse for David, recently drawn to the Communist Party, was the recognition that his uncle, although by character the antithesis of his father, was equally reactionary and anti-Semitic. They were both relieved when David hoisted his pack and left, but looking back once up the trail he thought Uncle Dan, standing so tall and handsome and still young after all at the cabin door, looked a lot lonelier than his father ever had.

One incident preyed on David more than any of this. He thumbed a ride and camped out one night with a murderer named Russ Hansen. A real mean killer only once by his account and he got away from that one, but he'd done time for a lot of other things and had to bump off a couple of guys for the cash not long ago and now he had the big reward notice with front and profile pictures in his pocket. He took a shine to the boy, enough to ask a favor of him, only for some reason he couldn't stand the name David so called him Lou from his middle name. He was driving a stolen car and he kept a gun on his knee through that long night to keep Lou or David or Tod from going until he got the promise out of him—the promise to turn him in and take the reward, "and have your chance, see. I see your face back there and I says, 'Russ, he's come. You're in.' You took one hell of a time coming too; me holding out like a goddam jack-rabbit with this fucking pain eating my guts out only I had to find the right one first. Listen, kid, you can skip the crap—your real name and your old man and all; skip it. You got the look, that's all I care, and I know you got to get far off out from under to get where you going to go. And this'll get you going, see"— he tapped the notice with the two pictures of himself, as if it were a tablet from on high and they two with their sardine can and no fire were its priests—"so how about it?" He was small, ugly, frightening, with rotten teeth and a crooked evil smile and a glint of craziness. There was a terrible smell mostly not liquor on his breath. The boy kept his face averted, sitting miserably on the damp ground, reeling with sleepiness but starting at every rustle in the brush. He thought most likely the man was working up to killing him and just getting the comedy out of it first, the way he was leering and pleading at the same. "I've had it, see, a lot more'n I ever wanted. Far as I'm concerned they ought to flushed the sperm down the toilet with their other liquids. A hot crotch and a fit of the wiggles and I'm paying for it, fifty-two years. Why me? Why not one of them other fifty million globs of pus? Was Doctor God in there with a telescope saying, 'That one there, push *him* through'? I'm the doc now and I'm doing the flushing." The boy said, "Would you mind if I stood up to take a leak, Mr. Hansen?" and his benefactor said crossly, "Hurry up. I got this pain. And call me Russ." He was becoming more moody and fooling with the trigger; the boy saw he wouldn't make it away so sat down again. "I got this one little trick to play on Doctor God, and pay him back for all the laughs he's got out of watching me, and I don't mean leaving my eyeballs to science. I'm going to send a golden arrow out over all the yowling garbage of his stinking world and blow it up good in his face, and I'm not taking no chances on specks of jelly or some cute little dolly lama baby either, none of that fifty-fifty and maybe get another like me. Lou, my boy, or whatever the hell your name is, this golden arrow I got up my sleeve is you."

He got to his feet, and with a deep ceremonial bow, the leer going more misshapen from a burst of pain in his guts, handed David the notice. "Now play me some music on that thing and make it hot." It was a penny whistle that trip. David played everything he could think of, jazz, hymns, Bach; the convict was sprawled blissful and drowsy on the ground with his hands under his head, but every time the boy started to fall asleep the gun would move. After an hour he began fooling with his pants, then rolled over and pushed the whistle from the boy's mouth, but as soon as that was over he wanted music again. David played till dawn, then they both slept a little, and parted. Russ Hansen was going to stay right where he was and wait and he didn't want to wait long. David was to hide the car a few miles away in case some human garbage came along and got a crack at the thousand bucks that were to be feathers for the golden arrow. "Solong Lou," Russ said at the car window, "and thanks. I mean it." He leaned in and winked hideously. "Give the big toilet a smack for me when you think of it, God bless it."

A couple of weeks later David paid him a visit, his mother meanwhile having sent him to a doctor in the hope that what was making him look so peculiar was syphilis, which in some way she was planning to hold against her husband. He knew the visit was going to be nasty but he had to do it. The leer and the wild hungry light in the eyes was all gone and the eyes now across the bars were like nothing but excrement, not even human, more like two little pitter-patters of sheep dung. There had been a picture in the paper of the man who got the reward, an attendant in a drive-in movie,

and he had eyes like that too. "Never saw him before," was all
Russ Hansen would say. He was in a private hospital cell and they
were coming in and out with all sorts of medicines, treating him like
a king, because he would be going to the chair after a while if they
could keep him alive long enough. The orderly looked confused.
"What did you say your name was?" he asked, and the boy who had
given another name outside said for the first time, the foulness
suddenly again in his mouth and nostrils, the strange name, "Lou."
"Well, I guess he don't remember you, you'll have to go." What he
couldn't decide in the seconds that were left or the years after was
whether it would have been better or worse to tell Russ Hansen that
the money wouldn't have made any difference, and maybe if there
hadn't been any reward he would have done what he promised, only
that way there wouldn't have been any promise because the promise
was to let Russ Hansen think he'd done one grand and beautiful
thing in his life. Unless it had all been a crazy joke. Nevertheless in
the face of even that sheep-dung death he felt he should say "I'm
sorry," not for what he had failed to do but more sincerely for all
the sins and failures of the world, and tried to, and said instead,
vehemently, "I hate you." They held him a long time for questioning afterwards and got most of the story, but nothing about the
golden arrow or that horrible contact of flesh, or the faceless vision of
evil that would recur often later but had come for the first time that
night out on the damp ground. It identified itself in some way as
his father, in the guise of Russ Hansen, yet was neither of them,
being grey and soft as a slug, without features or any skeletal structure at all, and it attacked by a slow engulfing in the manner of the
mouth of an octopus.

Something about David in the next year made his father think
he might develop some ambition after all; he discussed business with
him the few times he was home for dinner without company, and
for Christmas gave him a gold watch, which went into the treasury
of the Young Communist League. A lot of other people tried to
exert influence on him in this period, because of what Russ Hansen
had recognized as "the look," in spite of the slight distortion of
face left from the accident and the nose being a shade too narrow
for conventional handsomeness. Aside from the sexpots male or
female, a lady librarian, a teacher, a preacher, a doctor, a lawyer and
some nondescript others wanted to push him toward high-sounding
careers of one sort or another. But the day he was to make the

valedictorian speech at school was one of the times David wasn't
there, and his sophomore year in college he got hold of a big overdose
of sleeping pills and came out of it only because his roommate,
Corey Leonard, barged in a day early from a weekend. However, he
got through the four years in three and part way through engineering
school, only by then he was working nights and summers, in jazz-
bands or janitoring or anything to be paying his own way, although
he put it to his father as mildly as possible, without exactly quarreling. Sally, the girl down the street whose father also ran a corporation but a small one without subsidiaries, had been in love with him
for a long time and when he knocked her up he married her and
for a year after the miscarriage played it all straight, working for an
oil company in Texas, joining the golf club, going to the parties. He
was the white-haired boy, whom the company was going to send
back the next year to finish engineering school on a salary. Sally
was sweet and loving and loved the life they were having, except for
losing the baby and except for the times when she said, "What is
it, Davie? Why can't you tell me? Why do you always think I
wouldn't understand?" and except for some of his friends. He found
in the city his old friend Carl, who had also in the meantime been
in and out of the YCL, and was now drumming in a dance band
to work his way through law school. They found the friendship as
good as when they were twelve, began making music together and
hit on the idea of setting up a little greenhouse for some experiments
that intrigued them both. Sally pointed out what would happen to
David's job in a town like that if they went around with Negroes.
For his birthday surprise she gave him a terribly expensive tent with
pop-up cots and the latest compact outdoor cooking equipment and
even a little collapsible toilet, so he could take her camping as soon
as he got his vacation, and she got out the maps and made circles
around camp-sites all over the place. She had taken a course or two
in psychology and was sure that if he had a nice relaxed couple of
weeks like that, just doing his favorite things, it would make them
have another baby. She explained it to him, and also told her
girlfriend about it on the phone, with a lot of talk about what to
wear camping so as not to look too absolutely dismal.

The war intervened. He was twenty-three and had his only row
with Sally over his refusal to apply for Officers' Training. She cried
all night, got a job in Washington and after a few months wanted
a divorce so she could marry somebody else, who turned out to be

Charlie. Rachel was married to a ranch-hand that year and their mother was in a psychiatric sanitarium. Judith, at eight years old the spit 'n' image of the mother, with the same high dignity of brow and waving chestnut hair, wrote politely from boarding school to thank David for the doll and candy he had sent.

He had his camping trip after all, on a four days' leave in the Tennessee mountains with Uncle Dan, who was in the merchant marine and had already had two ships sunk under him. They hadn't seen one another for several years. David was just back from the Pacific and neither of them was much of a letter-writer, but when the wire came, about the convoy being held up a week so he thought he'd look in on Private Hines at camp, David's heart lifted sky high. The taste of guilt was gone, and Uncle Dan, the same old Homer plus a couple of detective stories in his pockets and a new repertory of stories dirty and otherwise in his slightly grizzled head, was in the best form ever. The boys kept him singing ballads in the barracks half the night. He had long ago taken to calling his nephew Luke after his father, David's grandfather, whose name had been Lucius, and the name stuck in the army after that night. He was going into sheep-raising when it was over, he said later beside their campfire. "Might even raise a family too, if we make it in time. We're slow starters, our kind. I'll be forty-seven next month." He smiled and in his smile as at certain other moments in their four days, when he would be watching a fish jump or tracing the honk of a wild goose, Luke knew the extent of his uncle's triumph, over the stings of worldly failure and most of all over the rancor and self-deprecation that had eaten into his vitals like a pair of twin foxes in his pockets after his parents' deaths, when he had had no choice but to see himself as among the weak and ineffectual of the earth, unable in the last squeeze to lift a finger, that is, produce a mere couple of thousand in cash, to save those he loved from the cold mercies of his sister and brother-in-law. Somehow he had come past that bitterness, perhaps through the recognition that his mother and father had taken a risk that it suited them to take, and only laughed good-naturedly over the fact that David Hines Sr. was right then making his biggest pile yet in government contracts for Q-ships. "Just so they keep the stuff coming, that's all I ask." Within limits, he had never set himself up to judge people, and whether or not Luke's father was across the line, the nearest he ever came to overt criticism of him was in connection with politicians, when he remarked, "I guess your dad's bought and sold quite a few of those," but that too was said with no more than a wry humor.

It was the fall of '42. The weather held mild and mellow through the four days, amid dronings of planes and sporadic thuds of explosions from the camp seventy-five miles away. They fished lazily and brought down only what small game they needed for their meals. Now and then they squatted in front of their shelter of branches to draw military maps and diagrams with sticks on the ground. Uncle Dan, an old poker-player, had been reading up on the Civil War in recent years, was much engrossed in strategy and was as likely to draw Vicksburg as Corregidor on the forest floor. But this was in short spurts; the map would soon be obliterated and the talk veered quickly away from personalities of commanders and ways of dying. They were sick of all that and might have stayed off it altogether but for the Jews. Uncle Dan, who had used to say "Jew trick" and "dirty Jew" without batting an eye, said he was thinking of studying Hebrew and becoming one now, and at the most unlikely moments would break out goddamning the Germans in an awesome bellow, so out of keeping with the general charity of his nature it looked like clowning. It drove him wild when he was on the subject to be a mere man and not even a combatant at that. He would have liked to turn himself into an armored tank, a whole squadron of bombers, something more in scale with his anger. Then he would simmer down, and grin at himself, to resume after a while, "I'll admit I've never liked doing business with them, but God damn it, those people, hunted like rats . . . piled up in boxcars, the gas chambers . . ." and his powerful woodsman's fist would come crashing down on whatever was handy.

The innocence of his rage was remarkable to Luke, who hadn't felt like striking anything or anybody with his fist for a long time. In the last couple of years, from about the time of his marriage, he had reacted to outrages of all sorts, as to most of what passed for pleasures, only with varying degrees of an ache that was settled and chronic. Yet it was mainly the fate of the Jews that had kept him, after some struggle, from being a C.O., although his most dangerous temper to date had been directed against a Jew. He found himself able to tell his uncle about that now, with no need to slur over the ideological gap that was still between them but no longer divisive as it had once been.

That had been in the period, beginning soon after the Russ Hansen episode, when his absences from home had not been just for wandering. He had made friends with a Jewish organizer in one of his father's plants, born Kaminski but who went by the name of Bob Kay, a bright-witted, magnetic, hungry-looking man in his late twenties, of vast dedication and fair book-learning, whose schoolmasterish strictness was shot through with bursts of uproarious comedy. His mimicries of Hitler, Roosevelt and Neville Chamberlain put his fellow workers in stitches. David adored him and had his first big love affair with Kay's younger sister Rena, three years older than he and as hot in bed as about the Party. For the first time in his life, the sensual and the moral jibed, experience was subject to understandable order; the terrors, sympathies, hatreds and hopeless will to decency of the depression years had found a groove that gave them meaning at last. He spent a lot of time in Kay's shabby little apartment, picking up a modest education in Marxism and doing small jobs for the union. He did more during the big strike in '36, when the National Guard was called out and several workers were wounded, but he was under orders from his friend not to get himself recognized so had not been rounded up that time. He was in other unions and other strikes in his summer jobs, in other parts of the country, and before he was half way through college had his bellyful of dirty work by commies and others, beginning with Kay. He discovered him making a secret agreement with his father, David Hines Sr.—one of the episodes the New Deal-minded reporters went to work on, since another union leader David had known well, an old anarchist named Riesman, also Jewish, was bumped off in the street by two gunmen that same week. Nothing was ever proved. Kay moved to a pleasant house in a suburb and when David finally sought him out there, in search of some straw for his loyalty even if it should be only a doubt, was a portly and affable liar, thirty pounds heavier and with the assurance of power visibly around him like armor, or the state of grace. Rena had thrown David over some time since for a Party functionary who took her along with him to the Spanish Civil War.

Kay's handshake was iron, his smile benign. He displayed the most ebullient pleasure in seeing his young friend again, was brimming over with modest pride in the closed shop and other victories achieved by the union, and darkened only at mention of the Riesman affair. It was terrible, he agreed, and those FBI bastards sitting on their hands but they wouldn't get away with it, his people were doing some investigating of their own as he had promised in his speech at the funeral. Incidentally membership had risen sixty percent the week after the funeral, people were that stirred up; it had been one great fist over the street at the close of his speech, a sight he would never forget. Then something in the young man's face caused a sea-change behind his glasses and with no pause whatever he was going on, "And I warn you, Hines, there's some goods I don't want to spill if I don't have to, but don't think I can't. We knew from the start you were spying for your old man, it served our purpose to let you hang around, but I'm giving you fair warning now . . ."

The young man hadn't yet looked far into the nature of his own anger, and still hadn't when he was mentioning these matters years later to his uncle beside the fire and the brook in Tennessee. He would be dropped twice more behind enemy lines and be stranded above the Arctic Circle with the one other survivor of his plane before he came to that, so all he said was that he had given his old friend and mentor a terrific wallop and gone off really not caring if he had left him dead. It turned out he hadn't quite, and Kay had chosen not to prefer charges. That was the second time David had felt the mouth of the octopus.

Uncle Dan nodded; he had had to deal with a few sons of bitches that way himself and was lucky he hadn't had his gun handy once or twice. What he'd like now was to get his hands on some of those Goerings and Goebbelses . . . On the whole Uncle Dan took a very favorable view of the human race, that is he had found people a lot more decent than otherwise, that was one thing. Another was that he was just about tops as a rifleman. An old woodsman he had known in his youth in New Hampshire had said to him, "You can't do everything in life, you've got to choose what you want to be good at—rifle or shotgun. You can't fool around with 'em both and be *really* good," and he had chosen the rifle and never regretted it. It was his third hand and eye; with it he had stood off beasts in the dark, and the comforts of religion, and provided through the years a great deal of his own food. He was sure of his aim and of what he wanted to aim at, and expected the same principle, or feel of the thing, to apply elsewhere. That marksmanship would not save the Jews, or that any particular Jew might be a son of a bitch, didn't prevent his drinking his evening bourbon from the bottle or tin cup with the same relish and moderation as before, saying merely, God damn it, there were some things a man couldn't stand for.

This old-fashioned simplicity of his uncle's nature was so unfathomably complex, compared to anything Luke had known in himself or his own generation, it made him feel old and at the same time young to the point of capers and handsprings on that trip, in which condition he found he was not missing Sally any more, also that he was resuming an effort he had dropped for a while earlier. It was something like a search for cleanliness. ". . . and then that year in Texas I guess I figured I'd just swim along with the stink, it wouldn't be my business . . ." He had never fully taken in until then Uncle Dan's powers as a listener. A strange gift, as far outside ordinary categories as the smell and taste of evil. It wasn't in his nature to meddle or advise; he was nothing like those listeners hungry only for tales of trouble, waiting to break in with the first-aid kit or their own stories. A large calm of natural-born generosity seemed to emanate from him at those times, of which one effect was on physical environment. The unique selfhood of things, the bark of a tree, texture of rock or soil, distinct ripples in the stream, the exact character of breeze or bird-call, became unnaturally vivid and separate in his presence even when he was paying them no mind; in fact it was often when he was exercising one of his innumerable physical skills, lifting his rifle, cleaning a fish, skinning a rabbit, pronging a rattlesnake—all his system was honed to a split-second speed and accuracy in such doings—that the power seemed most intense. No doubt that had been the basic trouble in the Hines household long ago; people too had a way of showing through their protective coverings around him. Luke felt he was breathing fresh air for the first time in several years.

They talked about women, the heads of some and the bodies of others and a few whole ones, Uncle Dan having one such in mind, "a good sport, straight as they come," to share his future as a sheep-raiser; and about Luke's tussle with himself over the army, and an earlier one when he had had the crazy idea of switching to divinity school—"and ended up that night in a whorehouse." He had suffered from a sense of spookiness all through his year in engineering school, and nearly left several other times for nothing, just to be shet of it and feel he existed again; none of which surprised or dismayed his uncle at all, although a man might as well hang for a thief as a clergyman in his opinion and he was naturally reminded of one of his yarns about the brethren, begging Luke's pardon. "And what has the good Lord done for you?" the preacher asked the last one in the tent, when the rest had all testified to the blessings received from the Almighty. This last one, who was blind in one eye, rose on his peg-leg and croaked through his harelip, "He ham near hur-recked *me.*" Luke began whistling, then they sang a few bars of "Rock of Ages" in harmony and recited a few verses of Ecclesiastes, and went back to whiskey and talk, laughing a little over this and that and broiling their trout, while the sky slid over into night and the stream made itself close by their elbows, each sound of it clear and messageless and of infinite significance. Luke even told about the incident of the sleeping pills, which hadn't just been due to particular kicks in the guts, political or sexual. There had been no one reason, but there was one word for it, which he found easy to say now—pointlessness. Corey Leonard never understood that, being more the adventurer stripe, and never joined much in the conversations Luke had had sometimes with other friends in college or out, about how not to spend your life sitting on your ass at a desk. Forestry tempted him most, but human faces always got in the way; perhaps if he hadn't seen so many in the depression . . . However, the best feeling and the best times were always with Corey, especially the year he and Rachel nearly got married, until with no explanation to either of them she walked out on him.

"I've had a good life," Uncle Dan said on their last evening—his first and only indulgence in that vein. "I've done a lot of the things I wanted to do. It hasn't all been foolishness." He meant that he had helped to get a little ore out of the ground and a few trees turned into pulp, had fought some forest fires, saved some people in a flood and once, what he was proudest of, had built singlehanded a good solid bridge that was still in use. Nothing else to speak of. "And when this is over . . ."

He would have been pleased to have for his epitaph what was in fact said afterwards in many places: *He was good company*—sometimes with the addition of "I wonder whatever became of him," because with all his drifting not many people had ever kept track of him for long. Often in later years, startled to recollection by some footfall or creak of branches, Luke would think, and for how many others did he move mountains too, who have to rack their brains for his name now? Then often he would see the blue heron, and his uncle's face as he watched it. It came over just at dusk, as though heavy laden, and so close over their heads they could almost have grabbed at it. They had their backs turned that way so were only aware of the great shape when it was nearly on top of them, and before it was ten feet past Uncle Dan had had time to flick his rifle up, as for any untoward apparition in the woods, and lay it down again. The heron continued unalarmed across the brook, sinking even further but with its foolish mortal-looking legs tucked back, then just when all power seemed off, veered up in a steep and stately surge to perch on the tip of a dead oak. A minute's rest, a small sacrifice of dignity, before the huge wings were in stride again and it was off over the woods as slowly as it had come, as though danger and sudden death had never been in the world. Uncle Dan didn't break his stillness with so much as a shift of expression until it was out of sight. "Well, he was a big fellow, wasn't he? biggest I've ever seen, I think. Getting ready to winter; must be a lake up over the notch there somewhere . . ." No tall thoughts; he was just engrossed in the actual bird. For several minutes his rough big-boned face was whetted with the pleasure of having seen it so close, and Luke watching him felt waves of fortitude—could you call it wisdom?—washing out from that pleasure, such as he had felt from no other presence in his life.

Corey Leonard was pulling wires all over the place to get him into his company but it worked out only a year later and then by accident, at a base in Africa, after Luke had been through another hitch in the Pacific and the episode in the Arctic. He heard with some months' delay of Uncle Dan's being lost with everyone else on his ship, not through enemy action, a week after they parted. He was on the second of several Q-ships that broke in two in bad weather.

Luke didn't do anything outrageously brave in the Pacific, didn't brood much, played a lot of jazz and picked up a girl now and then between rounds, did a good deal of reading of whatever books came to hand. He was popular and seemed so well balanced he was chosen for some of the nastiest jobs, but the worst trouble he had wasn't with the enemy but a poor bastard in his own detail, named Jacob Horn. Perhaps this guy wasn't a psycho exactly, anyway he was too good a fighter to dispense with, but nothing had ever been right for him; for one thing he was dirt poor and probably always would be except in the army, being too eaten up with angers to last long at anything in civilian life. Luke, fair-haired and handsome, life's darling to all appearances, with the glow of dawn and the aura of luck oddly recaptured and his own angers very much under wraps at that time, was *it* at first sight—the other, nearer enemy. Jacob needled him on all occasions, innocently sometimes, with a "Pardon my yacht" or "Ask Clark Gable," sometimes with more sinister insinuations; contrived a series of petty accidents against him and one or two potentially not so harmless; alternately strutted and sulked in his presence, took offense at anything, stood in his way even in combat and withal made some sorry plays for his friendship, having no other friends in the unit: it would be they two against the others, the two superior ones. But this shortly would slide over into a threat. "I can take it from them, they don't know any better, but you're different, and I'm warning you I'm not taking any of that stuff from a man like you that knows better . . ." Once in this vein he spoke the word murder.

Luke had had a little underdog trouble of the kind once or twice before and had learned that any response to the friendship line would foul things up worse. Although sorry for Jacob Horn, he played it coolly enough, suppressing his annoyance at having a board dropped on his head or being tripped at the edge of a swamp in full gear, and joining gladly in the accolades that came to Jacob, disliked though he was, for his prowess with his jungle knife and the bazooka. There was no grudging him that; he was one of the best, they all had reason to be grateful to him; besides he had been passed by the psychiatrists, nobody believed he would go so far. He was no crazier than many about getting in that extra whack at a prisoner, not that they were taking many. Luke kept his distance and his temper but it got harder to do. In his dreams he began seeing Jacob Horn coming at him in Jap uniform and shrunk to Jap size, and each time instead of going for him he was overpowered by a feeling of guilt toward him, and would go toward him humbly trying to explain and exculpate himself; once he got on all fours before him and tried to lick the hand which was in the very act of slitting his throat. These dreams had a muddling effect in waking hours, more so as the battalion had heavy losses and those who were left could hardly distinguish any more between sleep and waking, and in that condition, instead of the leave they were expecting, were flown off for a drop on another island. There had been a hitch of some kind about the replacements, one of those accidents that inspired various infantile jokes among Luke's friends, as over a huge pair of dismembered frog's legs sending out the orders from the Pentagon, etc.

So it came about that he himself made his worst dreams come true, or helped in it anyway. That day after the drop, coming on Jacob maniacally at it again with a prisoner, Luke knocked him off and shot the victim. It didn't come that night, nor the next. The real antagonist was close and silent as air; men were found knifed in their hammocks on several mornings, but when Luke's turn came and he sprang yelling from his brief doze that was only like a further degree of fever, he knew it was not that enemy, although Jacob had taken the trouble to put on a camouflage outfit and smear his face with grass. Or perhaps, which would also have been like him, he had been out repaying the Japs' visits and this other act was an afterthought. "You!" Luke whispered, but did not join with the others in shooting after the shadow in the dark, nor did he ever speak of the incident, knowing that Jacob would be on model behavior for a while and they couldn't afford to lose him. In fact he himself, with three others, owed him their lives not long after. Then came the occasion when he was to whisper "You!" again, with somewhat the same insane hilarity he had felt the first time. He could have bellowed like a bull if he had had the strength and nobody would have heard; the others must have been flung here and there over the ice fields; there was no sound or sight of them. It had been strange enough to discover in the hour of boarding that Jacob Horn was to be on the plane, since what was left of the platoon had long since been split up.

He lost consciousness again right away, and came to later with a start, to find he had no weapons and could move neither arms nor legs. He saw a glint of something in Jacob's hand and now he dreamed he was the Jap boy and the jungle was burning around them. It was only ice on Jacob's glove, in the light of a flare that had come down with the tail section nearby. Jacob couldn't walk either. On his hands and knees, during what seemed hours and perhaps was, he hauled Luke over to the wreckage and covered them with a tarp he had salvaged. Eventually, after more faintings and wakings, it was Luke who wormed out into the vile wind, over peaks and gullies of ice, to look for rations in the stuff littered around. He found some, also a foot and a head. He and Jacob slept in each other's arms and now and then in the intervals of pain were able to talk a little. There was still not much liking between them; they were merely bound by necessity, like brothers Luke thought wryly, and wondered if he had ever felt anything this close to love for his brother Charlie, and whether it would be better or worse to die with a dog for company. A dog if he had loved him would not eat him afterwards; it was hard to see what the human value was. Nevertheless he was perplexed, if not touched, to learn that Jacob who was not yet twenty-one was married and had two children. They figured very little in his mumbled attempts to make sense of his life, which in that extremity he viewed with neither complaint nor apology. "Sure I wanted to kill you, you'd insulted me . . ." "Never saw my father. My mother's a bitch and I married another." "You might think I don't like being the way I am. I like it all right. I've seen a lot worse." He was absolutely without patriotism, and uncrackable in his loyalty, even now in his spells of delirium; he had been one of the few back there on the islands who had never beefed about the fact of the war or the way it was run, that is beyond the lower echelons—he was always in hot water with any immediate superior; had nearly brained a couple of men once for making cracks about a visiting general; and now with his feet broken and frozen and coma near, in a last heroic exercise came close again to murdering Luke, in support of whatever principle it was that upheld him. They had been sharing the last cigarette until the thought struck him. He had been mumbling about some guys wanting it soft all the time, chickened out when it got rough, as if that changed anything; it was just the breaks, he could take it, if you got yours you got it and what the hell. "Can it," Luke said, "I want to sleep," and so nearly got his. "So you don't like it, I always said you were a commie or something . . . I heard you one night, you and your wisecracks and your nigger friends. You say you're for it or I'll . . ." "God Bless America," Luke said, "and get the hell off me." "I didn't say that, trying to make a monkey of me again, I don't give a fucking damn about America or South America either but we're in this thing . . ." "God bless this thing then," Luke groaned, shaking with laughter that didn't show and must have sounded like a death-rattle, then the wind ripped their tarp away and the next thing he heard himself saying was "Mother, Mother . . ." He had imagined her young, heart-wounded, loving, trying to shield him from cold as they escaped from something in a storm, on a beach; the loss of that love when he woke made him howl like a wolf.

Jacob got religion suddenly at the end. He didn't have much

vocabulary for it, just a smattering from way back, so he went on about forgiveness and sins and God's big warm hand that was going to pick him up and take him to the beautiful light. Luke didn't notice when Jacob died. Such loneliness overcame him when he discovered it, he felt himself spinning among the steely stars, lost to earth or any desire for it, in a universe that knew one word and was made of the word—*pain.*

The next words he heard were French. Father Bérard, who had seen the plane come down and spent two days looking for it, could speak to the Eskimos but knew only a little English. He cared for Luke for several weeks in the ice cellar where he had lived for seventeen years, and with the help of two Eskimos accompanied him two hundred miles by dogsled to the trading post. He worked for him in another way before that. For a long time Luke wouldn't speak. It wasn't the language; Luke knew some high school French and besides there was an Eskimo girl who could interpret after a fashion. It wasn't that he wanted to die either, but even yes and no had become senseless to him. He was aware of the priest moving gently about, a tall wraith, so emaciated he seemed made of the same stuff as his house, but strong, with a great scimitar of a nose and grey eyes neither particularly large nor deep-set but of extraordinary illumination and intelligence. For himself Father Bérard had no physical comforts and no longer wanted any, and his guest was aware of the efforts he made to provide him with a sealskin robe, fire, even brandy and cigarettes. He had set the broken bones, bound the head wound, and when Luke was out of danger confessed to him with his gentle smile, touched with the same delicate radiance that was about him in his devotions before the crucifix, that he had taken a big gamble in not amputating Luke's right hand. Still Luke turned away, and only much later forced himself at last, reluctantly and as though breaking a huge casing of ice around his chest and throat, to say "Merci."

They talked a great deal before it was over, only not about the girl, Booka. Father Bérard merely said in the beginning that his work took him to settlements quite far away and she was a good nurse; the rest he regarded or disregarded with an aristocratic tact, suggesting rigors and tolerances new in Luke's experience. So between the two of them he returned, more than to life, to a joy that almost seemed in both its contradictory parts, the sexual and the ascetic, beyond life. Outside of prayer, Father Bérard's life was all work. The school he had founded was taught entirely by himself; the second room of his cellar was the infirmary, the only one in a hundred-mile radius; he visited the sick and dying and drunk, said Mass, heard bizarre confessions. He could do it because he had trained himself to need very little sleep, and had no idea of strain; he made the word unnatural. So for a little while in the evening they conversed or played chess or listened to war news, after Luke had repaired the radio, like two men in the course of the most ordinary existence somewhere, and Luke could refrain from touching bottom or going under in his thoughts. His admiration of the Frenchman and doubt of himself stayed equally in the position of an atmosphere, something to be examined eventually but not yet, so he was very much off guard when Father Bérard asked casually one evening about the fight with his companion in the wreck, "the dead one."

What fight? He didn't understand. The priest took from a shelf of his cabinet the paratrooper's knife that he had removed from Jacob's body, more precisely from Jacob's back. "But it's impossible," Luke said. "There were only the two of us there." He hesitated. "I don't remember very well. There wasn't anybody else, was there?"

Father Bérard didn't even shake his head but just looked at him with such a tenderness of pity, it seemed to Luke that if his mother had ever looked at him like that even for a second none of this would ever have happened, there would have been no Russ Hansen, and even no war in the world. But as for what they were talking about, all he could remember was the terrible loneliness among the stars when he had found that Jacob was dead.

He talked a little more about it later to Corey Leonard, the last time standing on a cliff over the Mediterranean, when Corey said he was sending Luke back to Rome on sick leave. "There's something wrong with you, you need a rest. This fool diving every day; all these crippled children; I've got feelings too but it's getting the boys down . . . Just because your old man dropped dead." Luke kept his eyes on the blues of the sea far below, nearly black beneath them where he had just taken his daily dive, fading to turquoise and palest new-leaf green by the little beach. The outerworks of the old fortress they were occupying thrust down in a lovely geometry beyond the moat on that side; around to their left toward the harbor, out of sight, another great wall went down to embrace the village, mostly rubble now from the bombings that had preceded them. Freakishly the fortress itself, built in the sixteenth century, had escaped, and considering what a military anachronism it was, remained unaccountably grand, as well as beautiful. "You've got a guilt thing. You didn't kill him." "I did in my mind plenty of times." "Christ, if we were going to be convicted for our minds . . ." Corey laughed; so far, unless you looked close, the war hadn't seemed to dent his health and rowdy collegiate humor. "I killed him. I put a knife in his back." "Oh no not that one again!" He said what he had said before: self-defense; Luke hadn't even been conscious; everything indicated that Jacob must have gone for him one last time before he died . . . And secondly, what did it have to do with Luke's father who had come out fine from the Q-ship investigation, dedicated patriot, father with two sons in the service etc. and just happened to have a heart attack later. Corey changed the subject. "What a place! Wouldn't it be great to come back some time and just be here? Not alone, though." He made a sad face. "You may be right about her and me but she sure has a funny way of showing it." Rachel, working in a munitions plant and living with some guy, still wrote him now and then, and Luke was sure he was right, that she had never been out of love with Corey, and thought he understood now what had made her run away from him.

What he couldn't understand and wasn't trying to, looking down from that terrific height, was his own compulsion to strip down to his undershorts and run hell-for-leather over the edge every morning, to the point half way down where the pitch turned to sheer drop, and dive, from a lot higher than made sense for anybody outside the circus. He had never gone out to be a champion diver or swimmer either and didn't know by what luck he had gone on making it alive for several days in a row now. Then he came up by the same route, "like a crab" the people of the village said incredulously, having drifted back to their ruined houses or some of them now that the Allies were there instead of doing the bombing and the only German supply boats in the harbor were the ones on the bottom of it. So after the first day or two they heard about the crazy young American soldier who dived there where none of the invading armies throughout the history of the fortress had ever dreamed of trying to get up, and a few had sneaked around on the landward side to watch. Luke hated that, so went earlier hoping not to be seen and wished not to have to do it at all but he couldn't help it. The water was so clear, from the surface you could see the corpse, perhaps an Italian soldier or airman, wedged in the rocks forty feet down. He had not known before there could be such light or such color in the sea, and somehow the beach didn't tempt him but only that point under the rock wall where the blue was absolute and it was like going head first from the top of the Empire State Building, yet without there being in his sensation any recognizable death-wish. In so far as he could tell, he seemed rather to be hurling himself into life every time, which in another tempo was also what made him spend so much time with the children there. They would bring him presents, of crabs and wild flowers and bits of ancient pottery, and once for a joke one of them brought a little live octopus that was clamped like a jellied jewel around the stump of his right forearm.

Yes, Corey was partly right. Luke was losing his bearings; he had lost his taste for liquor in company, and for whipping up the kind of gay, gregarious evenings he used to be so good at. He was low in his mind; sometimes he envied the chaplain, or anybody with a regular religion. As for his father, that was true too though not quite as Corey saw it. What gnawed and burned at him, and flickered before his eyes like the pair of vipers the children had pointed out to him in one of the original underground arsenals of the fortress, was again dreams, never quite dispelled in daytime, only now they were of his father disguised in various enemy uniforms. Uncle Dan figured too, a sad ghostly figure unable to cross some invisible barrier, who kept pointing down to where Luke would see the other part of him, his body, wedged between rocks at the bottom of the sea. There was no accusation in this, but Luke knew it had been his fault, he had been a coward, so over and over in a mighty rage he strode through the hundreds of electric-light bulbs thrown up as a defense by the enemy, but the figure turned to a smothering jelly as his knife touched it, and to the sound of his father's dinner-table laughter he was himself absorbed into the soft hideous aperture. Sometimes his father's features slid over into Hitler's or those of the company psychiatrist, saying, "We are born of dirt, and to dirt we return. Follow me. Success is all." In daylight Luke was reasonably certain that if he had indeed knifed Jacob Horn it must have been when Jacob was already dead, but still now and then he would catch himself murmuring to a man only glazed by death, not quite gone, "I hate you!" and a stink of putrid flesh would seem to spurt from his own pores. It was only in the few seconds between the cliff and the sea that he felt clean.

Nevertheless he said to his old friend, whom it was rather funny to have as a commanding officer when the relation had tended to be the other way around in college, "Give me another chance. I'll be okay." The chance came that week, a hundred miles north of there, and Luke was a lot more than okay, until the whole hill went sky high.

"Where in hell are we?" he heard himself slowly muttering, because he had just imagined he heard English spoken. He was right. There was an American quite near him, who said in an Alabama accent, "You got the general location right." Luke was seized with joy at the sound, until he discovered he could neither move nor see; he seemed to be tied down and some kind of immense weight was on his head, although his lips had moved and he felt air at his mouth and right ear. He heard voices speaking some other language behind doors quite far away, and groans and breathing all around nearby. "Two weeks I been waiting for you to wake up. Got lonesome, listening to you." Luke asked after a while, "Can you see? Where's my face?" A kind of croak, of humor evidently, came from his neighbor. "You got one all right. Maybe not the one you're used to, but you didn't have much of that when you come in. My name's Pete Jenkins. Don't you want to know where you are?" "No." Pete told him eventually, as much as he knew; he had learned quite a lot of German in his long time as a plain P.O.W. before losing both feet in his last attempt to escape. As best he could figure, they were somewhere on the Rumanian border, not that it mattered. Things were cracking up and now nobody had brought food or water for a day and a half. "I wonder if I'm blind," Luke said. He didn't really care about that either, and Pete said he didn't know and then told him a funny thing about how they happened to have gone to the trouble to fix his face. It had been a big drunken medical joke, nothing else. It seemed the doctor, once a well-known plastic surgeon, had been demoted as a lush, all the way down to the lowest camp job, and had done that particular operation on a bet. Whether the patient lived didn't figure, but an old woman who did chores there had bandaged the head afterwards, with some help from other prisoners, because he reminded her of her dead son. "He was so beautiful. Like a young god . . ."

Pete was Luke's age, blond like him and about the same build, he said; was alone in the world, with no parents, sisters, brothers, anything; had a single dream—to spend the rest of his life in the U.S.S.R., "where they give you something to live for. Am I right? They make good artificial limbs there too, I heard about it. I wouldn't mind so much about the feet, if I was just in Russia . . ." And on and on, while Luke dozed and woke and wondered how long it took to go insane from thirst. Pete, who had been trying to make it to the Russian lines when the gangrene set in, kept working to make him say he would go with him when the time came, if it came; if they got liberated in time it was bound to be by the Russians and if the two of them stuck together, one with feet and one with eyes, they could get lost and end up there, in the promised land. It was like Jacob Horn's babble of God at the end, different words but the same paucity of vocabulary, stacking up to the same image. The big warm welcoming hand, the final comfort, *the answer*.

Pete undid the rags holding Luke down; he and a man on the other side had tied him earlier, because of his violence; so he could reach out to the face scorched with fever and left his hand a while on the emaciated arm, until the image of himself in battle returned, worse than thirst, to curse even that human contact. Over and over he was rushing up the hill with his grenades to the pillbox and the other one after that; there had been no stopping him; he had been the resurrection of Jacob Horn, a maniac, leaving out the torture bit which there was no time for anyway, but he could have gone on all night and over and over a pair of young blue eyes implored him from a bed of rosemary outside the pillbox. The thirst became a comfort, being merely physical, and under that distraction the little fantasy of long ago, of the frogs' legs commanding the war, expanded hugely and lost its childishness. There was still a Pentagon of sorts but transcending Washington as it did all space and all time, and the orders that went forth from the brainless reflexes housed in it made Hitler and Genghis Khan and Russ Hansen and David Hines Sr. and Jr. and the solar system into the least of the flyspecks in a whirligig there was nobody to appreciate.

Pete had begun moaning a little. Luke reached out to him again and this time left his hand there, overcome in spite of everything by a senseless impulse of friendship for this man he had never seen, who resembled him and was not going to make it, to see his dream come untrue. "Pete?" "Uh." "Do me a favor. You won't want your I.D. in Russia, like you said. Let me have it, will you?"

That night in the raid the staff, such as it was, disappeared. A Russian patrol found them the next day and Pete Jenkins was one of those who hadn't made it, but then there was nobody to care if he had or not.

Lucas, as he called himself now, had been making his way across the country from one bottle to another for about a month when he went into the bar in Indianapolis. He wasn't the only drunk around; aside from the usual, people were still celebrating the end of the war. He went into the darkest booth, from which, not being completely overboard, he could watch his sister Rachel waiting on the customers and now and then taking motherly measures about a child or two who wandered in from the back room. She hadn't lost her looks, although there was a sadness in her eyes and she sounded tired. The tall middle-aged man behind the bar was evidently the proprietor and her husband or the equivalent. She didn't notice Lucas until he started laughing. He was laughing about all the money that in spite of post-mortem litigation their father appeared to have left to Charlie; he had happened to see something about it in the paper, with no mention of other progeny except another hero son who was missing and presumed killed in action. She came and took his order, and when she brought the drink paused to say, "Feeling low, aren't you? And this isn't going to help either." He turned his face up to her slowly, she looked into it and smiled, also without hurry and as though tempted to linger, and later he heard her murmuring to an old man at the other end of the bar, ". . . that one down there in the corner. We've been getting a lot of them in here like that. I feel so sorry for them . . . He kind of reminds me of my brother, that we got the medal for."

Part Five

Part Five

I

BETWEEN THE TOWN MEETING, at which Lucas made a speech, and the big Labor Day affair when we were all on TV, the news came that Horace Beardsley had been killed in Korea. Alice Beardsley had been brought home and most people didn't know yet that she was dying of leukemia.

Myra Wienowski, fifteen, was pregnant. Mrs. Hollister was getting drunk more and more publicly. Work on the dam below the falls was starting. John Purser was so sore at Hester and her vegetable stand being on the TV show, he went home and set fire to his own barn. The famous Dr. Pryden was really famous all of a sudden and was off at a conference in Japan. The New Town Plan had some opponents but not many, anyway it had been adopted and Baldur's old house sheltered relays of architects. The goldenrod was in bloom.

Asked under the cameras for her opinion of all the grand new developments Beulah Wellman, with new teeth and hair ash blond, said the last opinion she'd had was a caesarian. That was for all the nation to hear—oh yes it was to be nation-wide, Jarvis had seen to that—and not another word would she utter.

Practically everybody thought it was the Minks, some said put up to it by Fred Leighton, who unearthed a lot of anatomical parts of Baldur Blake's old buried statues one night and stuck them with obscene messages in people's mailboxes. Then there was talk here and there of Baldur being a Communist and Fred Leighton having possession of a letter proving it, and other talk connecting him with the Wienowski scandal, not quite making him out the father when everybody knew that was the Seeley boy "but it's the influence, he has some kind of *hold* on these kids, he gives them filthy pictures and now look," as if Myra's mother then also fifteen hadn't produced her under the same conditions.

Baldur didn't mind. He was a whirlwind in those days, so was Lucas, so was everything around us, as though after holding out a few months against the fantastic Jarvis energy we had all suddenly been infected by it till we hardly knew our names any more; or rather as if even he, Chuck Jarvis, were not so much a person as a projectile of some sort shot in among us by much greater powers somewhere far away.

But he was very much a person as now, haggard, nearly un-recognizable from strain and sleeplessness, standing on the elegant hilltop terrace that I hadn't seen since it stopped being a barnyard and that had perhaps already been claimed by his creditors, he made his desperate announcement. "I wanted to be the one to tell you myself, Eva. You know why." Washed up; overextended; other such words; the Jordan project blown sky high. Apparently he had be-lieved until ten o'clock the evening before that he was going to bring off another of his famous manipulations. Now he was on his way to Canada. Oh, nothing criminal, and he'd work out of it all right, only it would be on the air and in the papers by noon and he'd rather be somewhere else.

"Does Baldur know?" That seemed, at the moment, the only part of it that mattered. Yes, Jarvis had gone across the fields to the studio first thing, before phoning me, asking me to meet him at his house right away. "And how did he take it?"

"The way I knew he would. He's not like the rest of us. Seemed mainly worried about me. I even got a feeling . . ." He searched my face, exposing for a second the full shattering novelty of his defeat. "He never said he was expecting anything like this, did he?"

There had been signs, I could see now, something ominous under the golden light of those busy afternoons, of our euphoria; under the prevailing sense of a grand and valuable activity such as Jordan had never been stirred by before in my lifetime, a sense of crack-up, even in objects. I can't have been imagining it all. One night when we were sitting at dinner as usual in the kitchen Lucas suddenly snapped at Dickie, "Stop jiggling! you're nearly making the cups fall off the rack!" I said, "He's nowhere near the rack, what's wrong with you?" and the next day when nobody was in there at all one of the cups fell off. Beulah, who followed current events on TV, said it was the Bomb, and if it could do that to a cup just think what it must be doing to our heads. "I sometimes wonder if I'm batty myself." "But Beulah," I said, "you always did. You've been saying that ever since I can remember." "Well," she said, looking quite pleased about it, "I've got more reason now."

But no, Baldur had never voiced a doubt of his friend's solvency, still less probity.

"There *is* no far-away any more," he had been saying a few evenings before. "That's the other thing we have to try to say with these hills, thcse houses. That and the other thing, not to be chucking out the past. Oh Lord we need it!"—going off on that again, his Memory theme, almost shouting, not at anybody in particular, he was just mulling as he did in chance minutes between seeing congressmen and magazine reporters and engineers and the rest, picking up each time with the same singleness and consistency as if it were a whole different set of brains in his head that dealt with the practicalities and interruptions. "How can our past live in us if we're not living in it? And if we don't . . . But it's happening now. When sick sick is everybody's joke, kill kill can't be far behind. IQ and know-how going up all the time while we turn into a nation of nuts—killers, more and more of them. For lack of a home." The word stopped him momentarily, while his doodling pencil picked up intensity—a thought for his town gate most likely; he still wasn't satisfied with his various models for that. "Funny word, come to think of it. *Home.* I wonder what it could mean, aside from inherited depth in time."

"I suppose you mean," said Mr. Farr, who had taken to dropping in several times a week and had been following hungrily as usual, "what it could be made to mean from now on. That might have changed one of those killers, if it had been there. Is that it?"

Baldur's thoughts seemed to have wandered for a second; he came back with a little start. "I guess so, yes. But for it not to be a lie. For it to shelter what we really and truly are—how do we manage that, with walls and spaces?"

"But we can't do without *some* lies, can we?" put in Mr. Farr with a more troubled urgency, which he hastened to smother under the look of sophisticated wisdom assumed with the brighter of his doubting parishioners. As he had whimsically confided one evening, he used the hurricane scale in figuring the doubt-intellect equation in each case; this was the second-degree look, rather an extreme tactic when adopted on purpose.

It was merely hectic this time, and I wondered what lies it scared him so to think of blowing up. He was only about forty, and hadn't outgrown an anxiety to do good and be good, only his handsomeness must have been a handicap at one time and now a good deal else was. Against the first, he had worn all through his eight years in Jordan a pair of black jumbo glasses like a spy getup, with lenses so mysterious, I had noticed he had to take them off for both near vision and far. Late at night sometimes, across the two fields bordering our brook, we would see the light go off upstairs in the rectory and after a while a little dim light appearing inside the church, back of the altar. He might have been only caretaking, but he did wear a certain gaunt wash and streaking of a man who has to spend some night hours tidying up his soul. Or perhaps just now he had been thinking of his unpretty, ailing wife, with her chronic brave smile and smell of chlorox, and of whatever praying he might do in that regard. It might be: Lord, let neither of us think I am more attractive than she, Amen.

"Trompe-l'oeil," Baldur went on in a reflective mutter. "It meant *trompel-l'âme*, didn't it? Those ceilings; an escape hatch, to take you into the celestial infinite, and that's necessary, and no more dishonest than what theater does or used to do in its grand times. So yes, you're right, to that extent we have to admit the lie. But look" —inviting Mr. Farr to bend over his doodle with him as his pencil sought out something further, "that's where water comes in. Water! Nothing does that kind of work so well. It *is* illusion, just as it's power, and we can channel it for that need as well as the other. The Romans knew it, look at the noise and congestion they lived in and the distance and quiet they put into it all with their pools and fountains. Inside and out. Oh I know, Eva, you're grieving for the falls down there. So am I in a way, though they don't contain my childhood as they do yours; that was in other streams. But what's left of them now, in that sense? You've seen the cars this summer—trailers, rubbish, radios; another glory, if we let it be."

He wasn't being ironical at all, and I was ready to take comfort from the fact, as Mr. Farr seemed to be too since he put in, though a shade wistfully, "You're so right. It's awfully debilitating, all this yearning for what used to be. If you could only convince me . . ."

"That we can make anything as good? Yes, we can, because to begin with, we have to."

"Tut tut," said the minister, suddenly removing his outlandish spectacles with startling effect, as if a clown were to lose his nose, only in this case it was solemnity that came off, "even for fourth degree I wouldn't dare try that. I mean, that the proof of God's existence is our need of Him."

Baldur laughed. "Maybe that would be your mistake. But there's no analogy. We can't make God a reality if He isn't one, nor apparently prove it if He is. But we *can* make an illusion of noble spaces."

"And if we're knowing it's illusion, what good will it do?"

"All the good in the world. The whole history of human dignity begins with the practice of artifice; the bison on the cave wall and so on—willful magic; that was our divergence from the beast. Only from one period to another we have to change the, well, the tonality, the key, of our suspension of disbelief." He crumpled the paper with its water-squiggles absently in his pocket. "By the way, that's the twelfth plane that's been over here while we've been talking, counting the helicopter. You see what I mean? We've had an illusion of quiet and privacy. And I suppose sometimes you must feel you're alone with God."

"Ah . . ." The minister put his glasses back on slowly, and smiled in sudden illumination. "But then there *was* an analogy."

Seeing him off at the front door I said, "Gordon, do you have to get yourself up like a raccoon?" He pushed the glasses on to the end of his nose and quite charmingly winked at me over them, then with no warning was saying in dead earnest, "And do you have to play possum, you and Lucas, pretending you haven't heard the voice of Christ waking you up?"

I was flabbergasted. He was so sincere he had even forgotten the hurricane scale, or at least which end of it I was at.

The traffic on the road too was suddenly much more and faster that summer. Before it had always been something you could count easily if you felt like it. Now our old trees by the road, my grandfather's trees that Lucas loved so, had the new and rather absurd function of breaking each passing roar into a rapid fire of whooshes, which especially on Sundays rose to the rhythm of some giant metronome about to race itself to pieces. Three teen-agers from Milford were killed just beyond the store one night when their car turned over, and two others the same week on the Danville road. One of the younger Leightons, a Mink, went off a bridge with a motorcycle, but lived.

"But there'll never be time," I said to Lucas after I had gone with him on one of his flights along the coast. It had been his idea to get up an exhibit of some typical housing sprawl around towns like Hackasaug, so he went with a photographer a few times when Jarvis could let him have the plane, and in the end the photographs did more than anything else to swing the town meeting.

"That would be the same as saying why bother," he said smiling, with the pleasant lightness and avoidance of revelation that was in all our private talk at the time. That was the nearest he had come to saying that he was in the Project head over heels, really hooked, not just trying out another personality as I had imagined sometimes.

"No. I just meant there's so much of all that horribleness, it has so much more power than anything else, it comes so fast. It seemed as if another ten thousand acres had gone just while we were up there today."

"I've heard French soldiers talk that way, about seeing the German tanks come down the road, in 1940. They said they got a crazy yen to bow down before them—the mystique of submission sort of thing. But well, you see . . ." He rumpled my hair, with a little kiss and grin, in exactly his old style only everything beneath and around the style was different. "How's the suit coming? Are you going to get it done in time?"

We had taken to sleeping in separate rooms, so he wouldn't wake me coming in from all the night business he had at that time, and outside of certain little bursts of ill-humor were being tender with each other.

One difference was we had a dog, or he and Dickie did, a setter puppy named Pogo. Then an old brown mare turned up in one of our horse stalls. It came out Lucas couldn't stand seeing her go for glue at the farm auction after Joe Yelinski's suicide, so Dickie and his friends began riding bareback around the fields. There seemed to be a lot of new children living somewhere near that he had taken up with.

Lucas was still working at the Beardsley orchards, and with the pears to be picked just then and hands scarce there was plenty of work, but then often he would only come home to change into a business suit and be off in the "company car" Jarvis insisted on leaving there. I was in a rush myself, without Nanny Beardsley to help get ready for the fashion show, which Mrs. Hollister had been hellbent on promoting, to be combined with the Garden Club and the Altar Guild Bake Sale and practically everything else in town that year, on Labor Day. A riot, as it turned out; no—worse; if there had been just the TV people and the Purser fire and Mrs. Hollister's condition and the Minks letting a truckful of poodles loose, it would have been rather a riot. Anyway I had to finish at least two fall models in time, not to have it just summer things, and it seemed there was hardly a girl or woman in town who wasn't itching to be in the show now that Lucas and I were so in, that was regardless of their figures and including the Countess and old Mrs. Dan Pickett, so most of the time I didn't half know what Lucas was up to in Hartford or Litchfield or wherever, and would just notice that he looked as much at ease in those city clothes as in his old dungarees.

He sounded natural too, like a man who has had a hand in large enterprises all his life, talking about state and federal funds that might be forthcoming and how to get around the road commissioner and so forth. Since the day of the storm and his moving over into this new life, the tic on the left side of his face had stopped; only now and then there would be a second's halt in his speech at some unexpected juncture, as between words usually run together, like supply and demand.

Still, I suspected that he was worrying about the trees as I was. It didn't suit them to be reduced to noise-breakers, or perhaps they were too slow for us, with all their "centuries"; we weren't caring so much about them any more; we could imagine not being heartbroken if they were cut down. Yet trees and memory were what Baldur was believing in. They were what our sudden passionate commitment was about, except as for Lucas it might be about something else too. He might be waiting for a new life for us to have time to be born of all this.

"Oh Christ!" Cluny said one day at a fitting. "And just when I've got my kiln finished!"

"What do you mean?"

"You don't really want to go on living here, do you, with these hordes coming in?" She gave me a rather mean little look; there had been some kind of bad edge between us off and on lately, and she seemed edgy anyway. But she had been more in the thick of the Project than I and all enthusiasm, running errands, painting posters, making propaganda calls on key people like the Picketts.

However, she had moods like this, and was having trouble with her children besides. At the moment they were both staying with her mother in New Haven so they could see a psychiatrist every day, after some incidents involving sex, theft and arson, of a mild variety.

"But Cluny, they'll be coming anyway. Baldur's right. If we don't do it this way and make it beautiful . . ."

"Who's your adman? You're as bad as Chuck Jarvis." But she changed her tone then and smiled at me with her old open friendliness. Anna, Boris's wife, who had made a living in Paris as a dressmaker at one time and was there helping me, looked relieved; she hated discord. "There's just one way to have peace and beauty nowadays," Cluny went on. "That's to be rich, stinking rich. The rest is bullshit."

"The simple life," Anna remarked out of her own little soothing brand of wickedness, and we both felt better for it. She and Boris had no heart for the Project, or against it. "If it comes, it comes," they would say, a shade rueful, a shade amused. "Any place left to run to is too hot or too cold." And Boris would add on occasion, "Thermostatically Connecticut is unreasonable enough," or with a shrug, "So we pull into our skins." Just the same they helped in small ways, out of feeling for Baldur.

Cluny soon had her drive and glitter back. But another day when we were alone in her garden, I working on the suit she was going to model and she pasting up one of her exhibits, she hit in another direction, looking quite ingenuous that time.

"What's this they're saying, about how you're going to get a divorce and marry Jack Pryden?"

"Who's saying?"

She just wrinkled her nose at that. "You mean it's true?"

I struggled, mainly against anger it seemed afterwards, but if it was that it seemed the anger should have been more against her than it was. "If it were, who do you think I'd have told, if not you?"

"Darling, don't be an ass. But how absolutely sweet," and she leaned over laughing and smelling faintly of geranium to kiss me on the cheek.

And all the time there was such a quietness around Baldur in his wild pace, even when his voice was loudest in the excitement of argument or of his own thinking aloud to somebody, you could feel the calm as something secreted out of his vital energies and almost to be touched, solid and pearly as a mollusc shell. I knew he was troubled or had been by something to do with Jack and what had happened at the lab, but that was either solved or short-circuited for the time being. We never spoke of it. In any case, in the crisis atmosphere of that month there was a lot that had to be bypassed. But if our house began to feel sometimes like a center of revolutionary conspiracy, there was a big difference, and at least in Baldur's presence nobody could forget it. Well, maybe Fred Leighton could and he was around too much for my taste, but nobody else.

Chuck Jarvis for one. That stillness of vision that emanated from Baldur had him practically mesmerized, or it might be only a chance phrase that worked on him: "to keep water clean and the wind in the trees," "the breathing-spaces of the mind," "the egg comes before the fern," when it wasn't more a gut blow though I heard Baldur take that tone toward him only once: "I wish you'd stop using that word 'basic.' There's only one basic requirement here, that's to keep the planet habitable and the human race from going insane"—so that he gave in on one point after another even when he had arrived with a blustering "NO! Positively no! This time, Baldie, we're not even discussing it . . ." First he fired his old New York architects and took on a young pair who talked Baldur's language; then agreed to start a whole new set of negotiations for land that would be a mile at the nearest point from any through road or possible future one, although his prime selling point on Long Island had always been that everybody could get from hearth to highway in a matter of seconds, and with all his vows to do everything differently this time it hadn't entered into his bravest dreams to forgo that; then broke off talk with his two most promising industrial prospects because they wouldn't accept the architectural veto, which turned out not to be a disaster since one recanted and the other was replaced in a few days.

"Sanity schmanity," he said on leaving Baldur one day. "Personally I think I'm nuts." But I had never seen him look happier or more confident.

I didn't remind him that he had made moves to betray Baldur, or at least slip something over on him, a few weeks earlier in the matter of the gate. It would have been unfair and irrelevant, when the liking and curious similarity between them had brought them, on both sides, to such trust; such understanding too. It was one of the odd facts of their collaboration that each had become the one quickest to grasp the other's thought, although actually we hadn't seen much of Jarvis. Mostly his trips to Jordan at the time were rushed and short, and if he brought women-friends with him, as Beulah reported, he wasn't showing them to us. Marilyn Jarvis never came any more, though he spoke as if they were still living together on Long Island.

The sketches and cardboard models for the Project grew day by day in strange and beautiful ways under the bewitchment, like plants under some daring new hormone treatment, or a shellful of Japanese paper flowers dropped in water. The egg and the fern were the forms most on Baldur's mind for a while, and they appeared in various ways and dimensions, not for any house plans but in their arrangements in the landscape, also as motifs in his gate design. I saw them a few times when I went up to Baldur's house or studio with a message—there was still no telephone up there—and understood then that the evening talk I heard was unimportant, a playtime thing and without much real correspondence with what Baldur was up to. Perhaps it was even deliberately misleading. It was curious to remember what a boring talker he used to be in the days when he had lost his own truths and had to keep shoveling words into the pit. Now it was for fun, although not in any obvious way evasive, and perhaps after all in the discussions with Mr. Farr and the rest of us, even in the presence sometimes of some pretty dense customers, he did mean to say what he meant, only his true medium was not words and without his having to or bothering to know what he was protecting, would not suffer the threat of the proximity of words beyond a certain point. Anyway the operational force, as the architects clearly knew and probably Jarvis with his unhomogenized brightness had known too from the start, was in his hands and his silences. A quick pencil line; a twist of paper or wire; few sentences exchanged, short and practical: "Too high here . . . We could try glass brick . . ."; zone of magic at work, like the area of magnetic influence around a buried meteor.

Once he deceived me. We had had a quick dip, he and I, in the willow pool, and were standing a minute on the bank afterwards, held by the cataract of afternoon sunlight, breaking and re-forming

and flowing through the leaves and down to the stream-bed the
color of lions if tawny could mean such a glitter and music, away
and away to our left, southeast, through hundreds of lifetimes before
ours but still in each particle of brilliance, for our eyes, absolutely
there. "God's money-bags," my grandfather said once, standing on
the same spot in the same late summer light, as usual trying to deny
his susceptibility in such matters.

My mother's flower-bed, which Baldur had led us to revive, was
close at my back, and without turning I knew precisely the light on
the delphiniums and the last of the summer's zinnias, which she had
been careful to keep quite far from anything of more delicate bloom,
such as cosmos or lupin; the pale yellow roses she loved most, apart
too; and nearer the house her other favorite, the clumps of cool but
blood-red patience. We had kept all her patterns, but it was the first
time, just then in the rippling quietness in which Baldur's vision
seemed to have an integral part, as if he had slipped over into the
realm of being that contained tree and stream and sky, that I had
fully admitted her there herself, with the sound of her hoe clicking
on the little stones and from her tired, willful face her one untroubled
love, the love of her flowers, pouring like another sunlight to make
them grow. And suddenly night, and it hurt me not to remember
what kind of dark and whether there had been stars in the pool . . .
For a second it was like brass and tympani gone wild, too loud. Then
I followed Baldur's gaze, still a little skeptical and almost smiling
in spite of the extraordinary vibrations of his seeing and knowing.
Together we watched a yellow willow leaf that had just wriggled
free from its twig, falling slow and erratic toward its last experience,
at last touching down as though in unbelief on the water where its
reflection had played all summer. There was something of a small
child's totter and forgetfulness in its descent, and childish rapture
in its sudden spinning dance as it was caught up by the wicked mirror, the only real leaf, for the moment, among so many dancing
images of leaves. It was carried off and got stuck shortly in a mass of
organic matter behind a log.

We walked back up the path still in silence, Baldur to return to
the studio, and with bitterness I recognized his absorption. He hadn't
been about to help me at all. Everything he had been seeing in the
brook, and in the instant of my terror that seemed everything back
to the formation of the first drop of water on the planet, had only
been to round out an imaginary landscape with buildings. Leaf or

other, it would be incorporated in what he went on calling, with puritanical modesty, a housing development—others were using more grandiose terms for it. He was living that design. His excursions, not around the world any more but into nature and himself, were in its service and had nothing more personal than that to do with us.

Traitor, I thought, banging my fists on the sewing-machine, and later didn't know if I was smiling at him or at myself.

On one level his contributions to the Project were wildly impractical. He was capable of thinking up a room without windows or stairs that would have had to go out through the roof, and the eager young architects, already half exhausted, would cry, "Damn it, Baldur, this isn't sculpture, it's houses! there has to be a wall to hang the toilet paper on!" "Oh yes, well, you can fix that," he would say and they did, with harder work than he seemed to realize, and between crises had to admit too that they erred more than he on the side of sculpture. It was they who in their desire to do something brave and new conceived of what he called "architectural drapery" and would have no part of. He talked only about the whole landscape in question as he used to about Michelangelo's David, as a "single fluid form" and "the only kind of strength worth trying for." He saw the houses all together against the hills and the hills against the farther hills as some such mobile but contained unit, in the material of which he counted also the movements of nightlight and daylight, as well as God knows what distances, between stars, down the brook, into the human mind—all everyday stuff, he would have said, to Michelangelo. Obviously in this case the "statue" must be to people's taste or they would destroy it, as they would have destroyed the Florentine David too, if it hadn't been comfortable to have around, though he had his own views on pleasing the public and got his best laugh of the season from the phrase he came across in a magazine, "The common man has a right to be common." He couldn't get over that; he laughed again every time he thought of it . . . But on what he took to be misconception of an art he was as stern and almost snappish as my grandfather used to be about "muddle-heads and do-gooders" who confused the nature of Law.

"Sculpture starts from the curve, architecture from the right angle. So they belong together and can borrow from each other up to a point, but crossbreeding makes junk—like anything that tries too hard . . ."

Fred Leighton had dropped in that evening and was sitting

around, for no apparent practical reason, as happened quite often, in pink shirt and purple spangled tie, looking more and more cross at the conversation, and more and more the company spy. What on earth was Jarvis paying him for? Another puzzle was that he and Lucas, instead of being at each other's throats as I had expected, seemed to be hitting it off very well. But Baldur went right on as though not even aware of any hostile element in the room. At least they had one thing in common. Fred too, out of quite different sentiments, and with gloating pride, kept referring to "the Jordan housing development."

Baldur didn't seem particularly aware of Cluny either, though she had made herself demurely lovely, in the navy-blue linen she was to model in the fashion show, and was being even more raptly attentive than usual. Lately she had been toning down her ribaldry in his presence, when she could remember to, and had taken on a certain studied work-of-art quality that reminded me of myself posing for him long ago. At the moment she was suppressing her intellectualism too, plainly hoping the talk would peter out in time for her to have a private stroll with him before he went to bed.

"One exception is the round temple, because it *was* a temple—not to put desks and beds in—and we could have our version of that. No, no, not a church: a thought-arrester, a spiritual circuit-breaker. Nothing new about that only of course we have to see it in a new way . . ." As usual when such a notion hit him and he didn't have a piece of paper handy, he jumped up to find one and began scrawling on it, still talking. "They weren't round anyway, of course, they were cylinders. The triangle is for temples too, tombs and temples, not quite the same thing. Besides, they're only understood in relation to the rectangle, the square preferably."

"Baldurdash," Cluny said, with a little grin so loving, everyone laughed, except Fred. Baldur had been as amused as bemused right along.

"A friend of mine once said—I remember we were looking at the Colosseum, that great tub—a circle absolutely imposed there so absolutely right—he said, a good criterion of architecture is whether any part of your body begins to feel uncomfortable in it; like a neck muscle; or feeling your posture strained. And that means a firm right-angle basis, regardless of accommodation to slope."

The conversation swept out to embrace the arch, the dome, the circular staircase, the curve of the earth—"and Jefferson's brick wall!"

Cluny couldn't resist putting in, the birdy girl-graduate student having to squeak up in spite of everything, with that excess in voice and eye so out of keeping with her innate grace—with sketches, in which along with the egg and the fern there kept figuring "the primordial beauty of ninety degrees."

"Like Bridgeport," said one of the architects, the Jewish one, making a Jewish-humor face. It was his home town. "There's your right-angle dream come true."

Fred Leighton had had all he could stand. With a look of glum belligerence, he stood up and demanded of the company at large, "What's wrong with Bridgeport?" Everyone looked at him in surprise, having forgotten he was there, but as nobody volunteered either to answer him or fight him, he had to content himself with sticking his jaw out further and saying, with an air of finishing off the whole evening's argument, "This town's been a dump long enough."

He had been waiting for a cousin of his, another Leighton, to pick him up, and a few minutes later when it started to rain and I went out to get the clothes off the line I heard the two of them talking, in low voices but excitedly, in the dark by the gate on the other side of the lilacs. Baldur's name came into it, and something about "the boss," Jarvis presumably, and I thought how predictable, if Jordan were about to have a second murder in its history, that it should come from a Leighton again. I waited up for Lucas, who came home after midnight, too tired even to look surprised at my coming in and standing by his bed.

"Lucas, you've got to watch out. Fred's working up to something, to get Baldur out of here. I heard him tonight. He's dangerous."

"Oh no he's not," he mumbled, pulling the sheet around his neck; he always treated bedclothes like a sleeping bag. "He just plays at it."

And was Jacob Horn just playing at it, I wondered; was that why you had to put the knife in his back? It was the first time I had thought of any part of Lucas's story as a reality; or more than that, the first time since my so-called marriage that anything in his experience had had for me, for a second, the reality of something in my own. But he was already snoring.

On another side of things Baldur showed himself as practical as Jarvis himself. The living room was strewn with literature on the latest synthetics, prefabs, etc.—anything to keep costs down. He wanted the houses as cheap as the ugliest split-level in Hackasaug, where the Pryden family fortune had been made. And more and more he seemed to be thinking of components, subject to more or less endless rearrangement, rather than shapes or structures made to stay put. In one set of sketches I found in a scrap basket, the floor of somebody's house one year was somebody else's wall the next; even the factories were to be potentially on the wing, and the town gate was sprouting wheels and feathers and eyes, perhaps to make fun of the whole idea. He worked it out with some wire clothes-hangers one night in the kitchen as I was getting dinner, and it did make us all smile, I couldn't tell just why. Lucas said it was a pretty lively egg and fern if that was still the idea. It looked to him more like peacocks on a merry-go-round.

"It was all for you, Eva," Chuck Jarvis was saying. "Not *all* exactly but I don't have to tell you, you know what I mean. I just never knew anybody like you before. My head-shrinker would have died laughing, me being so idealistic all of a sudden. As a matter of fact I wanted to tell him about it but he'd just jumped out his tenth-story window . . . Have a drink?" It was eight A.M. He looked so worn out I offered to get him one, but he poured it himself from the bar-cart just inside the door, and sank down with it into one of the white wrought-iron chaiselongues, expensively cushioned, that like all the items on the terrace had the chilling air of a top-price furniture display floor. He would never be a drinker, that was sure, only he hadn't slept all night, or more likely for two nights, having been to Dallas, Chicago and Los Angeles all in the last forty-eight hours, in the effort to patch things up. Not finding anything else to do for him I put an ash-tray beside him, and regretted it, he looked so surprised and grateful. I wondered what sort of women-friends they had been that he was supposed to have been taking there, since Marilyn stopped coming. "In case you're thinking this Jordan thing was what tipped over the applecart, it wasn't a drop in the bucket."

"You're mixing your metaphors."

He reached out for my hand and I left it there, in his. "I'm mixing more than that. The damnedest thing is, it would have worked here, it would have paid off, that's what gets me. You know something?" A bit of his normal flash and push were there, briefly.

"Every damn one of those crazy beautiful ideas of Baldie's was *practical*—can you believe it? I thought every time it was going to blow up the works, and I was wrong. We weren't going to lose on it, not after the first couple of years and I could have swung that with my little finger. It was just"—the desperation slamming back down, making his voice weak—"everything else." Like a couple of roofs collapsing after six months, at his latest Long Island project; he had had doubts himself about those specifications, only it meant about half a million dollars and he had let himself be convinced; somebody had been hurt. Of course that was only what started it, not the main trouble at all; in "this game," dealing with millions every day, when a lack of confidence sets in "it doesn't take much." If it had been just a rumor about those roofs, not even true, it could have had the same effect. "God, Eva, you'll never know how much I wanted this Jordan thing. For the U.S.A. For you."

That was a mix all right, intentional though and it was pleasant to be able to share a murmur of laughter with him.

I was thinking that if his "home" as he called it, on Long Island, was no more homey than this one he had really had a hard life. The sliding doors from the living room, if that was the word for it, were open and everything I saw there, except the overnight bag on the floor, was correct and rich-looking like the terrace, right out of the magazines and in fact interchangeable with quite a lot of other interior jobs around Jordan as of the last year or two: old English hunting prints, Aubusson-type carpet, golf trophy, three-masted schooner model, ten-dollar-a-yard mauve-pattern upholstery of country gentleman style, Steuben glass for the touch of modern in ashtrays, best Chippendale reproduction side-tables, and equally fine, so you could hardly tell the difference, a nearly perfect copy of the fireplace mantel that Marilyn had so wanted to cart away from our house. It was funny what an inferiority complex such a room could stir up.

"Nice, isn't it?" Jarvis said, following my glance. "That's one thing she's really great at. You should see the powder room. By the way . . ." He leaned forward and was handing me a document. It was the deed to our field, the one we had sold him the year before and that Lucas had worked for him that spring, with the transfer back to us, "for one dollar and other valuable considerations," dated several days earlier. He had taken the trouble to think of that, in the collapse of his empire. "I knew it meant something to you. They'll be taking over the rest of this place pretty fast . . ." Another corporation management, like every other farm left in Jordan since the night three weeks back when Joe Yelinski blew his brains out, and it would be like the mantel, nobody would know the difference: same cows, if any, same crops ditto, same tax dodge; Joe had been the last one running his own cattle farm. We had two thriving kennels, however, and somebody was talking about starting a cat hospital. My mind wandered to the space given to pet food in the store and whether it was more or less than used to be filled with fodder. Hardly looking at me, Jarvis said, "But we won't be quite strapped. I've got a few things in Canada they can't touch."

We, he said. As if I hadn't known since I picked up the phone, or long before. But I must have looked properly astonished, coming back from my sociological reverie.

"Honey, don't lie to me, there isn't time. You know you're not staying with Lucas, he's a fine fellow and maybe you should but you're not. You're too realistic. I've got a pretty good eye for people, I knew it all the time." He glanced at his watch, as if it were all settled and we were leaving together, right away. "I'll be good to your kid. He's fine by me. I love kids, I want a pack of 'em crawling all over me. You know, Eva baby, I doped something out about you one day . . ." He leaned toward me, sitting so close our knees were almost in contact, and I felt violently rocked by the dignity or whatever it was that kept him from wanting to touch me just then when he must have known that that was suddenly what I did want. He was smiling a little and in spite of the deep new lines and greyness of his face looked almost happy, as if his huge worries stacked up to very little after all. "You New England gals, you're all kooks. You wouldn't take me seriously before because you thought I had too much of the old exchequer—made you feel sinful or something. Right? Oh I know, you liked it when I sneaked you off to the yacht that time, and the champagne and the chauffeur and all—I was watching you. You'd probably have spent the night if I'd insisted. But not for real; I was too well-heeled; it just wouldn't go with your principles." He was so attractive, with all his fatigue, making fun of me, it seemed I had never looked at him closely before. Getting abruptly to his feet the next moment he made a slight beckoning motion and I followed him, docile as could be, into the house.

I didn't have to go far. From the overnight bag he extracted a razor, and after a bit of trouble finding an outlet, as if it had been a hotel room, plugged it in and began shaving, screwing his cheeks into appropriate planes and in the absence of a mirror deftly mapping his progress with one finger. He was obviously in the habit of talking business during that operation. The sounds came out with only a slight aberration. "But you see now . . ."

He had certainly had an eye for a view in grabbing that old house, among the many that would have been available to him at the time. Somewhat the same as from the old cemetery but much wider, without the woods to block it on one side. The whole central pattern of Jordan showed, a sprinkling through trees, just as I had imagined Jack seeing it that day in the spring when everything started, only more of it, from the Episcopal steeple and a speck of our roof low on the left, all the way over and up past the gas stand and Mrs. Hollister's great patch of Norway spruce to the white Yelinski barns, which had their own immense and contrary sweep of view at an angle off from this one but still, seen from here, looked scarcely higher than the Pryden and Beardsley and other Main Street houses in the lowland between, that being relative too to the still lower valley of the river-bed. A child's trainboard village, even to the little cars on the road; nothing was spoiled yet; the dam below the falls was hardly at the bulldozer stage and anyway didn't show in this view.

But nothing, nothing was the same as in the spring; good riddance too, a voice from the past, sardonic and twangy like Beulah's but unknown, was saying.

"Aren't you talking today?" His eyes contrived to make this not ridiculous, through the mouth's distortion, while the little machine went on finding its way like a caterpillar over his bristles. But it took me a second to realize that the grimace was more than necessary. He did want to shave and not waste time, but he was also being humorous. "I was saying, now that that obstacle has been removed, and all I have to offer you is . . ." Not funny at all then though with the razor still buzzing in one hand, he spread his arms out wide like a man being frisked, looking more tragically licked than at any previous moment, letting his tall heavy figure stand for the missing words: *my ruin, myself,* and at last stopped the current long enough to come and turn my face gently up toward his. "Will that do? Will that be enough?"

After a long look into a void I heard myself saying, in a voice unfamiliar and bleak, "I'm going to marry Jack Pryden."

He didn't look hurt or anything else, only a bit stiffer in the cheeks as he resumed work on them. I thought I heard some disbelief in his tone though. "You mean he asked you and you said yes?"

"Naturally." At a gleaming restaurant table laid for two, that had been waiting a hundred years in the clearing in the woods, beside the well, into which with fingers entwined and eyes too glimmering shy to raise just as in days long ago, we descend in our new beauty, to step forth at the bottom hand in hand into the passageway that leads to the enchanted land. "When he gets back from Japan . . ."

"Funny kind of engagement." He packed the razor, zipped the bag. "He got back two days ago." The phone rang, and went on ringing while he poured another drink, one for the road as all his manner indicated; it was only for a minute's windup that he twirled a deskchair around with his free hand and straddled it, looking at me across the back. "I saw him on his way through New York, with the government boys—they're taking over the lab. But of course you knew about that, it was set up before he left." As I said nothing he went on, again with some reservation that seemed to lie outside whatever injury I had done him, and outside what he spoke of, "It's lucky for him that Italian fellow pulled through."

"Are you insinuating . . . ?"

"Hell no. I'm admiring. He'd be no good to the world dead; no sense their both running the risk. His line's not so different from mine, or politics or anything else, when it comes to that kind of deal. There's no lily-white way to do any good in the world, once you get past the church social and I seem to remember some backstairs business even about that, on our street. That's where your Lucases flunk out. But doing dirty is damned hard work sometimes, I mean it's tough, and not just from the danger of exposure. Jack's got guts, that's all—brains too of course." It was all fast and fluent, in spite of the phone ringing a second time, and there was no hypocrisy in it; he was taking his disappointment in princely fashion, and really speaking in praise. "Where most people smell is trying to cover up to themselves; that's one thing I can't take. You know, finding something noble to do with the left hand while the right's pulling a fast one. Take the afternoon off to help the poor, endow a church, comfort the sick—you'd be surprised what people can think up, to look good to themselves." He made the face of somebody passing too close to a public toilet, got up with a glance toward the road to see

if any newsmen were there yet, then delayed once more to pull another document from his inside pocket. This one was yellow with
age and handwritten, nothing like the deed he had handed me. "To
show you I'm no angel myself, here, look at this. I've been hanging
on to it, just in case."

It was a letter addressed to Baldur by a painter, one of his old
Prix de Rome friends, saying he was sorry not to have seen him
for a number of years and asking him to lend his name to a society
of writers and artists: "if only to express the sympathy I have never
doubted you shared with the rest of us, toward the mass struggle."
I had seen the letter before. It happened to be one of the papers I
had idly glanced at years before, among the bushels of check-stubs
and other litter in Baldur's abandoned house, and of what conceivable interest it could be to Chuck Jarvis it took me quite a
long moment of staring at him to imagine.

"How perfectly ridiculous. Why, it's dated 1934—eighteen years
ago! and what if he *had* joined this thing? But there's no proof he
even answered, and I'd bet you anything he didn't, he'd broken off
with all his old friends then. What on earth could you be thinking . . ." I was seized by the conviction, which shook into a whirl
of little pieces everything that had happened not only that morning
but for some weeks, that Jarvis was off his rocker, literally insane.

He took the letter back with a touch of impatience. "The Senator
from Wisconsin is wrecking people with far less, as you know perfectly well. No"—having grasped the question I would have put—
"I didn't go and steal it myself, of course not. Fred Leighton picked
it up." After a pause he added with a trifle more hesitation, his first
admission of distaste in the matter, "I told him to—I mean, to look
around and see what he could find, that would serve the purpose."

"And when was that?"

"Right away, the day after I first met Baldie, that time with you.
It was after some party or other." It was indeed, and how vividly I
remembered his surprise and admiration in the studio and what
strange depths of confidence there had been between the two of
them almost from the first moment. "I knew I'd be getting him in
on this thing sooner or later, and one thing I learned long ago, it's
not safe to work with anybody, I mean anybody, without having
something up your sleeve in case of need. Matter of fact"—some
effort of energy he had been making gave out and he seemed to age
ten years all in one instant, under the new onslaught of weariness—

"I might have needed it the other way round, to protect him. There were bound to be people gunning for him, more than for me, once we got going. With this one little letter I could have made them look, as you said, ridiculous. Well, it's over now, for the time being . . ." He struck a match and snapped his fingers with pain as he let go over the ash-tray, the dry paper caught so fast. "I don't go along with the Senator's tactics, incidentally; he's doing a lot of harm. These things should be kept in proportion."

He hoped I would be happy, he said seeing me to the car, sound-ing only a shade rueful and altogether agreeable, and in the same tone, "It's not Jack's fault he's picking up all the glory right now. He's been damn decent about that; I saw a copy of his speech in Tokyo. He tried to give the Italian fellow half the credit, but the fool press, they're always wanting one name to play up or play down. Even"—again that curt obverse of a laugh, from rear nasal passage—"in biochemistry . . ." He flung the car door away from my hand and mashed his face against mine, one hand clawing my thigh as though feeling for a joint to break. "God I love you, I adore you, I'd have done anything for you! Can't you understand?"

The smoke plunging up from the Purser barn, not just the dry hay but kerosene too it must have been, way down in the valley. About four in the afternoon, when the fashion show was about to start and nearly everybody in town was still there at the center, milling around between the Town Hall and the Episcopal Church, so it was a bunch of picnickers with a New York license who brought the alarm, of course not knowing whose barn it was. Even after Cliff and Lucas and the others had gone off on the fire engine we still didn't know. Luckily the engine was there instead of in the fire house over be-yond the Catholic Church; one of the fire wardens had been giving children rides on it for a nickel apiece, down to the Civil War monu-ment and back, and the bell had been ringing along with their whooping and hollering off and on all afternoon, which was prob-ably what gave John Purser the idea. He had been working up to something in his rage ever since Hester, chatty and affable as always, had done her bit in front of the TV cameras that morning, but nobody thought anything of it when he drove off.

The last of the poodles had just been rounded up, except the one

that began howling hours later in the belfry. There were black ones
and brown ones and two or three white ones and some toy poodles,
all crazy with panic at the Minks' motorcycles roaring in before and
after the stolen or borrowed pickup truck, not to mention the air
rifles and cherry bombs going off all over the place as the dogs were
let loose. At least I suppose that was before the fire. It must have
been, since a couple of poodles rampaged over the Bake Sale counter
alongside of our stand, and as I helped Cluny get ready to go on in
the first model, Mrs. Pickett and the other ladies were still rushing
about after pails and sponges, with chocolate on their elbows and
cocoanut in their shoes. It was all from ready-mixes anyway, nothing
my grandmother or Mrs. Will Beardsley would have called baking.
At the moment the TV truck, which earlier had been on the church
lawn for the Garden Club show and in the morning had been all
over town doing the Congregational Church and the store and the
river and the best of the "genuine old colonial homes" including
ours, had drawn the crowd across the street, where the Occidentals
Five, with two electric guitars and Tom Seeley at the drums in spite
of the Wienowski scandal, were doing a pretty good job shaking
their last number off the ground.

Mrs. Hollister was wandering around with a dazed look and a
homemade banner reading "Down with Nicotine!" The Countess
had offered to substitute for her in introducing the fashion show,
which thanks to John Purser was about to not take place.

As far as TV was concerned, the whole day would never take
place. The show was canned, to be shown some time the next
month, and as the real little old New England village idea was all
tied up with the Project, or "Little Jordan shows the way," with
shots of the architectural and industrial exhibits and the landscape
in question, it would be scrapped with all that within a week. Poor
Hester's defiance and subsequent misery were for nothing. But
nobody could have been anticipating anything of the sort; the town
battle had been won and Jarvis looked as solid as Fort Knox. It is
something else that keeps the scenes of that afternoon from staying in sequence, or even staying distinct from the other big gathering the week before, the town meeting, that one at night and not
outside but of course upstairs in the Town Hall, and before Horace
Beardsley had been blown to pieces in a mortar attack six thousand
miles away.

Certain events seem to repeat themselves. The handsome sweating face of the TV announcer, who was the program manager too and Jarvis's friend, fills the whole scene and keeps being wiped out, over and over. At least if I were doing a TV show of him doing one of us that's the way I would have it, at about five-minute intervals; that was the way it looked. Perhaps it was just a face made to deliquesce, not the kind I was used to seeing around in real life, where an expression meant something. This one was so busy looking good, it didn't seem to have anything for even a smile to stick to, and whatever character showed through in off moments was of a small order and all in flux. "He makes you feel so silly," Hester had said that morning, with some discouragement, because she had thought it would be such fun and had gone ten miles to the hairdresser and worked hard filling the stand with her handsomest fruits and vegetables. "I guess John was right, but I'll be darned if I'll tell him so after the way he carried on. But they turn everything into nothing, somehow. Honestly, I feel as bad as if the stand had been wrecked. Don't you feel that way about your house too?" Still she got at least one of her ringing, high-spirited laughs out of it, of the kind that had always made her marriage to the sourest man in town look so improbable. "Imagine calling me a way of life!"

The man had been calling everything that all day, when it wasn't independent, tough-minded, democratic, genuine—rhyming with *bin*, not *whine*—or a wooden nutmeg.

Also over and over, but very slowly, as if the tarred street were being pulled imperceptibly back from under their feet and the short walk would never end, comes the procession of Beardsleys, all of them, traversing the some three hundred yards between the Beardsley house and the Town Hall. Nobody had thought they would come. Baldur and Lucas and I sat a few minutes with Will in his office the day the telegram was phoned over from the Western Union office in Wellford, but mostly he had been keeping to himself and people had just been leaving messages with Nanny or someone on the porch. But he was still First Selectman, and during his forty years in office had felt it his duty not to miss a general town party, beyond an occasional baseball game and except when his wife was dying. So he was there, straight as a poker as always, with Cliff beside him but nobody holding his arm any more than they ever would have thought of doing, walking toward the Town Hall exactly as he had walked there the week before to preside over the meeting and put in his brief, though for him extravagant, word for the Project.

The family kidded him a little about that the next day. Not that he could ever be accused of putting a personal interest above the good of the town, and he had sometimes been joshed for tending to the contrary. Nevertheless, it was plain he had been thinking of Horace all the time when he talked about Jordan having room for some small industries, "subject to reasonable regulation," and young men being driven away for lack of occupation. The rest of the family were doing all right, and Fred Nelson, Elizabeth's husband, after years of piddling carpentry jobs, was suddenly doing a lot better than all right, with a roaring business in old floorboards and hand-hewn chestnut beams from all the barns that were being torn down and another in new pine paneling made to look old, for which he turned out to have a great knack. The demand for both was so heavy he had had to take on several helpers that summer. Horace, whom his father had always called the businessman of the family, who was bored by the family orchards but miserable away from Jordan, was the one the Project was for, in Will's heart; and he himself wrote, answering his father's and little Loreen's letters about it, that it was just grand, a shot in the arm and too good to be true.

They walk in a wash of sun-speckles running through elm leaves down over their still faces, the elms along there not having succumbed yet to the blight. Their faces are the stones that only seem to move along in the flowing light, even the children's, even Angie's, although she was the one railing the most wildly the other day, partly because she was pregnant again and not quite herself so that for a minute she forgot about Alice, who was sitting there by the plants in the bay window and had just had what they all knew was her last birthday party. They were past hoping she would live to be thirteen; her face had become horridly swollen lately and her hair was falling out. "Where the hell *is* Korea?" Angie was sobbing. "As if John wasn't enough! What have we done to have to stand any more? Why can't this country mind its own goddamned business? I wish all those people in Washington were dead . . ." "Ssh, Angie," Nanny said, getting up to close the screen door. "You'll upset Poppa more, with such language." Alice had been staring at her aunt as if she had never seen her before, her curiosity turning slowly to a great silent shriek of terror, and I saw Nanny nearly break for the first time, wanting to snatch her up in her arms and hold her so tight nothing would ever harm her again, or so they would just vanish forever then and there, the two of them together. "Alice, honey," she said instead, sounding very like Mrs. Will long ago, "stop picking your nose." Then Angie remembered she had brought a kitten, a day late, for Alice's birthday and went out to the car to get it. Outside, some of the other children kept swinging and swinging in strange little fits and starts, one each on the two rope-swings and several on the double chair-swing that we used to sit in too when we were children and that nobody ever found time to repaint. A lot of things would be different if they could only swing high enough or hard enough, but it wasn't working well that day; they were embarrassed. "Uncle Horace got killed in Chlorea," Robin had said to us with a foolish smile, just trying it out, when we arrived. "*Kor*-ea, stupid, I keep telling you." "Well who cares, he's dead and I knew it before you did." "That's her father," the older Nelson girl said pointing to Loreen beside her, as if we didn't know. "But he's our uncle too, I mean was, I mean . . ." "And I know something else too," Johnny began, with a scared glance toward the bay window to see if he dared, but a thunderclap of looks from the others set him to whimpering instead, which in turn sent Loreen bolting out of the swing and across the lawn, to go and cry by herself in the hayloft. Her mother, the city girl who wouldn't stay with Horace in Jordan, had stopped writing to her long since.

The room Will called his office was so bare it looked almost tidy that day, because the favorite objects he kept there had all been borrowed by the Ladies' Committee for the downstairs exhibit at the Town Hall, in the low-ceilinged room always used for eats. Everything connected with the Project was on display around the main upstairs hall, the one for meetings, dances and such, with the stage at the end on which I used to play the ukelele in the school orchestra, and where standing all alone, aged seven and half dead with fright, I had to make my first speech, in front of the whole town, at the school exercises. "Theodore Roosevelt was a very great man," it began and that's all I ever remembered of it afterwards. The downstairs exhibit now was something nobody would have thought of before, of "Old-Time Jordan"—patchwork quilts, butter churns, anvils, Will's old carpentry and iron-working tools and pre-Revolutionary wagon parts, a dressmaker's dummy of around 1910, etc. From our attic had come my grandmother's wedding dress and a photograph of Abe Trowbridge, beaming from a wagon seat, whiskers flowing and portable cider keg aloft, behind his famous forty-pair team of yoked Devonshire oxen. In the show the picture was labeled "Mr. and Mrs. Abe Trowbridge on their way to the Danville Fair," but it was taken on what was then the dirt road in front of our house and the big-nosed lady on the seat with Abe's arm around her was really my mother. Mrs. Trowbridge had been dead two years in 1927 when my grandfather took the picture and never went to a fair in her life, though she was a most loving wife, resembling her sister who was Mrs. Will Beardsley, and full of quiet pride in their parlorful of cups and ribbons. It wasn't Abe's harmless gaieties around other women or his well-known barrels in the cellar that killed her either, but lack of vitamins, so the doctor said, all the years Abe was getting his from the cider. Anyway the exhibit was considered very educational and was a big success, even though Will was wry at the quantity of misnomers and Beulah said next thing we'd be showing pigs in a zoo like some place she'd read about in Westchester.

The season of the bees was over; the TV was off; it was very quiet, except for sporadic voices, kept low, inside or out, and now and then the creaking of the swings or a car passing. But that is not a main road and the few cars there were seemed to pass the house slowly that day in deference. A few letters, evidently from Horace in Korea, lay around the desk, along with town reports, the *Farmers' Almanac* and *Les Misérables*, open as always. Of the framed family photographs, hung against the stained and faded wallpaper, the most recent was of Horace in uniform, with his lopsided grin; having none of the others' musical talents he had made his way very young as the family joke-cracker, and with Angie, the most sociable of the children. Another picture, when he was about eleven, was of the three boys, and that was the last one of John, smiling in the wheelchair with a pet squirrel on one shoulder and a baby owl on the other, while standing behind him Cliff with the fiddle and Horace with the bow, heads together, pretended to play for him. By far the biggest photo in the room was one Mrs. Will had cut out of the rotogravure section and framed, the same year my mother rode to Danville behind the oxen, of Charles A. Lindbergh; he had been such a hero to her, apparently Will had never thought of taking it down.

He got up for us, with the habitual little plucking motion at his neck as though straightening a tie, nodded courteously toward some chairs and seemed glad we had come, but although his Adam's apple gave some preliminary jiggles as it did when he was about to sing, no words came out for a while. He had shrunk within a few hours; that was the only difference; his knobby old hand strayed once or twice to pull the shirt-seam back up on his shoulder where it belonged. "He gut through the whole war," he said at last, "without a scratch"—meaning what everybody did, Lucas's and Jack's war, unless they were old enough to still mean Baldur's war, anyway not thinking of using the word for whatever it was the telegram was about, and as if it might have been a shade less intolerable the other way, in the real thing, with the country understanding it more or less or at least acting as if it did. So Baldur, who hadn't sat down and had one hand on Will's shoulder, managed to say in a low voice, "I guess it's all the same, Will. The same war. Just keeping itself small for the time being." But he was really speaking on another level altogether, as neither Lucas nor I could have done, and Will's short nod was a reply in kind, as between two old men who have been friends too long to act out a pretense of sense or solace —when in fact they had barely exchanged ten words in thirty-odd years and their friendship dated from the evening three weeks back when they had their first talk about the Project.

They had had a good many since, some of them up at Baldur's house and studio, where Will went to study the architects' plans. Until then he probably hadn't been near the place since Baldur bought it, before I was born, nor given it a thought beyond the common talk around town. That was mostly about the naked lady on the wall, with the connotation that where there was one in stone there must be one or more in the flesh. However there had been nothing a First Selectman had to take steps about, like the still hidden in the woods back of the Leighton house during Prohibition; besides Will knew enough to take the talk with a grain of salt, considering Baldur's ties with my family and with Miss Pryden. But now it was as though the friendship had really made itself retroactive, over the whole time, and Will might have been stating as much in all simplicity when he got up, at the end of the town meeting, to second Mr. Farr's rather breath-taking motion. That was for a vote of thanks "to the man whose spirit and vision have made this Project something for Jordan to be truly proud of, a source of

hope where hope was nearly gone; who will have kept us from add-
ing our bit to the sickening, ruthless desecration of our once beautiful country. To Baldur Blake!"

There had been a sudden nervous hiatus, which was partly of
dismay among Baldur's admirers, in view of the tactics of the
opposition and all the ticklish business that had gone before. The
last speaker before the main vote had been Lucas, so there were
already some curious intensities simmering in the hall. I hadn't
managed to take in what he said myself, and even had an impression he was opening and closing his mouth without making a sound,
but I could see the rearrangements of feeling going on afterwards,
culminating in a delayed burst of applause that in some quarters
had a pitch almost of exaltation, most uncharacteristic of Jordan
gatherings. Even so, Mr. Farr's motion was something else again
and might have ended badly if it hadn't been for Will, toward
whom many eyes turned in a variety of expectations, but not for
long, since he rose at once and said, "Second the motion," in his
normal clipped business voice as though approving a school board
report. Poor Baldur had only gone to the meeting to put in his
vote, and then had to sit through an ovation, started by his following among the high school students and quickly taken up around
the room, even by some people who had argued against the Project
half an hour earlier. Among others the maiden ladies Miss Bean
and Miss Troy, who had become rather a scourge in their enthusiasm, were determined to have him lifted onto somebody's
shoulders, their own if necessary, and paraded to the stage. It took
two selectmen to stop them and Will apologized to him later for
his part in the inconvenience. "Darnedest thing I ever seen. Oughta
kept my mouth shut." Actually he looked rather pleased by the
fuss.

But in his office that day so soon after, in sunlight turned green
by Mrs. Will's trumpet vines at the windows, the color and empti-
ness making it like an operating room, I saw another depth of that
friendship opening out for Baldur. It can't have been one he had
bargained for—to have to remember himself saying: Yes, I hoped
you would be killed, it would have been so much easier; and being
able to say it because he and Jack had both imagined for a while
that night that the long refusal of their bond had been expiated
and like it or not, in mutual admiration or not, both of them had
accepted what they were to one another. Now his hand on Will's

shriveled shoulder, in the green little room where Horace's voice, Horace's smile were the only flickering life in an asphyxiation of pain, told him otherwise. He left without letting Will see his face again.

There had been some pretty sharp crossfire between Tony Rossi and his father-in-law at the town meeting, because Will's "reasonable restrictions" were going to kill off Tony's dream of a motel back of the gas stand, but he was walking and belonging with them now, his youngest daughter astride his shoulders. He was darker and stockier than Beardsley men, with a quick white smile and a restless quickness all over and eyebrows that Angie would try to smooth down with water or grease, saying they were two fox-tails dyed black. "A regular wop," he called himself cheerfully, "from little old Catania"—which even his parents had no recollection of but he liked referring to it, partly to tease his in-laws. Behind, the rest of their Catholic brood came mingled with the young Nelsons and Beardsleys, so it was after all not like the normal Sunday morning procession, although at first glance it seemed as relaxed. Alice with her puffy face, in the little white crocheted cap Nanny had made to hide the patches on her skull, was the only one holding a mother's hand at the start but then she fell back with the other children. It wouldn't have been like the family to plan to go all together like that, under the circumstances. The others must have just decided to drop around to the house when they heard Will was determined to go, just to be on hand, and so they happened to set out together, but it was nothing like a phalanx. There was some drifting out of line and nodding to people along the way and a natural amount of chatting and scolding seemed to be going on; one of the children had to run back to the house for something. It all looked quite easy-going, except for the same sense of river-rock in faces of so many ages, Tony's no less than the others, and the light and the black road running, leaving them still, though they kept walking.

The TV man hadn't noticed yet, and evidently hadn't been told anyway. He was busy moving his apparatus over to our side, for the start of the fashion show. But he would find out, there was practically nothing else he hadn't found out in a day, and there would be trouble, of what kind it was hard to imagine. Perhaps he would fade away for good and Jordan would be held liable for his liquidation. What a pathetic nonbeing and trifle of a thing he was, with his paid smile and silky babble, to be pitted against such a power of massed suffering. You had to be sorry for him. "Horace Beardsley just had his head shot off in Korea . . ." No, that was Dickie in the kitchen the other day, and his friend had said, "Who told you? You're just making that up, about his head." A new sound seemed to have been introduced, like the tread of all forty pairs of oxen still far away around a corner. It wasn't true, as Hester Purser had learned that morning, that the power was all on one side. It might be the other way around. The Beardsley men were unarmed, in shirt-sleeves, with their women and children; and about to spring on them was that huge organized force, equipped with trucks, lights, mikes, cameras, technicians, college degrees and inexhaustible cash. "'Where ignorant armies clash by night,'" I heard Miss Pryden quoting, and for a moment yearned for her to be alive. She would have broken this up quickly enough.

Across the road Beulah Wellman and Mrs. Howland, selling lemonade and doughnuts, had seen, and after we exchanged a look, were searching around for someone who would do something, stop the incredible collision, perhaps Mr. Farr, but he was trying to get Mrs. Hollister out of sight and into the Pickett house on the corner. First Selectman, has given a son, real old-timer, get that shot . . . But not yet, he still hadn't noticed, a young assistant named Pete was trying to tell him something he wasn't hearing because he had decided to take one more sequence of the fire engine full of happy yelling children on the last trip back from the monument. By what used to be the Jordan High School when we still had one in the days of one-room district schools, before busses, and was now the one centralized Jordan elementary school, Will stopped to speak with a couple who had gone over to him, and some of the family moved on ahead but then were somehow eddied back to wait for him. They had progressed that far, in fact most of the way, and the one apparently getting ready to stop whatever it might be was Lucas. On insistence from the Occidentals he had just played a number with them and still had the clarinet in his hand.

Cluny hadn't noticed either and was asking me for the third or fourth time, very pale from a night of emotions and pills, "What's he doing? Do you think he really isn't coming?" The navy-blue

linen, based on a design in a French magazine Jack had brought me
from New York, was my triumph and we had discussed showing it
last, but had decided to end with the soft Irish tweed suit I had
been up till all hours trying to finish; Anna was hemming it now
inside the Town Hall. Cluny, who had been sweet and adorably
funny about coaching the others, was going to show that too, if she
held out. As a model she was great, with her hybrid air of the
aristocrat drawn to the gutter, and an instinctive stage presence
that made her roll to the ball of the foot at each step, bringing out
a play of hips she never had ordinarily. She did it with a glint of
frigid amusement as though walking naked over the corpses of
lovers, yet without losing her normal frightened sensuality, which
did call attention to the dress. Fred Nelson had knocked the stand
together that morning. The six other models, from teen-age to
elderly, were ready and giggling inside. The triumph there, of another sort, was the appearance of rowdy old Miss Bean, five feet
one, with hair like the snippings from somebody else's and measure-
ments as for a set of barrel staves, in a fifty-dollar pants ensemble I
had made for her in July. She actually looked quite chic in it, and
was thrilled at herself. I had kept prices as low as possible, considering the materials, but still by doing several of the hits in series,
with easy variations, I had put quite a lot of money in the bank in
four months. It felt good, and the clothes weren't what you could
pick up anywhere, they had something of my own about them. I
had been suddenly happy and excited at the rehearsal the day
before, seeing the best of them together for the first time and seeing
how much had come from myself, not just from other people, to
open life up since spring. I wasn't in love, or wanting or needing
any love then, and had to make a big effort to play confidante
when Cluny burst in on me, in full tragic collapse, that night.

"Eva, I can't bear it! what has come over him? what has happened? what shall I do?" We were alone; she had arrived from
the studio, where Baldur had intended to work late, and Lucas was
out. She threw herself on me, sobbing wildly, so that I was obliged
to hold her in my arms as if there had never been any reserve between us. "I can't live without him, I won't! Oh Eva, you can't
imagine what it's been, all these weeks, I never knew anything
could be so wonderful . . ." Her delicate face was wet and ugly.
Reaching blindly for something to wipe it with she grabbed the suit
lining I was working on, but I managed to rescue it unobtrusively,

and found her a kleenex. In the subsequent arrangement I was on the sofa and she on the floor, beating her forehead against my knees. "I didn't feel I could talk to you about it before somehow, but you knew, didn't you? and I knew you'd want him to be happy —and oh, he has been, he does love me!" She said they'd had it all planned to go to Italy as soon as he could leave the Project, and have his new work cast; it wasn't safe for it to lie around up there in plaster, with all the vandalism going on; and it was at that point that she noticed for the first time that the plaster head was missing from our living room, and remarked on it, but luckily didn't give me time to explain. A new flood of tears overtook her. "Why is he doing this now? Why? Saying he's old. Of course he's said it before, but not like this. He's not, he's not!"—in two howls, the second distinctly canine. "If you knew how young he is, in bed too. I've known men of thirty who can't get it up like that. But I wouldn't care anyway. If I could just have one year with him I'd die happy, I wouldn't want anything for the rest of my life . . ."

She went on a long time in that vein, not expecting me to answer her questions or do anything but comfort her, until the end, when she did press for information. "Eva, you've got to tell me. Please. Something has happened in the last few days. Has some woman turned up that he used to know? or what?" So I brought her a glass of water and lied to her, saying no, I didn't think anything had happened. I couldn't say it was because Will Beardsley's son had been killed.

Lucas was walking slowly up the road swinging the clarinet, serious and a little abstracted, like when he got up on the platform at the town meeting; or rather, I began to see, the way he must look sometimes alone in the forest, abnormally quiet and alert. Cliff saw him and they exchanged a sober, friendly recognition, something outside of a smile, which on Cliff's side showed an innocence of any harm ahead, beyond the generalized pain of exposure, and just at that moment a diversion broke out. A three-year-old girl being helped down from the fire engine poked her candied apple at the TV man's face and in piercing rapture called out, "Way of life! way of life!" Immediately the whole mob of children went off like firecrackers, and with whoops and shrieks of laughter were fighting for the mike and screaming into it, "Lay of wife! Bray of strife! Day of plife! Clay of crife! Hife! Dife! Mife! Fife!" The announcer put up a desperate defense of his poise and property, and was eventually extricated. "Well folks, as you can see, there's plenty of good spirits among the young people in this town. If I get out with my toupee I'll be lucky"—and once more, this time taking with him a quite authentic look of panic-stricken joviality, he was wiped from the scene, but only momentarily. The truck was right beside us, and although I couldn't hear the urgent murmur of the man named Pete as he pointed to the Beardsleys, the disappearing artist, Jarvis's friend, seemed to rest his vocal chords by talking as loud as possible when not on the air. "What? right there? For Christ's sake, before they break up . . . And get that man out of the way." The man in the way, and not likely to get out of it, was Lucas, but before the assistant could leap from the truck to go for him his boss had had another thought. "Which one is the widow?"

It was shattering. Pete, after his fine work of spotting the shot and delving the dope, was a living tableau of lost promotions, but still not without hope. Very much the eager young lieutenant in the crux of battle, with a faint chance of holding the position, he moved a quick finger over the possibilities: Elizabeth with her spoiled figure, noble forehead and fair hair in a bun; gay Angie fresh out of curlers but pregnant and drawn; Nanny once the Juno of the lot, bearing her fatigue and double anguish inconspicuously in an old cotton dress. The scheme was feasible, as the program manager was on the verge of agreeing. Any one of the three women would do for a quick pan, with ambiguous commentary, suggesting a loss too sacred to intrude on further; then concentrate on the old man. But they would have to hurry. New formations were in process; already there was more than one man in the way; in fact there were several, and then I became aware that what was happening was not exactly accidental. It was more on the order of Paul Revere's ride, only strangely silent and slow. Perhaps Lucas had even looked directly at one person and another as he moved along, or it may have been only something in his face and manner that conveyed the bizarre alarm. In any case, one by one, men who had lived all their lives in Jordan had detached themselves from whatever group they had been in, and with their hands in their pockets, some of them chewing gum or dangling a cigarette, sauntered over to the space on that side of the Beardsley family, where two or three conversed a little but most seemed to be merely contemplating the weather. Old Dan Pickett was there, and Fred Nelson's brother,

a Howland, two of the young married Trowbridges, the leathery old
hermit who was a cousin of John Purser's, a Buckingham who was
only a distant relation of ours, a Wellman from down by the
Station, Art Choate with the empty sleeve from his run-in with a
corn-chopper long ago, and several more. At the town meeting
there had been a lot of strenuous fraternizing by the new people
in town, but right now none of them seemed to notice that there
was an event they were not in on.

From the Town Hall, not a Beardsley was to be seen. But even
before that, having evidently received the signal in the same
fashion as their neighbors, Will and the others in front, in an
equally careless and sleepy-looking shift, had come to be facing
the other way, while the mothers drifted around behind. For a minute all they presented was a ring of backs, as in some slow-motion
children's game, only the children were all inside. Then the view
was blocked, a trickle of silence went through the packed space
around them, and all the generations of Jordan seemed to stand,
a guard of honor for Horace. The TV man gave a disgusted sigh.
"It's no good without the *genuine* widow. Get this through your
thick skull, Pete. One thing comes first in this business, and that's
integrity." The next instant a poodle flew by his head, followed by
another, which to the accompaniment of gunfire crash-landed on
one of the lights, and after that all hell broke loose.

The Minks, minus the one who was still in the hospital from the
motorcycle crash, were all in Hallowe'en masks, so although everybody knew they had done it, there was an absence of positive proof concerning the theft, or forcible loan, of the dogs from the C-Me
Kennels, and the charge was finally dropped. Anyway the poodles
were all taken back home in the end and given sedatives, and the
only property damage was to the Bake Sale and a certain amount
of TV equipment. Besides, the Minks didn't even accomplish what
they meant to. The whole affair had been planned to bust up the
performance by the Occidentals, and the timing went wrong owing
to two of them being bitten trying to close the truck. Hester Purser
didn't get off so easily. At dusk, when the fire was out at last and
we were all standing around the black wreckage of the barn, wondering where John Purser could be, a beautiful long doleful crow of
a rooster sounded from the sky nearby. There he was, way up in a
hickory tree, stark naked and stark raving crazy, crowing at the
new moon.

II

I DROVE DOWN THE HILL from the Jarvis place faster than ever in my life on a back road, though not as fast as the two New York cars that passed going up, and tore for the phone. There was no answer at the Pryden house. At the lab the secretary said yes, he had been there but had left for Washington; he was expected back by the end of the month.

They were days of public letdown and nagging readjustment, after the first one when the collapse of the Project caused a general aimless scurrying, in which nobody seemed to have any other thought than to pass on the news. I didn't concern myself with any of it, and didn't work on the two or three orders I had for fall dresses. The weather turned in the middle of September, a little earlier than usual; before the maples had hit their peak of gold or the swamp maples were all red, a cold wind and rain beat a first big installment of leaves down around us, but enough stayed on the trees so that when the sun came out again the real kick of autumn was there, with its brash palette and smells suddenly piercing and haunted in the changed air. It was always my favorite time of year. I loved the feel of my skin then and the looks in other people's faces, and the way time, past and future, stopped being a line and as long as the leaves were falling was like a ball on a seal's nose. Even in the many years when there had been nothing I could possibly hope to accomplish with all the pickup of energy that went through me in jabs and vibrations, so unlike the treacherous stirrings of spring, I had had the same illusion off and on every fall: of projects and prospects, of imminent adventure of one sort or another, in which I would play a handsome part.

For several years after Jack's marriage the illusion always led around to some image of him in shocked admiration of me, consumed with regret at his mistake—and there it stopped. No matter how flaming the foliage, how bright my sense of self-improvement, I neither conceived of nor yearned for any happy ending beyond that. That single scene of recognition was the sole goal of the dream, and of course it is not true that this was only for the first few years. It took a somewhat different position in my life later, like a dog that has always slept at the foot of the bed and then moves off to the corner, but it never stopped. Lucas hadn't taken anything out of the change of season for me, in that respect. The first autumn that had left me dull and blind was this one.

A fine pair we make, I thought, watching Beulah sadly tidying Baldur's room in our house for the last time. The next day there would be only his packing to do. She wasn't wearing her new teeth, and had a rag tied around her new-colored hair, which had been done discreetly and when she tended it, framed her fine old face with becoming dignity. Now it was as if it hadn't been worth the expense. She muttered to herself about the pain in her back, and whereas she had had a proprietary touch for Baldur's personal things all summer, acted as if his brush and comb, the dirty sweat-shirt and muddy old sneakers on the floor had become the belongings of a stranger and almost inimical to her. I had told her it wasn't going to make any difference. He had never meant to move in on us permanently, and now that the architects had left and all the Project stuff had been packed up and taken away, it was only natural he should want to be in his own house. He would be dropping in every day and having meals with us whenever he wanted to. "It's hard for him, going up and down the hill so much, with all the work he's doing now. You can see how impatient he is to get there, in the morning . . ."

She pressed her thin lips in tight against the gums with a short shake of the head, mournful and stubborn, meaning "It won't be the same," and that all the years with "my boarder, Mr. Brown" she had lived for Baldur's knock at the door, so that she might give him a batch of her excellent cookies or a pot of raspberry jam. It was a wonder she had managed to keep her hatred of Miss Pryden from breaking into open violence at some point. But when she moved across the hall with the vacuum cleaner, to Dickie's room, I saw that she hadn't believed anything I said and what was weighing her down was a more general foreboding. "Kindergarten all right?"

"Yes, he was just scared that first day." Lucas was back, and she hadn't asked about his recent disappearance, very likely knowing I couldn't have answered if I'd wanted to. It hadn't been to Alaska anyway; he was gone only a couple of days and hadn't taken Dickie or Pogo, or even his rifle; and not to rescue his friend Corey from the jungle, after a month's delay. There had been some news or message in that connection, brought by Mr. Farr, that I hadn't been told about, quite a while back. It struck me that Beulah was probably on the right track in her apprehension, and all he was waiting for now was Baldur's moving out of the house, so that by the end of the week she might have lost Dickie as well. "And what are *you* idling around about?" she snapped, for all the world as though irked to have me following her around doing nothing, when I knew perfectly well she wanted me there to talk to, even more than usual. It was true that if I didn't get to work myself I wouldn't be able to go on paying her for the housework, but that was the last thing on her mind.

Baldur, at least, hadn't been showing any anxiety or afterthought, and treated the question of his change of quarters with nothing but friendly simplicity. He had turned back to sculpture almost at once and seemed as happily engrossed in it as during his first long fit of creation, in the spring. Of course the blowup of the Project was a disappointment. He didn't pretend it wasn't, and was worried too for a few days, when the selectmen were swamped by calls and pressures from new real estate magnates wanting to rush into the vacuum. However, none of them lingered long when they heard the town restrictions, which were going to stick at least for five years. So for the time being Jordan was protected from the typical exploitations, as it hadn't been before; at least that had been gained. "It was a great chance," Baldur said, allowing himself just that once a tone of real sorrow about it. "It might have been . . . Ah well," with a slow shrug involving the full length of both arms and the opposite of flippant, "it won't be the last." For him it would be the last, but of that he only said that disappointment was the life of art, as of politics; you never did what you hoped, and if you couldn't stand it you weren't fit for the business. He paid no attention to the new crop of rumors and accusations around town, in which he had begun to appear as a sorcerer diabolically to blame for both the conception of the Project and its death, and said nothing about going to Italy to have his work cast.

Cluny had stopped coming around, and made an excuse not

to see me the one time I phoned. I took it there was a lot she
wanted to forget, but when I ran into her at the store, after a
trek to Danville with Dickie for his polio shot, it seemed to me
she had done her forgetting pretty fast, since she had all the look
of a woman who has been satisfactorily screwed within the last
half hour. I happened to notice it because one of the strangers
who had been drawn to our house by the Project, a New York man
named Carlos Gibson with a house back of Fix Hill, had been
keeping a detailed notebook on all his sex life with his wife and
others for twenty years, and was always trying to read us entries
from it: times of and numbers of times per day; speed of orgasm in
relation to background music; variations of erogenous zones for
different income levels and age brackets with further subdivision
by skin pigment and cultural affiliation; effect of jealousy in wife
D. or self when exposed to copulation by spouse with other partner
at different degrees of proximity as versus same behind screen or
via tape recorder; agonies of a month of impotence; experience
with she-goat; and so on. Baldur encouraged him to read the first
time, and then laughed so hard Mr. Gibson, a rather small man
with bifocals and a crucifix on a chain around his neck, went off in
a huff, hugging what he called his "valuable contribution" as
though to keep it from being sullied by contact with such a mind.
Of course we had a hard time keeping him away later, as there
weren't too many houses in Jordan where you could discuss that
type of research.

Anyway, one passage dealt with visible physiological transformation of female as result of complete, as against partial, orgasm,
which was something I had never given much thought to or
bothered to observe in myself. The main symptoms were not to be
seen in a woman with clothes on, but the others were clear enough
and Cluny, stepping from her car that day, exhibited them all. Her
lips were full, moist and red without lipstick; her motions heavy in
a pride of languor, with legs a little spread and unwieldly, not as
from hurt but in protection of lingering sensitivity in the vaginal
area; her skin tone, normally rather dull, was freshened and re-
juvenated as by the most expensive facial; her shining grey eyes
swam in a liquid subtler than tears and conveyed the same gentle,
not quite focused condescension as her smile, in which there was
less recognition of me than savoring of her own queenly condition
of animal bliss. Not all of this was in Mr. Gibson's study; he went

in more for such items as temporary plumpness of cheeks, according to his statistics usually not lasting more than twenty minutes
but I didn't see how Cluny could have gotten dressed and up to
the store in that time. We said a cheery hello, like old friends in
a hurry who would be seeing each other soon, and went our separate ways.

Beulah, continuing her cleaning round, spoke of John Purser
being taken to Newtown, of various people who might hope to
succeed Will Beardsley, of a latest bit of gossip about Baldur. This
last made her very cross indeed; furthermore, she thought it was all
more sinister than we seemed to realize, especially with him about
to be all by himself up the hill. "I wish to goodness that Mr. Jarvis
had kept his fat nose out of Jordan and stuck to New York where
he belongs. It's been nothing but foolishness and trouble . . ." In
spite of the gloom of the day, this brought her by association to a
morsel that picked her up mightily and for a few minutes restored
her native spark and crackle over the follies of our neighbors. "And
say, that chorus-girl wife of his, you know what *she's* been up to?
It beats everything." She looked straight at me, hands on hips and
eyes aglisten as always before a particularly good one, and I couldn't
for the life of me tell if her glance meant only that or something
more. "You remember how she was going on around Dr. Jack Pryden downstairs here, that night I made a fool of myself dancing?
Well, would you believe it? She got him! She was hiding away
spending two nights with him right here in the Pryden house in
Jordan, beginning of last week."

I laughed. "Oh Beulah, you're making it up."

So that was what Chuck Jarvis had been too decent to tell me;
it gave me a respect for him that could almost have been taken for
love. I also felt something like gratitude to Carlos Gibson, for opening my mind to certain possibilities. If Beulah said it, it was bound
to be true, but it couldn't, simply couldn't be serious; it had to be
just a Gibson-type experiment.

The big month before he left for Japan, when we were in the
swirl of the Project and I in the other one for the fashion show, he
was also working full tilt and all hours on the materials for his paper
and then the writing of it, which came hard. We met only a few
times, briefly, without quarrels and without sex, but he phoned
whenever he could, and insisted on my meeting him in New York
the night his plane left. We didn't go to the old restaurant with the

red-checked tablecloths but to a glitteringly expensive one, with
huge mirrors and square yards of empty velvety space and a menu
like a jumbo-size wedding invitation. That was where it happened.
I had done my hair differently that night, straight up high from my
forehead with a purple bow on top to match my new dress, and was
wearing my grandmother's amethyst pendant for the first time in
my life. He broke into a wonderment of smiles as we met and
grabbed both my hands, as if he hadn't believed until he saw me
that I would really come, and from then on there was no break in
our happiness and such things as forks and knives seemed to do
what they had to by themselves, without our touching them. The
hours, I don't know how many, flew away as they used to that
summer long ago, but these were beyond any reckoning more wonderful, because we had come to them from such a waste of suffering.
The waiters seemed to tiptoe in our vicinity; the shining wineglasses
relayed the lights of our eyes down a thousand crystal corridors, to
where they merged in the one blinding revelation. There was no
more thinking or wondering to be done; we were there; we had come
through, to the very gate of our Persepolis, so that when Jack spoke
of marriage it was almost in apology for such a common-garden idea.
"You'll find Washington isn't such a bad place to live. I'll keep the
house in Jordan too if you like . . . Eva darling, darling, is it really
you?" He didn't explain about Washington or mention what had
happened at the lab or was going to happen to it.

I got home at five in the morning and every star in the starry
night sang for me all the way. It was the other side of the universe
from that terrible drive back from Briarwood when I had also
been alone, or the worse one years before when my head had been
just as full of his name but in despair and I found my mother
drowned. I had had no word from him since.

As soon as Beulah had gone home I set off in the car, with no
particular destination, but I found after a while that I was craving
to be by the river, so I turned off that way, not to the falls but way
up at the opposite end of Jordan, to the old picnic place where back
in the spring Dickie and I had had our lovely afternoon.

Lucas hadn't come in yet. It was midnight. Baldur and Dickie
and Pogo in his basket in the hall had all been asleep a long
time. On the bed beside me was a volume of Trollope I had pulled

out at random from my grandfather's bookshelves and had read half a page of in short pulls, over a couple of hours. Sometimes in the intervals it was the room that held my attention. It had taken on a strong and rather painful reality in the night quiet, which was intensified rather than broken by the slight counterplay of wind, an occasional click of a leaf on a windowpane or the little creak of wicker when the dog shifted position in his sleep, beyond the closed door. It seemed important to understand the room and come to terms with it if I could. It was the best bedroom, used by the heads of the family in any generation, and even at the lowest of Buckingham fortunes had always been handsomely furnished, more or less as it was now, for a long time with the same four-poster and brass-handled mahogany bureau and dressing table. The room at the back that we had given Baldur, my father's after Lucas and I married and my grandfather's when his lonely combats in the night had become too severe for him to go on sharing a bed, was just as large and had as good a four-poster, that one maple and from my mother's family whom Arthur and I had been too young to remember, and had the same southern exposure but not the fine eastern one out over the front lawn and the best trees, to the hills and the morning sun. My grandmother used to creep downstairs to fix her tiny breakfast tray and would take it back up to the dressing table, to be out of the way but even more from love of the light there in the mornings. Perhaps it went with the fact of her colors being blue and violet that she had so much of the morning-glory in her nature; that was the one hour of the day when she unfolded for herself alone, and required that solitude, as all the rest of the time she needed to be needed, in some sociable connection.

It was strange that there weren't more scars, more traces of misery in the room. There was nothing to tell that in her last year my grandmother moved with the rest of us to the row of cold little storerooms over the kitchen, to make room for the boarding school; of the tearoom period after her death, when we were in the Howland house, the only evidence was the loss of the pretty old-fashioned wallpaper, for which she had gone out in secret and sold her pearl brooch. We found it hatefully, and it looked deliberately, scratched and stained, and my mother, who was fairly sober that day, took it so hard she burst into the only tears I ever saw on her face. So for her last week she and my father slept in the room Baldur was about to vacate, and my walls had a coat of white paint in place of the little grey shepherds and shepherdesses I used to make up stories about. But we found the bedroom mantel and andirons, crated and ready to be stolen, left by mistake in the shed, and Lucas had laid the fire as husbands always had there after the first cold snap. The white curtains were clean and fluffy, the big hooked rug somewhat threadbare but right and comforting. What I couldn't find was the point in the room, because I felt it as a definite point and possibly a single object, at which something necessary was being withheld from me.

Now the summer was over there was hardly any traffic at that hour. I heard an approaching car half a mile away, and waited wide-eyed for the mysterious excitement of its passing. When we were little, Arthur and I, and the railroad track past Jordan Station was still in use, we used to wait that way for the eerie hoot of the train whistle rising and dying in the valley far away at night, and would fall into the perfect sleep of two rocks afterwards, wrung out by pity and terror. The car slowed for the two right-angle bends through the green. I turned the light off and sat upright as the sound picked up and kept mounting as if the vehicle itself, no longer a mere automobile but a beast of another order, were about to follow the thrust of its lights in through the south window toward the rectory. Then that side was snapped off and for two or three seconds the room was aflash in a series of lightning fan-spokes through the two front windows, from right to left, illuminating everything but too fast. I lay in the dark a minute while the noise dimmed away, my mind still keyed up from the disturbance and frustration, fanning out as fast as the car lights over the other upstairs rooms as if the thing to be found were in one of them, but there was nothing. The extra plumbing and army-type beds for the school, when twenty-two people slept in the house, had been whisked away in no time; the huge old bathroom at the end of the hall, strewn with celluloid ducks and sailboats, with the tub out from the wall on lion's-paw feet so you had to sweep under it, hardly showed where the partition and additional washbasins had been for a short while; in the little room next to it, in which Arthur aged fifteen had been found in bed with the maid, Dickie would be lying beside the teddy bear which he had taken back to his heart after the summer's difficulty, an arm across his sleeping face and bedcovers half on the floor. The two big north bedrooms, one closed up, one being used by Lucas, were furnished with heavy Victorian pieces of no value and accumulated odds and ends; various Buckinghams had been born

and died in them and I loved them in a way but without their
having a special voice for me. The cubicles of the kitchen ell, once
occupied by such as Bridget and the usually mythical "hired man,"
had gone back to containing all manner of junk.

One thing that had sprung into prominence under the split-
second probe of the car lights was the photo of my mother with
Abe Trowbridge behind the oxen, returned from the Town Hall and
propped, because I hadn't yet bothered to put it back in the attic,
against the dressing-table mirror, and when I turned my bedside light
on again I realized I had had a reason to keep it there. Not much
of a reason; just a teasing association I hadn't been able to get hold
of, and did now. It was something that happened a few minutes after
the picture was taken, almost to the day this time in the fall, in
the same wind and glow of leaves, when I was seven. The long
lumbering ox team, which I thought more thrilling even than loco-
motives although we would do almost anything to be taken to the
Station when the train was coming in, had just pulled out of sight,
after the ritual swig all around from Abe's portable cider barrel,
when Miss Pryden swooped down on us, in such a state of agitation
as I had never seen in her before and never did again. Her blond
hair unkempt and her sapphire eyes blurry with tears, she rushed
to my grandmother, crying, "I've just had a cable! Isadora is dead!"
My grandmother was duly dumbfounded and incredulous, because
she too through her California connections had known this Miss
Duncan they were always talking and whispering about, though she
was not at all a close friend of hers as Miss Pryden was. "She was
strangled by her own scarf, in a motor car . . . Oh Amy, think of it!
The genius! the loss! the one great woman artist of our time, gone
and so senselessly!" "And after that dreadful tragedy of the children," my grandmother put in in a tone almost as stricken but from
somewhat different considerations, the art of the dance and women
of genius not having quite the same title in her scheme of values as
in Miss Pryden's. They sat for a long time in the parlor commiserat-
ing with each other in surreptitious voices and shooing us away, so
that I learned only years later that neither friendship nor genius had
been quite the whole story for Miss Pryden, and that when she
spoke of "the magnificence of courage" and "the indomitable
spirit" she was referring to the paternity of her famous friend's
children. Their deaths in another accident, so distressing to my
grandmother, had not seemed to faze her particularly.

I did another hitch in Trollope, a sentence or two, while out back somewhere a shutter banged inconsequently in a puff of wind and the dry wistaria leaves scratched at the porch screen. The river had never been more beautiful than that afternoon. That was what I always thought in the fall, and it was always true. All along the steep banks the wild color leaped and flowed, cowhide, copper, flame and ruby, from ash and oak and birch and hickory, deeper and more beyond the reach of thought than anywhere else because set throughout in the dark comfort of evergreens, and because the deep places of the river, instead of merely doubling the brilliant images, gave them a quality of infinity. Nothing would change from this; nothing would ever need a new beginning; if one could only be taken into it body and soul, the so-called turning point of the year would be the point of perfect understanding of foreverness. I picked up an enormous yellow maple leaf, recently fallen since the light was still an active agent radiating from it as from the masses not yet blown from their boughs, and felt a fierce desire to stamp every one of the veins on my brain. But it was hard to concentrate in such a rush and richness of things. I gathered a small bouquet of leaves instead, and leaving my shoes in the car went upstream a way, from stone to stone. It was not as if I had been making a racket kicking up leaves in the woods. Once in a while a stone that looked stable would give and splash a little when I jumped on to it, but most of the time I made no noise and could hear all the different voices of the river, which was very low so that sometimes I was out almost in the middle. Then suddenly after not having my ears open to them the whole time before, I began to hear the birds, everywhere around me, so many and filling the air, the world, with such a complexity of trills and chirps and notes of every sort of mood and scale, I felt a sharp hurt of longing for Lucas to be there to tell me what they were and what they were saying. There weren't more than half a dozen birds I knew the names and the calls of, and the thought made me aware of loneliness for the first time since I had left the car.

I was missing Dickie too, more and more as I kept on toward the bend in the river, a place he and I had explored together in the fall of the year before. He was a lot more daring than I at "river-hopping" as he called it, and never wanted to stop even when he had landed on a slippery stone and hurt himself. He had been invited to a friend's house that day after kindergarten and was probably having a good time. Still it began to feel mean, and not that much fun besides, to be doing it without him. That I had at least that to thank my stars for I didn't know until a few minutes later, when I came even with the birch grove at the bend. Or no, that wasn't the only piece of luck; an unpleasant visit just before supper kept me from being alone with him, or with him and Baldur.

The unpleasantness, surprisingly, came not from Fred Leighton, who turned up looking for Lucas, but from quite a different quarter. The demise of the Project had worked on Fred in some peculiar ways. I had expected his taste of power and glory to lead him, after the abrupt end of that hope, to some vicious and possibly dangerous scheme that might involve us all; rumor even had him trying to worm his way into politics, by what means it was hard to imagine. But the week before when he pressed Lucas and me to go and see his new house he had shown no sign of having anything up his sleeve, and looked merely woebegone. At least temporarily, he had had the stuffing knocked out of him and didn't mind showing it, and that was a condition so far outside any picture held in Jordan in a good century of Leightons, it seemed more ominous than a plot.

His house, not quite finished though already painted flaming pink outside, was a diminutive ranch-type set only a stone's throw from the old homestead, which had never been finished either but in that case had long since settled for it, so that its tatters of tin and tar-paper on a base of old barn-siding at least had the virtue of an air of permanence. That establishment was swarming as always, except for a strange absence of children; only one naked-bottomed baby with a skin disease was visible in the dirt that passed for a yard. Fred didn't propose to take us over for introductions, but I had been there once or twice years before and recognized the old harridan screaming at somebody from the outdoor washtub as his mother, who had once gone for mine with a carving-knife, I couldn't remember why. Several grown nephews or younger brothers of Fred's, surly and in proper Leighton style occupationless, moved around the scene now and then like flies being stirred in molasses, sometimes stopping to tinker with one of the wrecked cars that took the place of a garden, but more often just dully loitering. "Pot," Fred said with odd candor. "We got a good little patch over there. But I about cut it out myself, seems to give me liver pains." The Mink teen-ager

who had gone off the bridge was sprawled bandaged and half asleep
on the ground by the door, beside a rickety bench from which an
old man leaning forward on two sticks orated in an angry mumble
that nobody was listening to; he must be the one supposed to have
done away with the traveling salesman when I was little, and to
have fathered several of his own grandchildren. A TV aerial of
exorbitant height and size, and makeshift shutters nailed across the
ground-floor windows, accounted for the children; it had seemed as
if the loud mechanical whines and gibberish issuing from there were
something permanent and unattended like the sky, but one of the
younger women suddenly got up and began yakking through the
door, to stop a quarrel or demand help with the bushel of potatoes
she was handling. Whichever it was, she didn't seem to expect any
result from her tirade other than to let off her own steam, and went
back to the task, not peeling but just cutting out rot, looking no more
nor less put upon than before.

In Fred's living room, also darkened but with brand-new Vene-
tian blinds, another bunch of children, presumably his, had their
white, vacuous faces turned toward what sounded like the same program, further duplicated in full daylight on a second large set in the
kitchen, where his wife was busy getting their dinners out of the
cellophane. She was a sultry sweater-girl type from one of the factory
towns down the river, who responded to his "Hey, Ruth! company,"
with a scream like a mynah-bird's—"What?"—and came out gnashing a wad of gum, not in anger it turned out since she seemed pleased
to have visitors and promptly turned on all the lights to show us
around, bringing growls of outrage and insult from the children.
We all had to yell. Along with the two TV's going full blast, the
house was being shaken by a roar of other machinery, constituting
Fred's chief exhibit and dearest pride. It was still too warm for the
new oil burner he showed us and the new vacuum cleaner didn't
happen to be running, but everything else was: washer, dryer, refrigerator, freezer, these last nearly hotel-size, and the stove-timer
and whistling tea kettle both went off too—not that anything was
being cooked; Ruth said it just made her feel good to hear them. It
was like a ship's engine room put by some dream logic in a small
boat, and Fred was haggard with dread of being torn from the dream.
"By Jesus," he shouted, jerking a thumb toward his sullen progeny,
"they're going to have the advantages or I'll know the reason why.
I ain't having no children of mine grow up over there," with another

thumb-jab in the direction of the old house, "like I did. Hey, Stupe, show the ring." Ruth was evidently used to having him call attention to more than her jewelry. Her pear-shaped breasts under a skimpy jersey came wriggling into prominence for us first, before she got the other message and held up a garish left hand. Actually she seemed a little less set up by the ring than by the plastic gladioli in a vase in the corner and the other object of honor in the room, an enormous doll in old-fashioned finery which they both quickly assured us had not been won in a shooting gallery but bought for cash. "Can it, willya?" the children were hollering by this time. "Cut the lights out, ya dopes. Y'already made us miss half the program." Lucas asked them what program it was and their faces all fell into the same blank, livened only by a truculence right off the old block. "How should *I* know?" one of them managed to blurt finally.

"Pretty neat, huh?" Fred said outside, before his discouragement towed him under again. "I could 'a' swore to Christ I had it made this time. I tell you, this is hitting me where I live and that ain't under the collar. I ain't told her yet but I can't even keep half the stuff if . . ." He stopped. It was a good place for a murder all right— five miles out from the center, with the wooded ravine across the road and a great stretch of uninhabited woods both east and west; even now there was only one other house even partly visible, a little new one half a mile up the highway. I asked him who had thought up the name Futility Farm that had appeared on a board at the entrance from the road a few years ago, and was still there. He said somebody in the family just saw the word somewhere and thought it sounded pretty with farm. "I kinda like it myself. But now . . ." His sallow face contorted with bitterness. "Christ, how can you figger such a thing? A setup like that, and straight as applejack, not even a crooked crotch in the whole goddam deal. To happen to guys like that!"

I naturally assumed he was only speaking of Jarvis but he gave my ideas another flip that later afternoon when I came home from the river. The other unexpected callers were Miss Bean and Miss Troy, who had taken to barging in all smiles and proposals in the course of the Project, but this time stomped through the front door without waiting for an answer to their knock and with high dudgeon written all over them. Baldur had come down from the studio a minute before; Fred had started to leave but changed his mind after being shoved aside in the doorway by the two furies in blue jeans. "I beg your royal pardon!" he snarled, while Miss Troy, tall and scrawny in contrast to her dumpling friend, glanced at him in contempt through her wire-framed glasses, her head tilted like a turkey-gobbler's. The couple were in the habit of cutting each other's hair and might have exchanged bits of it when necessary, but aside from certain acquired similarities of pose and tone, this was their only physical resemblance. However Miss Troy with her majestic profile was the shy one and Miss Bean, whom anybody would have taken for the weaker vessel, the real master in their house.

"Mr. Blake," she launched forth—they had not only been calling him by his first name before but flinging it around town as widely as possible—"we and our friends have been turning this over from every side, and we feel you owe us an explanation."

"Why certainly, my dear friends. Won't you sit down?"

"No, thank you." "Haven't time," Miss Troy corroborated with a woggle of her crest, and gave the floor back to her friend. "We've slaved, we've knocked ourselves out all these weeks. For what? For . . ." "A chimaera," prompted Miss Troy. An access of high blood pressure had reduced her voice to a quaver. "Exactly! A chimaera! We took your word. We assumed you'd investigated the financial responsibilities in the question. Now it turns out this Mr. Charles Jarvis we were supposed to put our faith in was nothing but a rank adventurer. As you must have known—" "should have known—" "from the beginning. It looks very much—" "very much indeed—" "as if you'd just been amusing yourself at our expense. I might add, to the very great detriment of Jordan, which happens to mean a great deal to us even if it doesn't to you." For her conclusion Miss Bean took a dramatic step forward. "We feel we've been sold down the river."

Fred let out a guffaw; it was a rare thing to hear him laugh. "Boy, what a kry-mera *that* would be!" Then to everyone's astonishment, interrupting Baldur who had listened patiently and was just about to get in a word, he added, "You dolls ain't fit to lick his shit."

Baldur put an arm across his shoulder. "Thanks, Fred, but it's all right. They don't mean it that way."

"Oh yes we do!" they both screeched together, out of their twin mind at the nature of the intervention. "We don't think it's going too far to say, Mr. Blake, that you have deceived us," Miss Bean continued alone. "And now it won't be long before we'll have to sell our house. You've opened the way for everything, anything! Jordan won't be fit to live in. Model architecture, rural planning indeed! Another Westport—that's what it's going to be. The whole scheme has been nothing but an invitation to—" "Riffraff," her partner supplied.

By this time some extraordinary white blotches had appeared on Miss Bean's leathery face, as from a corrosion of defective paint on a canvas, while under the same emotional stress Miss Troy's eyeballs had slid upward nearly to the vanishing point. Fred was getting ready to eject the ladies by the one method that came natural to him but Baldur, still courteous and half smiling, stopped him with a little shake of the head.

"And don't think we're the only ones who feel this way," Miss Bean was starting in again, in the tone of the spokesman for a vast segment of public opinion, when Fred cut her off once more. His arm muscles were twitching from the unaccustomed strain of resisting an impulse, and his face from the no less novel struggle to find words instead.

"Mr. Blake, you might not believe it but you done a lot for me and I mean it. I mean in the old schnozzle, know what I mean? And if you'd like these babes out on their fat asses . . ."

Baldur seemed on the point of saying something conciliatory, but if so, he thought better of it. Pointing to the door, in a change of stance as surprising as anything in Fred Leighton's behavior, he announced, "Ladies, the riffraff is here. You are it. Scram!"

This threw them into such confusion that their concerted mood and speech broke down and for a minute they acted less like a pair than a covey, seeking outlets in all directions. There being no alternative to the door, they chose it, and there Miss Bean rallied, though her anger had been suddenly emasculated by a wash of tears. "So this," she pronounced with a bitter look at Fred, "is the element that's been in the saddle. We'd begun to hear as much."

I recognized the pickup truck a long way off, over past the Town Hall on the road through the center, and lay still while it rattled on, around the half turn between the rectory and monument, into the last stretch. It was ever so much slower than the car I had listened to earlier and its lights were so weak they hardly brushed the windows. Then it had turned in and stopped, and I waited for the doors, one

slam at the car and a short creak and duller thud at the house entrance, before the familiar squeaks at three of the stair-steps; he was
carrying his shoes, although of course he would have seen my light
from outside. As always at the top of the stairs he opened Dickie's
door, and after a minute I heard that one closing, before the one
across the hall produced its own little distinctive groan, followed by
a slight bang because it was warped and hard to shut.

It was one o'clock. I pushed the book away, and now it was not
the room but the wind I seemed to need to understand before I
turned out the light. When I was little I used to fancy at night that
if you learned to listen to it and listened hard enough you would
know where the wind came from, and would try to make my ears so
keen they would penetrate way out across the hills, and find out,
though probably I tried most often in the wrong direction. Tonight
I didn't get far. Every time the wind fell, instead of leaving me soaring on my search in the night sky, it was replaced by the voice of
Lucas on the Town Hall platform, which I hadn't heard at the time
and still couldn't make sense of, and I was wanting to pull him down
all over again, before it was too late and he would be stammering
and plucking at the left side of his face. Everything in me was crying
"Don't! don't!" even when he was already up there, in front of the
whole town, serious but not at all ill at ease, his far gaze seeming that
once not an exclusion of others. On the contrary it could be taken,
and apparently was taken, as a friendly invitation to his audience to
come along and see as he did, wherever that might be, and that must
have been what the motions of his mouth were about. "Theodore
Roosevelt was a very great man. Theodore Roosevelt . . ." Over and
over, until he had finished and the hall, shaking off the initial hush
of bewitchment, broke into its thrilled applause. He must have said
something else. "We are a little island here in Jordan," I thought I
heard, but it didn't sound like him, unless he meant just the Buckingham house and our life as it used to be. "Baldur Blake is a very
great man . . ." No, that was Fred Leighton of all people, just this
afternoon, or Mr. Farr bringing on an ovation at the end of the
meeting. Lucas didn't talk like that either. I couldn't imagine what
he had found to say, or what kind of words had come to his mouth,
to affect people as he did that night. There were perhaps some facts
and figures in it; I saw him point once or twice to the big chart on
the platform beside him. But that can't have been all.

The hinge across the hall groaned again. He must be going to the bathroom or to fix the shutter in the ell. A bit of wind had strayed back from over the hills or wherever it might have been, and was shaking things a little, as though testing the security of the house. Then it was my door opening, very slowly; it was Zeno's paradox; this was one door that would never finish opening or cross the distance back to be closed. But it did. Neither of us spoke, and I didn't turn my face that way or raise my eyes toward him for a while when he was standing by the bed and I knew he was looking down at me. At last I did meet his eyes, for one long second. The little feeler of wind had been short-lived, and we were both so still, my eyelids seemed the only things made to move in the wide world.

I lowered them altogether, and the river began rising over me. I was lying on my back on the stones and it was flowing fast a foot deep above me, carrying leaf reflections across my face like trout. But this was not permitted. No matter how many times I lay back down or how hard I tried to stay, I had to go on through the same scene to the end, over and over. I had to get up and go on looking for dry stones to hop to, flat ones or round ones big enough to hold firm, all the way to the bend where I was no longer out in the middle but right at the edge, a few yards from where the noises were coming from; it was not just the one noise, of something moving on leaves. Probably they had gone in Cluny's car but the road was some distance away at that point and I didn't see it.

I knew the quiet rocks to retreat by. They hadn't noticed me, of that I was sure.

With effort, the lids resisting like adhesive tape, I opened my eyes, to find him still looking down at me, and it was as if I were seeing him again on the Town Hall platform, only my bed with me in it had been carried up there beside him. I couldn't think what on earth he could be searching for so carefully in my face. The river began rising around the bed, way up there on the platform in the second story, and apparently this was what the audience had been waiting for. A wild burst of applause broke out, and shouts of "Keep it up!" and "Hooray!" We must be playing our scene well, only it wasn't over, we would have to figure out the end, and then with awful desolation I discovered that what was holding the hall spellbound was not this at all but the scene in the woods by the river, in which I was only a spectator. "Hump it, boy!" they were yelling. "Go on there, get it in!" His pants were rolled up with some of Cluny's clothes to make a bolster, not for her head, but he still had on his blue and white striped T-shirt, the same one as now, and it was wet with sweat.

But now I was in the four-poster again and it was back in its proper place, in the familiar room that was still withholding its secret from me, but this was six years ago, just before I knew I was pregnant, and Lucas was investigating my features in the same way only not from a standing position. We had had one of our happiest afternoons, painting the chicken house, and were lying close together, about to turn out the light. Instead, he picked up the table-lamp and pulling it the length of its cord, held it right over our two faces, forcing me to gaze for the first time at the tiny scars and every hair and crease in his, while also for the first time his grey eyes went over mine in quiet, total scrutiny, not inimical, just in determination. I tried to joke, "Oh darling must you?" but he wasn't smiling any more than now. He said, "Yes, we must. Eva, look at me, all the way through. And let me see you that way too. I never have, you know." He never tried again. I suppose that was when he would have told anything, everything, without any Baldur to needle him, and maybe instead of being our salvation it would have wrecked us that much sooner. I had covered his face with my hand and laughing turned out the light.

It wasn't so much his heaving buttocks as the bottoms of their four bare feet on the red leaves, hers flung absurdly wide, that looked so peculiarly vulnerable, as though four Indian arrows might at that very moment be flying toward them from across the river, if I hadn't been in the way. The audience had faded out. It seemed unfair that I should have so far to go, with such difficult footing, and not be allowed to rest on the bottom of the stream. But I couldn't make it fast enough over the tricky rocks, not to hear. "Theodore Roosevelt to the life. A great man!" came the final applause from far away, and the arrows from the opposite bank were aimed at me, not at the soles of those other feet after all.

When I got home I found my bouquet of half-wilted autumn leaves on the car seat beside me; I must have gone on clutching them all the time.

I looked up to his eyes once more, and thought he was moving to leave. He bent over a little, and still looking at me from all his distances, passed a forefinger very lightly and slowly over my features, as Baldur might do to see if a statue were dry. Even after that he was not quite ready to go. The house creaked gently at one place and another, Pogo growled once in his dream in the hall, a small animal of some kind ran through the barberry under the window. Lucas sat down on the end of the bed and leaned just slightly, not with all his weight, against the bottom bedstead, well away from the ridges of my feet under the covers. Perhaps he was trying to show me that this was not the face of six years ago, or of six weeks or even six days ago. At the moment it was not even particularly handsome, but a trifle puffy, and somehow soiled.

"Dickie seems to be sleeping all right," he said at last.

I nodded.

After a pause, perhaps as long as all the time he had been in the room before: "Did the plumber come?"

I shook my head. We weren't looking at each other any more, and although the clock's ticking had become very loud on the dressing table, it felt as if time were crumbling like a hillside of shale and trying to put itself back together all the time. Nevertheless it was my voice speaking, eventually. "That story you told, you know, that night . . . how much of it was true?"

It was startling to see him smile, even if the smile was only a flicker and as far away as everything else. "Well, let's see. Scene one . . . scene two . . . Oh, let's say, sixty-four percent. Was that all you wanted to ask?"

"I just wondered what percent of you was here now."

"Of either of us." He got up, and this time the door opened quickly. "But I'd rather talk divorce in the daytime. Well, sleep well."

At two, acting on a hunch that turned out to be accurate, or perhaps I had been right about the fast little car that passed while Lucas was in the room, I tiptoed downstairs and phoned the Pryden house.

At the falls at nine, at the falls at nine; this time forever and ever. Nothing stopping me but Baldur, and who was he? Just the old preederome, whatever that was, standing between me and my true life.

"Mmm. Delicious," he was saying. "It's your grandmother's recipe, isn't it?"

"Mommy makes the best devil cake in Jordan."

"Don't talk with your mouth full," Lucas said harshly.

"You just did. You still are."

"Oh for Christ's sake."

I said, "You'd better have some more, Baldur, since you're going to start starving to death tomorrow."

"Who made the salad dressing, I'd like to know. I invite you all for shish kebab—how about Saturday?"

We all looked at our plates. I was ashamed of him, of his knowing he was lying. "Fine," I said at last, and Dickie began to cry. "I don't want Baldie to go away. Why are you sending him away?"

I thought Lucas was going to snap at him again, but he controlled himself. "He's not going far, Dickie-boy. Just up the hill . . ."

Baldur laid his great hand on Dickie's. "And remember you're going to earn a nickel a day bringing the mail up."

"What if there isn't any? Do I get the nickel anyway?"

Then Lucas turned savage. "For God's sake, shut up!"

We had tried hard to make a party of it, and of course had asked Beulah but she wouldn't come; she said she didn't like to eat with those new teeth in company. Then we thought of using the dining room but we never had in all that time and would have had to move a lot of furniture around so we didn't bother. Lucas came out while I was cooking and took a strong drink, without speaking to me. We had begun to have whiskey around in the Project period and he had been having a sociable drink now and then, but not by himself and he had no habit of a drink before dinner.

It seemed to be the trip to the studio that had unstrung him. We went up in the afternoon to help take Baldur's things, and I supposed he was thinking of Cluny on the couch there, not so long ago. A long narrow swirl of something like tin ribbon was Baldur's work in progress, barely started he said. The works of the spring, wood, stone and clay, he evidently considered as finished as they ever would be, and one, the long leaf-shape, was missing. He must have given it to somebody; surely not one of those dealer people. I noticed he was also still tinkering with his gate, in spite of having lost any immediate prospect for it. Propped on his welding table, it was a translation of sorts, in steel, of the one he had done in coat-hangers, and I thought it was about to remind me of something. But we didn't linger in the studio. More than our house it seemed to expose the lies we were all maintaining, and was uncomfortable.

At the falls at nine. Probably he had just fallen asleep when I phoned, but at least I knew from his voice that he was alone. He was going to be winding things up at the lab all day and then would meet me at the falls. Nothing else, nothing, standing in my way.

As we finished the cake, at seven-thirty, Lucas proposed a game of chess, which he and Baldur had played together a few times before and neither cared about particularly. He took Dickie up to bed first while I did the dishes, then when they were setting the men out I saw Jack's car out the kitchen window. It came to a mean skidding stop by the gate and I thought why wait, I could run out the back door right now and drive away with him and it would be over with, only before my apron was off he was taking some big object wrapped in a blanket out of the car trunk. In this way I was seeing him for the first time since the starry night, of wonder and resolution forever, in New York.

At the door he said, "Hello, is Baldur here?" and almost had to push past me to come in.

Around the chessboard the atmosphere was as of things stuck in glue but neither of the men got up or smiled or even looked up. They kept the lying pose of players absorbed in the calculations of the game, only in both faces, the old and the young, certain lines of bitter fatigue had suddenly deepened and become almost identical. Jack tossed his long bundle on to the sofa, where the blanket partly unrolled, exposing the missing cedar leaf.

"I found this, and your note. The house was locked. How did you get in?" I thought in another year or two he would be completely bald. He was more so now than when I had last seen him, and it greatly heightened his air of self-sufficiency.

Baldur looked up at last, smiling a little. "I used to know your house rather well in the old days." He scrutinized the board and even appeared to consider a move before speaking again, in a voice gone even softer. "I heard you were leaving Jordan. I thought you might like to have it."

"Thanks. But I don't expect to have much room in Washington. I really wouldn't have any use for it." With the briefest nod, and an expression perfectly undisturbed, he was already turning to leave.

"Jack, my boy, if you were thinking there were any strings attached . . ."

"Of course not. How could there be? I just don't want anything I don't need, thanks just the same."

I followed him out to the stoop. "Did you mean what you said? At the falls, at nine?"

"Certainly."

"Then wouldn't it be simpler if . . . you know, if you've changed your mind . . ." For a blinding flash of time shorter than my heart-beat I was the guinea pig, before the needle or the knife would touch; I knew all; I was all; I understood everything and the next instant, if there was any such sequence, understood nothing again.

"Darling, don't be silly. I'll be there." He was in an awful hurry to leave, and his smile didn't go so far as to make his lips part, but he blew me a little kiss and was looking rather agreeable than otherwise.

Nothing in my way; nothing else.

It would have been easier if there had been noise. The two kinds of breathing over the chessboard betrayed a twin nonattention, as I settled myself to pretend to sew. A careless move or two was made, before Lucas took advantage of a dog rumpus rather far off by the green, to go out and come back with the whiskey bottle. He set it between them, and more strangely, had brought two glasses. "I don't want any," I said, though he hadn't suggested I did.

"You know, Baldur," I said after a while, "I'm not sure you're wise to hang around Jordan at all just now. Things are rather steamed up. You've heard what they're saying. Of course it wasn't your fault, but still . . . I mean, just till it blows over." I was conscious of a quite diabolical impulse, and of reveling in it, as I went on, "Maybe you should go to Italy and have your things cast after all. It would be awful if anything happened to them."

It was a two-way thrust and was meant to be, throwing Cluny at them like that, but only Lucas responded, with what from anybody else would be called a dirty look. Dirty it was: petty, vicious, vulgar, so loaded with the squalor of the domestic wrangle at its most in-sensate, I felt I was looking into my own soul. A little surge of triumph went through me. This must have been what I had been hoping and working for all the time, as against his high-and-mighty rages and withdrawals—to see him not just as erring but debased, farther than I could be myself. How are the mighty fallen, Miss Pryden used to say, out of a more intimate knowledge of the process than I could have dreamed of at the time. But even her private "mire" was nothing to the soiling of Lucas Hines if that was his name, after a week's worth of outings or innings like the one by the river, at least one of them almost certainly there in our house: Cluny couldn't have gotten to the store quickly enough from anywhere else to be as puffed and anointed with sex as I had seen her that day. Now this evening, more than the night before, he was the smeared and swollen one. It seemed he must have been rather ugly all the time, only something about his glance and stance had kept me and everyone else from seeing it. His eyes looked now rather small for the size of his face and a certain flabby lopsidedness had become apparent at the level of his cheekbones, which made the little scars more weltlike. He was also licking and twisting his lips frequently in a disagreeable way, so that while his eyes had gone peculiarly dry his mouth looked oily. Or perhaps after all it was just the change in his posture more than anything that was suddenly giving him the appearance of a small-time chiseler or con-man, of one of the Leightons for instance; in fact he was sitting exactly as Fred had during the endless discussions of the Project, slumped and hangjaw, as if the weight of every part of his body were too much for the supports provided, and insolence and indolence happened to coincide in their demands on his frame. An ugly posture, as he was clearly wanting it to be.

I answered him with a nasty smile, to keep things equal between us, and only after a minute or two became aware that something had been happening to Baldur and that furthermore Lucas had known it first and done nothing about it. It was about over now, whatever it had been, perhaps a momentary stroke, only his eyes were a bit starey and seemed to have trouble detaching their gaze from the woodcarving on the sofa. So it was Jack's action, not my malice, that had disturbed him. Most likely he hadn't even heard me; for my part I had scarcely noticed what the bundle was and certainly hadn't taken in the extent of what Jack was doing to him. That it was total and atrocious I could see now, and what was exciting about it was to find that I couldn't have cared less. Baldur had bowed that low before his offspring, had brought himself to crawl like a thief into that house of such complex memory, to take nothing, only to leave as a gift a piece of his soul, which would shortly be flung back at him like so much garbage, in a rejection from which there could obviously never be any further appeal of any sort, and I was cool as a cucumber.

I wondered, in a trivial way, what would happen now to the cedar leaf-shape that early in the summer had looked so beautiful. He wouldn't want it after this, and I didn't, yet it would be awkward to burn it. Too bad it couldn't be smashed by accident like the plaster head that had been everything to me for so many years, so that looking back I couldn't imagine all that part of my life going on at all if it hadn't been there, and which it was now such a blessing to be without. I hadn't quite realized before how deeply that was true, what freedom had come to me with its disappearance, and I thought I must have been crazy to take it so hard at the time, even to trying to gather up the dust and little pieces of it. What a terrible power it had had, to keep the air out, to keep reality out. I didn't want ever to think of it again.

Lucas got up and put on a jazz record, quite loud, came back to his seat whistling to it, poured himself a drink in a curiously slow-motion series of movements, as though to force Baldur to observe the whole process with care, as in fact he was doing, though with a look slightly vacant and perplexed. He had aged since dinner, and looked like an old man trying to follow a scientific demonstration too difficult for him. His hands had been trembling for several minutes; becoming aware of it he tried to hide them on his knees, with an unhappy little glance at the record player as if that had perhaps been the cause. Lucas laughed, but stopped the record in a minute after he had tossed off half his drink. Then instead of going back to the game, which in fact had never been begun, he pushed the sculpture off the sofa and sprawling in its place began fooling languidly with his clarinet. There was a clear sarcasm in the muted and disjointed notes he produced, half of them from a Mozart piece that Baldur was particularly fond of, mixed this time with phrases from the record he had just had on.

"So here we are again. The beautiful people, with our beautiful ideas." He squawked out another few notes, stretched his limbs dog-fashion and let the clarinet roll to the floor. "You really had me taken in for a while there. I honestly thought you were believing it—all that common-man stuff, and how great it could be. I seem to remember I even made a speech for you about it. Jesus!" Baldur looked more specifically puzzled at that. "Now I have it on good authority you knew perfectly well what had happened on Long Island, and this whole thing was just a grand joke. You were about to cop out yourself and go live in Italy. Right?" So that was what Cluny had been telling him, and that he, Lucas, under Baldur's hypocritical influence, had overcome the dread and disinclination of years to make a public ass of himself at the Town Hall. I thought of Baldur watching the leaf fall in its golden death-dance on the willow pool, and knew the monstrous extent of this lie, and of my own perfidy in not minding it. "I don't hold it against you, Baldur," Lucas went

on more sullenly, "but I might as well get it off my chest before
you go. I mean the way you've been using me, beginning that night
in Wellford. I'm sure you remember it as well as I do, even if you
were plastered. I admit I was a sucker to fall for it and I guess
you'll admit your part. You can cut the Nero bit. You *were* using
me, weren't you?—all the time. It was natural, I suppose, in the state
you were in. To use anything that came along; for your own son. To
try to get something going there and save your own soul even if you
failed on his, before it was too late. I was the worm—the bait. That's
about the size of it, isn't it?"

"And me," I said, looking straight at Baldur. "What about me?"

It seemed to shock them both, as if they had forgotten I was in
the room. "You?" they both said at once, sounding so alike we all
giggled, although forlornly, and might have passed on to a very
different mood if I hadn't held to the point.

"It strikes me if anybody was being used it was me. Oh of course,
we were all three in it, Jack was supposed to come eating out of
your hand too. Luckily he has his own idea of being a man, without
a father figure for a guru. Oh well"—I leaned over and patted
Baldur's arm, just as my grandmother used to with him at the bridge
table, and I too had sometimes recently in other configurations—
"forget it. No harm's done." I was on the verge of saying what I
was going to be doing in twenty minutes but checked it for some
reason. "And I'm glad at least *you*'ve gotten some good out of it all.
You've done some fine work, made up for lost time; you'll be remembered. Nobody will have to know what went on here." My
voice had been rising.

"That's a good one," Lucas said, "from you."

In fact Baldur had never said or done anything to prevent what
I was about to do. For a second I did feel rather off base. Yet the
fact remained that all summer, even after he had told me the worst
about himself, he had been able to make me feel I was betraying
him—how, why, I might never know; and now his mere presence
gave me an image of myself as small and mean, just when I needed
every beauty and confidence. He was taking all the gold out of
my Persepolis.

"It's not a patch on yours," I said to Lucas. "Did you think you
were God's gift to the world before all this happened? At least now
you look like what you are. You ought to thank him for that." With
no shift of tone or feeling, only turning to Baldur, I blazed along,

"If it was doing good you wanted you could have thought of it long ago, and perhaps saved Arthur's life, and my mother's too. Instead of just your own. And it had to be so grandiose! Lucas is at least right about that. This power of yours, to get us all hypnotized over that fool Project. I suppose a person can't help his own delusions but it's not so far wrong, what they're saying around town. Admit it, Baldur: all this phoney democracy, this lovey-dovey gate of yours— you knew you were just pulling our legs, didn't you?"

"Well cheer up. It'll look good whirling around over a shopping center some day, with ESSO or FINAST blazing in it. Might make a few bucks." Lucas got off his new kind of laugh, more like a bark, and I could tell he was thinking not only of his excruciating self-exposure at the Town Hall, but perhaps more painfully, as earlier in the studio, of Cluny undressing for Baldur all summer up there. He must have made a first try for her himself some months back. "But skip it. That's not the point. As if there were one anyway. It's all shit." Even her vocabulary was rubbing off on him. "Come on, old feller, you're the talker around here. Got anything to say?"

"To say? No, no." He sat back with a little sigh, looking more himself again; not angry, not hurt, only so detached I wasn't sure he had been listening. But when he looked at us both it was with an immense charity. "I expect it's bedtime for old folks."

"Damn you!" I yelled, springing to my feet and not for the knock at the door. "Damn you both! Are you ashamed of nothing?"

Mr. Farr for once was too full of his own problems and decisions to notice what he had come in on, and helping himself to a drink began talking right away, as if it were our normal evening scene and the only agitation were his own. Pale, perspiring, with a hectic glow in his eyes, he announced, really only to Baldur, that he was leaving the ministry as well as getting a divorce. "Do you understand? do you understand?" he was pleading as I left and I thought, as I paused before the hall mirror, that in deserting God he had become, at least for this once, the god out of the machine, succeeding where we had failed; unless he was merely finishing the job. The corrosive little laugh I heard, undertoned by the thrill of some sinister abandon, came that time from Baldur. "I don't care if anyone else understands, but you've got to, it's all because of you. You opened my eyes, to all the beauty, the joy—to what a faker I've been, and the harm I've been doing with my lies, the little ones and the big ones . . ."

I swerved away just in time from the first of the two cars that came whirling in from the road as I turned out. It was packed with men, or boys, making quite a racket, and I couldn't tell if the second car was part of the same gang or was chasing it. Anyway I was quite sure it was Fred Leighton driving that one, although it wasn't his car. He was leaning out the window and trying to communicate something in a muffled tone to the ones in front. I didn't wait to see if they stopped at the house or went on up the hill, but I was way out the other side of the village before I heard the shot and it sounded like one from woods, rather than from a clearing or house.

Actually, what the sound instantaneously linked itself to in my mind had occurred an hour before. In his minute or two in the room, Jack might as well have been a man willfully committing murder with a gun; the intent was the same. And he too hadn't been alone in it.

III

THIS IS HOW YOU KNOW THINGS: from the clean running water descending the wrinkles of our earth. The earth pulls back unevenly from its stitching, faster or slower or scarcely at all, but the machine keeps humming. This needle's eye is open like God's eye, threaded now at night with a braided blackness alive with a swarm of star-lights that back home went out millions of years ago, they say. A fun-palace has jokes like that, so why isn't it more fun? The water is really there and now, I think, though we are on the surface being pulled back from it all the time and although on its table of time, which is partly rock in this place, it keeps stitching a brightness from unimaginable times ago. But if this were not our now we wouldn't have any, and we know we have. I know I have. We have to try to hear what the water says.

How clean and beautiful it is! It's not true it tells nothing; you have to be absolutely finished and desperate to think that, only we have to make ourselves part of the job and work at hearing.

Smell of weeds and iron in the autumn air. I pulled my sweater close. I was at the top of the great rock-slab over the head of the falls, the usual place, where Arthur started his run that time for the jump across. The stretch from there down around the bend to within sight of the old iron bridge, to the upper part of the swimming-hole, struck me with a sudden passionate stab of love, undoing months of accommodation. No other river, no other part of this river, would ever be like this for me: this is the cleanest thing, the loveliest water, in all this dirty world. I love it—every rock and tree and pool; I love it at noon when the fish go deep; I love the afternoon shadow spilling across from the western bank and the wild snarls of pine-roots in their crazy pride of life on both gashed-out prohibitive banks; I know the limbs to swing from so as to get down safely, down there at the deep part. Oh please God, let it stay. You can't understand anything, just anywhere. This is where I live, do you hear? For years and years I've been trying to find words for the colors of this running water in different kinds of light.

What is that owl saying? what does the water say? does the reflection of a star know when it has been drowned?

But it is going; it is nearly gone. Even if the dam doesn't back the river up right to here, erasing this beautiful green ice-age scar, there will be parking lots and stairways down and Park Department picnic tables etc. like the two already there by the bridge. As Baldur said. And it's not true the water can't be made to tell nothing; it can; if it loses its cleanness and secretness it talks like TV. Driving to Massachusetts we saw a little river like this one turned the color of curdled milk by the waste you could see pouring from the bottom or ass-hole of a paper mill, like a stinking white diarrhea that nothing could stop, and twenty miles downstream we were still seeing it and smelling it, and on the next river a new dam had left square miles of trees to die slowly of root-rot. Couldn't they have had the kindness to kill them quickly? A big old white farmhouse in the valley, only beginning to get wet around the porch, looked like a carcass the ants had been at.

You can ask if the river knows what is waiting for it; nobody stops you asking stupid questions; what you know is, pretty soon you won't care.

The spasm of possessive love had passed. I slid back into the night, as though it were to be my last and therefore I did possess whatever I chose to that was there, such as my own childhood and the cow that went over the falls and the delicious combined smell, very strong in the dark, of the turning leaves above and behind me and wet earth, iron and river-weeds below. This is my now. These tumbling apparitions of faraway fires are real specks to me, and really in the river.

It is important to see well and remember distinctly, my grandfather said; otherwise you wallow in sentiment and that is disgusting. The rock reef, for instance, toward the west side of the middle of the swimming-hole: for some reason my least favorite spot here, perhaps because the shadow reaches it too early and makes me think of water-snakes. Still, I've climbed out on it, how many times—say for a minimum, thirty times a summer for twenty-eight years because I remember being helped to it by my father the first time when I was four; that makes eight something, eight hundred and forty times: I'd have guessed more, and I was forgetting the two summers away. The spiny outer ledge is never exposed, slopes steeply down at the lower end, is slimy in the middle and jagged so it makes you bleed at the upstream end. The main ledge only goes under in a big flood. It has a cleft with sand in it, big enough for three to sit, two comfortably, the third at the right where it narrows like a knife-point; approaches slippery there but better than frontal one which is too sharp. Several buttresses at each end underwater. I think of that one rock as more brown than grey, but that must be wrong; the diving rock not quite directly across the river is grey. You don't stand to dive there except from the lowest shelf which doesn't count; you can't walk down either, it's so steep; you have to run and once you start running you're in for it because the sharpest reef of all is there offshore parallel to the western one, most often in summer about six inches under water. From there up to the bottom of the spillway must be—I'm not good at distances, Jack or Arthur would know—seventy, eighty yards, and half that way is where part of the current breaks off to the east bank and goes backward so you can float around in circles. The spillway, or curving funnel space facing the Moses Rock against the cliff outcropping, is so narrow I never could see how so much water goes through it; it thunders in high water, drools in drought-time when you slide down on your stomach using your hands; in between you go fast and can get bruised, not quite clearing the rocks, which change position a little from year to year at the mouth of this passage. Solid ledges form it on both sides above, and upstream from that is the gentlest and clearest place, the wading pool unless a fisherman is there.

Three of the big loose rocks marble-striped; a great deal of mica in the pebbles on the bottom and some white ones; moss mostly farther upstream but some there, only on the western bank. Rather dull section and hard to maneuver from there to the rough pool at the bottom of the falls, probably two hundred yards or so in all.

Arthur was one of the best fishermen, from the time he was ten or eleven. He would spend hours casting here and there along the river, alone and serious, and there was no blame in him. It is strange to think of the moment when he reels in, then bends to pick up his creel, before moving on to another spot, his motions are so unhurried and quietly grave and self-contained. From what complex appraisal has he made this large decision, in such serenity? You wouldn't think anything ugly or dirty could be waiting for him.

The trout is waiting for him and doesn't know it, in the shade of the rock we call the whale-rock. It might be asleep, flicking only enough to hold in the slight current there and complete its camouflage, and who knows from what kind of appraisal the body then decides to bend and flash straight for the spurt to speckledom. There must be words for these colors in sunlight, the trout's and the water's: if new maple syrup had the consistency of a hummingbird's flight, if the human soul turned to absolute good . . . There must be an explanation of blue sky requiring certain flecks of pink in the scales, along with the silver-to-green spectrum, depending somewhat on the nature of stones beneath him; he rarely goes where the bottom has been ground to pebbles or sand. But it is not feeding-time now, unless something extra good came along, perhaps one of the flies Arthur was tying last night. He lies crosswise to the current and in dozing majesty rides it back to the shadow, which makes him brown.

How old-fashioned; how stale. From hatchery to freezer to septic tank, that's the way to look at it. The trout has a lot in common with love in our time.

Nevertheless I sort out the many voices of the falls and wish I could hear the voices of my mother and father and grandmother and grandfather, once more. I have tried and tried. They come out before me, in the night, above the falling water, like actors one by one speaking their lines. That is not the way they really were. Yet I love them, I love them all in my fashion; surely they should be able to speak to me. If the light of a star can travel so long, so far, it doesn't make sense that such realities as they should be gone from the universe.

"You are getting cold, Eva. You should have worn a warmer sweater. I'm afraid the poor child has come down with a chill."

"Let's go to the spring, Eva, and get cool . . ."

"It's all right, girlie, an old man's bound to be in the way."

"Granite. Do you even know how to spell it?"

"Grandpa, take me in the sleigh. Please. Look how deep the snow is. We could go right over the fields in the sleigh."

"I don't see how you can stop them jumping in the hay. Children always do."

"Mommy, the fishes like me . . . I'm afraid."

A horrible black mass was approaching the falls, like the corpse of the old woman in black they used to tell about, in the Robinsons' well. The cow wouldn't have looked like that, it would have been trying to swim I suppose, they said it was killed by the actual fall. This is thinner, longer; it twists and turns as though fighting the suction but not like a live thing; an old tree-trunk. A broken limb lunges up black from under the black roiling water, and then I see the whole log has the shape of a distorted cross and is not altogether a dead thing because Baldur is lashed to it, alive and about to be carried over the falls. Oh my God save him, somebody! Jack! Arthur! Lucas! do something. But the shape writhes again and instead of going down lengthwise as it was about to, somehow slams across and gets stuck, right over the top of the drop, where it takes all the pounding of the river-power forced in to the one three-foot-wide opening.

It may teeter and tremble there all night or longer, and there, that's better, it's just an old tree-trunk with a certain grotesque resemblance to a cross, already pretty well waterlogged. Where it got loose from, the trout will miss its shade tomorrow, though not as if it were summertime.

I looked up at the stars in the sky, I mean away from the twinkles in the moving river that are in the same relation to me as the trout-speckles in a sunlight twenty years ago, up to where actual lights indicate positions of what used to be. The owl and I must find our directions in all this, even though the needle won't stop for us and every instant is a goodbye to what we thought to understand, as we spin away and away. But certain phenomena are recurrent. That mild whirlpool by the far bank, not really visible in the dark from so high up but I know it is there, has been forming in more or less the same pattern all my life. The falls make such a tangle of echoes through the gorge, it is like sunlight through woods in a wind, and the owl's call is quickly lost in the smash, but the original note is clear and firm as a horn. It only sounds, as they say, chilling to our ears, because of some primitive awe of night as the time of vampires and such. I think he knows I am there and is not alarmed; he may have just finished disemboweling a rabbit or young mink. Over the tumbling water-noises I can hear a frailer night-bird too, close at my back and then farther off, two piercing plaintive notes repeated, perhaps a warning of the owl.

No love, no anguish of mine has any power here. If I did understand what the river tells it wouldn't change anything. Only mathematics and human stupidity prevail.

I won't go with my mother; she doesn't love me enough; she always loved Arthur more, even when he was to blame. She would be annoyed if I went her way, down among the fish and the stars. I could yell my head off and none of them would hear me anyway. You don't see constellations spelling Welcome Home. But there is no fault in the running water; it has no blame, and blames no one.

I was taken with a sudden fit of shivering. My midget flashlight showed that in about a tenth of an inch, speaking of the minute hand, it would be ten o'clock.

Of course that wasn't where I meant to go. But something had to be very wrong at the Beardsleys', for the lights to be blazing upstairs and down at that hour, and in fact the house had been dark when I went by a long time ago, except for one bathroom light. So I had to pull in there. The rope-swing on the apple tree looked lurid in the glare from the dining-room windows, against the push of the dark. From the open barn door the smell of the new hay came fresh and strong across the lawn, as sweet as a phoebe's call, just like long ago when John was fiddling in his wheelchair by the window with a tame squirrel on his shoulder.

It wasn't what I expected. Alice hadn't gone into the final stage they had been told to wait for, when fever would set in. She was asleep upstairs, or at least in bed. The other children were standing around, too hopped up to be shooed back to their rooms so Nanny wasn't trying at the moment, and they all wanted to help tell how Bill Tobin, the sheriff, had called from our house and Cliff had driven Will over there, both of them with pants on over their pajamas. They had been back only a few minutes.

"But what . . ." They weren't saying that anybody had been killed, though from their looks it could be anything.

"But where have you come from, Eva?" Nanny asked, with a hint of some new consternation. "We thought when you came in you must have . . . Where were you? didn't you hear anything?"

"I had to take a dress to Stonefield." She and Cliff both quickly looked at the floor; from Stonefield I wouldn't have come home past their house. "Down at the falls end so I came back that way. For God's sake tell me . . . Baldur?"

And when they had told part of it I said, "But Lucas was there, he wouldn't let them, he must have done something . . ."

That time it was old Will, pajama top showing over an aged sweatshirt and his little Adam's apple going like a spark plug above that, who looked away. "Dunno." He might have been drifting off to tend his bees.

Baldur, however, hadn't been hurt, and it appeared that Mr. Farr would live. Fred Leighton had gotten off with a burned hand and a broken nose. The studio was wrecked, that is everything inside; they had saved the structure. Bill Tobin had found somebody to take the casualties over to Wellford hospital while he and his deputy started booking the offenders.

"A bunch of them fool Minks was there," Will said, "and goshdarned if they wasn't the ones trying to *stop* it! Goldarnedest thing I ever heard of. Fred Leighton, he brought 'em. Must 'a' come to Jesus or sumthin'."

"It was the Oxi . . ." "Oxi . . ." "Doodles!" "Dentals, stupid."

"The same ones that was so hot on Baldur Blake they was for carrying him around the Town Hall and all. They're who did it. Not a one of 'em over sixteen." At least his grandson Tiny Rossi hadn't been there, having deserted the gang a while back.

"They're a real hot band just the same," Robin said and began shaking like a drummer until Cliff snapped him up short.

Mr. Farr was the one who called the sheriff, after a first dash up the hill in his car behind the other two; that must have been just after I left. Then he went back up again right away, evidently alone, without Lucas or Baldur, and got in the fight and was shot in the chest with a .22, nobody was certain by whom but it was an Occidental, no doubt about that. An accident, possibly. The gun, the only one there, belonged to one of the Leightons and a tug of war was going on with it as Mr. Farr took a stand in front of one of the statues, which had been thrown out the door. Several were already in pieces by then and a boy was going for that one with what was probably Baldur's own axe, since the Beardsley story was that the boys, who'd been out doping somewhere, had set out unarmed except for a wrench or two. The worst damage was just from

the two gangs fighting each other all over the place, and where
Fred got his was trying to save, of all things, Baldur's refrigerator.
The fires weren't too bad. They were started by cherry bombs and
Fred and his boys put them out before they got to the walls.

But then there was the other scene I had to hear about, at the
front door of our house, when Will and Cliff arrived.

"Was Jack there?" I asked quickly. "Jack Pryden?"

"No," Nanny said, "they didn't say he was. He wasn't, was he,
Cliff? Why? Was he there when you went out?"

"No but I just thought, he might have heard the shot or something; you say you heard it here. I mean," I blurted as if somebody
had hit the words out of me, "because Baldur is his father. He might
have wanted to help."

"Help who?" one of the boys said, not in any childish innocence.
It was sharp and sullen. But Jack hadn't invented leukemia; he had
done what he could for Alice. Nanny gave him a hush-up look.

"His father!"

"Didn't you know that?"

Will had, it appeared, and wasn't going to dwell on it. "No
matter, that's ancient history. Addie Pryden lived's best she knew
how, I expect, like the rest of us. No, there was just . . ." There
he didn't seem able to go on. Cliff told me, though it went against
his grain too to speak of it, or to have seen it.

Just Baldur and Lucas, standing at the open door being pelted
with tomatoes and not doing a thing about it. What had happened,
he said, was that when Bill Tobin and the helpers he picked up on
the way came waving their pistols at the front of the studio, three
or four of the boys cut out back and made it to their car, and then
figured there was time for a little more fun before the sheriff caught
up, especially with all he had on his hands up the hill. They'd had
the bushel of tomatoes with them and perhaps hadn't planned
anything worse than that in the beginning; anyway they were having
such a good time they didn't even notice the Beardsley's car for
a minute.

"But Lucas," I said again, more weakly, "he must have . . . You
know how mad he gets. He can't have been . . ."

Cliff was looking at his hands, miserably. "Seemed like Lucas'd
just gone off his head. He was standing there beside him laughing
like a nut, laughing his head off, and they were getting him in the
face too and everything. Gave him one right in the eye and he

didn't even wipe it. Been drinking, looked like." He wiped his own face, wearily, around the eyes, and went on more to Nanny than me, as though suddenly too oppressed by all that was happening to speak to anyone but his own wife. The strain had brought a suggestion of hollows, as in a much thinner face, under his eyes and cheekbones, and gave him a strong resemblance to the older of his two dead brothers. "But Baldur Blake, that face; I never saw such a thing! He wasn't laughing, and he wasn't minding. I wouldn't say he was asking for more either. He was kind of, you know, lifted up; gone on beyond, some way. Like when you've dreamed something so many times, maybe since you were a little fellow, you know it all beforehand. It's just the way it's going to be." So then I knew the nature of Cliff's dreams, since he was a little fellow, under the long shadow of John. "Standing straight up the way he does, with all that red goo plopping down his forehead and shirt and all . . .

"The boys were yelling 'Zam!' 'Wham!' 'Bingo!'—all that. And then all of a sudden it seemed like the fun went out of it. I heard one of them, I think it was that Bud Raymond, say something about quitting, and it sure looked like they wanted to only they didn't have the nerve before. That was when we came up. I got one of them. The rest skittered off back by the brook."

"Oh Lord," Nanny said, "whatever comes over these kids nowadays? Why does everything have to be so awful? Children, that's enough now. You get to bed."

"Did you hear what she said?" Robin went up whispering. "That means Dr. Pryden's . . ."

"Ssh."

To get next door I drove three miles around, up over Mrs. Hollister's hill and down the back road by the old cider mill, so the Beardsleys would see me start off in the right direction. I could see from their porch that there were no lights on over there, in the Pryden house. I left the car in the woods.

What does the river say?

It says desperate women should carry pearl-handled revolvers and get their pictures taken. The house was locked. I thought Baldur must have felt just about as silly when he went in earlier that day with his present, probably by the same entrance, that is the high pantry window reached from a garden bench on the little kitchen porch and giving on to a laundry tub beside the refrigerator. It was a big joke among Miss Pryden's friends. She always left it unlatched as an insurance measure against her famous penchant for losing her keys as well as her glasses, but she couldn't ever have maneuvered it with her dumpy legs and anyway, like everybody else in those days, she never bothered to lock the house unless she was going on a long trip. I couldn't remember when there had been a latch that worked on that window, and Jack hadn't cared to fuss about such things.

It wouldn't be like him to think of winding her eight-day Tiffany clock on the mantel either; the woman who cleaned for him must have done it. It made itself my untrusting companion. We didn't seem to be getting on very well, the clock and I, as I sat stiffly in the dark on the sofa, just as I had sat to have tea with her that winter day ages ago, out of equal necessity and with no clearer purpose. Yet we had to reach an accord; it was the only voice, and I the only presence to give meaning to the time it told, in which however there was no continuum, merely a planless succession of ticks and tocks that for all I knew might bring us to dawn and full daylight without any change in our situation. The French word for ghost played around my thought: the *revenant*—in, of course, Miss Pryden's intonation, not mine, so that the pretty peal of the quarter hour took on an extra ring of merriment, from her view of such notions. I the living, not she, was the one returning to that room, and she was not too unkindly mocking me for it, as for so much else in my behavior. If there had been a poodle there, it would have backed away from me with its hair on end, until she consoled it with a cupcake. It was useless to remind the clock of the ignoble-looking character I had seen, around this same time of night, storming out from that same pantry, only by the door instead of the window and in an odor of syringa in place of fallen maple leaves.

But surely I was not the same person I had been at eighteen. The clock agreed, that could not be, without explaining. It is only in the river that certain phenomena are really recurrent. I was better dressed now, my hair was tidier, and that revolver idea, for instance, was new. It didn't have a pearl handle. It was just the old one she used to keep hanging in a holster from her bedpost, that

Jack and I had shot tin cans with one afternoon, for fun. The idea didn't extend to using it, naturally. The gilt pendulum behind its little glass door over the mantel kept annoying me with the image of an object, nothing more, but it was insistent, to the point where I half thought if I went upstairs and got the thing from the dressing-room shelf where it was now and took it out to the garbage can, the waiting, if that was what I was doing, would be easier. I was just seeing it there, the way I saw Jack's shoes in their tidy row below it and his monogrammed brush and comb on the dresser, only more so. But I didn't want to go upstairs. I didn't want to move at all.

I wished I could hear something besides the clock, and after I don't know how long because I wasn't counting the chimes, I did. Not any little outside noise, such as I was used to hearing from our house at night; I had blocked them out too. It was a slow drip, caused by a defective washer in one of the kitchen faucets, at the back of the house. I could have stopped it, by going and turning the faucet a little tighter, but that was not in the *donnée*, as she used to say, of the scene, any more than it was for me to wonder, in any precise way, whether Jack would actually come home that night, and if he didn't, or for that matter if he did, what I proposed to do. I forced myself to come to terms with the drip as I had with the clock, and derived a curious peacefulness from it after a while, so that I felt quite resentful when the car did come in the drive and I had to brace myself for the irregularly timed noises of the garage and pantry doors and the key in the lock and steps and his groping for the light switch. At least there weren't any voices. He was alone, and if he hadn't changed his mind at the bottom of the stairs and decided to come back for a nightcap, would have put out the light there without noticing me.

"Why, Eva . . . What on earth . . ." He was beaming in no time, and beside me, bending to kiss my cheek. "Darling, I'm so terribly sorry, I honestly am. Will you have a drink?"

I didn't say anything. He went for his, talking, and sat down with it at the other end of the sofa.

"I tried to get away and make it but I just couldn't. I was having dinner at the Stone Hearth, that dreadful place. Some friends of mine were on their way down from Boston . . ." It was true, I was sure of that, and too feeble even for him. He gave up and looked glum. "Have you been here long?"

"Why don't you ask me how I got in?"

"I suppose I gave you a key, didn't I?"

"No. That must have been Marilyn Jarvis."

He laughed. The clock was hammering. "You don't need to worry about her. She's fun once in a while, that's all. And frankly, she's a lot better than you are in bed, for me I mean. I dare say you're fine with some of your other men."

That was said in a pleasant conversational tone, and his eyes in their incredible blueness met mine blandly with no after-regard. A blueness more difficult than noon sky or the black river at night. There is no way of finding your way in such a brilliance of blue; there is no way of telling what it tells. I wanted to hear the little pendulum again but it had stopped its not very cordial communication with me, and the glass door looked more decisively shut. It was in fact locked, I remembered; a tiny gold or gilt key to it, to be used once a week, had always been kept under the clock, and most likely was still there.

Jack hadn't heard what had happened at Baldur's studio and our house since nine o'clock; the inn where he had been was some twenty miles away, and it was curious, I noted as I had sometimes before, how providential all his friends were, as well as mysterious in other ways. They always turned up just when they were needed, to keep him from dealing with something uncomfortable. "What a mess," he said with a sigh when I had told him the gist of it. "But he asked for it. It doesn't surprise me. Sow phoney love, reap slapstick." He grinned, more relaxed than in the first few minutes.

"You mean any love."

"We seem to have had this conversation before." But after filling his glass again he sat down closer to me and laid his hand a moment on my knee, then let out one of his sudden laughs that I had always loved. "Tomatoes! What a sight he must have been!"

I pulled a little away and wasn't looking at him. "Do you happen to remember the last time we were together? I don't mean tonight when you took back the sculpture, whatever it is. In New York . . ."

"Of course I remember. It was idiotic of me; you should have known better. I regretted it very much."

"Until you wiped it out."

"I suppose so. But don't snipe at me, darling. You know it's no use."

"One more thing." There was a strange tactile attraction in his new baldness and the shave-cut of the scanty hair, almost all grey, that was left. He must have known it and played it up on purpose. It made the purity of intellect around his features, that used to strike me in his moments of repose or reflection, more marked than ever, giving a thrill of actual beauty and even of some far-reaching sweetness to the effect of his face. At least it was so just now, and my hands yearned to caress that perfect fit of skin to skull; no hair, no hairdresser could achieve that artistry. "That afternoon," I went on quietly, "when you left the lab and took Alice Beardsley to the hospital . . . It was so Sanseverino would go ahead without you, and take whatever it was you were going to try together that day, and maybe it would destroy his brain. That was the reason, wasn't it?"

I don't know what hovered a second, besides irritation, on his face, making it a little less sublime than a minute before.

"If you mean I'm not a natural-born do-gooder, certainly not. That's bunk. Scratch the old virtue-scab any time, on anybody, and out comes the stink: people in love with themselves. If that's what you admire . . . But we've had this conversation before too." He smiled at me, recovering his friendliness. "As for Sanseverino, I told him to wait for me. In fact I ordered him to."

"You knew he wouldn't."

"That was his choice."

"That's why you couldn't leave the lab just to play golf . . ." "Which I don't play . . ." "Or something. It had to be for a better-sounding reason; a sick child, a neighbor in trouble. Better-sounding to yourself, I mean."

"I'd say," he smiled, "that it sounds rather worse, not better, the way you put it. A pity I don't play golf. That would have done the Beardsleys as much good and me a lot more." He had come to sound rather bored, as though his mind were not really on anything but wanting to be alone and in bed, but whether by some lingering affection or just for decency's sake he felt obliged to go on, lackadaisically: "My dear sweet muddlehead, are your motives so single and pure in everything you do? I should say definitely not. Show me one person's that are. Just who are these moral paragons you suggest I emulate? President Truman? Pope Pius the Wily? Baldur Blake?" He stared through his highball at the light, in mild transient amusement. "Certainly I try to use my reasoning faculties. That's what we have them for; that's the difference between man and the ape. We all weigh profits and losses in what we do—the risks and the costs—and the brighter we are the more sensibly we do it. That's all." As was not uncommon with him, his indifference and condescension parted abruptly like a fog, leaving in the blue gaze that met my eyes the kind of light usually taken to signify overmastering tenderness. "You, for instance, are partly in love with me, or think you are, because of what you imagine to be my money. I wish it were as much as you think. You're a very ambitious girl, my dear."

The drip in the kitchen had stopped, perhaps he had tightened the faucet on the way in, but the clock had become very loud again. It was inviting me to use its key and walk through its little glass door, as a person might slip through the surface of the river, into the place of perfect clarity, where no owls call. On the other side of time, the star is one with the star's light and the ghost with the living self. The glass doubled and became blue, it was his eyes, and something very peculiar had been happening in them, although on the surface their look was fixed in precisely the half-humorous affection of before, as though the pendulum had been removed at that instant. But something like a steel sliver, a nearly invisible weapon if it was not an aperture, seemed to have appeared in them, so that the wrinkles of his smile looked like an old-fashioned frame of artificial leaves and flowers, designed to play up those two points of lethal transformation. It had grown colder in the room, and I thought he laughed a little at my attention as he turned his left hand, which was resting on the sofa beside me, slowly palm up; as if I didn't know the palm of his hand, with its strong, oddly simple lines, as well as my own, and perhaps after all he didn't even remember the stories of the supernatural that we all used to scare ourselves with long ago. The palm was as hairless as his pate.

"Ah well"—with one of those charming grins, I knew, though our faces were averted—"as the fellow said, we all have our defects. Mine is just being wicked." Then with an inflection quite different, a bit ironical: "Were you looking for something?"

In a visionary flash, on the order of the one I had experienced at the door of our house earlier in the evening, it had just struck me, with a force of absolute novelty as if I had known nothing about his work before, that the object of all his research was the human brain. But I had no sooner felt myself on the verge of whatever large comprehension the fact entailed than I had fallen into the panic of a trapped bird, and it must have been then that I got up and crossed to the fireplace, evidently to feel for the little key under the clock. The glass door and his eyes and the surface of water were all the same; we live trapped behind these transparent barriers, plastic it might be, fogging them with every breath, while all cleanness and truth wait for us beyond them on every side. I was sure I had been looking into the eyes of one who lived *over there*, where I yearned to be. Yet at the same time that I heard him asking if I was looking for something, I was hearing the rather similar voice, only imperious as his never was, and female, saying, "Eva, do help me find my keys, there's a dear . . ." and what I passionately yearned for was to be the one to find them, so as to merit her smile and thanks.

Everything looked different from the ceiling; luckily the walls ended all around in a Victorian molding, wide enough for me to perch on comfortably. The light funneled up sharply from the two shabby table-lamps that were on, being the ones connected to the switch. The whole room looked shabby, and the nearly threadbare patches in the rugs and upholstery and the lopsided sag in the armchair where a spring needed repair showed up to an embarrassing degree. Nevertheless a dinner party was in progress around the corner in the right-angle extension of the space, no doubt a bedroom in the original farmhouse before some Pryden or other had the partitions knocked out, that served as the dining room. There, all was an elegance of light and laughter; a battle of polished wits, set off by some quotation from Montesquieu, rivaled the exchange of leaping brilliances between the polished silverware and the diamonds in Miss Pryden's hair and at my grandmother's throat. My grandparents, of course, were at the main table, along with eight or ten other guests in evening dress; only my mother and father, in drab workday clothes, were eating from kitchenware at a card table set off by itself in the corner. If anything was left after the platter had been around it was set down for them, and they smiled in wan gratitude; otherwise they did without. The baked Alaska didn't last that far. "Oh, are *they* still there?" the hostess murmured to the maid in annoyance. "Well never mind, they won't notice. And don't trouble with the Meissen demitasses; the Cantagalli will do. They're probably used to breakfast cups with their dinner."

The children were playing games upstairs. Or no, we were there in the living room and it was not we at all but little Addie Pryden and her brother Forrest in knickers and a velvet jacket, with a few others, including the Buckingham children. The long-faced boy of censorious mien, whose tension broke up in that rare, astonishing smile or in some sudden practical joke that put the others in stitches, must be my grandfather, with beside him his little sister who would die the next year of diphtheria. The smaller ghost figure looking sadly on from outside the circle was evidently the brother whose mysterious death had already occurred, causing such grief, no mention of it would be allowed for two generations. But now the old rascal Joseph Pryden was reading family prayers, and all was ponderously stilled. ". . . and pray for us now and at the hour of our death." "Amen." "Amen." "Amen . . ."

There was a very young bird up there beside me, still with baby-feathers so its breast was not yet yellow like mine, who kept wanting to fly and didn't know how. The children would grab him if he fell. I hopped closer and got him under my wing, gently pecking the nonsense out of him, until gradually he snuggled in against me. I felt his little heart pounding against my breast. "Sleep, my treasure," my blood murmured to him. "Sleep, my sweet baby. Sleep." My grandmother, lovely in her jewels and upswept white hair, twinkled up at us, her lips pursed in a little conspiracy of love, to say she would keep the secret; we were safe.

A horrid moaning swept the room. There of all things was Miss Pryden dragging herself on all fours across the Persian carpet, tears washing down over the bright red streak where she had just been whipped across the cheek, to clutch at the legs of an insolent-looking black-haired gentleman who was standing with his back to her by the mantel. "I'll do anything!" she was sobbing. "Anything you want. Is it just money you want? Take it! Only don't leave me, my love, my life . . ." She looked like some kind of spaniel that had come in from a bad time in the swamp, muddy and whimpering. The room had filled up meanwhile with similar couples, all enacting the same drama, some in evening dress, some in farmers' work-clothes. Cluny, on the floor like the other women, was naked. She was desperately grabbing at the legs of a man about a hundred years old, with a shawl around his shoulders and what used to be called a steamer rug over his knees, which his nurse kept tucking back in, with a disapproving cluck at the young woman who couldn't stop pulling at it as she begged this aged Baldur for his love. Except for the money part, her words and gestures were almost identical with Miss Pryden's. The one departure from the general scenario involved a younger Baldur, and a second Miss Pryden, gaily playing chess at a card table by the window. After making the winning move, she laughed brightly, removed her dowdy dress, pink silk underpants that hung to her knees and boned brassiere-corset combination, and clearing away the pairs of anguished strangers who were there, laid herself on her back on the sofa. Her flesh had a fish-belly pallor; her breasts, on which the flat smudges of nipples betrayed a total absence of sexual interest, fell away to each side like two child's balloons half filled with water. The next instant, however, her nudity was covered by diaphanous billows of pale blue lace. Baldur, the good loser, bowed whimsically, let his pants down and proceeded to the operation of paying up. "Of course, I can't guarantee to conceive the first time. There might have to be a repeat performance." "Very well. I've no objection." He had paused to part the lower strata of the negligee, which drifted back over his head, and push her knees to the sides. "You don't mind if I look in first, do you?"

The moaning had turned to the sound of wind through trees, and there is no music so wonderful. My little one had stopped trembling and become tiny in sleep, close under my wing. "Be safe," my heart sang to him. "Sleep. Sleep." May my feathers shelter him, until the hour of my death. Let the owl pierce my heart but never his.

The evening star had slid down behind the black woods a long time ago; it was very late. There was only one couple left, a trim-built blue-eyed man with young skin and a middle-aged look sitting on the sofa holding a highball glass, and a young woman with fine chestnut hair growing to a widow's peak, weeping and pleading with him from the floor at his knees just like all the others. Probably the two were about the same height but her rather full breasts and broad shoulders made her look bigger. Her well-made red slacks and white silk shirtwaist had become crumpled in the course of her desperation, a strap on one of her sandals was about to break, and a little old-fashioned turquoise pin had fallen from her lapel and was lying unnoticed on the rug. It was a pity to see her spoiling her looks so, and so uselessly. Now she was hugging his bony knees, her once-pretty face turned up to his in the classic flower-pose, in this instance more like an offering of wet mash. "Jack, I want to go with you. I'll be anything you want, I only want to be what you want. *Please . . .*" etc. etc. "You too," hooted the owl. "Tee hee," breathed the tree. The river gave a goodbye gurgle; the beautiful woods parted and drifted away like halves of a chiffon negligee.

A terrible power drew me back into the Eva on the floor; the little glass door was letting me out and locking itself behind me. There was no bird against the ceiling. But it was supposed to be so clean and clear on that side! A black log is stuck over the falls; push it down; get the revolver. Somewhere there is that perfect clarity.

"I'll leave Jordan!" I cried in the exaltation of despair. "I'll leave Dickie! You were right, I don't care. I'll never see him again if that's what you want. Jack, darling, I only want you!"

"That's very touching. Very sweet, Eva dear." The slivers were gone from his eyes. He spoke fondly, and the touch of his hand passing lightly once over my forehead and hair thrilled me with sudden pain, as from metal left outside in winter.

Again I cried out, this time in joy, as if he could understand, "I was wrong! I went the wrong way!" This, this is my purity! I felt my beggar's smile verging toward radiance. "We could go right now. I'd get a divorce in Mexico . . ."

He was shaking his head. "You see, darling, I'm going to have a rather important job in Washington. It just wouldn't be your kind of life."

I imagined a dying person, very old, might sound like me when I asked after a while, "Research?"

"Better. Pushing researchers around." He seemed uncertain whether to elucidate, but did shortly, in a sudden sunshine of candor that surely would have melted stone, it was so engaging. "You know I haven't had an original idea in a long time. I'm not wicked really; just dried up. So I'm afraid I'm not going to be all that famous after all. But I'm still brighter than most in the business, and I'm enjoying myself. You'd never be satisfied with that." He reached out once more to touch me, taking my chin in his hand to make me look at him. "I'm so damned fond of you, Eva. Don't let's muck it up. And now don't you think you'd better run along and let us get some sleep?"

I remained in a heap at his feet. "I wouldn't care if you never did anything. If you were just a bum. I'd have a dress shop and support us."

"That would be jolly."

"Oh, I hate her! I hate this house! If only she'd been a real mother to you, and you'd had a real father . . . If only you'd let Baldur reach you the way he's been trying to all summer . . ."

Not his eyes only, his whole body went taut with contempt. "These idiot *ifs!* This disease of the conditional! If I were a Negro; if I were a great composer; if this were a hundred years ago . . . For Christ's sake leave us the dignity to be what we are and be responsible for what we do. Life is tiresome enough at best, without all this stench of relativity and personal mishmash. Obviously if either of us had been born a Zulu we'd be different people; it happens we weren't." The flare-up passed, leaving a flicker of amusement of a new kind. "Or if you like ifs so much, there are some that are more interesting. It could be, for instance, that the human race is killing itself off by overdevelopment of the brain, as many other species have by hypertrophy of some organ or other—tail, legs, muscular structure. It's quite possible. And *if* it were so, then work like mine would be in the front line of destruction. Society ought to be working, not to cure mental retardation but to develop it—to save humanity, as they put it. Of course it's true our kind of research could be used for that too, as well as for anything else, but that's not the way it usually gets applied down the line, when your friends the Salvation Army boys get hold of it." He looked at his watch, yawned, stood up. "Well, it's just a theory . . ."

I didn't seem to be able to get up. From my face a new burst of tears began falling on his shoes, and I wondered if he would polish them that night or wait till morning. "Jack, please, please," I sobbed, perfectly in my role, "I can't live without you. I can't!"

He smiled down at me, pleasantly whimsical. "Shall I get the revolver? But come to think of it, which one of us would you be using it on?"

I sprang to my feet, and hurled from all moorings, like a falling star, started for the stairs, just as the phone rang. It was still on the little table by the door, near the foot of the staircase in the entrance hall, and I was somewhat surprised to find what strength fury, as they say, can give. I succeeded not only in smashing the instrument but even in pulling the wire loose from the wall, hearing in the process a few seconds' worth of a not unknown woman's voice in confusion and alarm at the other end. Then the lights flashed across the glass panels at either side of the front door and the far more familiar sound of a pickup truck was in the drive.

"Well, this is where you wanted to be. Can I go now?"

"Wait in the kitchen, please. If Miss Pryden permits, of course. I shan't be long. Come along, Carrie, hurry up."

The duck, being dragged by a string around its neck, tried to flap back from the doorsill. Baldur made a couple of wild grabs for it and finally swooped it up and came in with it under his arm. Lucas, after making a slight sarcastic bow, seemed about to leave but instead collapsed in the armchair. They were both drenched. Evidently they had washed up, since the episode at the house, only by falling in the brook, no doubt in an effort to catch the duck. They were globbed and stained with tomatoes, with seeds clinging to their hair.

"Stop this nonsense," Baldur muttered, but let the struggling bird go. A new annoyance had distracted him and brought him to his tallest, most reprimanding posture as he stood staring around the room. "Adelphia, what are all these dreadful people doing in your house? I thought I was invited for a competent game of bridge, in the usual company. Do you think it's fair to me, to waste my time among strangers? Ah well, I suppose I have to put a good face on it . . ." He groped his way toward a chair by the window and was about to miss it when Jack caught him and helped him down. "Aren't you offering any refreshments today?"

"Sorry. The bar's closed." He was full of scorn, and for once not relishing it particularly.

Lucas waved the half-empty bottle he had come in with, not the same one he had started on after dinner. "You've had enough, old boy. But I haven't. You can get me a glass, Doc, while you're at it."

"Adelphia, do get the cards out, I can't wait all night. Garçon, un whiskey! Subito! Don't they speak *any*thing around here?"

"Well, well. Another Jack—and nothing wrong with this Daniels fellow. That's better than this rotgut." As Jack hadn't moved, Lucas was helping himself at the sideboard, having left the bottle from home on the table back of the sofa. Baldur lurched to his feet, had hold of it at once, and got in a long swallow before the two overpowered him, Lucas making a crazy pass at holding his arms while Jack poured the remainder of the fifth into the upholstery.

"Where is he sleeping tonight?"

"In a ditch, I guess. Or in the Buckingham mansion. Fine accommodations there, for transients anyway. I wouldn't say much for it in the long run." Leering, Lucas tumbled on to the wet cushions. "Had a little trouble over there tonight. You may have heard about it. Nothing out of the way for old army boys like us, n'est-ce pas, Baldie? Just a noncom myself. He's a lew-tenant"—with an ugly wink at me. "Stand up and salute, old boy, like you were doing a while ago. Did my heart good to see that. A real old patriotic murdering U.S. son of a bitch. Like this." He struggled to his feet and in a parody of Baldur's stance, with the Jack Daniels over his heart, banged his muddy heels together while whacking his tomato-stained forehead in a left-handed salute. A fit of coughing overcame his raucous laughter as he fell back onto the sofa. "It was some show, though, folks. Sorry you weren't there. Why we must have had half a company standing us off out there, till the relief came up. Giving us everything they had. New kind of Russian shells they're using, red, with a lot of little seeds in 'em. But me and the lew-tenant here, we held 'em off. Didn't give an inch. Whites of their eyes and all that. I expect there might be a little decoration in it for the two of us, what do you say, Baldie? Well merited too if I do say so. Boy we really gave it to 'em . . ." He slumped back, eyes closed, and began to snore.

Baldur, sitting very straight, had ignored the account and apparently forgotten the little scuffle before it. In professorial solemnity he announced, "I've been gleaning some exceedingly pertinent and interesting information . . . But for pity's sake, Adelphia, where are the cards? Haven't you even set up the table?"

I pulled out the old mahogany card table, actually used more often by Miss Pryden for anagrams and in one period mah-jong, and set it up before him. The cards were in their same old drawer. "You're dealing, Betsy," he said with impatience, so I took a chair by him and dealt four hands. He made the motions of picking his up and sorting it but most of the cards eluded him.

"Art is a devilish business," he said crossly, as though blaming it for both the behavior of the cards and the thickness of his voice. "You have to be very careful all the time, wielding such a powerful force. The absurd thing is, nobody has ever measured exactly how powerful it is; it could be done, the instruments could easily be devised, matter of fact I've been giving some thought to it myself. Safety measure of the first importance. And all they can talk about is their stupid bomb shelters—dugout, fallout, ridiculous. Art's the danger and there's no maybe or some day about it—in the wrong hands of course—and it's with us right now. Atoms be damned; nothing to 'em; just a fad; another fifty years they'll be old hat like everything else. Except art. That's the danger. That's the old girl you can't stop. Power of volcanoes there and it's liable to backfire, that's what they can't see. Create an appetite for beauty, order, form"—he cleared his throat rapidly several times without effect—"and then don't satisfy it, what have you got? Sheer, total destructiveness. Here, Carrie, come here. Heel!" His lips made a blubbering motion intended for a whistle. A bit of webbed foot was showing under the sofa. "Ah, there you are. Well, let sleeping ducks lie. As I was saying . . ." He fumbled at his cards, threw down the two of hearts and sat back waiting for the next play, his eyes wandering furtively toward where the bottle had been. "I'm still waiting for my drink. Terrible service here.

"As I was saying, where was I? Oh yes, there are some very stupid architects at the Academy. I never have anything to do with them if I can help it. Go around measuring palazzi all the time, you know. Of course proportion has to be learned, unless you're born with the greatness to have it like absolute pitch, but where's the genius of the thing? do they measure that? Goda'mighty, they don't even know it's there, or if they do have a glimmering . . ." Seeing that I had played a card he threw down another without looking at it, causing several others from his hand to fall to the floor. He stared at them a moment, perplexed. "I think I've lost someone. A beautiful lady. She was kindness itself, as I remember . . . Hmm. Very kind indeed. I think I used to call her my water-lily. Yes. There were beautiful lights in her face, it was always pale, her face, and she had a way of lifting it up like a water-lily. Of course it wasn't yellow. A white face, that's it; very white. And gentle white hands, always drifting . . . I did a sculpture of her once, happened to find a fine large piece of local fieldstone but it didn't wear well. It was a mistake. I believe I called it Niobe. Was that the one we just burned in the fireplace?"

Lucas wasn't altogether out after all. He opened his eyes half

way and said with surprising crispness, "No, that was wood. And
it wasn't a lady. Wasn't anything in particular. Kind of a leaf. And
don't say I helped you. Had enough trouble tonight without nearly
setting the house on fire. Well, thanks for the hospitality. Sorry
I can't stay . . ." But he didn't make it off the sofa.

"Ah, yes, stone. That would be difficult to burn. Though Rome
was mostly stone. I wonder whatever became of it. But I wish you'd
stop interrupting . . ." He heaved to his feet and made his way over
to the bottle that was propped against Lucas, and this time nobody
stopped him. There wasn't much left in it anyway, and Jack was
the one who seemed asleep now, on the settee beside the broken
telephone. "I was telling you about eglantine. Or was it Elephan-
tine. The island of. Extremely interesting. The name does in fact
derive from elephants, and as there were none in that part of upper
Egypt after the Fourth Dynasty, various theories about the anti-
quity of the cult in question have had to be revised. Now whether
it was in opposition to the cult of the crocodile . . ." His voice
trailed off; he made his way back slowly to the bridge table. "Very
limited sense of drapery the Egyptians; curious fact. You have to go
to the Greeks for that . . . Most astonishing thing is the intense
development of significance in drapery in the Roman adaptations
from the Greek, alongside all the obvious borrowings, but there
was a great deal more to it than that. They've been badly under-
rated, those Romans; people think they were just practical, laws
and roads and that tommyrot. Now look at the significance of the
seventh pleat in the skirt of Venus Anadyomene, or Venus at the
bath, same idea. That's a late Hellenistic development of extreme
importance. Mystical number, seven . . . Late second century, as
I remember; sorry I'm a trifle hazy on the dates just now. The
seven-fold versus the six-fold skirt—a revolution! The Greeks had
no such conception at all; they were the rigid ones when you come
right down to it. Of course each separate fold represents an attribute. Chastity wasn't one of them, for better or worse . . . That
comes with Christianity, makes for the confusion and finally disintegration of Renaissance drapery . . . Why my dear child, you're
crying."

He reached over the table to take my chin in his big hand, and
stared at me with a fearful directness, murmuring, "Who are you?
where have I known you before?" The great gnomish crags of his
forehead were infinitely comforting; hall after hall of time opened

in perfect clarity, as through the strongest telescope, beneath them, out along the path of speeding light, clear to the dead stars. No river was as knowing as those eyes. What kind of joke had he been pulling on us? what was he telling me? It was like the night in the spring, at Wellford, and perhaps we were going to have to begin all over again, but none of us could have borne that. Yet in those far clear corridors, colorless like running water at night, I seemed nearly to glimpse the unity we had been after, whether process or place I couldn't tell, and I thought he was saying, yes, it wasn't foolish to try, all these smithereens can be gathered up and put together again, in a better whole. But I must have gone the wrong way once more, because where I found myself was nothing like that at all. I was back in that awful time in the Howland house, having lost everything, only worse than ever now. I was trying to make my mother look at me, and re-create for me in her eyes the precepts it was my birthright to have from her whether they would ever suit me or not, when in her ignominy and despair what she could stand least was to look at anyone, especially me. I could even see the half-used cans of food every which way on the dresser along with laundry and bills, and hear the rattletrap pressure cooker in the corner on the floor. Then I came to have tea with Miss Pryden in this room, and saw Jack's wedding photograph. What water or stars would ever bring these pieces, or Lucas's either, into any sense again?

"Water-lily," Baldur muttered, still holding my chin.

"No," I said, half choked with tears that there was no reason to try to stop any longer. "That was somebody else. Before I was born."

"Just like your hands, her hands . . . She wanted a child so much, a child of mine, they said she died of it. That's rubbish. People don't, you know . . . Are you sure?"

His change of tone had somehow penetrated to both Jack and Lucas. They had gotten to their feet, groggily, and Jack was now at Baldur's side, getting ready to eject him by some means or other.

"That," I said, and it came out as in a spasm of rage, "is your child. Your son."

Baldur looked slowly up at him, and I was sure it was with the same unnerving perspicuity he had bent a few minutes before on me. He spoke with the patience of great dignity. "Who is this gentleman? I don't know him."

"Cut the comedy, Eva, for heaven's sake." He yanked at Baldur's arm. "I don't think your friend here is in condition to drive. If you can still walk, come on, I'll take you to your boarding house or wherever you're going. Sorry there aren't any beds made up here. But you'll have to hurry up."

Baldur made another attempt to whistle. "Carrie! Come here! where has that blessed duck gone?" He shook his head, frowning severely. "Artists should never have children. Ridiculous indulgence. I don't mind their coming to pose once in a while if they'll sit still and keep still, but fidgeting is intolerable. They all do it." When he was nearly upright a new train of thought plumped him down again. "I'm working, you see, to create the perfect fold. The seventh. I'm referring to drapery, of course. It's never been done. The Renaissance got sidetracked very quickly into meaningless effulgence—too much money and power around; corrupting, you know. The artist couldn't keep clear of it. But I tell you it's devilish. Have to fight for your peace and privacy every minute, the least little thing and you can work for months, years, in the wrong direction entirely. I've had to start over at least five hundred times . . . Well, I'll tell you something. I've nearly got it. I'm on the right track this time and if they'll leave me alone for one more month, even a week with luck . . . " He cleared his throat, and croaked loudly for the garçon.

"But now about Ephesus. Shouldn't read ahead—you might miss something; I did though, this once. Wasn't cheating too much, I'd have gotten to it in another week if they'd stop interrupting me. Carrie there, she's pretty well trained, but even she comes pecking around sometimes when I'm reading . . . Fascinating parable, if you want to call it that. Have you ever considered the burning of the temple of Ephesus?"

That time he stared straight at Lucas, who answered without smiling, "No." He was looking suddenly almost sober, and rather sad.

"Herostratus was the fellow's name. Herostratus B. Blake. I'm joking, you understand. He and I are different kettles of fish altogether. Absolutely. And do you know why he burned it? You there, by the way, bring me that whiskey!" He pointed an expository finger at each of us in turn. "He burned it, because, he hadn't been good enough, to make it. Get the idea? He was, I forget the Greek word, what we call, a failure. And that's the moral of the story, if there is one. Failure's bad business; very destructive; leads to burning temples and that sort of thing . . ." His head was sinking, his eyes closing, but he jerked himself back up to mutter, with a certain desolate pride, "But I, Baldur Blake, am creating, the perfect . . ." Lucas was handing him a glass of water. He tasted it, ruminated over it with growing anger, rose trembling to his full height. "Cheat! Fourflusher! it's adulterated! Show me the . . ."

Part Six

Part Six

It was about half a mile beyond the old cemetery, over the other side of the hill, that I began to notice the animal tracks in the snow. That part of the lane, probably a pretty good road when George Washington rode over it to have his nap or whatever he had in our house, was just a relic of a woodcutters' track now. Still, occasional passage of hunters or hayers or surveyors had kept the wheel-ruts fairly clear, and made a path for the strange convergence of the animals. It took me a while to see how strange it was. In the beginning there seemed only a normal number of prints for a clearing, of deer and field-mice and foxes, and I didn't pay much attention, although they all went in the same direction without any of the usual circlings and backtrackings. But more and more came in from under the laurel thickets and over the heavy beds of ground-pine on either side, all with the same peculiar mark of single purpose, so out of keeping with the natural conflicts between species, I began to feel I was in an animated cartoon.

It was late March. In the two weeks since my money gave out and I came back from Europe, this was the second time I had left the house, not counting a few brief early-morning trips to the store, where I could still charge. Probably it was Beulah Wellman's letter from Florida that drew me out on my aimless walk, giving me a sudden revulsion from the hammering and bulldozing and city voices of my new neighbors next door. It was cold and lowering, with another snowfall on the way and the afternoon sun a dim spill of water-color ahead of me; the sap must have begun to run in the swamp maples but the branches crisscrossed the sky like cracks in a ruined veneer, and the crunch of my boots in the crust was merged with icy cracklings from everywhere around. Now and then the little piercing cheep of a bird that had lasted out the winter there, or the great groan of two branches rubbing together, stopped me a moment, as if I were being followed. But except for a couple of chipmunks, I didn't see any of the animals that were no doubt watching me, the interloper in their mysterious scene. There was just a strong sense of suspended activity around all the lairs and dens and shelters I was noticing, once I began thinking about them, under rotted stumps and overhanging rock-slabs and along the half-ruinous stone walls that marked open fields long ago.

Even the lower part of the lane was still impassable by car, but that hadn't kept the young couple who had bought Baldur's place from coming over for the day to work on it, leaving their car near our gate at the bottom as he used to in winter. Mrs. Hollister's house had been sold too, after her family got her moved permanently to a nursing home, and of course the Jarvises', and Mr. Raymond the real estate man had told me with great satisfaction that he expected to finalize the deal on the Pryden property that week. That "home," as he called all dwellings, had given him a pain in the neck; it was cranky and overpriced and not even genuine colonial, with bad closets, an antiquated kitchen and no separate dining room. He really had to pat himself on the back about that one. However, his euphoria was more general than that. He had done more business in the last six months than in five years before, largely as a result of divorces among the new people, which was fine as it spared the buyers the nuisance of a remodeling job like the one going on next door to us. He had come to see me as soon as he heard I was back, in such a state of swollen confidence, he didn't think to mention the role of his son Bud in the scandal there and up the hill a few months before. Nor did he ask if I intended to sell. His only fear was that I might give an exclusive to one of the Wellford agents, a suspicion that darkened when I declined to show him around upstairs. The downstairs he covered pretty thoroughly without asking, approving and frowning at this and that, and he reported as a point in his favor, showing the kind of initiative he brought to his business, that he had gone over the outbuildings from A to Z while I was away: the barn wasn't worth turning into a garage and would have to be destroyed but the beams would get a good price; the chicken house would

make a fine recreation or guest area, etc. The house itself, he
wanted me to know, was "a beaut. You probably don't realize,
but this is the real old American thing; there aren't many of these
left any more. I bet you anything that's the original doorway out
there. And that mantel, got a date on that? Of course you have to
discount . . ." He went on about shabby plaster, outmoded furnace, floors in need of reinforcement; still, with all that land and
the asset of a good mortgage, and considering the quality of his
clientele, he was bound to come up with a handsome offer. He
had been phoning me nearly every day since, lately in a tone of
reprimand, as if it were indecent of me not to let him bring his
house-hunters around.

Beulah had accepted the first bid he got for her, let him dispose
of all her household belongings too through an auctioneer in Danville, and was gone, I gathered, a few days after me. "I just hope
I die quick," she wrote in her correct country hand from the motel
in Florida. "It was all the changes in Jordan made me do it, you
know. It just didn't feel like home to me any more. This is so
much worse I can't tell you. Who are these people anyway? Eva,
I never knew anything so awful as getting up mornings here. Sometimes I just lay there and skip breakfast. Well Eva, you have
got worse troubles I know and you're young, makes it worse. You
do the best you can and forget me now. Your friend, Beulah T.
Wellman." She didn't mention Baldur or the short service at the
cemetery, where the goodbye she had to say was of such an order,
selling her birthplace right afterwards must have seemed of little
account.

Mr. Raymond also tried to pump me about Cluny's house,
which he would have loved to add to his list, but I didn't know
anything about it. Evidently she was hanging on to it for the time
being, in spite of her marriage. He didn't ask if I were still married
or where I might go if I did sell or anything like that. It was as if
both the house and I were already practically finalized, and had
never had any other significance than to provide him with a deal,
like Hester Purser and the TV people. Even in the European
hotels and cafés I had just come from I had never felt quite so
obliterated, but it was worse still to see the new owners at work
around Baldur's house on my way up the hill. The girl, with one
small child toddling around in a snowsuit and another on the way,
called "Hi," and looked hurt at my walking on with a vague smile

and wave of the hand instead of stopping for a neighborly chat. Apparently they were waiting to have the new baby before moving in, and from her eagerness to make friends I guessed they were already feeling a bit dubious about moving to such a godforsaken spot, although Mr. Raymond had probably told them, as he had me, that most of our land up the hill would undoubtedly be broken up for building lots as soon as I came around, as the greater part of Baldur's acreage was, so they could expect plenty of neighbors before long. They had started demolishing Baldur's split-rail fence, thinking it perhaps unfriendly-looking or just useless or too much in log-cabin style. There were bright new café-type curtains at the downstairs windows, and out in back the husband had a big bonfire going on the snow with trash from the studio. But they would not find what was, as far as I knew, Baldur's only remaining work of sculpture—the poor weather-pitted and featureless Niobe, which for some twenty years had graced their stone wall with her grief and nakedness, and was now in my cellar. I had seen to that before I went away.

The old graveyard was unexpectedly peaceful. Somebody had done some scything and tidying up there, for the first time in years, during my absence, and that created a slight disturbance, relating as it probably did to the sudden vogue for beautiful old New England cemeteries in general. A rash of rubbings and quaint obits had run through the cocktail set in Jordan last summer, after the big national magazine article on the subject, and in American get-togethers in Europe I had noticed that words like "heritage" were in fashion, very like brand names for perfume or canned fog. "Everybody should have the right to choose his own brand of tradition," an American Legionnaire said to me in Rome, in a nightclub called for some reason, being alone of its denomination, "Eternal City Post Number 4." I never did figure out either the name or the remark. Anyway, *sub specie publicitatis* as my grandfather might have said, even though I was alone and nothing had really been changed in the plot or its lovely view, the old bones and stones seemed to have become transitory and a trifle hectic, reminding me of Carlos Gibson's studies in sex. The thought "It isn't spoiled *yet*" broke up the old comforting human flow of the past there as it did the voice of the river down in the valley, and made me not want to linger. But that had nothing to do with the summer night's episode, between a brown and a grey headstone of which the hundred years' discrepancy had seemed at the time a little arch for shelter from eternity. Pale stems of poverty grass showing above the crusty snow were all the life of the spot now, as of the other graves and the spaces between them, under the bleary winter sky. My couch of a half hour had nothing to distinguish it for my feeling from the others that were for all time, any more than the little announcement I had seen in an American paper somewhere, perhaps Paris, did from the other pages of the newspaper, except that my mind filed the item—a few lines on the wedding in Washington of Dr. Jack Pryden and Mrs. Lillian Pryden, for the second time, after a divorce of two years.

However, before walking on I climbed up on the icy stone wall to look down one last time on the rolling landscape in its wash of blacks and whites, where my whole life was held by the roots like one of those bare trees and that I needed to feel for a little while longer as my own true place, even though it took the snow in its magician's skill to hide what was happening to it. Barely out of sight on the hill facing me five miles away, just over the Jordan-Brookbury line, there was already an enormous trailer settlement called Mobil Homes Estates, with a two-acre junkyard for cars alongside and the asphalt esplanade of a burgeoning shopping center after that. I had driven Baldur over to contemplate it, before the Project blew up. But that was probably not the only reason why my old dream of the great white bird, of which the scene was always the same one half way up our own hill, had so completely abandoned me. I could re-create it when I tried, from a distance, seeing as in miniature the ponderous beautiful bird nearly succeeding in the flight that was to be so wonderful and the little figure that was myself in her re-actions, but I didn't understand it or care about it any more. I couldn't see what the ecstasy and the heartbreak had been about.

A faint whine rose at intervals from the black ribbon that was the road, of which a few loops showed, two of them through the dip of what had been Baldur's place, separated by the tops of the tall spruce and cedars marking the newer cemetery. I almost wished the little crying sound of the cars could have come instead from the four recent graves there, the smallest one, for Alice Beardsley, only a month old; it seemed unfair that they should be as quiet as those others on top of the hill, from so much longer ago. Even so, they were no quieter than our house now. Cliff had taken the mare and disposed of the ducks and cats for me when I left, and Pogo had never really been mine. It seemed as if my months of travel should have left some echo in my mind, but except for one hour, relating to Baldur, they hadn't. Planes, trains, clanging foreign trams and restaurants, proposals of this and that, the voices of all sorts of pickup acquaintances, had receded into instant stillness like the toys in the closet at the end of the upstairs hall.

Perhaps some day I would be different and would manage to do it all differently. I hadn't been in a mood to initiate much on my own so hardly did any sight-seeing unless I was invited by people with cars; on the bad days I would just drift into a bar and wait. I had spoiled a few excursions by an antipathy to anything associated with Miss Pryden, such as Notre-Dame and Carcassonne, and others from an aversion to sex, which I often thought I would overcome: I didn't plan to sneak away from the tent in Dorset or the hotel in Athens as I did. Of course that wasn't all. Somehow I would have to pull some use for my life out of so much ruin. I couldn't see the way just now, but I thought I had had a hint of it on one of the few expeditions I did undertake alone, which I didn't quite tell myself were more like pilgrimages—to what we used to mean by the *preederome*, or perhaps they were to all the works that sprang from it, only to vanish like a single mirage, at the end. I felt a need to look at some of the old saw-horses of sculpture that Baldur had adored in his youth, those of the curled-up photographs, especially the ones by Rodin and Michelangelo that he used to go on so about. I hardly knew why when he had scarcely mentioned them in the last phase and by now they were such common property I couldn't see them without horsehair moustaches and batman's wings. It was refreshing in a way but not much help, till the last.

That time, expecting another comic-strip experience, I went to the dark frigid little church that must have been exactly the same when Baldur was standing there in his passion, how many times he probably wouldn't have known, before I was born. It was partly the name, San Pietro in Vincoli, that drew me first. Saint Peter in his time of darkness and terrible trouble, in chains and about to have his head cut off, was a person I could feel for and somehow converse with, unlike the great amorphous triumphant one connected with the Vatican, even though Michelangelo had to do with that too. Anyway I didn't feel like communicating with the whole world and got depressed in the big basilica. In the lonely intensity of the little church, as soon as the leather-padded door thudded to behind me, I became aware of some strange multiple and pounding reverberation, as from the river below the falls in Jordan. I didn't see how it could come from the famous Moses, which I hadn't spotted yet and was prepared to find as gibbering as other things of the kind—works of art, I was coming to think, were like gorillas in zoos: they went crazy under too much gawking—and it was certainly not in key with the cheap Virgin Mary I was seeing, although she startled me with a most unlooked-for burst of reality, which in her case took the form of compassion. I hadn't expected pity from that quarter, or from any, and was rather undone by it, especially among such heroic-scale males as Peter and Moses and Michelangelo—and God for that matter, whatever He was. But it was only the Moses that Baldur had worshipped there, long ago.

The reverberations led me to it, or so it seemed. There it stood, or sat, not fig-leafed with a banana peel, nor smoking a corncob pipe; it was just incredibly itself, the way Michelangelo left it, and in its marble silence it was nearly blowing the roof off. Actually Baldur had had various criticisms to make of it and cared more for the David as sculpture, and in his last year in Rome I believed he had drawn away from Michelangelo in favor of the Byzantines. Nevertheless, I felt sure that there had been times in that same spot when he too had felt like a sparrow, one half eager to be crushed if it could be by that awful gaze, the hardest thing in sculpture he used to say, or that great hand's reaching down a second from its repose in a stone rope-tangle of beard: as indeed he was crushed in what mattered most to him, later on.

A few thin organ notes squealed out among the vaults, paused, were repeated more playfully before flowing on into the movement of some antique piece, joined gradually by the deeper ranges of the instrument, reminding me of how the river would be soon when the melting snow began swelling its tributaries around the hills. No mass was in progress; someone was just practicing and in a minute broke off again, to go back a few bars. But the dimmer set of echoes persisted apart from the organ and from the muffled traffic far outside, and although related to the statue seemed not to emanate from it alone. Then slowly it dawned on me. The Moses Rock above the swimming-hole appeared and grew before me in a grandeur and portent altogether new, not as a piece of Connecticut granite reminiscent of a drawing in a child's Bible, but as if it were the real thing on Mount Sinai, with the commandments fresh from on high writ-

ten that very morning by the hand I was now seeing. Something like
this, I thought, some need to obey the message written in all rock,
the prophet's or the apostle's or the ones along our river, even if
the words were to be under water for all the rest of history and
nothing we did would seem to endure, were what had made Baldur
come back and live again for those few months. He had been betrayed once by himself, and the second time by all the rest of us.
But there must be some part of his vision that could be brought together again, to hold against my own and the world's desolation.

A boy's choir, high and invisible like the organist, began their
part of the rehearsal as I started to leave, so I sat a while in a back
pew to listen. They would have to be a little younger than the Occidentals, but they were of the same species and probably no better
when they weren't singing. However just then that was what they
were doing and their flat piercing voices, in conjunction with several thousand years of accrued artistry, made in that empty place
such an absolute statement of beauty, of the kind just short of a
shriek, I was able to cry for the first time since the hour before
Baldur fell dead across Miss Pryden's rug. I hoped there were differences among tears and that these were worthy of the office I felt
was being sung for him, his actual burial having been without music
and without tears except for a few sniffles from Cluny.

I tried then to relive, but could do no better than review, that
occasion. As badly as in happening, it flunked its raison d'être, perhaps because that was where I had last seen Lucas and Dickie; they
already had Pogo in the car, probably without Dickie's knowing why,
and didn't go back to the house afterwards. Cluny's big scene of
grief had been the day before in the funeral parlor, where she carried
on as though no consolation had come before his death or ever
could after it. At the grave the lines were read perfunctorily by the
Congregational minister, Mr. Farr being still on the critical list
at the hospital, before a group including the Beardsleys, Fred Leighton in bandages, and to my surprise Miss Bean and Miss Troy, who
had evidently had another change of heart. There were also two
of the old ladies I had seen him playing bridge with at the boarding
house in Wellford, who kept up a running conversation through the
service, one of them asking repeatedly who it was they were burying. "It's our friend Mr. Blake, you remember . . ." "Oh. Well it's
a pretty place. I wonder where he's living now. Who did you say
was in that jug? It's somebody's ashes, isn't it?" A still older lady, in

black, frail, arthritic and of great beauty of face, turned up with a driver in a rented car from New York. I had never seen her before, and beyond a courteous murmur she spoke to no one, keeping strictly to herself in her sorrow, of which the marks were heavy and the story from too far a past for anyone there to have heard of it. Boris and Anna had been lent a house for the winter in the south of France, where I spent Christmas with them, and had left before Baldur's death.

Beulah's few tears came later, when she suddenly sat down at our kitchen table as though hit by a club. She was ashamed of them, and of sitting down in daylight for anything but what she always called "a bite" even when it included pot-roast and a full line of vegetables, but it took her a minute of working her wrinkles this way and that to get herself in hand. She got up looking very angry, dried her face on the dishtowel, and refrained from speaking of anything that had been happening.

I set out for home, if I could still call it that, a few hours after the visit to San Pietro in Vincoli, so it must have been that same night, during a stopover in London airport, that I saw the honey-mooners being swept like Jonah into the whale, only in a spume of smiles, rice and flowers, into one of those giant caterpillars through which the airlines squeeze us out for our departure from earth. Another of their devices, the plate-glass wall separating me and my fellow passengers from the happy two and theirs, seemed as it always did an instrument of some computer-type Last Judgment, reshuffling souls every few minutes for lack of a moral basis. But Cluny, stunningly groomed and in mink, didn't look at all worried by that, or by whatever reasons might have made Chuck Jarvis prefer to avoid the publicity of a wedding in the U.S.A. just then. It was at least plain that they weren't, as he had put it, quite strapped, and that what started on both sides as a second-best had quickly grown into the best. They vanished in the direction of Stockholm, in a radiance of tender joy and a faint aura, I supposed, of geranium.

It was beginning to snow, but in sparse sidewise-drifting flakes, not enough to obscure the tracks of the animals. The lane leveled off over there, with steep little dips and climbs along its winding westerly course, among woods too thick to give any distant views although the general attitude was at least that of the old cemetery. The prints, even the tripod ones of the rabbits which were among the few I could recognize, were mostly of an ambling gait, rather than the all-out sprint our presence usually precipitates. It struck me I had never seen a wild rabbit when it wasn't frightened, or any of the others for long; just for a little while sometimes I had watched a beaver or otter going about its chores, or a deer grazing, before they heard or got wind of me. Lucas would have taught me how to be closer to them and begin to understand them, if I had let him. In the beginning he used to want me to go out in the woods with him, with or without a gun, but I always thought I was too busy or said I was. He would have guessed right away what the weird procession might be about, and could have put a name to every hoof- and paw-print. I couldn't even tell a skunk's track from a coon's and fancied I was seeing both only because it was probable under the circumstances, since everything with fur seemed to have passed there, and quite recently too. It had snowed only a few days before and some of the traces had been made in snow already settled, without the blur of steps in powder. I wondered if the animals had gone within sight of one another or more warily, and for a few minutes sat very still on a log, hoping to find out, but it was too cold. I had to move on, trying to lessen the racket my feet made, which could keep so much life in abeyance on every side.

Not paralyzed though. Brush stirred; jays squawked; a spot of white flashed into sight and away. If only they would let me see them! I had a superstitious feeling that if Dickie had been beside me they would not have found me so ominous, and wished I could know what the mothers among them were saying to their young and how, by what rubs and nudges or contact of nostrils or fur. Once last spring, before everything happened, he and I had come on an awful scene of carnage around the mouth of a fox-den—hide, feathers, entrails, snakeskin, parts of all sorts of skeletons—and so like fools we hated the fox. Now I would have been grateful for a moment's trust from any creature with a natural law to obey. As it was, the best I could do was to study their footmarks, where they came in at the sides as there had come to be too many to distinguish on the main path. I would look them up in a nature book later. The tiniest hieroglyphic, two pinhead dents made by not much more than the weight of a butterfly with a thread's worth of tail-line behind them, was the one that looked the most hurried; the littlest mole or vole would sink in more if it were going slowly. But that was perhaps so it wouldn't be left behind, more than a skittering for its life. I had never heard of any bobcats being left in that part of the state, so didn't know what to make of the large catlike tread, or the one like a heavy dog's, unless there were a pack of dogs gone wild such as occasionally made trouble in the few remaining chicken houses in Jordan. The woodchucks were still hibernating, but I thought one small claw-tipped print might be of a possum, or perhaps a porcupine though they were mostly gone from the region too. Of course there was nothing as big as the bears and even moose my grandfather said he had seen up there when he was young, but quite a few deer had passed, mostly rather small, along with a hoi-polloi of still smaller creatures.

An ark waiting up ahead?—only the members of species weren't two by two. Or an exodus of some other kind, set off by a signal that hadn't yet penetrated to humans? Or we might be the evil to be fled from once and for all: the animals were fed up with us and what we had done to their habitats and by common consent were walking out on us, in a migration that would end in mass suicide when they swarmed out of the temperate zone or into the ocean. But this was too close to no fooling. What a world, what a landscape —flattened out to nothing but the human dimension! I saw what Baldur meant about insanity. The horrid image shifted to a happier one, of the three of us huddled for a night in one of those black lairs, mercifully healed, past all accusation and forgiveness. We grow fur, grow hoofs, paws, wings, anything that doesn't run with poison against its love. I had tried often in those months to hate Lucas and nearly did when I thought of certain things, not just his fornicating with Cluny in our house and bringing the bottle out in front of Baldur that night; the smile he used to have when he had quit a job was just as bad. Now the craving was so tactile, I thought I would gladly have offered my brown juicy eyes to the woodpecker in place of his grub if I could have touched just once the faces of my husband and child. But no, I was stuck with eyes to see and my thumb-proud hands, fit for nothing but to be modeled in plaster. Whatever he had been or done, I was the one who had forfeited all rights. There were to be no gratuities, even for a night.

A longing came to stop the senseless business of sticking one foot out before the other, on a path where every footprint but mine was there for a reason, whatever it might be. To lie down and let the cold kindly put me to sleep. But that was not to be allowed either; the writing on the rock forbade it. I trudged on, trying to stop the equally pointless exercise of wondering where the two of them were, or ever would be. Some day I supposed there would be a communication about divorce; that would be all.

It wasn't generally known around Jordan. I gathered people had thought we had all gone off somewhere together after Baldur's death, only Mr. Raymond with his real estate nose had had hunches and put this and that together when I came back alone. But Mr. Farr, when he was there packing up after his time in the hospital, had apparently spread some curious report of a visit to Lucas's married sister, whoever that was, so the situation was slurred over, and more strangely, there were still a lot of people backing Lucas for First Selectman and expecting him to be there to run. Cliff Beardsley told me about it. "Any word?" "No." "Me either." After a while I said, "There won't be any, Cliff. You know that." He came to help me start the furnace and get the water on, and I walked up once to visit with Nanny, on account of Alice and having been away when they buried her. It wasn't a time for questions and Nanny wasn't the questioning kind anyway; nor was she the kind to crack up, under anything, and she hadn't, but she looked drained and bent and the life had gone out of her voice, as from Cliff's too. They were people having to push a big load away from in front of them all the time, to speak or move, and old Will for the first time seemed to be a little bit in the way and to be knowing it.

Nevertheless, when Cliff sat in our kitchen with me a few minutes, I understood that it was they, he and his father, who had done the stalling for Lucas, in case there was a chance of his coming back, even though Cliff was talking about maybe moving to Vermont or even Canada after the old man died. Too much had changed in Jordan, it just wasn't their place any more; besides it was getting too hard to find labor for the orchards, and a lot of their farmland was already being taxed as "potential residential sites." I thought what I was really hearing was that if Lucas had stayed with him in the business he wouldn't have lost heart so, to the point of pulling up stakes that went as deep as theirs, so that his dim hope had to do with more than just wanting to see a decent successor to his father's forty-year era of town control. Lucas's behavior and condition during the attack on Baldur had evidently been hushed up;

the Beardsleys would never blab about it, and the boys were in disgrace, as being indirectly to blame for Baldur's death a couple of hours later. A movement of guilt and revulsion had set in around Jordan after that night, all to Lucas's benefit, if he had been there to make anything of it. "Seems like Baldur Blake's kind of a hero again," Cliff said with a wry smile, which was no belittlement of Baldur but only a comment on the ways of public opinion. "Damnedest thing, a lot of them are even talking about reviving the Project business, getting new backers and so forth. So they figure Lucas is their man, the way he spoke at the town meeting and all. He's Mr. Clean. Well, they're not so far wrong at that, only . . ." He got up to go, perplexed and sad, and for all the sorrow of his own weighing on him and waiting for him at home, plainly wishing there were something he could do to leave some cheer with me. "You know you gals are always smarter'n we are. Nanny said a funny thing. She thinks these two godawful crazy things—I'm not talking about Alice, we just have to live with that some way or other—I mean about Baldur Blake that night here and the Leighton story, she said they might just end up looking like the salvation of Jordan. Got people scared; made 'em sit up and think for a change. But I don't know. Maybe she's too optimistic. I hope not, for Fred's sake. Poor son of a bitch."

This they had written me about, along with the curt news of Alice's death and the birth of Angie's baby: how Fred Leighton and his wife had been murdered in their sleep with a shotgun by their three children, the oldest a boy of eleven, who had taken the car and what money there was in the house and driven nearly to Waterbury before they hit something and were arrested. They said they had done it because their parents wouldn't let them stay up for a late late show. For those two of the new gravestones a collection had been taken up.

"You'd better tell them," I said at the door, "Lucas won't be back."

"No . . . I suppose not."

I was thinking about Baldur's sculptures, not the old dead and buried ones but those of last summer, because something about the wind through the evergreens and the loneliness of the stone walls in the snow had brought them suddenly to life for me, when round-ing a bend I came on the end of the trail, and the end of my fine mythology. It was the town dump. The animals had been trekking over there after garbage. We had gone on using our own dump as everybody used to, and I hadn't bothered to inquire what land had been taken for this purpose a year or two earlier; I had even for-gotten there was such a thing. A road had been cut in at the other side of the clearing, off from the now black-top branch road that wound across the back side of the hill to join the main highway at the bottom, where the railroad used to be. It was from all the way over there that Arthur and I long ago used to hear the lone-some shriek of the locomotive at night.

The peculiar thing was that instead of fading out under this gross discovery, the works of art that had been re-creating themselves in my mind became all at once a great deal more vivid than before. I couldn't understand why, but it was as though they had clicked open for me at the sight of all that trash and I were somehow able to move around inside them, one after the other, while at the same time the sense of the trees and of the long-lost train whistle also grew more, rather than less, acute. In particular the last version of the gate model, with its writhing steel spokes or plumes or ten-drils, its intimation of some large serenity always in the act of rising out of torment, grew as large as a real city gate and began to exercise its intended function of protection and welcome. Why, it was something like Ezekiel's wheels, that was it: concentric, caught in a flash of arrested motion, with the ferns turned to wings and the egg to their firmament—grand word, that, he had once remarked, we shouldn't let aviation do it in. Yes, it was full of eyes "round about" as the prophet said, and I could have sworn the glory and noise of rushing waters were round about it too. Yet it was simple and solidly put together; it would have worked.

It was not set on the ground but was somehow rigged, as Bal-dur had envisaged, to float rainbow-fashion at about the height of the tympanum of a cathedral, only instead of being the portal to the ideal city, it framed in this case a vista of rusted-out bedsprings and pots and pans, rotting mattresses and stacks of old newspapers, broken furniture, every sort of cracked and superseded domestic object thrown aside by the march of commerce through the homes of Jordan. There was no smell; the snow and the animals took care of that, and apparently some burning was done once in a while, though there was no sign of any recent fire. The vision of the gate persisted, a final ironic caprice of Baldur's imagination, and as I watched, waiting for it to go, a young doe wandered under its arch and after holding its nostrils to the wind, began to lick something in the litter at its feet. Salt, presumably; there couldn't be much else in such a junk-pile to attract a deer. It was quite relaxed in its foraging, and yet I felt sure it had seen me before lowering its head and must know I was still there. Except for the head, I was surprised to find it rather an ungainly animal in repose, with a ratio of rear to front quarters almost as cumbersome as that of a cow. The snow had increased for the moment to a flurry that whitened the doe's coat in little streaks and patches on top, making her shake herself and rub a fetlock across her face once or twice, before she gave up, and after another quiet casing of the scene, and me, ambled off. Just at the end she cast off her homeliness in a great bound, and it was like the transformations in fairy tales or the leap of the human heart in happiness, to clear the wall at the edge of the woods.

The peacefulness she left in me was strangely like a feeling of homecoming—God knows to what, with everything that could mean home wrecked or about to be. In any case it seemed to embrace the ugly expanse of rubbish strewn before me as much as the beauty of the doe's spring and her not having been afraid of me, and to give a reason for the clarity in that unlikely place of the gate, the cedar leaf, the dozen shapes in plaster that had gone the way of the plastic containers and toothpaste tubes I was seeing, only through willful violence. I saw the works, and their own unwantedness, as part and parcel of the frightening joke I used to see in the depths of Baldur's eyes, and the joke was on all of us, himself included, since what it amounted to was just an extreme effort to keep the faith while not telling any lies. Not to kid ourselves, about what art, home, love, Jordan, anything could ever mean to us again, and yet to keep capable of love, of work, of hope. Surely it was something like that that he used to try to say in words, but the sculptures were his real speech, and even they had never said it as powerfully to me before they were destroyed as now in vision over a field of frozen débris, in conjunction with the trees and the deer that faced an extinction as ruthless and total as theirs. *Memory* . . .

charity. Who said that? It had been like a voice not far away, through the snow, but no one was there, it must have been only the wind in the trees, which now played another trick on me. It blew the dead sculptures away, and over the dump now slowly having its sores and sad stories soothed to a semblance of peace and beauty by the falling snow, as the graves must be over the other side of the hill, there appeared before me the scene from the past that had been my main point of torment through all the years since.

Evidently I had fooled myself about it that afternoon at the beginning of summer, under the influence of Miss Pryden's syringa. I must have just seen enough to drive it deeper and give it a trickier power over me; anyway this was the first time I hadn't muttered Darling, Darling! when I thought of it. Jack the rescuer! how crazy can you get?—poor defeated man, what a time I had given him! The scene itself, which I now saw quite whole and clear, was about as interesting as the rusted and burned-out tea kettle I had had an impulse to pick up and blow the snow off of in my musing stroll around the edge of the dump. Anything to delay going back to the house, where I had a strong feeling Mr. Raymond was going to be waiting for me, and now that dusk was coming on and the snow was falling faster there was even a slight and half-inviting chance, commandments or not, of my becoming lost over there, as Arthur and I were once in a blizzard much closer to home, only this time nobody would be out looking for the children. My beloved brother, how handsome and good and finally destroyed he was that last night of the school, as what seemed to us both the incredible worst happened before those hundreds of eyes, in the barn that had been fixed up as an auditorium and that Mr. Raymond now proposed tearing down. Just sixteen, he had come home only that afternoon from the disciplinary school in Massachusetts where he had been sent in February after being found in bed with the maid, so he had had no warning. It was he who found our mother passed out in her cubicle over the kitchen at dinnertime, and arranged for one of the teachers to substitute for her, and later struggled with her all the way over to the barn, right to the rickety platform that was our stage, as I started my opening speech in the *Malade Imaginaire*. I still felt the buckram ruff scratching my neck when I thought of it. Probably he should have knocked her out, but that far he couldn't make himself go against her mother-power. He stopped by the curtains serving as wings, and we exchanged a long helpless look, the last true communication of our lives as it turned out, as she stumbled on in her mad array, barefoot, with a smile of idiotic inquiry and surprise, to mumble something about a "nice party" and very slowly sink to her knees and then, this motion seeming no faster than the other, altogether off the platform, at Miss Pryden's feet.

By this turn of events I was prevented not only from showing off my French accent and talents as an actress, but also from playing the slow movement of the "Moonlight Sonata" later on and doing cartwheels in the gymnastic finale. As there were only fifteen boarders and twenty-one pupils in all, including me, the performance was to have been a mixed bag. Of course as far as I was concerned it was all to have been for *her*, for her alone, to earn at least her unqualified admiration. Instead of which none of us was ever to speak to her again, except for the winter afternoon four and a half years later when I called and had tea with her. Hester Purser was one of the few kindhearted people who ran up that night, while Miss Pryden made her imperial exit, to take care of my mother, and later wanted to comfort Arthur and me, but she searched for him in vain in the fields and everywhere. He didn't turn up for two days.

No, the scene had nothing to tell me any more, and probably never had mattered—it was only one episode in a process, and nothing would really have been changed if it hadn't occurred—except as I had drowned it a thousand times in my fantasy of love, the way you would drown a kitten with your bare hands. There were many times and pictures that deserved to be more vivid than that— for instance my mother hoeing among her flowers, tired and beginning to have a backache, on a particular afternoon. With a mock groan Arthur came and took the hoe from her so she could rest, and my father picked a little cinnamon carnation to put in her stringy hair, and they all looked at me with the same indulgent, loving smile at my stupidity in having forgotten and having been so greedy for a different shape to their lives. Why, it was like a victory celebration. Of course, they would want me to do better than they had in this way or that, if I could, and have better luck, but by what standards had I been thinking of them as the vanquished ones? Even if I did do better, I still might have less claim than they to have my face absorbed into such a garden, and that was not really a new ending.

I clearly remembered the smile, and my own, and the strange meaning of it among us for a minute.

But just then what I wanted most to see, in every detail, was
Lucas's life—everything I had kept him from telling me while I
trapped him in my silence and my enormous lie. My God, I had
given birth to Dickie to trap him; I hadn't wanted to be left alone,
after all. Lucas, I love you, I said aloud into the snow, and it was
strange to be drowning nothing and just speaking under the stress of
the truth. The recording of his voice from somewhere in my brain
switched on, as engineered by Baldur, the night the head in the
parlor was smashed and we were swept into the Project; and soon
it was not his voice telling but the actual life taking place for me,
with the speed of light or of dreams, thirty-four years' worth in
leisurely detail scene by scene, character after character, in what
couldn't have been more than a few minutes. I knew before it was
over—all, all of it, and more that hadn't been told: the months of
impotence in the third year of our marriage, the look that must
have come with a particular experience in geometry at age fifteen
and a game of mumbly-peg at seven—I knew that for better or
worse I had crossed a line of absolute division in my life. Whether
I ever arrived at any happiness or not, whoever Lucas might marry
some day or might be in love with now, I had at this late date at
least had an intuition of who he was, and nothing would ever be
the same again.

In fact the old tea kettle I was holding had already become
quite different. So had the other things in the dump, reminding me
of the magic of such places for Dickie and how he could never come
home from a trash-heap without his arms full of "treasures." They
had begun speaking to me, all these broken and worn-out objects
with their histories, asking for nothing but appreciation: saying look,
this is how I was made, I am an old orange-squeezer superseded by
frozen juice requiring a can-opener instead of me and here I am
with only one small nick, not bad for a glass thing in a houseful
of children; not to complain, you understand, it's the way of the
world, but just as a matter of record . . . Or no, it was Lucas's voice
again, guiding me, like a guide in a museum, among the cast-off
objects and other phenomena too, a deserted bird's nest, a bed of
creeping Jennie. He was only pointing out what they were and how
they got that way, but the meaning of it was: how could we love
one another, until we understood that our stories were part of this

one and that Dickie was right to cry when we spoke of turning in the old Chevvy against a new car even if it had to be done, because it carried a piece of our lives. The ugly plush sofa on which somebody fell asleep with a cigarette, the birch leaves that twinkled for the young finches last summer and are turning to compost under the snow, the dim early star a Phoenician sailor saw about to be blotted out by the storm as it is now, the kettle without a handle and the handle without a pot, all life-touched things and beings outlived like these or not to be conceived for ages to come, share our place here and our significance. Baldur's gate too, what was left of it; that was a surprise. I had wandered over by the entry road, where the young couple I had passed earlier must have thrown a load of stuff from the studio just that afternoon, and when I kicked a little at the new snow it appeared, bent every which way and with several parts missing. Somebody had really worked at wrecking it to that extent; I couldn't twist it at all with my hands. I had an impulse to take it away with me and make a treasure of it, but it declined the honor. I am not this trash you would like to weep over, was its message. Whatever life I have is in you now, and in Lucas, and perhaps even a little in Jack and in those young ones who wreaked their poor rage on me.

So I dropped it, sadly, and gave the place back to the animals; they would have it to themselves at least for the night, unless the weather kept them, as we say, indoors. For some reason I was thinking of Lucas's two sisters as I headed back, I suppose because I hadn't admitted before to knowing anything about them, whereas actually Mr. Farr, when I visited him in the hospital after Baldur's funeral, had told me quite a lot; he had been in touch with them for a year. Corey Leonard, it seemed, after losing a leg in his jungle adventure, had found his way back to Rachel and persuaded her to marry him in spite of everything; she had been supporting her three children, one of them half Greek and one half Negro, by running a laundry; they loved their new crippled father and it was a happy family. But it was the baby of Lucas's family, Judith, whom he had scarcely known by sight, who had set out to find him, after her marriage and their mother's death in a mental institution. She was the one who started writing to Mr. Farr, and sent Corey Leonard to visit us, and had been waiting all those months for word from Lucas himself. His reputation for violence, and what he had chosen to do to the self he had been under the old face, before the war, called for that much discretion. But what a lovely girl, Mr. Farr said, remarkably like Lucas, the same eyes and smile and voice although her hair was dark; and the way he said it, with pain unlike the physical one he was in at the time, made me wonder if his meeting with her might have worked along with Baldur's influence to bring him to his own violent decision. And perhaps Lucas at last . . . It comforted me to think of Dickie having two aunts, who would love him. I hoped it was true.

I lost the track over and over, and fell on stones and deadfall in the dark; the snow had begun to blow furiously and pile into deep drifts. At one time I must have been half a mile off course, in the woods, and later when I was ready to give up I found I had been right by the road and what I had stumbled on was one of the old gravestones at the top of our hill, only I had come on the graveyard from the far side. My nose and thumbs had stopped hurting and I wondered vaguely about frostbite. Nevertheless I went on absurdly clutching the tea kettle and twice groped in the snow until I found it when it had flown out of my hand; that one treasure, or fetish, I had to have, to keep going. And yes, of course, when I saw the lights I thought it was Mr. Raymond waiting for me with papers all drawn up ready for me to sign, and I knew what I would have to do. Instead there came a wild barking through the cluttered air and Pogo was doing his best to race toward me up the hill, and in a minute Dickie was in my arms. He had flown out without a jacket or boots and I thought he would catch his death of cold but it was more likely we would both catch our deaths of joy. I unbuttoned my coat and held him tight against me while we both babbled, he of where had I been and what had happened to his ducks and when would dinner be ready, only not of who had brought him there, and that I didn't dare ask. I took a few more steps before falling with him, which made him laugh in spite of the cold. The wind whipped angry curtains of snow around us, and from them the form and face seemed not so much to emerge as to take shape, as though made of their substance, but it was the real Lucas, all of him, flesh, blood and spirit and all its history, who stepped out from the whiteness saying, "Eva . . ." and the grey eyes looking close into mine, not quite ready to smile, put no more or less of a question than the water in our spring.

"I've started the fire," he said. "Down, Pogo, good boy. Yes, it's all right now. She's here."

The next summer, near that spot in the lane, I happened on a squashed disc of rusty metal. It was the old tea kettle, flattened by one of the bulldozers that had started working on the hill.